THE
W⦿RD
CHANGERS

D1570435

THE
WORD
CHANGERS

A Novel

Ashlee Willis

 CONQUEST
PUBLISHERS

Conquest Publishers
A division of Conquest Industries, LLC
P.O. Box 611
Bladensburg, MD 20710-0611
www.conquestpublishers.com

ISBN: 978-0990397908 (eBook)
ISBN: 978-0990397915 (paperback)

Librartyof Congress Control Number: 2014941932

Published in the United States of America

For Mom and Dad, who taught me to see the worlds beyond the one we live in, and for Lacey, who was by my side in each of them.

THE
WORD
CHANGERS

CHAPTER ONE
A Bewildering Beginning

The moment she began to fall, Posy forgot everything except her descent. She even forgot how she had come to be falling in the first place. Everything behind her grew faint and far, and everything in front of her seemed a black void. Gravity worked backward, and her racing speed slowed. Now she floated, like a dry leaf, or a page torn from a book. Gradually she felt nothing at all.

And the entire time she was falling, she could hear voices, hollow and wide-flung, pulling her back from the precipice. Posy lifted a heavy hand to swat awkwardly at her face.

"You've come at last, my dear," said the voice nearest her. "And about time, too." Posy attempted to open her eyes, only to find it difficult. Was that the brush of a feather on her brow? She groaned in frustration at the weighted feeling she couldn't shake.

A woman's voice came faintly from a distance. "Will it work?"

"Well, their looks are quite different, I must say." Now a man's deep tones.

"It was what Your Majesty wanted, if I may remind you," the answer came smoothly. "And after all, it is much too late now to send her back."

"Let us hope it is only for a short time," the woman spoke again, with a slight accent of distaste. "But see. The princess begins to wake."

Why are they speaking so strangely? Posy's thoughts crawled sluggishly into her head, *And it is almost as if they are speaking about me ... Did someone just say ... 'Princess'?*

Only last night—*was* it only last night?—Posy lay in her own bed, listening to the sounds of unhappiness down the hall. Crying hadn't stopped her parents from arguing. Praying hadn't ended their hate for each other. Fists clenched into the pillow she had pulled over her head had done no good either. Of course it hadn't.

All the same, something deep within her had clamored and quaked for a change. Something inside had whispered that things could not remain as they were. Perhaps this was the answer. But she thought it more likely it was all a horrid mistake.

Solid arms went around her, pulling her to a sitting position. "There we go, my dear," said a man's voice next to her ear. "What a scare we had, didn't we, Valanor? We thought we were going to lose our princess."

There was no doubt about it now. Someone was calling her princess. Posy's eyes snapped open at last. What she saw almost convinced her she was dreaming, if everything hadn't been so real and so unbearably bright. She had not seen a place like this before. What had she been doing before all this happened? Why could she not remember?

Standing around her bed were several individuals. The first one she noticed was a large man, tall and broad, with ruddy cheeks and a full black beard streaked with shots of gray. His must have been the arms that had moved her, as easily as a doll, up on the bed. He was smiling broadly at her through small, intent eyes as he rubbed his hands together with the anticipation of someone a fraction his age. Next to him stood a tall slender woman, breathtakingly—*coldly*—beautiful. Her white-blond hair fell over her pale shoulders and shimmered like fairy dust down the back of her exquisite gown. Posy blinked at the sight of the gold crown on each of their heads. A group of people—servants from the look of it—surrounded the two of them, all peering curiously at her. *Just as the students in biology class all stare at those poor frogs in their glass tanks,* Posy thought with a grimace.

"Did ...?" she began hesitantly. "Did someone call me—Princess?"

"Indeed! And how are you, my dear?" the man said, who seemed to be the king.

"I—I—am all right, I guess. Although—"

"Ah, good!" he boomed before Posy could say more. His grin widened, his white teeth gleamed. "Nothing to put you down for long, eh, Daughter?"

"Daughter?" Posy murmured in confusion, looking from the king to the queen and back again. She bit back a panicked laugh. A vision of her own mother and father—nothing like these two—swept through her head and was gone. What *had* happened? she demanded of herself harshly. But she could remember nothing clearly. Nothing but ... but ... Posy sighed in frustration. The memory was just beyond her grasp.

"Yes, my daughter," the queen repeated, her rich voice filling the corners of the room. "You had a fever, and we have been worried about you these many days. We even feared for your life. But you have proved the doctors wrong and are on the mend at last."

"No," Posy shook her head, "I am not your—"

"You may not remember, Princess," a smooth voice, neither the king's nor the queen's, cut in. "They say a fever can chase many memories away, even keep some away forever. You were on a hunt with your father and mother, the king and queen, and the lords and ladies of the court. It began to rain. You, being the excellent horsewoman you are, decided the rain would not stop the hunt. You pushed on. But alas, that very night when the hunting party returned, you took ill with a delirious fever and have been abed ever since. You have regained consciousness only today."

Posy heard these words with astonishment as she looked around the room for the person who had spoken them. At last, her eyes alighted on the stone windowsill. On it sat a great gray owl, at least twice the size an owl ought to be, sitting with feathered chest thrust forward, a self-satisfied expression on his face. Surely, she thought to herself ... surely the *owl* didn't just ... . But even as she doubted it, the creature spoke again.

"But now, here you are," he said soothingly, as if he were calming a distressed child, "and we all rejoice that you are restored to us."

Posy stared, open-mouthed, but the creature merely gazed back at her placidly from where he perched.

"Yes, yes," bellowed the king rather impatiently. "So we will leave you to rest, my dear. Come, Valanor." He took the queen's hand. "The Kingdom awaits us, you know." And they swept from the room.

The Kingdom awaits us? Posy snorted under her breath. Had the man really just spoken those words? They seemed theatrical—like those you'd hear in a fairytale, or read in a ... Posy froze.

"In a book," she said aloud, though the room was now empty.

Memory flooded her then. Once again, she could hear her parents down the hall, just as she had countless times before. Their voices rose and fell in anger, traveling through the house and into her room like an endless, waking nightmare. She remembered the heavy tread of her own feet as she launched from her bed, heard the jarring of her parents' bedroom door as she ripped it open. And she had screamed at them—screamed to stop them shouting at one another, screamed to quiet the fear and anger that reared up inside of her. But she had seen their faces turning toward her, and their expressions had gone from shock to anger and then a disappointed sadness that was worst of all.

"How dare they?" Posy turned sideways and whispered into her pillow. "How dare they get angry. They were the ones hurting *me*. And hurting Lily, too."

Posy felt a thrill of sorrow, thinking of her little sister. Lily was only eleven. To Posy's 15-year-old mind that was much too young to be subjected to the bitter misery of what their parents' marriage was doing to their family. She had hoped Lily had heard nothing of the wild interchange of that night, when her parents shouted cruel words at one another, and she shouted cruel words to them in turn.

Tears pricked behind her eyes. Yes, she remembered now. Anger and tears had etched such deep grooves into her young heart that she hated the very thought of them. Anger and tears were what drove her out of the house and straight down the street to the library. Peace, and silence, and books. Posy clung to these things.

And that was where she had discovered the book. She had found it innocently enough, she supposed. The library was an old one, to be sure, but she had thought she knew all its dusty corners and sagging shelves by now. But somehow, yesterday, she had found herself in an unfamiliar place. And down the dimly-lit aisle she had chosen a strange, musty book, with a scrolling, antique font. Posy had chosen it for the lettering. It had reminded her of the covers of the fairytales she had read as a child—the ones that made her feel like a character in a kingdom far away from any troubles she knew in her own world. And she had certainly needed such an escape.

Her fingers could still feel the grooves of the book's title, her hands the heaviness of its spine. She had opened it, and ... and ...

The thought that came to her next made her suddenly sit up in the unfamiliar bed. She didn't dare say it aloud, to herself or anyone else, for it seemed so bizarre. All the same ...

Posy looked to the windowsill, intending to question the owl, but he was gone. A young maid in a simple gray gown approached Posy's bed and began to straighten her covers in a fidgeting way, as if she didn't know what was expected of her. The girl wouldn't look into Posy's face, even when Posy asked her for her name.

"Olena," the girl said, keeping her chin down and her eyes on her clasped hands.

"Olena," said Posy, thoughts of her own soft-spoken sister making her voice gentle, "I think you must know that I am not the princess, whoever she is, don't you?"

Olena's gaze shot up at once and her frightened eyes looked straight into Posy's. "Yes! That is to say ... no! Oh, Princess! Please don't ask me such things!" And the girl flew from the room as if she were escaping something horrible.

Think, Posy said to herself. *Think hard. Where are you? How in the world did you get here? What were you doing last? Shouting at Mom and Dad—telling them to shut up, telling them I hated them. Yes, I remember that much. Then, at the library ... finding the book, yes ... taking it ... feeling so strange .... Opening the book .... But that means ...* Posy's mind swam and spun within her head. What *did* it mean?

Ashlee Willis

"You are within the book, yes."

Posy started and turned toward the sound of the voice. The owl had returned and was sitting on the windowsill as if he had never gone, his soft gray and white feathers gleaming.

"In case you were wondering, which of course you have to be, you are within the book. That is really all I am at liberty to tell you for now, for things are a bit complicated within the Kingdom at present. Well, *very* complicated, in fact. I might tell you more at another time, but I don't know when. It can't be now. We need more privacy and I need more information. You will have to be patient, Princess."

"But why are you calling me Princess?" burst out Posy. "You must know I am no princess, and certainly not the daughter of any king and queen. I don't think you realize where I actually come from .... It's nowhere like this!"

"Oh, of course it's nothing like this," the owl scoffed, ruffling his chest feathers. "No world is like this one. We are characters living within the Plot. And now you are one of us. But I can say no more—not now! I will find you when the time is right. In the meantime, *Princess,* I suggest you go along with whatever happens. It might be much less than pleasant if you decided to start talking and asking questions. No one asks questions here. You must follow the Plot. The king will have it no other way." The owl made ready to fly out the window once again. As he turned, his head swiveled around toward Posy and he said, "I am Falak, the king's chief adviser, if you have need of me. But you won't, because there is nothing else to say now." And he spread his great wide wings and dived off the windowsill and out of sight.

* * *

The thought slowly came upon Posy that perhaps it was no bad thing to be believed a princess. In fact, the more she thought of it, the more she liked the idea. How many times had she wished for just such a thing, as she sat curled on her bed enwrapped in a book?

As she lay on the enormous, soft bed underneath a silken coverlet, she began to feel very comfortable. Her fear and ignorance as to the way she had come to be in this strange place began to matter less and less. The owl had told her to play along, and she was only too willing if that meant living as a princess and forgetting the worries of her other life, which already seemed so far away. She determined that she would enjoy this adventure, even if it turned out to be a dream after all.

One thing worried her as she began turning things over in her mind. If this was a book, and it was full of characters, where had the *true* princess gone? And what if she came back and found Posy had taken her place?

CHAPTER TWO
Inside the Book

Posy slept as though she was exhausted that night, though all she had been doing was lounging in the princess' grand luxurious bed all day. When she awoke, she felt almost as good as new, though she still had a nagging feeling in the back of her mind that things were not as they should be.

The maid named Olena appeared as if by magic and began to help her dress. When Posy had woken the day before she had found herself in a simple white gown. The worn jeans and long-sleeved T-shirt she had remembered previously wearing were nowhere to be found.

Olena helped Posy into a pale lilac-colored dress that felt like froth on her skin. It fell in folds of material that flattered Posy's figure to great effect. She found herself staring into the mirror, not able to believe she was looking at herself.

Posy had never thought much of her appearance and had secretly thought herself rather plain. Her brown hair fell past her shoulders, always a bit wild because of the curl in it that she never seemed to be able to control. Wide green-gray eyes set in a pale, unexceptional face. Her figure ... well. "Late bloomer" was how her mother always kindly described her. But she had always accepted her flat, slender shape. The dress she wore now revealed a figure she hadn't known was there. She blushed and turned away from the mirror.

She had gazed into the embellished mirror long enough to see a few things, though. The dress made her awkward new curves seem graceful. Her hair had a softness and her eyes a brightness that she didn't recognize. Posy still didn't think she could be called pretty, but she could look in the mirror and smile at her reflection now, which was more than she had ever done before.

After Olena had swept back Posy's hair and laced it with tiny flowers, she told Posy she was finished and free to go.

"But go where?" Posy asked.

Olena fidgeted nervously and stared somewhere past Posy's left ear. "I—that is to say—perhaps ... yes, perhaps you should see your father about that."

"But, Olena, my father is not here. He is somewhere far away—not here. Whom should I see? Do you mean the king?" Posy couldn't help herself asking, though she knew perfectly well whom Olena was referring to.

Olena's hands jerked and she began wringing them together.

"Well," Posy said at last with finality when she realized the maid wasn't going to answer her, "I will speak with the king, then." And she picked up her skirts and swept from the room, feeling a thrill as her voluminous skirts swished around her ankles and her delicate slippers padded the marble floors.

Shutting the door behind her, Posy realized this was her first venture beyond the princess' bedroom, and she felt a growing curiosity to see more of this kingdom she had fallen into. *A book*, she told herself incredulously as she traversed the wide halls of the castle. *I am in a book—that is what the owl, Falak, told me. How can that be, when everything here is so solid and real?* Posy slowed her pace and ran the tips of her fingers along the stone wall of the corridor. Real, hard, cold .... not a dream. Posy's mind reeled.

"Daughter!" boomed a voice Posy immediately recognized. She took a deep breath before she turned and smiled shyly at the king, who was coming swiftly toward her. Posy had no idea how to respond to this large man as he towered over her and appraised her with his intense charcoal eyes. Her heart beat faster as she bowed her head slightly and lowered herself in what she hoped was a proper curtsy.

"Your Majesty," she murmured, barely daring to look back up into his face. She didn't know whether she was in awe or whether she wanted to burst out laughing at the absurdity of the situation.

"Oh, yes, quite proper, quite proper!" he beamed on her. "How well you have recovered, my Evanthe."

"Evanthe?" began Posy.

"We will have to begin the Plot again now, won't we? This time a bit more carefully, wouldn't you say? We don't want any more riding accidents, or any more straying from the lines. What would the Kingdom come to, eh?"

"Riding accidents?" Posy asked. "But I thought I was supposed to have had a fever ..."

"Ah," the king gave her a conspiratorial grin. "Yes, yes, a fever, of course."

How could he have forgotten what happened to his own daughter in such a short time? *But then*, Posy reasoned, *I'm not his daughter, am I?* Was it possible that she looked so similar to the princess Evanthe that she was truly being taken for her?

"But my name is Posy," she finally said cautiously. "Thank you for having helped me recover—I'm still not quite sure what has happened, it's all so confusing. But I am sure I'm not who you seem to think I am ... Your Majesty," she added as an afterthought.

The king looked down on her for several moments, which seemed to stretch on, until finally he took a step closer to her. He took her arm gently in one of his large bejeweled hands and leaned toward her, closer and closer until his mouth was almost against her ear. "Now, we can't have that sort of talk, my dear." His smooth voice was deadly as a knife wrapped in satin. Posy's heart began to pound as his grip tightened on her arm and his voice hissed just above a whisper. "People will begin to think that your injury did you a lasting harm. We follow the Plot here, my daughter, and if you stray from it, you will greatly regret it. You are my daughter, Princess Evanthe. I am your father, King Melanthius, ruler of the Kingdom and every creature within it. Your mother is Queen Valanor. You would do well to remember everything I tell you ... sweeting." The king's voice brightened abruptly as he spoke the last word and released her arm from his painful grip. Posy took one stumbling step backward. He reached a hand up to brush back a strand of her hair in a fatherly gesture, making a *tsking* noise. "Such a shame, your memory loss! You must meet with Falak as soon as possible to relearn the ways of the Kingdom, my dear. It seems you have forgotten a great deal indeed." He turned on his heeled shoes and walked away from her down the corridor without another word.

Posy released a long shaky sigh and realized she had not been breathing. Had the king just threatened her? It all happened so quickly—his manner changed so swiftly—she almost could have believed it never happened at all. The king—indeed, the entire Kingdom—saw her as the princess Evanthe. Whether or not they actually *believed* her to be the princess did not seem to matter. The

Ashlee Willis

thought made her shudder.

She wondered how she could have let the farce go on so long. This was her second day in the book. If she had known it would come to this, she would never have done it. Then she remembered the king's voice, his breath on her face and his steely hand on her arm, and knew it wouldn't have mattered anyway. Coldness seeped into her fingers and toes as she realized she was trapped. This was becoming more of a nightmare than the pleasant dream she had believed it to be.

* * *

When Posy had spoken to Falak before, the owl admitted she didn't belong in this book—she was certain she hadn't imagined it. She had to speak with him now, she told herself urgently, before things got even more frightening. She lifted her skirts around her ankles and started down the hall. A guard stood outside a pair of massive polished wood doors, and she slowed to a stop in front of him.

"Excuse me," she said carefully, not knowing where to begin.

"Princess Evanthe." The guard swept a low bow and then straightened. Posy noticed he was not looking into her face, just as Olena had done.

"I wish to speak with Falak. If you could show me where to go, please?" When the guard hesitated, she added, "King Mela ... my father wished me to speak with him."

He gave a short nod and said, "Oh, yes, Princess. If you would follow me."

The guard led her down so many hallways and up so many

twisting stairwells that Posy was completely lost by the time they came to a stop. Before them stood a low arched doorway, wooden and riddled with knots. Posy attempted to catch her breath as the guard rapped lightly on the door. A noise came from within, and the man lifted the latch and entered, with Posy close behind him.

Though it was mid morning, the room was unsettlingly dark. A cursory glance about the large room revealed to Posy that all the tall windows were covered with thick drapes the color of a midnight sky. The only light in the room came from a fire roaring in the stone hearth on the far side of the room. The ceiling curved into a dome far above their heads. There were bookshelves that appeared to be carved from the trunks of great trees, branches thrusting out from the sides of them and curling into the room like searching fingers. Posy spotted Falak on one of these branches, his enormous round eyes flickering with firelight. He was so still that Posy realized she had been looking at him several moments without seeing him.

"Princess Evanthe to see you, Chief Adviser," stated the guard, who was already bowing and backing out of the doorway to leave.

"Very good," said Falak evenly. "Won't you join me, Princess?" He spread his expanse of wings and glided from the branch to a chair near the fireside. Posy walked across the room and seated herself in the chair opposite.

"The king sent you?" Falak said. Posy was relieved to hear him refer to the king this way instead of saying "your father."

"Yes, he did," she answered, "though I wanted to come and talk to you anyway."

"Oh? And why was that?" the owl tilted his head almost imperceptibly to one side.

"Because ... well, you told me yesterday we needed to speak—that you would speak to me—"

"When the time was right. When I had gathered more information. That time has not yet come. I can tell you part, but not whole. You will have to be patient, Princess."

Posy searched his face and asked slowly, "Why do you call me Princess when you know I'm not?"

"Because whether you are Princess Evanthe or not, you are now a princess, and a princess is what we need to follow the Plot and save our book."

"What?" Posy said incredulously. "But why?"

Falak blinked. "I will tell you what I can."

Posy nodded expectantly.

"Our princess, the princess Evanthe has disappeared," the owl began, and his huge eyes leapt with reflected firelight. "She has always been here for the Plot. She has never strayed until now. But when the day of–when a certain day came, she was nowhere to be found, and we discovered that she had run away." His voice was low and sharp. "We do not know what caused her to leave. We do not know why she has betrayed us in this way. We only know that the Plot, and the Kingdom, cannot go on without her. The Kingdom has indeed been in uproar ever since we discovered her missing not four days ago. Though you are from another land, I am sure you can understand how a Plot cannot continue without one of its characters, yes? Our very lives have hung in the balance. King Melanthius and Queen Valanor have been beside themselves with worry for their daughter and with distress about what will happen to the Kingdom if she does not return soon."

"So if everyone *knows* she is gone," Posy said slowly, "why am I being treated as the princess? How did I even get here?"

"Ah, yes." Falak ruffled his feathers and stuck his downy chest out a bit. "That is due to me. Well, to be honest, I was aided by a good bit of luck as well."

"*You* brought me here?" Posy's voice rose in astonishment. "But how? How in the world did you do such a thing? How did you even know I existed?"

Falak shifted his clawed feet on the arm of the chair and cleared his throat, "I dabble–I am not proficient at all, you see–but I *dabble* in magic. I suppose you could say that I barely even do that. I merely study it, as a curiosity, of course. But I had learned, through my years of study of certain magical laws within our Kingdom and the Plot, laws that apply not only to us characters, but to those outside of our realm as well. We call them the Infinite Laws, for they apply no matter what story you may come from."

"Even to me, and the story—I mean, world, that I come from?"

Falak nodded slightly. "You see, it is too complicated to explain to someone who has not studied it as I have–and that is why His Majesty left it to me–but in short, there comes sometimes what is called a Requirement. Now, Requirements can occur in both this world and yours or others. When they occur in either realm, there are usually two ways events can unravel: either the Requirement tends to disseminate and resolve of its own accord, or, if it is not resolved, it creates havoc and trauma. Our king is not the type who will stand idly by on the hope that something will take care of itself, and neither," the creature's eyes glinted fire-orange, "am I."

Posy watched the owl closely as he spoke. She wondered just how much the king relied on his chief advisor, and how many decisions Falak himself had made for the Kingdom.

"The Requirement I speak of is, of course, the princess' disappearance and the continuance of the Plot," continued Falak. "We had a great need, you see. And here is the crux. In my studies I had learned that it is thought—though never, until now, proved—that if a Requirement occurred in two separate realms, and they were aligned—rather like an eclipse—then they might meld and solve each other. I hope—yes, I do believe—" His smooth voice became pitched with excitement. "—that this is what happened when you were brought here. You are the answer to our Requirement. And we, possibly, are the answer to yours, whatever it may be."

Posy stared rather open-mouthed at Falak for several moments. She shook her head in disbelief and said, "But you're wrong. I don't have a ... Requirement."

"Indeed?" Falak seemed unperturbed by her answer, and Posy knew he wasn't fooled. She had of course had a need—there was no use pretending to herself she hadn't. But was *this* the answer? It seemed ludicrous.

"Yes," Falak said sharply. "I see in your face that you know it is true. It is as I thought. For the first time in the history of the Plot— or perhaps anywhere—a Requirement eclipse took place. You see, Princess, you are here for good reason—for a purpose."

Posy did not know how to respond to this. It was outrageous, yes, but not more so than everything else that had happened to her in the past couple of days. She was beginning to miss her parents, however little they may care that she was gone, and she was quickly tiring of this.

"Well, I have stood in as the princess," she said slowly. "Now what? As the king so kindly reminded me, I don't know the first thing about the Plot, and most likely I'll mess it up, and you won't want me in it anyway."

Falak eyed her without expression for several moments and said, "That cannot be helped. You will, of course, make minor slip-ups in the Plot, but they will be of no consequence, so long as we get to your purpose. Once a reader comes, it will be only three days you need remain here, then you will be free to go."

"It only takes three days for my part to be over?" asked Posy suspiciously.

"Yes."

"What happens to me, then? Am I even a major character at all?"

Falak straightened up on the arm of the chair and gave her a stern look. "Characters are all equal, for without one of them, how could the true Plot continue?"

Posy rolled her eyes. "Okay, maybe you're supposed to say that or something, but Falak, we all know there are major and minor roles in books, right? So, am I a major one or a minor one? Being the princess, I thought I would be one of the main characters, especially since the whole kingdom has gone crazy since she ran away."

"Your role," Falak said stiffly, "is pivotal to the Plot. Without it, the Plot would not survive."

"So, major," Posy said, then smiled when Falak drew his owlish brows together in silence. "What do I need to know about my character, then, since apparently I'm stuck here until I go through with this? Is there any type of script I need to look at?"

"No, no, nothing as conventional as that. Follow me." The owl swooped across the hazy room to one of the tall shelves carved straight into a tree trunk. He indicated with his wing a bottle, one of seemingly hundreds that lined the shelves in the chamber. "This will give you explicit directions for everything you need to do or say. Just take it and open it after you leave my chamber. The rest will happen of its own accord."

Posy reached her hand up to grasp the crystal bottle. "It's a pity I'm not a good actress. My part as princess will never be believable, you know. I hope your readers don't mind a bad performance!" She laughed.

"Our readers," Falak said, his voice almost mournful sounding, "are very few, unfortunately. Dark fairy tales are no longer as popular as they once were. And you do not need to worry about acting—fortunately for all of us, readers take care of that part themselves. As long as you deliver your lines and place yourself where you are supposed to be when you are supposed to be there, the reader's imagination fills in all the blanks. As long as the words to the Plot remain the same, and clear, all will be well."

"Yes, of course, I hadn't thought of that," Posy said. "But"—she looked at Falak—"you said 'dark fairy tale.' What do you mean ... 'dark'?"

"Oh, a story that is real, I suppose," he answered carefully. "A story with tenacity, and strength. It has light that is bright, but shadows that are deep."

Posy wasn't sure that answered her question at all. "So, this one doesn't end happily?" she asked with growing apprehension.

"That depends on who you are speaking of. For some, yes; for others, no. It is the Plot, and we follow it, or we would not exist."

Why did he keep saying that? His eyes glowed as he studied Posy for a moment before adding, "There are things I wish to tell you, Princess, but as I said before, I cannot—not until I know more. I will come to you when it is time. Now go." He flew up, up, so far into the domed ceiling that when Posy tilted her head back to gaze at him, he looked like a phantom gliding against the blackness of the sky.

Ashlee Willis

CHAPTER THREE

Imposter Princess

Opening the crystal bottle was like an enchantment. When Posy unstoppered the lid, it gave a slight pop, and then blue, misty light spilled gently over the bottle's mouth, falling around her legs, moving up around her skirts and flowing into her hair and eyes. Her skin tingled as the mist's delicate fingers ran along her spine and across her scalp. She shivered as pleasant warmth filled her from head to toe. It was when the sensation faded that Posy began to hear the voice, very softly telling her what to do. *Walk down the hallway, dear. Yes, that's the way. Now head down that staircase and make a right, then a right again. Come on, now, don't dally, Princess.*

She supposed when the time came, when a reader opened the book, and it was time to play her part, the voice would give her words to say, too. At least this way she wouldn't have to memorize anything—that was a huge relief. The mist led her to her own chamber. Once she arrived, it stopped speaking to her, though she did listen for a while to make sure it was gone. "Well, what do I do now?" she said to the empty room.

The mist immediately appeared, swirling above her head. It made a *tsking* noise at her and said lightly, *We have no reader at present, silly princess, so you need do nothing unless you wish to.*

Posy moved across the room to one of the high windows, carved like a gash into the side of the stone wall. She gazed out across two more towers, lower and smaller than her own, a courtyard, and beyond that, what looked like stables. Fields stretched beyond the sprawl of the castle, and beyond them Posy saw a dense line of forest, far down a sloping hill.

Her thoughts must have been waiting for such an opportunity of silence and solitude, for they seemed to descend on her now. Words spoken, things that had happened, seemed to come together in her mind.

First off—the princess had run away. Falak had told Posy that her part in the Plot was pivotal. Everyone knew Posy wasn't the princess, but they wouldn't admit it—wouldn't even look her in the eye. Why, *why* after so long, had the princess Evanthe run away from the Plot? *Why else*, Posy asked herself, *than to escape what it held for her?*

Posy felt her body suddenly grow cold. She shivered and moved away from the window toward the hearth where a fire had been lit. Sitting in a high-backed chair, she stared into the bright flames. She just had to know the answer, she decided.

She sensed it was horrible, the thing the princess had run from. She saw it in Falak's cool gaze, in the king's threats, and even in the darting glance of her maid and the guards in the hall. For it was Posy who now played the part, it was *she* who would face whatever was to come. Falak said the story would end happily for some. But for others …?

"Is mine a dark ending?" Posy murmured to the mist that hung shimmering around the bedpost. Her heart was pounding to hear the answer. But all she heard was silence.

* * *

Ashlee Willis

The day wore on and, despite her worries, Posy grew bored. She paced the marble floors of her room, her lavender dress swishing around her, and she gazed upon the bright tapestry murals hanging on the stone walls of her bedroom until she had committed them to memory. Olena brought Posy's lunch on a gold-embellished tray. Posy thought, as she watched Olena place the food on the table by her fireside, *perhaps it will all taste like nothing. What can food taste like in a book?* But when she took her first bite she was overwhelmed with bursts of sensation and incredible flavors. "Oh, no," she said aloud, smiling at Olena, "I will be ruined for normal food after this." Olena's eyes grew round, and she nodded awkwardly before curtseying and rushing toward the door to make her escape.

Posy sighed. "Olena, before you go, could you tell me something?"

The girl turned, her blond curls trembling on either side of her pale face.

"When do you think my father and mother will want to see me? I mean the king and queen. You see, my head injury made me forget so many things." Posy put her hand delicately to her temple, grimacing a bit for effect. It had been a head injury, hadn't it? Or had it been a fever? She couldn't recall, but it didn't seem to matter to Olena.

Relief spread across the maid's face at the normalcy of the question, and she smiled. "Well, Princess, it is customary for characters to wait until a reader comes to begin their roles at all, but it is never much opposed if members of the royal family, such as yourself, choose to roam the castle or the grounds to find amusement in the meantime. The king himself likes to organize hunts, and throw an occasional ball, between readers."

"And what do *you* do while waiting for a reader, Olena?" Posy asked curiously.

"Oh, my lady, I have much to do. We have to keep the castle scrubbed and shining in the event that a reader opens the book. The Plot has to be ready to spring into action at every possible moment. You never know if the reader will open the book at the beginning or in the middle ... they're so unpredictable!"

"What is your role in the book?"

"I am your maid," she said as if the answer should have been obvious.

"And what is your name in the Plot?"

"Why, it is Olena, my lady."

"So you are a character, but the character is also who you *really* are?"

At this Olena looked still more puzzled. "My lady?"

"Hmm. Well, never mind." Posy licked sauce off one of her fingers and tried to ignore Olena's stare of horror. "I suppose since I *am* of the royal family, I will take advantage of my freedom and walk around the castle grounds for a while. If anyone asks where I am, you can tell them what I'm doing."

"Very good, my lady," Olena curtseyed one last time and disappeared quietly through the doorway.

Posy stood up with renewed energy. If only she had known this hours ago! The castle had to be extremely vast, and the grounds full of wonderful places to explore. As she headed for the doorway of her bedroom, the mist piped up, rushing over her shoulders and into her ear, *Darling girl, you are not going to venture out in those shoes! And without a wrap! For shame, Princess!*

"Oh, um." Posy looked down at her light fabric slippers. She quickly exchanged them for a pair of smart-looking little boots she found in the scrolled wooden cabinet by her bed and grabbed a white fur cloak with a fluffy hood and threw it over her shoulders.

Posy enjoyed getting lost, really, although she knew in this castle full of guards and characters and mists, she could never really be alone. Nevertheless, she instructed the mist to stay in her room. She preferred to find her own way this time. It consented with a disappointed sigh.

After seemingly endless twists and turns down hallways that all somehow looked the same, and down several treacherously steep stone staircases, Posy finally emerged from the walls of the castle and into a courtyard. Sun spilled onto her and she sighed with pleasure. But the wind nipped at her cheeks and nose, and as she made her way across the cobbled courtyard and past a bubbling fountain, she pulled her cloak tightly about her shoulders.

Posy didn't know where she was going. She just walked, a feeling of freedom overcoming her after being confined almost entirely in her room for two days. She eventually came to the outskirts of the gardens and saw the stables ahead of her.

"Good afternoon, mistress," a young stable boy called to her and bowed as she neared one of the high wooden doors where he stood brushing a horse. "Would you like to ride today?"

"Oh, I, uh ..." Posy was taken aback. She never rode a horse in her life, and she knew without a doubt that now was not the time to learn. "No, I don't think so today. Thank you, though."

"Lad, what must you be thinking, asking the princess such a question?" A new voice emerged from the darkness of the stables and the speaker strode out into the sunshine. "After the accident that she has just recovered from? I wouldn't be surprised if she never wanted to see a horse again!"

Posy looked up into the face of a young man about two or three years her senior. His hair hung in silken black waves to his shoulders, and his dark eyes swam with amusement and something like mockery as he took in her appearance from head to toe. He was certainly no stable hand, obviously, judging by his clothes and his way of speaking. *Arrogant,* Posy thought with a frown.

"Oh, excuse me," his voice invaded her thoughts. "It *was* a head injury, wasn't it?" His dark eyes bore into her, gripped her as if her response would answer more than what he asked.

Posy turned away from him, lifting her chin. "No, I won't ride today," she said haughtily. "But that certainly doesn't mean that I won't ever ride again. Thanks for your *obvious* concern, though." She turned to leave and caught his eyes still on her. Their intensity made her want to squirm, or to run away. Instead, she swung to face him and said, too angry and flustered to care, "Isn't there something you should be doing? Somewhere you need to be? You're ... annoying." She tried not to think about how childish the words sounded.

The black-haired young man gave a snort of derision, then shrugged and said, "Have it your way, then. Evanthe always did. Why should her ... *replacement* be different?"

Posy's mouth dropped open, and the hand of the stable boy next to her stopped brushing the horse in mid stroke. She watched the young man's back as he strode indifferently back into the stables. No one save Falak had yet been so blunt with her about her role here, and the fact that she was so out of place.

But she had seen something, only for a moment. Something had happened, behind his black eyes, so quickly she could almost convince herself it hadn't been there at all. But not quite. What had it been? Fear? Sadness? Confusion? Perhaps all three. Posy suddenly felt deflated and empty.

Bells clanged raucously from a high tower somewhere as Posy made her way back through the gardens and into the castle.

* * *

Olena was waiting when Posy arrived back in her chamber. "My lady." Olena dipped a short curtsey and said, "I am here to tell you dinner will be in an hour, in the Great Hall, with the king and queen."

"I am to eat with the—with my mother and father?" Posy asked. "Is that ... usual? I mean, did I do that back before I had my—er—sickness?"

"Oh, yes, on occasion, Princess, although not always. Usually it was when—" Here she stopped a moment as if wondering if she should continue. "Normally His Majesty wants to sup with his family if he has something important to say about the Plot or one of the characters."

"I see. All right, then. Can you help me get ready?"

"Of course, miss. I will help you change, and dress your hair for you."

For the next hour, while Olena worked on fashioning Posy's hair high up on her head, using hot tongs to make small ringlets around her face, Posy's mind wandered. So, she would face the king and queen tonight. She had not seen the king since their alarming exchange in the corridor that morning, which now seemed so very long ago. She didn't feel apprehensive exactly, but a nervous anticipation tingled through her. Maybe she would learn something more tonight.

When she was ready at last and stood before the mirror, Posy was captivated by what she saw. It wasn't Posy at all, she thought. Perhaps everyone truly *did* believe she was the princess, if this was how she appeared to them. Beneath the pale shade of powder Olena had covered her face with and the delicate curls hanging to her shoulders, Posy searched for recognition of the self she used to see in the mirror.

Now she thought of it, what *had* she looked like? Something in this book, or maybe in the castle, seemed to hang over her, threatening to make her forget all she had known before. Posy attempted to bring up the image of her sister in her mind, her mother, her father, her house. She realized with a feeling of dread that she couldn't. A cloud—a sort of fog—fought to cover things in her mind. She could feel it, tucked at the edge of her consciousness. She suddenly knew she had to leave this place as quickly as she could.

* * *

The mist led her to the banqueting hall, commenting on her appearance between directions. Posy nodded absently as it swirled about her shoulders like a cloak and murmured, *I do believe that dress makes you look a bit taller than normal, dear.*

"That's great," Posy said absently, her mind elsewhere.

"Daughter!" King Melanthius' voice rang down the length of the enormous vaulted room as Posy walked through the doors.

Ashlee Willis

"Come—come down here quickly now. Let the queen and me get a look at you!"

Posy made her way as gracefully as possible past all the empty tall-backed chairs lining the long table. She looked up into the king's face with some trepidation, wondering how to behave with him after their last conversation. But his face gave away nothing; indeed, he looked as if there had never been a harsh or awkward word between them. He smiled sincerely at her and scooped her hand into his large one, kissing it. Then he pulled out a chair for her.

"Evanthe, my darling," the queen smiled placidly, her long white hands resting upon her lap. "I am so glad you are feeling well enough to join us this evening. Your recovery has been nothing short of a miracle."

Posy felt cold when the queen spoke. It was as if her words were a script or a pretense. Even a mask.

"Yes," Posy said, "I am feeling much better. Thank you, Your Majesty." She found that though she had referred to the king and queen as her parents to Olena so as not to upset her, she couldn't do it to their faces. They were most certainly not her parents, and she could not imagine them ever being so.

The king took his seat at the head of the table. The queen and Posy sat across from one another further down the table. Melanthius looked upon them both with a generous smile. "We are expecting a reader any day now, you know."

"We are?" Posy blurted before she could stop herself. *How can they know when a reader will come?*

The king raised a black eyebrow. "Why, yes. We are *always* expecting a reader. It could be tomorrow—it could be in a week.

Who knows? But we will get one, make no mistake. Our story will be told, princess. My story, your mother's ... yours."

"And ..." Posy took a nervous breath, "what is my story, Your Majesty?"

The king's dark eyes squinted at her, and his mouth instantly drew into a tight line. In panic, Posy tried to change tactic.

"That is—with the accident, I have forgotten many things. I know that when the time comes for me to play my part in the Plot, I will do so. I just ... I would like to know ahead of time what is expected of me." There was no reason the king should grant her request. Nevertheless, she had to ask, even if she was refused.

Queen Valanor gazed at her husband, and he frowned, drawing his bushy eyebrows together. "I believe I will tell you, Evanthe, since it is understandable that with your memory loss, you will want to be reminded. Tonight is not the time, though. Perhaps tomorrow afternoon? In my audience chamber."

Posy nodded, relieved. If the king was willing to tell her of her own part in the Plot, it might not be so bad after all; although Falak had said it was a dark tale. Food appeared as servants swept into the room and conversation lagged for several minutes as their efforts were bent on eating. Just as Posy was beginning to breathe more easily, the great doors at the far end of the room flew open with a bang. Posy just managed to keep her mouth from dropping open, but her eyes widened in astonishment when she saw who strode into the room.

He, however, did not seem surprised to see her. His mouth pulled into a smile that didn't reach his eyes, and he said in the mocking voice Posy remembered, "Ah, Sister. Good evening."

The king growled, "Kyran, you are late, my son. We have started

Ashlee Willis

without you."

Sister, thought Posy, *son.* Her heart quickened, and she kept her eyes on her plate. So he was a prince—*the* prince of the Kingdom. No wonder he had spoken to her as he had in the stable yard. What must he think of her, pretending to be the princess Evanthe—pretending to be his sister? Who would know better than he that she was an imposter? Posy flushed in mortification. When she finally found the courage to raise her eyes, she found Prince Kyran as calm as she was uneasy. He was busy consuming his food, ignoring her completely.

"Is that all you have to say to your sister, Kyran?" the king challenged, his small eyes on his son's face. The prince went still, and Posy felt her ears burn. She wanted to say, "Never mind—it doesn't matter!"

The prince lifted his dark eyes, and the look in them told Posy all she needed to know. Kyran knew without a doubt that she was not the princess—she could see that plainly enough—and he seemed to hate her for it. How could he not?

But when he turned his gaze to his father, Posy saw even more. The mockery he had directed at her had at least been open; the things she saw in his eyes when he looked at Melanthius made her shudder, and sent an unexpected pang of sadness into her heart. There was no respect there, and much anger. Posy felt fleetingly that perhaps there was a strange bond between her and the prince after all.

Then the prince's face became a mask, and he said, "I'm glad to see you are better, Evanthe." His voice was as blank as his expression. Melanthius nodded in wary approval and went back to cutting his meat.

The Word Changers   33

Posy had never felt as relieved as when supper was over and King Melanthius stood. She was sweating beneath the snug bodice of her dress, and she had hardly gotten a morsel down. The king and queen bid her and Kyran goodnight and walked down the wide candlelit corridor arm in arm. Kyran turned swiftly on his heels and went the opposite way without a spare glance at Posy.

"Wait!" Posy surprised herself by calling. She walked quickly to catch up with him as he turned a scornful look on her.

"I know you despise me," the words tumbled out of Posy's mouth in her haste to justify herself. She knew enough by now, though, to be cautious, and she kept her voice low. "I am not the princess Evanthe. Of *course* I'm not! I don't want to be here at all! My name is Posy, and I'm not even from this book—this world—*whatever* this place is! Your father ... he ... I tried to explain to him, but he ..."

"He wouldn't listen?" Kyran's face was still unreadable.

"No," Posy shook her head. "I tried to tell him who I am, but ... he wouldn't believe me."

"Wouldn't believe you—or wouldn't allow you to speak the truth?" the prince's face broke into a bitter smile. "You see, my father the king knows exactly who you are. Do you think he would mistake his own daughter any more than I would believe you are my sister? He merely wants you to take Evanthe's place. What does it matter if everyone in the kingdom knows you are false? The crucial issue is whether the reader believes in you or not—not the other characters. The Plot—that's all that matters," contempt dripped from his voice.

"So," Posy looked at him questioningly, "did you know your sister was going to run away?"

"No. I found out along with everyone else—after she was gone."

Ashlee Willis

Posy saw sadness creep into his dark eyes just before Kyran looked down at his boots. "If she had told me—perhaps I could have stopped her. Or perhaps ..." his voice faded.

"Yes?" Posy asked quietly.

"Maybe I would have gone with her!" Kyran raised his eyes to Posy's in defiance. "It's not as if my father would have cared, really. Even now, Evanthe's absence is only a burden to him. He doesn't think of her safety. His only thought is for the part that was left open with no one to fill it. How can the precious Plot go on without her? Well, I suppose we're lucky you're here. At least my sister won't have to go through with it again. Whenever a reader comes, she has to do it, over and over, every time the book is read. Why didn't Father see she was bound to run away someday?"

"What?" Posy said slowly, her heart racing. "Go through with what?"

"So you don't know? Well, I suppose you wouldn't. If you were told, you would run away, too." Prince Kyran laughed derisively. "Never mind. Don't worry your pretty head about it." He patted Posy's curls patronizingly. She angrily swatted his hand away. Fear was gripping her like a vice, and she clutched at his arm before she could think.

"Prince Kyran," Posy said, "you have to tell me what it is. What will I have to go through? What's my part in the Plot?"

His face became serious, but he shook his head, the ends of his black locks brushing his cheeks. "I cannot," he answered simply. "I am sorry for you, Posy. But you must ask my father or someone else to tell you. It would be as much as my life is worth to tell you this and risk your running away as well. I can't have that laid at my doorstep. My father will probably try to give you a runaround story, but don't let him. Demand the truth. When you find out, if you still want to stay, come and speak with me. Next to my sister you will be the bravest person I know."

* * *

So, Posy thought, shivering and huddling under the thick layers of blankets on her bed, *I am awaiting a terrible fate.* The words made her want to laugh ... almost. *A terrible fate.* A phrase to be printed on a book jacket, to draw the reader in. She suddenly felt so alone that it was like a physical pain. She curled into a ball, uncertainty and fear eating at her. The last thing she was aware of before drifting into a disturbed slumber were the silent tears that trickled down her cheeks and onto her pillow.

CHAPTER FOUR
Midnight Meeting

Posy dreamed of feathers ... a voice, smooth and imposing. She heard wings flapping and thought she saw her parents among them, behind them, and Lily, her little sister. She tried to call to them, get their attention, and found her voice choked within her throat, muted. Something was tickling her nose, and she lifted a sleep-heavy arm to whisk it away. It moved to her cheek, her ear, until at last she was thoroughly awake. She sat up in bed, breathing hard, certain someone was in her room. She looked to the window first, thinking of Falak, but saw nothing other than a bright crescent of moon, astoundingly large, and a bright scattering of stars.

Rubbing her eyes, Posy took in the room around her. The fire had almost completely died in the hearth, and the air held a creeping, merciless chill. As she reached to pull her blankets closer to her, a folded paper slid down from where it had been placed on her chest. Posy seized it and opened it, turning the page toward the light of the moon.

Come to the Audience Chamber immediately. You will learn all. Let no one see you.

There was no seal, no signature or indication of who might have left it. Olena slept in the room next to Posy's, and for a moment, Posy thought about waking her. She decided against it, amused at the thought of Olena on a midnight escapade through the castle.

It was probably something the real princess Evanthe would never have dreamed of doing.

Posy didn't dress. She couldn't have if she had wanted to; her clothes were so complicated they required a second person's assistance. Her gown was long, but she threw a heavy robe over it and slid into her slippers. She would have preferred her boots, but somehow she thought stealth might not be a bad idea. *Where are you going, dear?* The mist swelled sleepily about her head as she went to the door.

"The Audience Chamber," Posy answered quietly. She had forgotten about the mist. "Could you lead me there?"

Why, yes ... I suppose ... it is so late, though. Very unusual. But just as you say, Princess. You will need your candle, though. I am faultless at giving directions. There's no mistake about that, of course, but I cannot take the blame if you walk directly into a wall or tumble down a staircase, all because of thoughtlessness.

"Oh, yes." Posy knelt to light her candle in the glowing embers of the fireplace and then placed it on its stand.

Very good, the mist said, but Posy thought it still sounded rather disapproving. *Now here we go.*

A few minutes later Posy hesitated outside of two high, magnificent doors. They were solid gold and inlaid with every type of rare gem. On one door the gems spelled out the letter *M*; on the other, *V*. "Melanthius and Valanor," whispered Posy softly, touching her finger lightly to one of the diamonds that winked in the glow of her candle.

You know, the mist said thoughtfully, *you may not want to enter through that way. Those doors are very ceremonial, not to mention very heavy. Perhaps the side door? Over this way, dearie, to your right. There you are.*

Posy spotted another door, wooden and plain, almost hidden in the slope of the wall. *Usually for servants,* the mist explained in her ear, *but much more practical, I think.*

"Yes, thank you," Posy nodded, stepping up to the door. *Practical,* she thought, *and cautious.* After all, the note had said no one must see her, hadn't it? She began to feel nervous, and she thought wildly for a moment that she had made a terrible mistake. What if this was her part in the Plot? What if she was to be led to this very room and murdered in some cruel way? And here she was, walking right into it. Her hand hovered over the door handle as she thought about simply running back to her room and staying there, but then she heard voices. They came from within the chamber, so low they were almost inaudible. A dull warm light glowed from underneath the door—she hadn't noticed that before.

She hesitated, not knowing what to do. Was one of these voices that of the one who had summoned her? Or was it coincidence that someone else was meeting here at this time of the night?

Posy turned the knob of the door as slowly as possible, then eased it open, thankful that its hinges didn't groan. Silently, she padded into the room, pressing her body against the wall where the deepest shadows fell. Across the wide expanse of the marble floor was a high sort of platform, with wide stone steps leading up to it. On top of it sat two magnificent thrones of shining gold. Two rows of miniature golden trees—statues, Posy decided—ran the length of the wide aisle that led to the thrones. On the curving branches of two of these trees sat Falak and another owl, smaller than Falak, with red-brown feathers. King Melanthius paced in front of them before his throne.

Heart racing, Posy crept closer, padding silently in her slippers. She dropped quietly to her knees and began crawling, rather gracelessly, toward the speakers, hiding within the deep shadows of the stone columns along the border of the chamber. When she was as close as she dared, she stopped and sat on the harsh, cold floor, pulling her knees to her chest and clamping down her jaw to keep her teeth from chattering with fear and cold.

"We cannot know when a reader will come. Even the Author doesn't know that," Falak was saying.

Melanthius shot him an angry look and growled, "Do not mention the Author to me. He has abandoned us—that's if he ever existed to begin with. *I* am the ruler of the Kingdom now. *I* am the keeper and protector of the Plot."

"As you say, Sire," Falak conceded smoothly, his round orange eyes fathomless in the candlelight.

"What say you, Egbert?" Melanthius gestured toward the other owl.

"Majesty, I must say I agree with Falak in part," Egbert answered solemnly. "A reader may come this minute, or perhaps in a year, but it will make little difference to the Borders and the lands beyond them. The creatures there are wild; they are not a part of the Plot, yet they rise up against you. If they threaten us, and invade the kingdom, and a reader comes ..."

"Then all will be lost," Melanthius finished, his eyes glinting.

"Yes," agreed Falak, nodding his head emphatically, "How could the Plot carry on if the Wild Folk overran the Kingdom? Even now, without outright war, they threaten it by trying to cross the Borders, by challenging our way of life. What if one of them was to get into the Kingdom while a reader read our story? What then? The

Plot would be destroyed!"

Melanthius turned red. He slammed a large fist down on the arm of his throne. "It will never happen!" he shouted, oblivious to the look that shot between the two owls. "We must declare war," he said, "but it must be outside of the Kingdom, far beyond the Borders of the Plot. Readers must not be disturbed when they come. Characters must be allowed to carry out their parts in peace."

"Yes, yes," Falak said with a hint of impatience, "but how will you account for the absence of your armies if they are far away fighting in a war that has little to do with the Plot?"

Melanthius gazed at Falak several long moments before he said softly, "Why, you will think of something, Falak. You always do. You will tell the characters whatever story will keep them pacified for the time being, and if a reader comes, we will all act as if this was how the Author intended the Plot to be. As long as my people believe I am the one who controls the shape of the Plot." His voice lowered to an ominous whisper. "As long as they believe the Author has forsaken the Kingdom, my place on the throne—and yours as my advisers—is secured forever."

Listening to the king's voice, Posy knew that this was something Melanthius had done before—perhaps often. Deceiving the characters, deceiving the readers. Prince Kyran was right to despise him. Posy rubbed her hands up and down her arms trying to stop herself from shivering. Something more than the chill of the castle was wrapping cold fingers around her heart. She was horrified at the reality of whom the king was, and what he was doing. And she was confused at Falak's part in all of it. She had thought she could rely on him, but it seemed she was mistaken; he was the same as King Melanthius.

Her ears perked as she heard Falak say, "And what about the princess Evanthe, Majesty?"

"What about her?" grunted Melanthius. He stopped pacing, and Posy heard the exhaustion in his voice. His broad shoulders slumped, and he dropped into his throne. "As far as I am concerned, she never left at all. The girl who is here can take her place and be done with it."

Egbert ruffled his feathers a bit and cleared his throat. "Your Majesty, pardon me for suggesting this, but … what if the girl goes through with the sacrifice and, when a reader comes again, decides she doesn't want to go through with her part again? What is to keep her from running away like Princess Evanthe? Can we expect to keep her here indefinitely?"

Posy felt her body go rigid.

Melanthius straightened and replied, without looking at either owl, "And why would she not want to go through with it again? Especially when she knows that in a book you cannot truly die? She might be sacrificed a hundred or a thousand times, but she will always be here again at the beginning of the Plot! Besides—" The king turned slowly in his chair and directed a thunderous gaze at Egbert. "—you know very well that is not why my daughter left the Kingdom. A traitor she might be, but a coward—never."

"No, I—" began a flustered Egbert, but Falak cut him off sharply.

"We know she had reasons of her own that made her betray the Kingdom and yourself, Majesty. And we know"—he shot a significant look at Egbert—"that we must never speak of them, now she is gone."

"Yes, yes," murmured the king, a shadow crossing his face for a moment. But then he stretched his arms above his head with a great yawn. "Thank you for meeting with me," Melanthius nodded to Falak and Egbert. "I wanted a chance to speak with you before I addressed the rest of my advisers. I think tomorrow we will have a council of war. We cannot let the Borders be threatened. Perhaps all we need do is offer threat in return, and that will be an end to it. Perhaps there will be no need for full-blown war at all," Melanthius finished hopefully.

"Perhaps, Your Majesty, perhaps," sighed Falak without much conviction, spreading his wings and gliding from his perch. "We bid you good night, then, Sire."

"Yes, good night, you two." Melanthius stifled another yawn before grabbing his candle and disappearing into the darkness at the far end of the chamber. Posy heard a door open and close. From her place in the shadows she sat motionlessly, trying to still her breathing.

"You may come out now, Princess," Falak said calmly just when Posy thought he and Egbert had surely gone. "You forget there is not much in a darkened room that an owl does not see or hear," Falak said. Posy got to her feet with an effort, feeling cold all the way to her bones. Dread making her speechless as she stood and regarded the two owls with eyes nearly as large as theirs.

"Do you understand what you heard?" Falak questioned matter-of-factly. Posy began to shake her head slowly, as if in a dream.

"No, no, I don't!" she heard herself burst out. "At least, I understand you are no friend of mine at all, and King Melanthius is not far off from being ... well, *evil*!"

"My, you are beginning to sound like your predecessor, Princess," observed Falak levelly. "But, like her, you are mistaken in at least one thing. You *may* call me a friend, for I have your interests in mind. Now—as for King Melanthius—though some might not call him evil, he is indeed not well liked in the kingdom, and swiftly becoming even less so." Falak and Egbert exchanged smug glances, and Posy lowered her eyebrows.

"But why would you wish for the king to be disliked?" Posy asked suspiciously. "You are his Chief Adviser. If he goes down, you go with him ... right? And what about the Plot that everyone seems to find so important? And ... and *what about me?*"

"Your part—" Falak said, and his voice held a note of calculation. "—as you now know, ends in death." Posy choked down the cry that tried to escape from her. Falak continued, eyeing her face, "I told you this was a dark tale, Princess. And you are not the only one whose part is to die; there are many, though lesser, characters. But the Plot decrees that the only way to stop the death of many is for the death of one who is of great importance—you. That is why you are sacrificed. But if I have anything to do with it, this will never happen."

"Wh—what?" Posy stammered. "You would stop the Plot? *Can* you stop it from happening? Wasn't it already written by an author somewhere?"

"I will certainly try to stop it," he nodded, adeptly veering around her second question. "But you must wait for my signal. I will send Egbert or one of my other trusted owls to your room in the next night or two. And you will escape this place."

"Escape!" Even in her distress Posy knew how unlikely this was. "With the princess already having run away, they won't let me five feet away from the castle grounds! Especially after all the trouble it took to get me here! Falak, you of all people—er, owls—should know that."

"Yes, and that is why you could never do it on your own. That is why I am helping you," he sighed with exaggerated patience and hunched up his gray-feathered shoulders. "You will simply have to trust me, Princess. Now, there is nothing more to say. Back to your room quickly before you die of a chill and save the king the trouble of doing it himself."

CHAPTER FIVE
Escape

Posy woke the next morning resolved. Whether something in her dreams had made up her mind, or the slow panic that had been welling up in her had finally driven her to the edge—she knew what she must do.

Knowing the king had a late night, Posy rose early, hoping to be up long before him. She called Olena to help her dress, then summoned the mist.

"Take me to the Audience Chamber, please," she asked.

Again? Oh, dear, well, I suppose ... There is nothing of much interest there, though, I can tell you.

"Oh, uh ...." Posy glanced around. "Could you please not mention to anyone that I went there last night?"

Secrets?! Hmm. This castle is full of those, my dear, the mist answered wistfully. *Why, even I have a secret or two of my own, you know. I will keep yours for you, never fear. Now come along.*

As Posy once more trod the twisting corridors, her mind hummed. It wasn't that she didn't trust Falak, she told herself; it was just that it wouldn't hurt to have someone else on her side, too. A woman. A mother. Someone who would understand and have sympathy. In short—Queen Valanor.

This time Posy motioned to the guards who stood outside of the formal golden doors and entered through them with her chin held high. She saw with relief that the king was nowhere in sight, but the queen sat upon her throne at the far end of the chamber and was already at work listening to a straggling line of petitioners. When they saw Posy enter, though, they parted for her, and she walked the length of the room to stand before Queen Valanor.

"Daughter, how nice to see you," said Queen Valanor benignly. "Do you wish to sit with me as I see the petitioners today, dear?"

"No," Posy said with force—maybe too much force, for the room became eerily quiet and the queen's face froze. "I wanted to speak to you myself. Actually, I have a sort of petition for you, I guess you could say."

"I see," the queen said stiffly. "Well, then." She lifted one elegant white hand and waved it, sending everyone in the room shuffling dejectedly toward the door. When the room emptied, Valanor eyed Posy with her cat-green eyes. Her light lashes sent shadows down her cheeks as she squinted in calculation. "Will this be a petition I may grant you, daughter? For I hope it will not be a waste of both our time."

"I don't think it will be," Posy explained hastily. "A waste, that is. But I do hope you can help me. I wanted to speak to you without the king here."

"Your father," the queen corrected smoothly. "Why would you want to keep something from your own father?" If there was a warning in her voice, Posy chose to ignore it.

"He's not my father," she said boldly. "You know it, and he knows it—probably everyone knows it. I know why I am here. I know the real princess has run away from a horrible fate, and I don't blame her. But you are her mother—her *mother*. Don't you care about how she feels? Don't you care about the reason she left the kingdom?"

The queen stood from her throne and towered above Posy. "How do you know all these things? Who has been speaking to you?"

"I cannot say, Your Majesty."

"You *will* not." The queen's pale cheeks were tinged with two bright spots of pink. "Do you know the reason she left the kingdom, girl?"

No *daughter* or *dear* now, Posy noted grimly.

"Yes, I do. She left because she was being sacrificed, over and over again, every time a reader came. How could you let that happen to her?" Posy's face darkened with anger. "Don't you love her?"

"This is none of your concern, I am afraid," the queen said in a deadly soft voice. "The princess had a role, she was a character like the rest of us, and had to follow the Plot. We would be nowhere without the Plot; Evanthe knew that. She had willingly fulfilled her role many times before she ran away. No, that was not the reason she abandoned us. You have not been here long enough to understand," she sneered. "How dare you, a stranger, come into our world and tell me, the *queen*, what to do."

"And how dare *you* take me from my own world and use me against my will for your own horrible Plot!" returned Posy quickly, her voice rising to a shout. "I thought I could trust you—a woman. I thought maybe you would feel more deeply than the king, that you would have mercy on me, knowing your own daughter is in danger. But I can see I was wrong," she finished coldly and bowed her head in defeat.

"Oh, yes, you were wrong," Queen Valanor said, her voice slinking across the marble floor toward Posy like a writhing snake. "You were very wrong to come to me like this. For now, we know not to underestimate you. The king will be very interested to know how you feel." She snapped her fingers sharply, and two guards appeared from the sides of the room. "Accompany the princess back to her room and see that she stays there." She looked down at Posy, and her smile was sickly sweet. "I am afraid our princess is feeling a bit put out today, and she will need to be confined to her room until I give you further notice."

* * *

So that was that, then. Posy was a prisoner. She walked across her room and peered, glaze-eyed, into the great mirror. She wanted to shout at her reflection, shake herself by the shoulders and say, "What have you done?" She had ruined everything. Why had she been so trusting? Why had she taken such a chance? Simply because the queen was a mother and a woman? She was also the wife of the king, and his co-conspirator. Posy knew that now—too late. Falak would not be able to help her escape, and she could very well be dead in a few days' time. *Dead.*

Posy flung herself onto the wide bed and began to cry, feeling very much like a child. She had barely slept the night before, and she was tired, so tired. She was tired of trying to work things out, tired of guessing what she was to do, tired of being here in this strange and horrifying place with false people everywhere she looked. She threw her arms around a pillow and hugged it, letting it soak up all her tears until at last she sank into oblivion.

* * *

"Falak is rather upset with you, my lady," a voice said close to

Posy's ear. She awoke with a start and sat up in a room darkened with the long shadows of evening. A fire roared in the hearth, so Olena must have been here recently, but had not woken her. She had slept all day! Posy peered around the room. Near to where she had been lying, perched upon her bed, sat a smallish snowy-white owl, with gray-tipped wings, peering at her with midnight eyes.

"Who are you?" she asked.

"Nocturne," he answered, puffing out his chest. "Falak sent me to aid your escape. It seems, though, that you did not want to make it easy on yourself." He shook his head back and forth disapprovingly.

"I—I thought I could trust ..." Posy's voice faded. "Well, I was wrong. I learned my lesson. There is no one I can trust. Maybe not even Falak."

"Hoo-*Hoo*!" cried Nocturne indignantly. "Falak is the *only* one you can trust! He may be the king's Chief Adviser, but he has a vision for the Kingdom that goes even beyond what the king himself wishes to do."

"Oh?" Posy answered, raising her eyebrows. "Just what is Falak's vision?"

"He knows what most of the characters only dream of ...." Nocturne stopped and eyed Posy suspiciously as if she would coax secrets from him against his will. "But I cannot tell you—those are things meant for the ears of King Melanthius and his advisers only."

Posy's eyes widened. "But I have heard people speak of the Author. What does he have to do with it all? Doesn't he choose how the Plot goes? Wasn't he the one who wrote the book to begin with? That's how it is with stories where I come from."

"Oh, the Author may still be here or there .... We do not know, really. But none of us has seen him for years and years. The characters believe he has abandoned his book. Falak says we must uphold the Plot ourselves."

"And what do *you* think, Nocturne?" Posy scrutinized the little white owl closely.

Nocturne shook out his wings uncomfortably. "I ... I have often thought that perhaps ..." He stopped abruptly. "No. We cannot dally with this talk now. Falak would have my tail feathers if he knew I was speaking to you of these things! Of his plans! Please ..."—he hesitated—"do not mention it to him?"

"Of course not," Posy answered with a smile, feeling rather more warmly toward this creature than anyone she had yet met. "I am interested in how you think I will ever leave this room with guards posted at my door to watch my every move."

"Oh, that does make things difficult, but by no means impossible. Come," Nocturne flapped to the window. "Open it," he commanded.

Posy swung open the heavy shutters. "I hope you don't want me to tie my bed sheets together and climb down," she said with a laugh.

Nocturne made a guttural noise in his throat. Posy wasn't sure if it was disdain or laughter. "Indeed, no." He perched himself on the windowsill and said, "Ah, here we are."

Posy squinted into the night, which was clear and crisp. The night breeze felt refreshing against her tear-stained cheeks. She saw one small cloud in the sky, dark and low, which looked a bit ominous. Even as she watched, it was coming closer to the castle.

"What is that?" she asked, pointing.

"That, my lady, is your escape," Nocturne said smugly. If owls could smile, he would have done so as he took in the astonishment on Posy's face.

"Why, it's ... they're ..."

"Owls, yes," Nocturne nodded. "Only some local ones hired for the job—none of them royal advisers, mind you; that would be undignified."

Posy watched with fascination as the owls swarmed toward her window, closer and closer, a great pulsing mass of wings. "But how are they my escape? What are they going to do?" she asked incredulously.

"Well, you are obviously too large for a few owls to carry, aren't you now? So we had to enlist around one hundred of them, just to be on the safe side. You are shorter than Princess Evanthe, but she was slenderer, so it was hard to judge."

"You mean, these owls helped the princess escape, too?"

"Why, yes, they did. And proud of it, they are! You ought to hear them talk about it—well, I can tell you, I'm sure their friends are sick of hearing of it by now—I know I certainly am. All their high talk about furthering the Kingdom—bah. It's Falak who deserves the credit for it .... He arranged everything."

Falak? Posy's thoughts halted to a stop. Falak had arranged for the princess' escape? Impossible! Hadn't he told her that very morning he didn't know why the princess had chosen to desert them, to betray the Plot? What could it mean?

"Ah, here we are now. Look sharp." Nocturne dove off the windowsill and back into the room to perch on the end of the bed. Posy just managed to move sideways out of the opening of the window as the throng of owls all came flying and flapping into her room in a deafening whirlwind of feathers and hoots. She knew it would be a miracle if the guards stationed outside her door did not hear the commotion.

"Now, fellows," Nocturne's voice rose above the shifting and the ruffling as owls perched on every possible surface in the room. "We must help yet another princess to escape. You fellows did a re-markable job last time." Nocturne winked at Posy. "So I know you can do it again. We will be taking her to the stables. That is where Falak is waiting for her."

"But how—" began Posy, but Nocturne held up a wing to stop her.

"Come over here now, if you please, and sit in the middle of the bed."

Posy looked at all of the round gleaming eyes staring at her cu-riously. She knew that even if she did not completely trust Falak, she had nowhere else to turn. Falak himself had said it the night before: she would *have* to trust him. She walked across the room and settled herself into the middle of the great bed. The owls im-mediately began to close in around her. If it hadn't been so bizarre she would have burst out laughing. The owls began crowding each other, sinking their claws into the edges of the blanket Posy sat on, and she understood then what they meant to do.

When they had taken hold of the blanket, the company of owls all began flapping upward until Posy was funneled down and her legs and arms seemed to fold in on her as the blanket went up on all sides. She closed her eyes and tried not to cry out as she tum-bled backward into the blanket cocoon. The owls flew across the room toward the open window.

"Not a hoot now, mind," cautioned Nocturne as loudly as he dared above the incessant flapping of wings. "We must be as quiet as we can!"

Too late for that, thought Posy as she felt a rush of cool air through the fabric enmeshed around her. She opened her eyes. The first things she saw were her own knees, for her nightgown had folded backward. She had undergarments on, but still she scrambled sideways, tugging at her gown to pull it down again. She soon found it was impossible to maneuver into a comfortable position. So she lay quietly, knees pulled to her chest, trying not to think about the possibility of the owls losing their grip on her. She gazed upward through the opening where the owls' claws and wingtips were just visible and saw the white moon staring back down at her.

Posy remembered a time when she had looked up at the moon in another world—her world. Was it not so long ago? The moon here was much larger. The stars twinkled with patterns that jumped out at her. A mermaid waved at her, far above, and swished its graceful tail, sending a shower of falling stars cascading across the black canvas sky.

At last, the owls began to slow and descend, and Posy felt the ground beneath her back, and then a mass of blankets rippling toward her face and covering her in a mound.

"Well done, well done, fellows!" Nocturne's muffled voice came through the blankets.

"Yes, indeed," Posy now heard Falak's voice. Posy pushed the blankets aside and got to her feet, feeling a bit dizzy. The group of owls flew away with one movement, gliding back into the dark as if they had never been. The night seemed strangely silent now. Posy turned to Falak, but her gaze focused on the person behind him, just leading a horse from the stable.

"No!" Posy's voice was low with panic. "He's found out!" she said urgently to Falak, unable to take her eyes from Kyran as he sauntered over to them. Her body was ready to run. But where could she go?

"Oh, you mean the prince," Falak answered calmly. "He knows all. Don't trouble yourself."

Kyran barely spared her a glance, though, and immediately turned to Falak. "Why am I here?" he demanded. "I'm assuming it was you who summoned me? I'd know your cryptic, unsigned messages anywhere, Advisor."

"Yes, I did," nodded Falak, unabashed at the prince's accusatory tone. "We have great need of you, Prince Kyran. This is not your sister." He spread a wing toward Posy.

"Of course I know that!" Kyran said through gritted teeth. "Do you take me for a fool?"

Falak blinked and continued as if Kyran had not spoken, "Your sister the princess Evanthe left the Kingdom and the Plot cannot go on without her. I am allowing this young woman to leave, though she was brought here for the purpose of fulfilling the princess' role."

"And why would you do this, Chief Adviser?" Kyran scoffed. "Out of the goodness of your heart? Because you care so deeply about her well-being?"

"Because we must find the real princess," answered Falak shortly. He gestured toward Posy and Kyran. "And you two are going to find her."

"*What*?" exclaimed Posy.

"Would you rather be back in the castle, then, awaiting your fate?" Falak asked innocently, eyes wide. Posy had no reply.

"Why do you think I need to accompany her?" Kyran asked Falak skeptically. "If she leaves alone, no one would think twice about it, since we all know she is not the real princess. But if I left, too ... my father would surely send out a search for us!"

"Not if I advise him against it," answered Falak smoothly.

"That doesn't answer my question," the prince said. "Why me? Why must I go as well? What have I to do with it?"

"Why, Prince Kyran, I thought you would wish to find your sister! I thought you would want to bring her safely home!" Posy detected a subtle tinge of mockery in Falak's voice. She thought it would be wise to watch this creature, this owl who was so close to the king. How did they know where his true loyalties lie?

"Safely home?" burst out Kyran. "Wherever she is, however horrible it may be, she is better off there than here; that is certain! And you know it!"

"Prince," Falak said quietly, his voice heavy with a secret, "it is not known for certain, but it is thought that the princess has gone beyond the Borders and into the Wild Land itself."

Kyran's face blanched when he heard the owl's words and Posy saw fear flare behind his eyes.

"I think you know what that means, Prince," continued Falak. "I think you know the genuine danger she puts herself in, going to that place." Kyran gave a silent nod. "So you see why we must find her and bring her back? Her fate in the Kingdom would be nothing compared to what she might face in the Wild Land. And who better to find her than her own brother? Her own brother who knows her mind and her thoughts better than anyone else? Who better to guess at where she might be?"

Posy saw the determination on Kyran's face then, and knew he had decided to find his sister, even if it meant going against his father's wishes. *And*, she thought fearfully, *I am to accompany him to this Wild Land, whatever that might be.* The situation felt wrong, all wrong. She had not known exactly what would happen after her escape from the castle, but never would she have expected this. Never would she have wanted it. Now she was forced from a bad thing to something even worse: a journey to find a runaway who had no wish to be found. A journey to a place called the Wild Land, which had made the prince himself turn pale with dread.

"Can you ride a horse?" Kyran turned to Posy and demanded.

"N—no, I never have before." She suddenly felt like crying.

"Well, then, you will have to ride pillion with me," he shrugged. "It will make our progress slower, and the horse will tire more quickly, but it can't be helped. Come on, then." Kyran turned to Falak and nodded. "I suppose you will be in contact with us somehow or another?"

"Yes, I will send Egbert or one of my other owls to you if there is news or if I have instructions for you. You must remember, though, that once you are out of the Kingdom, beyond the Border and into the Wild Land, I will have no way of knowing where you are. The mist cannot follow you there. Then it will be up to you to contact me—and you *must* contact me. If I do not know where you are, I cannot protect you."

Kyran swung onto his enormous black horse and reached down for Posy's arm, raising her easily into the saddle behind him.

"You will find provisions in the saddlebags," Falak said.

"It is not a journey I would wish to make," Kyran said suddenly, looking straight into Falak's hooded orange eyes, "But I do it for my sister. I hope you are not scheming for yourself, Chief Adviser. I hope this chase will not prove to be pointless or contrived."

Falak widened his eyes and ruffled out his chest. "Prince Kyran," he said, "you insult and wrong me. I work for the good of the Kingdom, as I always have and always will. That is my solemn promise to you."

"I suppose the good of the Kingdom means going behind the king's back and sending his son and heir into danger, eh?" Kyran said, his horse dancing circles in anticipation of flight as Posy clung to his waist in terror. "Ah, well, we will see." He flicked the reins and said, "Go on, Belenus." The horse turned and trotted through the stable yard, its hooves thudding dully on the beaten-down earth.

Posy turned to look once more at the castle, its great white towering walls glowing eerily in the moonlight. She sent out a silent wish that she would never have to return there, that her escape would not lead her into further danger. Somehow, she felt both of these wishes were futile.

Falak perched silently on the fence, his large changeful eyes the only thing indicating he was not a statue. He watched them as they neared the shadows beyond the castle. Posy turned and lifted a hand to him in farewell. His eyes flashed, once, and his owlish expression turned to something full of menace. Something—Posy sucked in her breath—full of hate. A shiver racked her body and was gone, and with it the feeling of dread. The moonlight, Posy told herself with a yawn, could play many tricks.

Ashlee Willis

CHAPTER SIX
The Quest Begins

Kyran and Posy rode all night. Several times, Posy's head drooped and her cheek fell against Kyran's back as she grew weary. When she became conscious of it, she snapped back up, alert, shaking her head to drive her fatigue away. She couldn't help admitting to herself, however begrudgingly, that as much as she disliked Prince Kyran, it was rather comfortable riding with her arms around his warm torso and having someone strong to lean against. Twice she felt the muscles of his stomach tighten as he leaned to pat Belenus and she had a pleasant sensation which quickly turned into red-faced embarrassment at what she found herself thinking. She wished she could keep her mind on where they were going, but she found herself closed in on her own thoughts. At last she decided conversation would keep her awake, and her mind from wandering.

"Do you know where we're going?" Posy started, realizing too late that the question might seem to imply distrust.

Kyran shifted in the saddle and grunted.

"I am sorry," Posy tried again, truly contrite. "It's just that I am afraid. Can you understand how I must be feeling? My family is a world away—literally—and I'm in a book. I'm an outlaw and a runaway, and I'm on a journey with someone who can't stand me!"

"Well, as heartrending as your self-pity is to me, I can't say that your fate is any worse than mine," Kyran answered snidely. "Actually, it is much better than mine, I'd say. If you had stayed at the castle, at least you would have had a glorious end in sacrifice. My life has no such meaning, according to the words of our story. And now that I am run away ... my father ...." His voice faded. Posy felt a surprising twinge of pity for him. She did not have to imagine what it was to be on the wrong side of the king's wrath.

"He will be angry," said Posy quietly.

"He will be outraged. But Falak will calm him; he always does." Posy watched the back of Kyran's head as he shook it and sighed. "Falak is the one ... he is the one who truly governs the Kingdom, not my father."

"But it is Falak who is helping us!" Posy said. "And it is Falak who brought me from my world to this one so I could fulfill the princess' role."

"Yes, so don't you find it a bit odd that now you are here, he wishes you away again?" He shook his head again, his black hair brushing the back of his neck. "I only wish I knew what he was scheming. He has too much power. Not like the old days. The owls weren't always royal advisers, you know."

Posy blinked confusedly. "So, let me get this straight," she said. "The Kingdom is where the Plot takes place. The Kingdom is ruled by your father, King Melanthius. Everyone in the Kingdom is a character."

"Yes, yes and yes," Kyran answered impatiently. "I would have thought you'd been here long enough to figure those things out by now. How do they do things in your story?"

Posy laughed and said, "Not like this, that's for sure." She continued her earlier thought. "So, if the Kingdom is part of a book, and the Plot is the same every time a reader comes, how can there have been a time when Falak and the owls weren't royal advisers? Has the Plot changed from what it used to be?"

"Well, yes, I suppose ..." Kyran's voice was uncertain. "At least I've heard stories by those who remember, although not many are brave enough to speak of it to me. Everyone knows if it were to get back to my father that there was talk of the old days... well, let's just say, it wouldn't be good."

"He wouldn't kill them?" Posy asked.

Kyran's still, silent back was answer enough. She shook her head. This king wasn't a king at all ... he must be a tyrant.

"It was so long ago, though," Kyran continued at last. "It was when the Author first wrote the Plot. Too long for many to remember now."

"And the Author," Posy pushed on, "Where does he come in? Why does everyone talk about him as if he used to be around, but isn't anymore?"

"Well, think about it. Once the Author wrote the book, would he need to stay within it any longer? He just leaves the characters to fend for themselves. Whether he does this in other books, of course I do not know, but this is what he has done with us."

"Are you sure?" Posy was skeptical. "I'm not an author, but I know that if I created characters and a story, put my work and my heart into it, I wouldn't just walk away. I've heard people in my own world say that when someone creates something, they are always a part of it."

"That makes no difference in what we have to do," argued Kyran. "What does it matter if the Author is still in the Plot or not? Will that help us find my sister? Will it make my father and mother ... change?"

"But it *does* make a difference," Posy said quietly. Things were not right in this story. It didn't take any great insight to see that. Posy had heard Falak tell the king the Plot would be destroyed if changes were made. And here was Kyran, telling her it had already been changed, and probably more than once. Was Falak merely trying to keep his Chief Advisor position secure? And the business about the Author confused her even more. Surely, the characters must believe that an author existed. They were aware they were in a book—where did they think the book had come from? No, she felt sure they had to believe. But she thought they wanted to forget—*tried* to forget. Especially the king, who, it seemed, wanted to take the Author's place as—what had he called it?—"keeper and protector of the Plot." No, things here were not right.

Posy yawned again. "How long will we travel tonight?" she murmured, feeling her eyes begin to droop again.

"Not much longer. We are heading for the nearest village, only another couple of miles away."

"Village? Is it one past the ... the Borders?"

"Oh, no. I've no idea what's past the Borders. No one does. The Borders extend along the line of forest that you likely saw beyond the castle. But it stretches far throughout the Kingdom, and the Wild Land can be entered anywhere along it. But I wish to visit the village first. I just have an idea ... some information I'd like to get, before we head for the Wild Lands."Posy didn't ask what his idea was. She was tired, and she had an idea he wouldn't have told her anyway. They rode on through the silent night.

Kyran halted his horse suddenly, and Posy's eyes flew open. *Have I been sleeping sitting up?*

"What are we doing?" she asked groggily, peering into the darkness.

Kyran's voice held a note of his usual sarcasm. "Well, I thought you may want to change from your nightgown before we enter the village."

"Oh." Posy looked down at the ruffled, full gown she wore. How had she not frozen? When she began to dismount, something fell heavily from her shoulders, and she saw Kyran's thick riding cape heaped on the ground below them. How he had managed to get that on her as she slept, and from his position in the saddle, Posy didn't know. But for some reason she found she couldn't look at him. This unexpected kindness made her suddenly awkward.

"Check the saddlebag for a change of clothes," suggested Kyran, leaping from the saddle and reaching down to sweep up his cape in one fluid motion. "Falak usually doesn't forget much."

Posy dug into the bag and sighed out thanks to Falak, wherever he was. He had packed a plain, thick dress, nothing like any of the form-fitting, frilled dresses of the princess' that she had been wearing. Posy was longing for something more comfortable, and less revealing. She grabbed the wad of clothing and looked up to find a place to change. Kyran was a step ahead of her. "There," was all he said, gesturing toward a high stone wall that separated the road from the wheat field beyond.

Posy clambered over it and dressed as quickly as she could, shivering violently in the chill night air. "I won't be wearing *you* again," she muttered to the nightgown, dropping it like a fluttering white ghost onto the ground.

As she approached the horse once again, Kyran looked oddly at her. "I suppose it wouldn't do me any good to ask whom you were speaking with just now."

"Speaking with? Oh!" Posy flushed. "I was just talking to my ... to my ... nightgown."

"Your ...?"

"I was," and she couldn't stop the burst of laughter that came out then, "I was telling it goodbye." She supposed it was exhaustion that made her feel so giddy, but she didn't care. The look on Kyran's face as he stared at her only made her laugh harder. His jaw had dropped open—was laughter so uncommon in this story?—and a strange look had crossed his face. But only for a moment, and then his face transformed as he smiled at her, and laughed too. It almost made Posy completely sober again to see him change so much. Seeing him smile like that did something strange to her and she felt the sudden need to catch her breath.

"Evanthe always has hated those frilly nightgowns," he breathed. "I used to tell her"—and he began to laugh again—"that between those things and corsets, she was more of a warrior than I. She was always longing to wear what I did. She even tried, once." His voice lost its mirth then, as he remembered. He fell silent, turning to stroke Belenus' neck. He finally continued, quietly. "And that was only the beginning of the things Evanthe fought against."

Posy drew a slow breath.

"Evanthe and I have always been children. Well, I am eighteen, and Evanthe is sixteen—not really children, I suppose, but we're seen that way by most. In a book, the characters don't age, you see. We always have taken what happens in the Kingdom as natural." The prince pushed back a lock of his black hair. "I think it has always been there in the back of my mind, the fact that things didn't have to be as they are now. But how was I to know? I'm a prisoner of the Plot, too. My life is spent pointlessly dallying around the castle while waiting for another reader to come."

"But Evanthe knew, didn't she? She knew the Plot *could* change without being destroyed," Posy asked softly. "That's the real reason she left."

Kyran raised his dark eyes to Posy's face, and for the first time Posy saw openness in them, no mockery or cynicism. She saw ... *Kyran.* He nodded his head miserably and dropped his gaze to his hands. "Yes," he murmured, "I think she did know. She never spoke with me about it ... if only she had!"

Posy shook her head. "If she had made up her mind to leave, she wouldn't have wanted to put you in danger by telling you."

"Yes, you're right. That's exactly what Evanthe would have thought and done." Kyran looked up at Posy, scanning her face with an odd expression on his own. "How would you know that?"

"Because," Posy said, and she felt sadness overwhelm her, "I have a sister as well, and I would do anything to protect her. I know. Even if it means protecting her from those you thought you could trust."

Kyran got up from where he sat and walked to Posy, his dark eyes brilliant with a new emotion. He took her hand and bent over it, his shoulders slumped. *He's going to cry,* Posy thought with a feeling of panic. She didn't know how to deal with her own tears—how could she respond to his? But he didn't cry. He lifted her hand to his face and kissed it. "I am sorry," he said, his voice heartfelt. "I am sorry I have been cruel to you. I was only angry with my father and mother—not you. I didn't even know you. Angry that my sister left, without a word to me." His eyes looked down into hers, and Posy felt her heart flutter like a wild bird in her chest. When was the last time anyone had cared so much about her feelings, or asked her forgiveness for something they had done to hurt her?

An alarm inside of her seemed to be buzzing ... *danger*. This wasn't something she could afford to feel, not in a story like this, not knowing she eventually would have to go back to her own world. She fought it, shoved it away.

"Do you forgive me, Posy?"

She could only nod, hoping the words she couldn't seem to speak were plain enough on her face for him to see.

* * *

So, there was peace between them and they had found common ground. That is what Posy told herself. They had found a sort of comradeship. Both of them had been hurt. Both of them had been deemed unimportant, their voices and hearts silenced in the scheme of others' plans. Each of them had a sister whom they loved and wished to protect. With such strong cords to bind them together, where was there room for the skepticism of before?

They came to the village soon after. Along the cobbled street, the tiny cottages were cloaked in the silence of night and sleep.

"We will stay here tonight," Kyran whispered over his shoulder. "A stretch of the Border is not far from here, and we can enter the Wild Land from there in the morning."

As they made a turning in the road, Posy saw craggy hills stretching beyond the village and downward toward a darkening of trees. The forest grew thick around them. It threw jagged, dancing shadows across the rocky ground.

Kyran reined in Belenus swiftly and turned to place two fingers on Posy's lips, mouthing, "Be silent." He turned again and pointed silently, and Posy could feel his back stiffen in alert. She squinted into the darkness and after a few moments saw what Kyran was seeing. Dots of lights moving—lanterns. The dim outline of men and horses. Several tents scattered in the shadows of the woods, not visible to the casual eye.

"They are soldiers. The king's soldiers." Kyran's voice was a mask.

"Why are they here?" Posy asked quietly.

"I have no idea," he answered unhappily. "We have never had soldiers patrol the Borders before now. Why now? And why have I not heard of it? Now we will be unable to get into the forest—at least here. Perhaps if we moved a mile or so further ..."

"Kyran ..." Posy said uncomfortably as he wheeled Belenus around on the path. "I ... I heard something—something your father spoke of, with some of his advisers."

"What?" Now he was all attention. "When did you speak with my father?"

"I wasn't speaking with him. He didn't even know I was there."

"You were *spying* on him?" Kyran turned in the saddle to give her an incredulous look.

"No!" Posy said swiftly. "I received a note—I think it was from Falak, but it wasn't signed. I was to meet him in the Audience Chamber. But when I arrived there, the king was speaking with Falak and Egbert. They spoke of holding a council of war because of trouble on the Borders ... trouble with creatures from the Wild Land, trying to cross into the Kingdom and interfere with the Plot."

"Why did you not tell me of this before!" hissed Kyran, spurring Belenus on toward the inn that was the only place in the town with lights in the windows. "A council of war? And Falak knew of it? I *knew* he was a traitor to the Kingdom."

"Falak knew I was there listening," Posy explained quickly. "I think he was only pacifying the king by what he told him. I don't believe he thought war was a good idea. And Falak was the one who rescued me, remember? He could have left me in the Plot to die, couldn't he?"

"Posy," Kyran said with forced patience, "You do not understand. You have not been here long enough." Posy thought she had heard these words before. She sighed. Kyran continued, "Hardly anyone here is whom they appear to be. We are—all of us—actors and deceivers. My father and Falak are probably the worst. If Falak rescued you, and if he sent us on our way to find the princess, you can be certain he has his own reasons. Whether his reasons coincide with ours, or with the king's, or with anyone else's ... well, that is hard to say. But he would never do anything out of mere kindness—not Falak. He has sent us on this journey for a purpose, and most likely not the one he told us. If I had *known* of the council of war before we left!"

"And what would you have done if you had known?" Posy asked, hurt that Kyran thought she was so naïve.

"I don't know," Kyran said, shaking his dark head. "But I am sure there is a connection. I am sure there are reasons beyond what we are seeing now. We simply have to get more information."

"But where will you get that?"

"Here." Belenus came to a stop.

"At the inn?"

"What better place for gossip?" Kyran said, swinging his leg over the front of the saddle and sliding down. He pulled Posy down after him and began to tie up the horse. Posy groaned as she straightened her stiff legs.

"You'll get used to it," Kyran reassured her without turning around. "Now come on."

* * *

The smell of sweat filled Posy's nostrils as Kyran led her through the inn's low wooden door. She didn't cringe from it. It was an honest smell, here in this homely, warm place. And beyond the smell of it, she could smell stew cooking on a fire somewhere. It made her stomach want to howl; she felt she hadn't eaten in ages.

A middle-aged rosy-cheeked woman bustled up to them with a cheerful smile as they entered. "Well now, and what can I get you to eat tonight? Or have you come only for a room?" Posy suddenly remembered whom Kyran was, and wondered if it was possible anyone might recognize him. She saw he had brought a plain green cape, and had pulled it tightly over his clothing, which may have given him away.

"Food and a room, if we may," said Kyran, producing a gold coin. The woman's eyes widened for a moment.

Two rooms, Posy wanted to nudge him, but she couldn't seem to find the strength. The warmth of the room seemed to seep into her, and she found all she wanted to do was sit in a comfortable chair next to a fire. But it wasn't to be for now. As the woman walked away, she saw Kyran's eyes become alert, though he didn't turn his head. He was listening to something, Posy thought, and she soon heard it too.

A man was sitting a few tables from them, with a group of other men, near the back corner of the room. His broad shoulders and bulging muscles set him apart from any other person in the room.

His voice was not raised, but the look of anger on his face was hard to mistake.

"And now they are here, *here*, where our own wives and children live," he was saying, his eyes moving from one man in the circle to the next.

"Yes, but they have done nothing yet, and perhaps they will be gone as swiftly tomorrow as they came two days ago," another man interjected.

The large man waved a hand in the air in abrupt dismissal. "You are a fool if that is what you believe."

"Alvar," another man said in frustration, leaning forward, "I am as concerned as you. There are certain ... items that will be unavailable now that the king's men are here, and that will make it difficult for me to make ends meet. It will make it difficult for many of us." Several men in the group nodded and made noises of agreement. "But what can we do? You know very well we are helpless to do anything against this."

"Helpless," Alvar's low voice seemed to growl, "is not a word I am fond of."

"And nor should you be." Posy heard Kyran's voice from next to her, and realized he had been inching them nearer to the group of men. He pulled out a chair for Posy and then seated himself next to her.

"And you are, young man?" asked a white-haired man with a grizzled beard. He sat straighter in his chair.

"My name can't be spoken here, gentlemen, but you may trust I am a friend. And I agree with your friend Alvar here. You are never helpless. That is a word for cowards."

Oh, no, Posy thought.

"A coward, is it?" One of the men rose menacingly from his seat. "None of my other ... *friends* call me a coward."

Alvar motioned impatiently for him to sit. "Not to your face anyway, Garin."

Garin stared at the larger man for a few moments, then threw back his head and laughed. Alvar smiled, a thing that seemed to turn him into a different person altogether, Posy thought; someone not quite so terrifying. Then he directed his gaze at Kyran once more.

"Where do you come from, boy? And why have you turned up here, now?"

Kyran smiled. "I'm afraid I can't tell you that either."

"That can only mean one thing," Alvar said. "You must be a character well-known to everyone. Eh? Otherwise, why not tell us?"

"Perhaps," Kyran's face gave nothing away.

"And why have you shown up now, only two days after the soldiers?"

"That's a mere coincidence, I assure you. I am as curious and ... concerned as you are. It has never happened before, has it?"

Murmurs of denial moved throughout the group.

"No one has told us a thing," Garin said angrily. "The king treats his characters as children. No, as prisoners. What has happened that he feels the need to station soldiers near our village?"

"The Wild Land creatures are trying to destroy the Plot," Posy heard herself say as if in a dream. Every head turned to her in silence. Kyran gave her a look she couldn't interpret.

Alvar spoke first. "Well, young lady, I don't know where you got that information, but if it's true ... well, it'll be the first sign of anything *real* happening in this story in an age."

Whatever response Posy had expected, it hadn't been this one. She found she was staring at Alvar. His short-cropped hair shone fiery red in the firelight as he threw back his head and roared with laughter at her expression. "Think I'm a traitor, lass?"

"No," she whispered, suddenly feeling weak. How many hours ago had supper been? Too many.

"But a traitor to whom?" Kyran asked. "The king or the Kingdom?"

"Can you tell me without riddles what it is you mean, boy?"

"I don't speak in riddles," Kyran fixed a look of intensity upon Alvar. "I only say what I mean, that following the king no longer means doing what is best for the Kingdom or its characters. You know it as well as I."

The circle of men grew strangely quiet. Posy saw downcast eyes and tight lips. But she noted that even if they were too fearful to admit the truth, they would not deny it. That was something, wasn't it?

"Alvar is right to question the king," Kyran continued, heedless of the men's awkward behavior. "The king takes too much power, and the power he is entitled to, he abuses. And the characters have been weak and afraid and ignorant. Think of the Plot ... really think." Kyran gestured toward the man with the white beard, the oldest in the group. "Do you not remember a time when things were not as they are now?"

The man's expression turned blank, but not before Posy had seen it—that flash of remembrance, that recognition of the truth. Kyran had seen it, too. "Yes," the man nodded, "the Plot has changed right in front of our faces, despite the king's claim that it must never change or waver. It has been so long we have forgotten. A fog has covered our eyes from seeing the truth."

"The truth? And what is that? Young man, if you have any secrets you wish to tell, tell them now!" The old man had lifted his eyes to Kyran now.

"It's fear," Kyran said quietly. "You are afraid to admit what your heart already knows. That the king is not the author of this story. He is no longer even the protector of it, for he has changed it for his own good. And we have more power than we thought. We may not be able to write the story, or change the whole—but *we can make a difference.*"

This proved too much for the men. One of them rose and left the group silently. Posy heard the word *treason* muttered by someone. And the innkeeper, short and round, came rushing forward from where he had been eavesdropping some distance away to say, "Now, now, I cannot tolerate this talk any longer. I won't have words like these spoken in my inn. If you want to commit treason against the king and the Plot, do it elsewhere, far from here."

The group was dispersing now, the men laying their copper coins on the table and departing for their own homes and beds. Posy felt the room spin around her. It teetered sideways, and her vision blurred. She didn't think she lost consciousness, but she slumped in her chair, her hands held to her head as if to steady it.

The woman who had greeted them at the door, the innkeeper's wife, hastened across the room. "Oh, for shame!" she said with an accusing glance at Kyran. "Sir, how could you let your wife come to this state? She must be tired to the bone, and hungry besides." She called for a maid and told her to prepare a room.

"Posy, are you all right?" Kyran's voice held deep concern as he reached for her hand.

"Brother," Posy's voice came thickly as she tried to sit up in her chair. Her hands were shaking. "He's my brother, not husband. You're my brother," she looked at Kyran.

"Ah." The woman gave each of them an odd look. "Well, never you mind, love. We will take care of everything."

Posy was bustled and bundled off and up the dark narrow stairway. When she turned to look over her shoulder, she saw Kyran, leaning forward across the table, speaking with the only man who had stayed behind. Alvar.

Ashlee Willis

CHAPTER SEVEN
A Whisper of War

Whether she was more tired or hungry, Posy couldn't decide. But when the innkeeper's wife dropped her gently onto a bed, in a small room where a fire had been lit, her body began to sink into sleep without another thought. Sometime later, she was woken by noises of movement in the room. She squinted through her lashes to see two maids, one carrying a tray of steaming food, and the other leaning to tend to the fire.

"He's handsome, there's no denying that," one of them giggled.

"Yes," the other agreed. "He is that. But I wouldn't get my hopes up if I were you, Shannon."

"And *why* not?" Shannon turned from the fire with her hands on her hips. "Perhaps his sister will put in a good word for me, if I play my cards right."

The other girl gave her an odd look. "Hmm. So you believe that story, do you?"

"What story?"

"I mean that they are brother and sister."

"Why shouldn't I believe it?"

"Well, Meriel told me she'd never seen a brother look at his sister in such a way. She didn't believe it for a minute. But she won't say anything, though, and neither will I. Perhaps they are fugitives from the Wild Land? Or perhaps they are running away to be married? No, I won't say a word other than to wish them good fortune."

"Thadra!" Shannon cried, then clapped a hand over her mouth with a glance at Posy, apparently asleep in the bed. She lowered her voice. "You must be a fool if you think they are anything but brother and sister. I will say, though, they don't look much alike. He's handsome as the day is long, and she's a plain little thing. But he never gave her a look that was more or less than brotherly if you ask me." She vigorously shoveled ashes into a bucket, sending up a black cloud around her.

"Stop that, Shannon, you'll make a mess—what are you doing? Finish up so we can leave. And," Thadra turned a doubtful look on the other girl, "you never had a chance to see the way he looked at her. Meriel says if her husband had looked at her like that she'd have married him in a month instead of two."

Shannon stood from the fire, bucket in hand. "Two months, was it? Would no one else have her, then, that she only waited two months for that lump of a man?" And both girls doubled in giggles as they rushed from the room.

Posy was awake now, and the smell of food lured her from the warm bed. The maids' words had brought confused thoughts into her head, but she pushed them away. She had barely had time to sit and begin eating when there was a light knock on the door. Kyran poked his head through. Posy motioned for him to come in and he crossed the room in a couple of strides to sit at the table with her.

"So?" she said.

"So …." His thoughts seemed far away.

"What were you and Alvar speaking of down there?"

He shrugged.

"Listen," Posy said, fixing him with the threatening look her mother had given her many times, "I'm here, I'm in this. I'm risking my life too. Don't you think I deserve to know what you're up to? What is it you're planning, Kyran?"

"We spoke of ... well you heard most of it. We also decided that perhaps it's time ... time to –"

"Time to *what*?"

"To make some changes ourselves. To try to break away from the Plot as it is now."

"Kyran –"

"No, hear me out, Posy. I know what you are thinking. You think we are searching for Evanthe."

"Well, *aren't* we?" Posy gave him an incredulous look.

"Yes, of course. But it's more than that. Evanthe ran away for a reason. For a principle. She didn't believe in the Plot either. She wouldn't speak of it much to me—I think she thought it would keep me safe not to know. But I'm no fool. I could see her unhappiness in our mother and father, and in the way things were. She didn't run from fear of what she must do ... but because she knew she was basically a slave. None of us has a choice as to our parts here—*none*. And as hers was the pivotal role in the Plot, who better to rebel, to throw things into chaos?"

"Kyran." Posy tried to keep the panic from her voice. "We are meant to find Evanthe, that's all. Not start a revolution." What would happen to her if war broke out in this place?

"A revolution is just what Evanthe wished to cause by leaving, don't you see?" Kyran explained patiently.

"But where would she go?" Posy asked. She had no idea what the extents of this world were. Did it drop off as you reached the edge, like the margins of a page? Where could Evanthe hope to exist beyond detection?

"She went into the Wild Land, Posy. I know it. Falak may have questionable motives, but he spoke the truth there. I know Evanthe. She's always had a curiosity for that place, an instinct that it wasn't what we all believe it to be. And we must follow her there quickly, for I believe Falak won't be off our tail until we are beyond the Borders."

"But he wanted us to let him know ..."

"Posy! Do you honestly think I would let him know anything of our movements? This is our quest now, not his. And we don't do it because he commanded us. I don't trust him."

Posy knew it, too, really. She felt the same, the intuitive doubt in Falak's intentions. But she wasn't ready to write him off yet. Neither, though, was she willing to argue for him.

"You are tired." Kyran's dark eyes took her in. "Get some sleep. My room is next door, although I won't be there for a while yet. I've a few things to do," he said vaguely.

"Hmph," Posy said, rising from her chair and moving toward the bed. "Things?" she asked. "Things like amassing an army, I suppose." She smiled. Kyran's silence, and the look he turned to her, made her smile freeze on her face as her heart began to pound.

"Kyran ...! You *aren't* ..."

"Trust me, Posy," was all he said, and then slipped out the door, silent as a shadow.

* * *

The light that flooded through Posy's window the next morning was almost unbearable. She opened her eyes and tried to sit up in bed, but let out a cry, as the light seemed to pierce her head with pain.

The innkeeper's wife, Meriel, came bustling in with breakfast, a smile gleaming on her round face. "Such news!" she said.

"News?" Posy groaned.

"A reader!" she burst out. "We have a reader at last! Surely you could have guessed it, dear. I imagine you and your—er, brother—will need to be getting somewhere soon so you can begin your roles." She didn't wait for an answer, but continued a bit pensively, "When a reader comes, our whole world changes, really. Everyone springs into action. The sun becomes brighter. The wind becomes stronger. I remember a time," she said with a sigh, "that these things were said to happen not because of a reader ... but merely because the Author had written us. That," she finished slowly, "was the meaning of our lives."

Posy remained silent. She didn't have to ask if those times had gone.

"Anyway, dear," Meriel said, snapping out of her reverie, "I just thought you would be excited at the news. We here in the village certainly are. When a reader comes, our businesses do better, our services are needed more often, and we all live so much better, I can tell you. People flock toward the castle, and our inn gets double the business it usually does."

"But why do people go to the castle when a reader is here?" Posy asked.

Meriel gave her a questioning glance before explaining, "Why, they may be needed for the Plot, you see. All these characters, most of which have no part to play in the Plot at all other than being mentioned as part of the Kingdom—they wish to play better parts, that's all. Oh, there will be parts that are minor, of course—characters that have no names at all, such as kitchen help or gardeners. But it is agreed among us that those lesser parts are not played by the same person twice. Those who wish it may have a turn."

"I see," Posy said. She was thinking, *proof again*, proof that the Plot can change, even if in minor ways. Right under the king's nose, too. She wondered what they would do for the princess' role, now that Posy was gone as well. She imagined the castle was in an uproar. Posy snapped back to attention when she caught Meriel staring at her as she stood thinking to herself.

Just then, the door was flung open, and Kyran stepped into the room. The innkeeper's wife excused herself and left the room.

"I've just come from Alvar's house," Kyran said immediately after the door closed.

"His ... house?"

"Yes. We had to speak. We have decided it is best to make a beginning ... to start gathering followers. We will find those who are unhappy with the Plot as it is, with the council of owls ... "

"And with your father as king?" Posy put in.

"Well, yes—I suppose—"

"Anyone who will wish the Plot different than it is will inevitably put blame on King Melanthius, Kyran, you must see that," Posy said gently.

"But they will remember he was once a good king, wise when he was not under the influence of Falak."

"All the same ... he has changed—he is different now—and that is what the characters will see."

Kyran grew silent, and for a moment Posy thought he was angry with her, that he would deny what she had said. He proved her wrong.

"You are right, Posy; they will blame my father. Perhaps I can change their minds about him, if he is put under better counsel. Perhaps I can speak with my father, and he will agree to change. And perhaps not. That is a chance we will have to take." His voice was strong, but Posy detected the uncertainty in his face, in his eyes, and she felt the urge to reach out to him. She suppressed it and went back to eating her breakfast.

Kyran explained to her all that had passed between Alvar and him. Alvar had sent a note to the inn and Kyran had met him at his house early that morning. It turned out Alvar had long been unhappy with the Plot, the king and the council of owls. He told Kyran that he and several others had met numerous times to discuss what was to be done. They always arrived back at the same inevitable conclusion: war. Talking of war seemed to make Kyran's face transform, Posy thought. It hardened and seemed to glow. She supposed this was how most men reacted to this sort of thing, with a sense of duty to a better cause, and imagining victory to come. But she found she could not. It frightened her; not only the violence of it, but the things it might bring about for the Kingdom and its characters. Whether she liked it or not, she was part of that Plot now, and its welfare concerned her. War was a huge decision, that once embarked on could not be taken back. She reminded Kyran of this.

"Yes, Posy," was all he said. "I know you mean well. But don't you see? It is no longer in our hands. That is the very thing Alvar and I spoke of. The war is no longer our choice. Skirmishes have been happening everywhere, even as near as two villages over, and you saw yourself that my father has stationed soldiers to guard the Borders. There is no longer a question of war, for there *will* be one.

The question now is: who will be victorious?"

Ashlee Willis

CHAPTER EIGHT
Unexpected Treachery

The swish and flapping of wings made Posy and Kyran both start and look toward the window. Neither of them saw anything for a moment, and then Kyran leapt from his chair and reached to the floor. He picked up a parchment that was lying there, folded and sealed in red wax with the imprint of a claw.

"Falak," he said rather grimly. He opened the letter and read it quickly, then flung it across the table toward Posy.

A reader has come, as you will have guessed by now. The princess' maid, Olena, is playing the part of the princess Evanthe for now, as there was nothing else the king could think of to do with both princesses gone from the castle. She is deathly afraid and has to be prodded along constantly, so my hope—painful though it may be—is that she will play the part so ill that the reader will grow bored and stop reading the Plot altogether. I pray you, though, find Evanthe and bring her back as quickly as you can. When you both disappeared, the king flew into a rage such as no one has ever seen. He even threatened and blamed me, which he will come to regret. He will doubtless send out searchers for you, though they will most likely not venture beyond the Border. So, get you there quickly and don't return without the princess.

*The king has held a war council, and it seems war is indeed
inevitable. I should not wish either of you to come to harm.
Once you are beyond the Borders and the mist of the Kingdom can follow you no longer, you will need to contact me.
Please do this at intervals, so I know of your progress; find
one of my brethren and send him on with a message to me.*

-- F.

"Oh, poor Olena!" exclaimed Posy with pity after she was done reading the letter. "She has to play my part! She will be so afraid!"

"I'm sure she will," Kyran said absently, plucking the letter out of her hand and throwing it into the fire. "But we won't find out, for we won't be contacting Falak again for whatever reason. I don't want him knowing where we are once we are past the Borders. Are you ready to go?"

Alvar was waiting for them near the inn, sitting atop a wagon looking as severe as he had the night before. As they approached, the smell hit Posy like a physical force. Manure. It filled the back of Alvar's wagon along with other unrecognizable filth, the sickly sweet smell of it making Posy's nose wrinkle in disgust. Alvar laughed when he saw her expression and said, "It's a necessity, Miss, if you wish to get past the Borders undetected. It's one of the only—ahem—legitimate reasons for crossing into the Wild Land."

"What are the other reasons?" Kyran questioned, handing Posy up into the seat next to Alvar and climbing in after her. "The ones that *aren't* legitimate."

"Well," Alvar hesitated, urging the horses on down the street. "There are some—I won't name names of course—but some get their livelihood from the Wild Land. There are healing herbs, game, and lumber there. Too close and too tempting to be left to nothing and no one. But it is forbidden to go there unless empty-ing refuse just beyond the trees. The king," he said with a wry look, "must have his Kingdom looking and smelling clean I suppose. Al-though it may be more difficult than I thought."

"What do you mean?" Kyran looked up, his eyes sharp.

"The encampment is heavily guarded, and more so every day. Just this morning I saw more troops marching past the village. And there are owls, too." He flexed his great arms and shook his head. "Interfering pests."

"So what are we to do?" Posy asked, eyeing the cart with a build-ing sense of dread.

"Ah, that's simple, Miss." Alvar leaned forward confidentially. "This is my neighbor's cart—my neighbor is ... well, he makes a good bit of his money off fruits of the Wild Land. So he has need of a wagon like this, he does."

"A wagon with manure in it?"

"No, no," Alvar smiled. They had come to the outskirts of town, beyond the last of the houses and shops. Alvar reined in the horses and leapt nimbly from his seat. "A wagon like this," he said, yank-ing on a rope that extended from the side of the wagon bed.

Posy and Kyran climbed down and bent to see what he meant. A sort of trap door had swung downward from the bottom of the wagon, and Posy could see a dark opening beyond it.

"A false bottom," said Kyran with a nod. "Well, Posy, are you ready?"

It was a tight fit, and Posy was more than a little uncomfortable. Alvar loaded them in, pushing two bags in after them.

"Your food," he explained. Posy wondered if he had thought of it himself or if Kyran had given him money to buy it the previous night. He also tucked a blanket over the top of them, "In case the manure seeps through," he told them. Posy tried not to gag.

"Hep," called Alvar to the horses and with that they were off to the Borders, the forest of the Wild Land, and, Posy thought grimly, most certain danger. Posy had noticed one of the two horses hitched to the cart was Belenus, Kyran's blue-black gelding. She supposed Alvar was going to unhitch him when they got safely to the forest, then take his own lone horse back with him. Posy gave an involuntary shiver. They were trusting much to the soldiers' inattention.

Within fifteen minutes, they had reached the encampment of soldiers. Kyran whispered into Posy's ear, and she felt his breath blow a wisp of her hair against her cheek. "Do you think you could see out of the slats on your side of the cart, Posy?" he asked. "I am turned the wrong direction and am wedged so tightly I don't think I can move."

Posy couldn't move either, but she could tilt her head sideways, just enough to place her eye even with a space between the boards of the wagon. She had a narrow view of the soldiers they were approaching. The noises of the camp surrounded them now, the clank of metal, the occasional rough shout of orders or the hoot of an owl. Posy squinted through the boards. She wasn't sure what she was looking for.

Then her body stiffened. She and Kyran lay so close he knew something was wrong right away. "What is it?" His tone was sharp and alert.

Posy swallowed with difficulty and whispered hoarsely, "It's Falak. He's here!"

Silence for a moment, then, "Are you certain?"

"Yes," she answered, certain indeed. He was perched on the hilt of a sword that had been thrust into the ground, overlooking the activity with wide yellow eyes. "Why is he here? What is he doing? Has he followed us, do you think? He told us he couldn't come with us—he had things to do at the castle."

"He lied," said Kyran shortly.

"Well, he knows we are near, at least. He knew we were in the village this morning—that's where he sent the note. And now here he is, almost like he's waiting for us." Posy heard the panic in her voice. She found herself remembering the malicious look on Falak's face as they rode away from the castle. She hadn't imagined it, had she? No, she did not trust him now. Suddenly, the small space seemed unbearable, and she fought the urge to begin squirming.

Posy turned her head again and peered out into the crowd of soldiers as Alvar steered the wagon slowly toward the forest edge. He had tried to take a path on the outer edge of the camp, but he was still close enough to draw attention. He had not yet been challenged, but Posy saw that men were starting to give them questioning glances. Even if they weren't concerned about what he was doing, thought Posy, they couldn't possibly miss the way this wagon load smelled. If only they could get past Falak!

That's when the shout came.

"You there!" one of the commanding officers demanded, breaking through a small group of soldiers. "What do you think you're doing, bringing all that filth into our camp?"

"If you please, sir," said Alvar calmly. "King Melanthius himself has decreed that we are allowed to dispose of our waste just beyond the Border. I am merely taking a load there now. It will take no more than a few minutes, I promise you."

"Oh, no, you don't," the commander said, shaking his head once. "The king might have decreed it at one time, but that is over now. No one crosses the Border, coming or going. Don't you know we will soon be at war with the Wild Folk?"

"I have heard as much," Alvar conceded. "But what am I to do with my wagon load? Dump it in my own yard?"

"Why, yes, for all I care," the commander said with a cold laugh. "Now away with you. I believe we have a reader, and every last character is needed for preparations."

"No, no," said a voice, smooth as glass. With a flap of wings, Posy and Kyran heard Falak approach.

"There is no reader," said Falak, "not anymore. The princess' performance was very poor, and I think she bored our poor reader to tears! I hope most sincerely that will never happen again." His voice sounded very pointed, and Posy suddenly thought, *He knows we are here. He knows, and he is speaking to us.*

"Now what do we have here?" came the owl's dispassionate voice as he surveyed Alvar and his load. The commander briefly explained, and Falak said offhandedly, "Well, I suppose it won't hurt to let one through. After all, he has made the trip from the village, and it would be a pity to send him all the way back without having accomplished his errand."

"But, Councilor ..." the commander began, but Falak silenced him with a shake of his feathers and a dark stare. "As you say," the man finished shortly and moved aside for Alvar's wagon to lumber by.

"He has let us through," Posy said softly to Kyran. "He knew we were here, hidden—I know he did. And he is letting us through."

To her surprise, Kyran said nothing for a long time. She turned to look at him, their faces inches apart. Bars of light moved across his face through the wagon sides, but his eyes glinted in the dark. Posy knew the look in those eyes; she had seen it only once before, when Kyran had spoken of war. His dark eyes were hard and far away, resolve written in the set of his jaw. She didn't know what it meant, what he was thinking, but when she opened her mouth to ask him, the wagon jolted to a halt. They were in the forest of the Wild Land.

* * *

"All right now," called Alvar as quietly as his forceful voice could manage. "We are in the clear." They heard him make his way off his seat and then heard the scratching of the latch on the belly of the wagon as he unhitched the trap door underneath them. "Watch yourselves, now," he said just a moment before they both tumbled out of the wagon and onto the damp layer of leaves that covered the forest floor.

Kyran grasped Posy's hand and helped her to her feet. She brushed leaves off her dress and cloak while Kyran and Alvar went to work unhitching Belenus. They worked swiftly and didn't say a word. Posy looked about her, amazed at how dark it was within the thick trees of the forest, when they had just come from a sunny field minutes ago. Posy saw that Kyran was gazing about them into the shadowy trees, the muscles in his body taut and his eyes sharp.

"What is it?" she moved nearer to him.

He only answered her with a short shake of his head. His gaze had centered on a spot some distance from them, the place through which they had just driven the wagon. A second later, he shoved her roughly behind him as his voice came harshly in her ear, "Stay behind the wagon. Take Belenus and run if the worst happens." Then the quick scrape of his sword as he unsheathed it and motioned to Alvar, who was already there beside him, a knife in each of his large hands—surely a sight to frighten anyone.

Then she saw what they had already seen. Two soldiers were making their leisurely way toward them through the trees. But their nonchalance didn't fool Posy for a second; she saw the deadly intent in their eyes even from a distance. *Stay calm, stay calm*, she told herself as she gripped the sides of the wagon until her knuckles were white; *you are in a book, you can't die—can you?* But she wasn't *in* the book anymore, she was not in the Plot. They were beyond the Borders now, and she didn't know what rules held sway here.

Without a word, the two soldiers drew their swords. When they were within range, they didn't waste a moment, but lunged into attack, so swiftly that Posy let out a short scream. But the soldiers had met their match. Kyran, as the prince, had been trained to fight, and Posy saw quickly, with an odd breathless feeling, that he probably could have taken on both soldiers alone. Alvar made up in power for what he lacked in technique, the muscles of his arms bulging, his lip curled in a snarl. They circled and struck, parried and slashed, until Posy became dizzy.

I'm being the stupid girl, she thought suddenly, thinking of stories and movies she and Lily had always talked and laughed about. *The stupid girl who hides and screams and waits for the men to fight. Well, what if they fight, and don't win? Hiding and screaming won't do me much good then.*

But she didn't know what else to do. She was terrified; she had to admit it, no matter how she hated the principle of the situation. And she had no weapon, even if she had wanted to fight. Her eyes focused in front of her, instead of beyond, at the wagon and the manure. Well, it was something, wasn't it? Too scared to be disgusted, she thrust her hand into the dung and came up with a large solid clod of it. She lobbed it as hard and as straight as she could into the face of one of the men as he pressed Kyran back toward the wagon. Surprised, he took a step back—for a moment his eyes had closed in an instinctive reaction. With dizzying swiftness, Kyran took advantage of the moment, and in a few more, he and Alvar had both soldiers pinned to the ground, sword and knife at their throats.

Kyran's voice came low and threatening, straight to the point. "Who sent you?"

One of the soldiers, who looked to be the same age as Kyran, glared into the prince's face and remained stubbornly silent. The older one spat into Kyran's face and sneered, his upper lip curling to reveal a mouth of yellowed teeth. Kyran grunted angrily and bore down with his sword, drawing a faint line of blood along the man's neck. "I suppose," Kyran said, "that not answering my question is worth your life, you think? It's so important, then, this information? Or are you just a character, with no mind of your own, following orders blindly?" He waited a moment and then snarled into the soldier's face, "I said *who sent you?*"

But it was the young soldier who spoke. "I will tell you," he said, his Adam's apple bobbing nervously under Alvar's knife point. "If you will let us go, without harm."

Kyran nodded slowly. "Tell me," he said.

"It was the Head Councilor, master Falak," said the boy, squirming and looking about him as if he thought Falak would fly from overhead and strike him down.

Posy felt her stomach drop and found herself shaking her head in disbelief, eyes wide. *Falak.* The very one who had sent them on this journey. And now he was trying to kill them. Even if she had thought the owl was untrustworthy, she never would have guessed at this sort of treachery. She couldn't see Kyran's face, for his back was turned toward her, but she knew him well enough by now to recognize by the stiffening of his back that he was as shocked and enraged as she.

"Very well," he said at last, rising to his feet, the tip of his sword held solidly against the man's chest. The soldiers stood as well, and Alvar adeptly relieved them of their weapons. "Did your master give you a reason for killing us in cold blood?" said Kyran. "Or do you follow such morbid orders as these without knowing the reason?"

"You are traitors to the kingdom," growled the older soldier.

"Oh, I see," said Kyran. "How so?"

This question seemed to stump him for a moment, but he quickly recovered. "If Falak says you are, you are. Who am I to question? He is the right hand of King Melanthius himself."

Kyran took a step toward the man and said softly, "And do you know who *I* am?" He waited until both men were looking at him in nervous expectation. "I am the *son* of King Melanthius himself, that's who I am."

The young soldier blanched, and Posy thought his eyes would pop out of their sockets. "Y-you? The prince? B-but, why are you here? And ... and why would Falak try to ...."

"Kill me?" Kyran suggested helpfully. "Yes, I would like to know that myself. You both know we will be at war soon. Do either of you know why? It is only power, only selfishness on my father's part, and Falak's as well. They don't care for you or for your families. But since you take orders from them, and have no thought for a better life, you had best get back to the encampment and tell your master we have escaped. He'll be wanting to send another assassin after us, I suppose."

"I'll tell him we killed you," the young soldier's words tumbled out. "I'll tell him you are all dead, and he won't have a need to send anyone else. For he *will* send someone else, you are right. He is determined to kill you before you finish your quest."

"Hush, fool." This came from the older soldier as he shoved a rough elbow into the boy's ribs.

The boy glared at the older man and said, "It would be to your benefit to let him think they are dead, as well. For if he learns that we have failed, it will be *our* necks. What other choice do we have?"

The soldier considered this for a moment. He didn't make any movement of agreement, but he grimaced, and Posy could see he knew the boy spoke the truth. It seemed to Posy that his life was worth more to him than following Falak's orders. She was glad of this, for his sake and for theirs.

"I thank you," said Kyran ironically, with a slight bow of his dark head. "Now get back to the camp before reinforcements are sent." He tossed them their weapons. "You will have to have these if you wish to convince him you killed us. I trust I won't be seeing you again?"

"No, indeed," the boy shook his head energetically.

As they walked away, back through the trees toward the encampment, Alvar called after them, "If you ever decide you want to fight for the common characters, and a free Plot, come and speak to Alvar in the village."

"Alvar, you shouldn't have!" Posy said anxiously. "If they know who you are, they may decide to turn you in to Falak or one of the other owls for rebellion!"

"I'm willing to take that chance, my lady," Alvar said. "Two voices of soldiers who have doubts can be easily turned into hundreds, if they talk like I suspect soldiers do. And we could use some well-trained men for our army."

Kyran nodded approval as he sheathed his sword. He then went to Alvar and grasped his shoulder. "I thank you, friend, for all your help. I'm truly indebted to you. As soon as my quest is finished I will come back to help you raise your army."

"But ..." Alvar shifted uneasily. "You ... are you really the king's son? Are you the prince Kyran?"

"Yes," Kyran answered calmly, with a sigh. "I am the prince. That is how I know for certain that the way we are ruled is wrong, and that what we are choosing to do is right. I hope the fact that I am the king's son doesn't make you think differently of me, Alvar."

"Not at all, Your Majesty—it was just a shock. I—I had no idea." He ran his palm over his cropped flame of hair and shook his head. "Indeed," he said quietly, "the Plot is changing before my eyes now."

"So now you can raise your army in my name if you like; perhaps that will rally more soldiers for you," said Kyran, thumping Alvar on the back. He pulled a great emerald ring off his first finger, the only one he wore, and placed it in Alvar's great paw of a hand. "Use this as proof that I am behind you." Alvar stared at it a moment, and Posy thought he might try to give it back, but he nodded and closed his great fingers over it, tears in his eyes. Kyran

Ashlee Willis

cleared his throat and turned to adjust his horse's harness, but Posy ran over to Alvar and threw her arms around his middle. His muscles stiffened, and for a moment it felt as if Posy was hugging a boulder. Then his body softened, and he put a massive arm around her gingerly, as if afraid he would crush her, patting her shoulder lightly with his large hand.

"You saved our lives, Alvar," she said, releasing him and tilting her head back to look up into his face. "I wish you luck and safety in raising an army. You have taken a great risk helping us, you know."

"Oh, miss," Alvar's voice was gruff, "I'd do it a hundred times over if it won our cause, as I know you and the young prince would."

"Now," broke in Kyran's voice matter-of-factly, "Alvar, you must get back to the village as quickly as you can. There's no telling if Falak will swallow the story those soldiers are going to give him. Be safe, my friend. Your life is changed now … you will have to always be ready for danger." He reached out a hand to shake Alvar's and they exchanged a look of trust.

"And you." Alvar grasped Kyran's hand, and then nodded to Posy. He heaved the wagon up until the pile of manure spilled onto the ground, then jumped into the seat and flicked the reins. He headed into the forest, finally disappearing into the shadows. He would have to go a good distance to avoid going back through the encampment again. Now that Falak was to be told they had been killed, their original plan would not hold.

Kyran turned to Posy and raised an eyebrow. "Saved our lives, did he?" he asked. "Did I do such bad fighting, then, that I get no credit?"

"No!" Posy felt her face flush. "I meant that he saved us by smuggling us past the Borders, that's all. Of course you fought well,

Kyran—you know that."

"Mmm," Kyran nodded, his dark lashes flashing over his eyes as he looked down, busying himself with their saddlebags. "I suppose I will have to find a way to save your life, then, if such an embrace is to be the reward for it."

Posy stared at his back for a moment in astonishment, and then turned quickly away, her face burning.

Ashlee Willis

CHAPTER NINE
The Wild Land

So now to decide if *everything* Falak had told them was untrue.

"He is the true power in the kingdom, not my father," pointed out Kyran as they rode through the forest. "I believe he would like nothing better than to be the only councilor my father ever listened to. I believe he's not far from that goal now ... that is, if it weren't for my mother. She is a force to reckon with." Kyran's expression was wry.

"And there is one more tiny thing you are forgetting," Posy said wryly. "He tried to have us murdered in cold blood. There's always that, if nothing else convinces you he's bad news."

The corner of Kyran's mouth quirked as he threw her a look. "Yes, there's always that. I suppose that doesn't leave any room at all for trust, does it?"

"Not much," Posy agreed. "But I don't understand why he wanted to have us killed? Why now? If he wanted me dead, why not just leave me where I was in the Plot? Why send us away?"

"But Posy, don't you see ... the real question is, why try to have us killed *at all*, anywhere? Falak knows, as does every character of the Plot, that though he kills us now, we will only be there again at the beginning of the story. What can he have hoped to gain by it?" Kyran bit his lip, shaking his head. "It doesn't make any sense."

"Well, I can tell you, I'm certainly not turning around to go ask him," Posy laughed.

Kyran paused, turning to glance at her over his shoulder before he said, "Girls from your story must not be contradicted often, for you speak what you have to say rather ... forcefully. As if you take it for granted that you will be heard and considered."

Posy smiled at him, but her smile quickly faded as she thought about how it truly was in her life. She never took it for granted that she was heard. In fact, she never expected her opinions or words to be cared for or wanted. And this from those who were supposed to love her the most. She felt a wave of self-pity and sadness, familiar and sickening. She looked up to see Kyran was still turned, looking at her closely.

"What did I say?" he asked. "I would never want to cause you grief."

This brought back the smile to Posy's face. Only Kyran, only a character from a book, could say something like this and make it believable, and charming.

"You haven't," she said. "Others have perhaps, but not you."

He nodded. "I know," was all he said, and somehow, she knew he did.

They rode through the forest a while in silence. Posy gazed about her at wide tree trunks with their curling bark, the soft bunches of ferns growing on the forest floor. The sun was high, somewhere above the treetops, and its light filtered through the leaves, dappling everything around them. This Wild Land didn't seem so wild. But it did feel far different from the Kingdom. The colors weren't so bright, perhaps, but everything seemed real and solid. The smells of earth and damp leaves filled the clear air, and Posy took a deep breath of it. This was a real world, the Wild Land,

and her mind felt a certain release, as if it had been imprisoned before, and she hadn't even known it.

"Speaking of girls with strong wills and great bravery ..." Posy said at last.

"Were we?" Kyran asked, and Posy heard the hidden smile in his voice.

"Well, we had been talking about me, so I just assumed ..." she gave an innocent shrug.

This caused Kyran to throw back his dark head and laugh out loud. Posy smiled and laughed as well, continuing, "I was actually going to speak of your sister, Evanthe. Perhaps the answer lies with her."

"The answer?"

"The answer to why Falak might want to kill us. Your sister ran away, supposedly into the forest and beyond the Borders of the Plot. Now we are also beyond the reach of the Plot. Doesn't it seem suspicious to you? Like maybe Falak is trying to get rid of all of us?"

"But he can't get rid of us, Posy," pointed out Kyran patiently. "I mean, he might—but we'd come right back again, wouldn't we? We're part of the Plot, part of the story."

"You yourself said Falak does everything with a purpose in mind. If we could find out what the purpose was! You're sure ... absolutely certain ... that we can't be killed?"

"Yes, of course I am! Don't you think I've watched my own sister get sacrificed dozens of times? And she always came back again."

"All right, yes. But that was part of the Plot, right? Something the Author said would happen. What if it was something the Author didn't write down? Something a character—like Falak—took into his own hands?"

They were riding deeper into the forest, and the light seemed to be slowly ebbing away somehow. Posy could see Kyran's profile in front of her, and she didn't like the look that crossed his face after she had spoken.

"What is it?" she asked.

"Something I remembered," he said slowly. "Something I heard a long time ago. I'm not sure who told me, where I heard it ... but ...." He paused and knit his brows, thinking hard for a moment, trying to recall the memory. "It's a very hazy memory. Must have happened generations ago. Something to do with things happening outside the Plot. I can't remember for sure, though."

"But what *do* you remember of it?" questioned Posy urgently.

"That's all."

"That's all?" Posy's voice was incredulous. "You mean all you remember is that *someone* said *something* about things that happened outside of the Plot, but you don't remember *what*?"

"Exactly," Kyran said with a sigh. "That's no help, I know. It's just that ... well, I've felt different, this past hour or two. It's like something here is making me ... remember things. Oh, just little things," he said quickly. "But things I had long forgotten. And now this ... this memory of what happens beyond the Plot. I feel certain it will come to me eventually. The air is clear here, and light. Don't you feel it? It's as if the air I've been breathing all my life wasn't even air at all ... it was heavy and thick. I had to fight through it every day. It muddled and confused me, made me slow and indecisive. But all that's swept away here. At least, so it feels. Now my mind is my own again."

Something in his voice made a shiver go down Posy's spine. His words, free and content, were like harbingers of something new, sounding clearly through the silence of the forest, and she thought the trees leaned in to listen to them.

"I feel it too," she whispered.

* * *

That first night in the Wild Land forest, under the blanket of trees and the clear white eye of the moon, was to remain in Posy's memory forever, for its wonder and terror both.

They had ridden all day, making their way deeper into the forest. However, a strange thing happened as they went further into the heart of the Wild Land. Kyran's horse, Belenus, became nervous, and once or twice refused to respond to Kyran's command. It troubled Kyran more than he wanted to say, Posy could see, and at last in frustration he announced they would stop for the night, though the sun had not yet gone down.

Kyran began to build a fire as Posy drew their blankets and some food from the saddlebags Alvar had packed for them. She looked around into the darkening trees, and if she had thought they listened to Kyran's words earlier that day, she didn't doubt it at all now. They leaned and swayed to a movement all their own, not commanded by the wind. Posy's hand idly stroked Belenus' dark mane, her eyes transfixed. She didn't see the moment of change, it came so gradually, so naturally, where shadows and moonlight met on bark and dirt and leaf. What her eyes saw flowed together, like a silent song, and suddenly, there they were. Creatures like trees, like the forest itself. Posy didn't know if they had come from the trees, or from the bushes, or from the floor of the forest. She was frozen, watching them, but not with fear.

"It's the Wild Folk," Kyran's voice came in a soft breath at her ear. "Evanthe used to read of them, and she would tell me .... But I never dreamed they were real."

"What are they?" Posy asked, never taking her eyes off the procession that moved in and out of shadow.

"Creatures made from the land itself. They are a part of it, more truly than any other who lives here. Only look at them, Posy." His voice held awe.

They were people—or at least their forms were similar to people. They had limbs, face and body, but their arms and legs were long and slender, gnarled like tree branches. One had skin covered with patches of green moss, another had eyes like acorns, and still another had hair of supple leaves flowing over its shoulders. They moved with the grace and silence only a forest could hold, creaking and swaying. Posy drew in a shaky breath as the last of them disappeared. The shadows around them seemed to sigh.

"Where were they going?" she whispered still, though they were gone. "They were heading back where we have come from, toward the Borders."

Kyran only shook his head, a troubled expression on his face.

* * *

Later, after they had eaten, they were sitting, with blankets wrapped around their shoulders, in front of the fire Kyran had built, Posy said suddenly, "What do *you* think?"

Kyran turned at the intensity of her voice and raised his eyebrows. "Think about what?"

"You know Princess Evanthe better than anyone. You loved her better than anyone. So—where would she go?"

"I don't know," he answered.

"Yes, you do!" answered Posy forcefully. "Just think about your sister, who she is, what reasons she had for leaving." Kyran's face clouded in thought and Posy continued. "Put all those together, and you might have at least an idea of where she could have gone. If she's smart, she won't be just wandering the forest. She had to have a destination."

Kyran was silent for a long time. Finally, he said slowly, "Evanthe is brave—that is her strongest characteristic. She is opinionated, but soft spoken. She is smart, and not just from reading and having lessons. She is wise—wiser than I ever was, that's for certain." He shook his head. "But those things are just ... just traits she has grown into ... they are not *who* she is."

"Who is she, Kyran?" Posy asked quietly, thinking now of her own sister. Posy knew Lily better than anyone. Her mother had often joked that there might as well be no one in the world but the two of them, as far as they were concerned. Posy had always been surprised when she heard the resentment in her mother's voice, as if this closeness with Lily was somehow wrong, or unhealthy. But she wondered, too, that her mother hadn't suspected the cause of it.

How can we not cling to one another? thought Posy with a sudden surge of anger. *What else is there to cling to, after all?*

Yet her mother was right for all that. Posy and her sister were two halves of the same whole, and a single look between them usually spoke more than hours of conversation. But putting the heart of her sister into words? She didn't know if she could do it.

"She had eyes that saw things," Kyran said. "Eyes that *knew*. I could see from watching her she knew what I was thinking, no matter what I said. And she never had any fear of admitting it. She saw long ago the trouble in the Kingdom and the poor decisions of our father. She spoke of things to me, said things that should have made me suspicious if I hadn't been too lazy or stupid to understand what she was truly speaking of." He paused, knitting his dark brows. "That heavy air in the Kingdom, that haze we all live in and move through .... I feel sure Evanthe could see through it more clearly than any of us. She knew the Plot had been changed. She knew things weren't as they should be. That's why she left. Not from fear of her fate, but because a stand *must* be made by someone. And that's who she is," he said, straightening as he spoke, a new expression on his face. "She's a girl who won't wait for someone else to do something, someone else to change or fix things, if she can do it herself. Making things right," he breathed. "That's what her heart always wanted. Yes." He gave a slow nod, and Posy saw something like dread, or fear, rising behind his eyes. "I think I know where she has gone."

CHAPTER TEN
Night Attack

Light and dark shine from the trees,
A threat to give a soul release.
Light and dark are mixed and stirred
Until one over the other is heard.
Light and dark, the self same face,
Until a soul can pierce the Place
Of death and life's struggling embrace.
The emerald of trees will light the path
To the center and heart of truth at last.

"All right, what's with the weird poem?" asked Posy, after hearing Kyran recite the poem in a voice that made the forest seem colder. She pulled her blanket tight around her and moved closer to the fire.

"It's a poem we used to hear long ago. Evanthe was always infatuated with it," Kyran said. "I always thought it a bit morbid."

"Well, *yeah*," Posy said, widening her eyes. "But what is the point of it?"

"The *point* is what the poem is about. It's about this forest, and a place within it. Somewhere that no one has ever been and returned from, at least so the tales go. And I will say, most in the Kingdom don't think much about it at all, let alone believe in its existence. I don't know how the rumors of this place began, or when, but I can't remember a time when I wasn't aware of them. They are always kept quiet, though, for my father never liked talk of the Wild Land."

"What is the place called?" Posy asked curiously.

Kyran's face darkened as he answered, "The Glooming."

Posy felt a shiver trickle down her spine at the name. "So the princess was infatuated with a poem about this place, and now you think she's gone there?"

"It's the only place we ever had a true consciousness of, outside the Kingdom. And it was a place that held the deepest good and the deadliest evil, together. She was fascinated with the idea of such a place. But everyone spoke of it with fear, when they spoke of it at all."

"But Kyran, *why* would she go there? Surely she wouldn't have gone there just out of curiosity. Would she?"

Kyran smiled wryly at this. "No," he said. "I think you are right. I think she must have had another reason." Belenus neighed softly behind them, and Posy felt gentle drops of water on her skin, falling from the trees, echoing eerily as they slid and splashed from one leaf to another. "If we assume that she left because she wanted to help the Kingdom change ..."

"Then it's pretty obvious why she went to the Glooming," finished Posy.

"Oh?" was all Kyran said.

"Yes. Something or other about light and dark being the same until someone can 'pierce the Place' ... whatever, whatever." Posy waved her hand. "So basically she thinks she can be the one who goes to the 'Place'—the Glooming—and make things right. Recite the poem again," she demanded. Kyran did.

"Yes," Kyran said at last, and Posy didn't like the look on his face. "I think you might be right. The poem is saying that good and evil appear to be the same. The only thing that will separate them is when someone goes to this place and ... well, I don't know what they must do." He sat in silence, his dark head tilted down looking at his hands. The flicker of the firelight cast dancing shadows on his face.

Posy pulled an arm from her blanket and reached to Kyran impulsively, putting her hand on his. "We will find her," she said with more heart than she felt. "We will." When he didn't respond, she continued, "Do you know how to get to the Glooming?"

"I've never been there, of course," Kyran said with a frown. "The poem says 'the emerald of trees will light the path,' but I'm not sure what that refers to."

"All the trees are emerald," Posy said dejectedly, gazing about her. "That is either a lousy clue or one that is so genius it's incomprehensible."

Kyran chuckled without much spirit. Suddenly he leapt up and grabbed a half-burnt log from the fire. He took it with him to a cluster of nearby trees, holding the log's glowing embers up for light. Then he reached out a hand and swept a finger down the bark of the tree on one side.

"What is it?"

"It's moss," he said.

"All right ... so?"

"Well, I'm not sure how consistently moss actually grows on certain sides of trees, but the country folk in the Kingdom always used to say it would grow on the north side faster than any other side of a tree. Do you suppose that means, since the moss is emerald, we should head north?"

"If that's true," said Posy, shaking her head, "it's the most obscure clue I've ever heard. If I had to figure it out on my own, I'd be wandering around in the forest for the next hundred years or so."

"Well, I'm not completely certain that's it, but it's all we've got right now," was Kyran's rather demoralizing reply. "And anyway, going north will lead us deeper into the heart of the forest, further into the Wild Land. So that's something else in the theory's favor I suppose." He shrugged and began moving to lie down next to the fire. Posy began running her fingers through her tangled hair, trying not to think about how badly she needed a bath, and how good it would feel to be able to brush her teeth.

Suddenly, Kyran was there beside her. "Here, let me," was all he said. He had a bit of twine in his hands. He ran his fingers gently through the last of her tangled waves, and then began braiding her hair loosely. He tied the twine at the end and let the braid fall against her back. It was quickly done and over with. Posy mumbled thank-you as she watched him walk back over to his blanket. He turned and smiled at her, and she made herself take a slow breath.

"In ages past, before the Plot had changed," Kyran explained, "we always braided our horses' manes before going into battle."

Ah, Posy looked down. *That was that, then.*

* * *

The rain that had started before, dripping and weaving its way through the high branches and leaves, had now slowed to an uncomfortable drizzle, cold and damp. Posy pulled her blanket over her head, getting as close to the fire as she dared. She thought this day, the things spoken of and seen, the cold and the rain, would make sleep hard to find. But she was wrong. Her body sank into dreams even as she closed her eyes.

In this world, this story, it seemed she would dream about the world she had left behind. For she saw her own house, tall and white, as if she approached it from the front street. She saw her porch, the familiar chipped stairs and shaky banister, the mailbox that her mother had hand-painted with tiny flitting bluebirds years ago. There was even the solidly normal charcoal grill pushed into the far corner of the porch. And there were her parents in the window, and she had the thought that they would be happy to see her. She had been gone so long. But they only stared, expressionless, until she felt she would cry, until she wanted to bang on the windowpane and break the glass. And where was Lily? Why couldn't she see her?

She didn't have time to panic, though. No time for being lured further into the places this dream could lead. She was being shaken awake, gently but firmly. Kyran's lips were pressed to her ear, his voice a deadly whisper as he pressed the cold hilt of a long knife into Posy's hand. "Wake up," he commanded. "We have a guest."

* * *

The world spun into focus then. Kyran hauled her deftly to her feet, and his words hit her like cold water poured down her back. She barely had time to register the scrape of Kyran's sword as he unsheathed it, and the outline of an enormous creature beyond the shadows. It was on them in an instant, its roar exploding into the quiet of the night. Posy saw the dull flash of Kyran's sword as it swung outward, but she knew instinctively, as the cold of the night seeped into her, that this would be nothing like his fight with the two soldiers of yesterday. They had been men, and they had been visible. But the forest was so dark, with their campfire now burnt to embers, that the only clear glimpses of the beast were when it bellowed, and fire and smoke blasted from its mouth in a horrible cloud of dust and flying cinders.

While Kyran and the creature circled each other in the shadows, Posy crept to their campfire and began stirring it, hoping that the light would aid Kyran, hoping that perhaps it was a creature afraid of fire, like ones she had read of in books. She worked feverishly, feeling panic as she heard the sounds of Kyran's clashing sword and the clatter of something thudding heavily against his shield. When the fire was stoked enough that it began to burn brighter, Posy turned, the knife clutched in her sweaty hand, and froze at what she saw.

It was a monster. Its head and neck were like a bull's, only twice the size of one. Its immense neck rippled as its muscles tensed. Masses of matted tangled hair hung thickly around its face. And its face ... Posy's breath caught in her chest. Such an expression she saw in those eerily human eyes as they flickered and followed Kyran with stony, deadly intent. Its front legs were not those of a bull—they were pawed and moveable, swiping through the air with a combination of power and swiftness that was terrifying. A tail rose from behind it that was no tail at all, but a large serpent, nearly as big around as Posy, writhing and twisting itself toward its own head where Kyran fought, hissing and lashing its forked tongue in fury.

The monster lowered its head, swaying back and forth bizarrely like a marionette. Its slanted eyes glinted, taking in Kyran with a look that already held triumph. It played with him now as he tired and reeled from the heavy blows he had sustained. It pushed him slowly toward the darkness of the forest, away from the clearing and the bright flame of fire. Posy knew if they disappeared there, the forest would swallow them. The darkness would mean death for Kyran.

Posy heard her own voice breath out a word. "Help." It held all her desperation. She saw the faceless Author in her mind, the Author whom many characters believed was a myth. If anyone could help them now, wouldn't it be he who wrote this story to begin with? After all, wasn't he meant to help these characters he had written?

A wind stirred, breaking the stillness of the air. It came from the blackest part of the forest, straight toward them. Posy watched as the monster turned to sniff the breeze, then hunched down, cowering in fear as if the wind held a threat in it. Posy watched it back away from the trees, toward the fire once more. *Toward her.*

Kyran bore down on it, seizing his opportunity, for an opportunity it was, and Posy knew it may be their only one. If it had come of her cry of help to the Author, it was up to them to make the best of it. She didn't know how brave she would have been on her own, but now there was something in her stronger than her fear for herself. It was fear for Kyran.

She gripped her knife like a lifeline, staring down at its long blade for a moment, as if willing it to do as she wished. She began moving toward the monster's snake-tail. Kyran battled the head, and she hoped the tail would stay turned his way until she could do what she knew she must.

As Kyran cried out and spun his sword toward the bull-like head, Posy ran, launching herself toward the back of the creature and the base of its serpent tail. It was surprising how easy it was. The blade almost seemed to know what to do within her hands, and it sliced neatly through the snake as she lunged and brought it down with all her strength. There was silence for a moment as the serpent lay twisting on the forest floor. But when the bull's head turned its uncanny yellow eyes upon her and saw what had happened, it let out a scream that Posy felt to her bones. It turned on her in an instant, but in that instant, Kyran was there. He flung himself between Posy and the beast, and his sword sunk into the monster's great chest. It fell with a ground-rattling thud at their feet.

Posy stared at it, numb to any feeling but disbelief, then suddenly felt the unexplainable urge to laugh. She put her hand up to her mouth to stop any noise from escaping. But when sound burst out she found she wasn't laughing at all, but crying, weeping, with the fright she should have felt minutes ago but was feeling now instead. Kyran threw down his sword and hugged her to his chest gently. He pulled her away from the dead beast, and it receded into a shapeless dark mass beyond the warm circle of warmth from their fire. He kissed her wild and matted hair, smoothing it away from her face.

"Sit," he said, seeing that Posy was shaking violently. "You must eat something."

Eat? Posy felt the blood drain from her face. She watched in her mind as her knife slid across the serpent's throat with a sickening hiss. She shook her head, lowering it, thinking she might be sick.

"No," Kyran amended quickly. "No food then. But some water, at least." And he held a flask to her mouth and watched as she drank.

"I understand, you know," he said quietly when she was finished, sitting next to her on the hard ground. "To kill ... is a horrible thing. But a person's mind can get past it, eventually. My first kill was a man, not a soulless beast like this."

Posy turned her tear-stained face to him quickly, waiting for the shudder in his body, the hesitancy in his voice that bespoke the horror he must feel. She saw neither, only a calm sadness in his eyes.

"I'd never kill anyone in cold blood, Posy," he reassured her, "but battles are necessary sometimes. Wars will happen between men. Defense of yourself and the ones you love is ... the most important thing."

"Yes," she said quietly. His life was worlds apart from hers, so different it wasn't worth comparing. But still ... she knew what he meant. She knew where his words had come from, and she knew they were true. Perhaps the differences between the two of them were not so great after all.

Kyran's eyes sought out the creature, which lay at an odd angle in the distant shadows. "I hope ..." he began, and then stopped.

"What?"

"I hope that monster wasn't another proof of Falak's ill will. I hope that was a natural encounter we had tonight."

"Oh," Posy breathed. She hadn't thought of that.

"Wherever it came from," he continued, staring into the fire, "I fear that the closer we get to the Glooming, to the center of the Wild Land, the more dangerous it will become. I pray I can keep you safe, Posy."

The firelight lit up his dark features as Posy looked at him. Her heart skipped a beat when she saw the way he was looking at her, with tenderness, and sadness too. He brushed the back of his hand on her cheek and gave her a crooked smile. For a moment, she thought he would do something more—wished he would—but he only drew his hand back to run his fingers awkwardly through his black hair as he turned from her.

Posy lay wrapped in her blanket, her back to the fire, and she cried silently. Not for fear or relief, not even from the shock of what she had just seen and done, but for the sadness she could feel gripping her. She knew in her heart she couldn't stay here in this story—she knew a time would come, eventually, when she must go back to her home. And now her eyes cried, and her heart cried, at what she knew she must leave behind.

Ashlee Willis

CHAPTER ELEVEN
Revelations

It was a dark room, and the darkness rippled like black velvet upward toward the vaulted ceiling. A polished stone table was piled with neat stacks of papers and quill pens. Falak sat behind it, on a wooden perch made for the purpose, and King Melanthius sat across from him, his great arms crossed and a thunderous expression on his face.

"You said that you would have them returned to the Kingdom and within my castle within days, Falak. Where are they? What is taking you so long?"

Falak eyed the king dispassionately and answered, his voice serene. "Your Majesty, you know what chaos the Kingdom is in right now. The looming war with the Wild Land has been foremost in our thoughts and plans. Your wayward children are a bother, of course, but they do no harm where they are."

"No harm? *No harm?*" roared Melanthius, rising from his chair and leaning across the table to thrust his face menacingly toward Falak. "What do you take me for? A fool? Every moment they are gone makes me lose face with the characters of the Plot. Am I to be seen as such a weak ruler that I cannot keep either of my children within my own Kingdom?"

"Sire, it is not known beyond the castle itself that the prince and princess are gone. Everyone has been told to address the new girl, Olena, as the princess for now, and it has been passed around that the prince is ill and stays within his rooms."

"These are sad and pathetic excuses, Falak. Unlike you, I would have thought," the king answered. "I always thought you the most cunning owl of my council, the wisest in your advice and plans. But now I begin to wonder. You know as well as I that it is common gossip that the prince and princess are both gone. These lesser characters have been taught that I uphold the Plot. What must they think now that they know, or at the very least suspect, what has happened? No!" He pounded a large fist on the table. "I won't have it. You get your scouts out there now, and you find them. If they are not back soon, I will take matters into my own hands, and perhaps we will give you a trial as a common character for a while. One owl can easily replace another, eh?" Melanthius directed an evil smile at his chief councilor.

"As you say, Sire," answered Falak stiffly. His great owl eyes flashed dangerously for a moment.

"Good," stated the king as he pushed back his chair and stood to leave. "Soon," he repeated. "I want them back soon." He strode across the vast room and disappeared.

Falak stayed unmoving for many moments until a faint flapping sound heralded the appearance of Egbert, circling down into the room from one of the high windows, open to the night. "And so?" he immediately asked, alighting on the chair the king had just vacated.

"And so," answered Falak, "the king has just asked me if I think he is a fool. My answer is yes."

Egbert smiled slowly, although he glanced sideways as if fearing they would be overheard. "In what way, Councilor? For I fear there are so many ways he can be a fool."

Ashlee Willis

"He demands that his children be returned to the palace soon. I think he means a matter of days."

"But that can be done easily," protested Egbert.

"It *will not* be done!" Falak's voice silenced the other owl. "If our plan is to succeed, they must continue. Are you such a dolt that you don't see that? If they are returned safely, to fulfill the Plot, and within the Borders, our plans would be doomed. It cannot be," he shook his head back and forth resolutely. "Evanthe, Kyran and the new one, Posy, must stay outside of the Borders—they must fulfill the path I have laid out for them. I will tell Melanthius it is the fate of the Plot—I will tell him ... whatever I must to ensure things continue as they are. Sometimes"—he gave the other owl a harried look—"I wonder if I have taught the king too well. He begins to believe he is the one who truly upholds the Plot, that he has the strength to make changes. I think he may even begin to believe he is the Author of this story."

"Only *you* are strong enough for that," put in Egbert faithfully, ruffling his wings excitedly.

"Yes, only I," Falak's great eyes became pools of darkness. "The king thinks he can threaten me if I do not do this for him. Threaten *me*." Falak's voice hissed in disgust and outrage. "Well, we shall see who comes out triumphant in the end."

* * *

The morning sunlight trickled down through the roof of leaves overhead and speckled the ground. Posy rolled over to look at Kyran where he lay on the other side of the burnt-out fire. His eyes were closed and he slept still, his blanket askew on top of him, his mouth slightly open and a lock of his silky hair strewn across his face. Posy smiled. What must it have been like for him, to live with the constant knowledge that no one would protect him if he didn't protect himself? She felt a sudden tenderness toward him, the urge to defend him against future pain.

"What a face to see upon waking," Kyran's voice came from below her. "It looks as if you are trying to solve all the problems of the world. Is it not a little early in the day for such serious thoughts?"

"And you must dream of teasing things to say, since when you wake they're the first things out of your mouth," Posy returned with a grin.

Kyran chuckled as he rose to bank the fire. He reached into one of the saddlebags and handed Posy a small loaf of bread and an apple. "We will eat as we ride," he said, hoisting the saddle over Belenus' back. So the day began.

* * *

They rode until the sun was far above them, stopping only once to stretch their legs, eat a scanty lunch, and fill their flasks in a cold creek as they passed. Posy felt drowsy as the afternoon sun shone down on their backs, and her head drooped against Kyran's back. She didn't know if she slept long—it seemed like only moments later that she felt his body tense as he reined in Belenus. His hand slowly reached for his sword, though he didn't unsheathe it.

Posy opened her mouth to speak. Though Kyran's back was to her, he immediately let out a low "Sshh" to quiet her unspoken question. His dark eyes swept the shadows that the trees cast beyond them, and he silently dismounted, motioning for Posy to stay where she was.

He walked, barely making a noise on the mossy forest floor, to a large tree some distance from them. Its roots dipped and rose from the ground, large and gnarled, like so many trees in the Wild Land forest. He thrust his arm beyond them, where an embankment dipped out of sight. A shout rang out as Kyran dragged a man from his hiding place. Posy saw right away the man wasn't armed. Indeed, he was barely clothed. His weathered face was streaked with dirt, drawn with weariness and fear. But Kyran had him by the throat. He was taking no chances.

"Please!" Posy heard her own voice shout as she nudged Belenus forward toward them. "Don't hurt him, Kyran! He looks harmless." She felt an unspeakable pity for the man standing before them. He would be about her own father's age, she guessed.

"Posy, I had no intention of hurting him. Only of questioning him as to what he does here. No characters live within the Wild Land, so I understood." He gave the man a small shake in the way of encouraging him to speak.

"You are right," the man said in a strangled voice. "I am a character. Perhaps I have no business here in the Wild Land, but I wouldn't leave my family to the consequences of the Plot, no matter what we may find here beyond the Borders."

"The consequences of the Plot?" Kyran loosened his hold on the man a bit.

"The attacks," the man continued, a wild look in his bloodshot eyes. "There have been battles along the Borders, and the king has declared war on the Wild Land at last. There is no place for us there now. Everyone knows if the Plot begins to change, the destruction of our story is not far behind."

"Yes," Kyran gave the man a strange look, "everyone knows that, don't they? So," he turned to Posy with a significant glance, "the king has declared war."

She only nodded. They had known it would come to this.

"And your family, man? Where are they?"

The man's face became blank, but not before Kyran saw his eyes flicker sideways, toward the place beyond the tree roots from where he had just been pulled.

"Ah," Kyran said, releasing him. "Well, tell them they may come out. I won't hurt you or anyone who is an enemy of the Plot."

The man massaged his neck, giving Kyran an incredulous look. "They will not come out," he stated loudly, "I have no way of knowing if I can trust you."

"I suppose refraining from killing you wasn't proof enough?" Kyran smiled. "Well, have it your way. I can understand your desire to protect them well enough. Are there many others like you roaming the forest, then?"

The man shook his head. "There may be a few, I suppose, who made it away when we did some days ago. But the Borders are so closely guarded now, there is no telling who will make it through now, though I fear many may soon wish to. Things are different ... oh, much different from the days of long ago. Yet much is still the same."

"What do you mean?" Kyran asked, drawing his eyebrows together.

"The king sent soldiers back then too, you know," the man said, sighing. "Long ago. That is when the Plot first began to change. There were battles, though war was never actually declared. Power changed hands, as a result of these battles, and the Council of Centaurs was driven from the Kingdom and into the Wild Land, to the deepest part of the forest."

"The Council of Centaurs," Kyran and Posy said together. Posy's voice held surprise, but Kyran's eyes had a strange look.

"Yes," the man nodded, "Most will not remember them, because that is what living in the Kingdom does to you. There is a magic there that makes you forget the change—or nearly forget it. We only began to remember after we crossed the Borders. The magic was lifted from us, and we remembered how things used to be ... who we had been before everything went wrong. Has this not happened to you as well, now you are away from the Plot?"

Kyran opened his mouth to speak, but closed it again, his black eyes hard and glistening. "Yes," he finally conceded stiffly, "I have begun to remember things."

"We couldn't live a life that meant nothing," the man explained quietly. "We couldn't bow to a king who would change the Plot to include his own daughter's death. Such an unnecessary thing, just to create sadness and darkness, things to attract readers."

It was slight, the change on Kyran's face. So slight that anyone who did not know him would never have seen it. But Posy saw it.

"Surely," the man said, looking acutely at Kyran as if taking him in for the first time, "You must know of all this, though, if you are characters."

"Yes," Posy nodded, dismounting and leading Belenus forward to where the two men stood. "But we had not until now heard what you just told us. We did not know the extent of the king's cruelty. Can you be certain this is true—that he would wish to ... sacrifice his own daughter?" She hated to say the words—hated more what the answer may be—but she knew she must, for Kyran's stony face told her he would not.

"Ay," the man nodded sadly, "it is as true as I stand here."

"But how can you be sure?"

"It is simple. I remember a time when her death was not necessary. It's astounding—like being awakened from a lifelong dream. The magic of the Kingdom no longer clouds my eyes. When the Council of Centaurs was forced from the land and into the forest, the Kingdom took an unpleasant turn from which it has never recovered. The owls have gained too much power this past age. I see it now." Malice flickered across the man's face. "I fear the king will one day be a puppet on the throne, and any hope of the goodness that used to be in him will be gone forever."

Kyran made a sudden violent movement, then turned and walked a few paces away, his back to them. Posy cast a nervous glance at the man, who still stood as if waiting for dismissal. He only wanted them to leave, she could see. He only wanted to be back with his family. He didn't seem to care—or even see—that Kyran stood here, a silent, horrid pain coming from him like a wave.

But when Kyran turned to them, he smiled. Posy felt everything shift, when she saw his smile, for it was a mask covering broken pieces.

"It is time something was done," he stated, hand on the hilt of his sword as if he would throw himself into battle at any moment.

The man shook his head sadly. "The Wild Folk who live within the forest have been gathering for weeks to form an army of their own, but they are no match for the king's soldiers. Their numbers are too many, and they have been trained to fight."

"But the army *I* speak of will be formed from characters themselves, those who live within the Kingdom now and who see things as you do, clearly." This got the man's attention. He lifted his head.

"Who are you?" he asked. Kyran looked a bit taken aback by the abrupt question. "I have told you my story. What is yours?" The man's eyes bore into Kyran's.

"I am a friend," Kyran said at last. "And if you listen, and watch, even greater changes than those you have spoken of will happen in the Plot soon, you can be sure of it. Perhaps"—Kyran gave him a sad smile—"you and your family may find you can live there again one day."

They gave the man some of their food—enough to feed him as well as the family that still hid out of their sight—and they set out on their way once again. Posy twisted in her saddle as they disappeared from the trees. The man stared at them as they went, and beyond him, Posy saw the heads of two small children pop up between the tree roots where they were hiding. For some reason the sight of those two floppy blond heads made Posy's heart yearn for everything to turn out for good more than any of the words the man had spoken to them.

CHAPTER TWELVE
Battle in the Glade

Strangely, horribly, it was as if a rift had been hewn between Posy and Kyran. The knowledge of the king's treachery, his betrayal of his own child, stood between them, so solid that no other thought or word could get through. Posy didn't know why it should do so. She didn't understand why it had anything to do with what was between the two of them. But it did, all the same. She could feel it crackling in the very air around them.

Thoughts of her own parents came to her mind. And into her mind, quite vividly, flashed a night not long before she had fallen into this story. Another night of arguing; another night that hatred had seeped into the walls of her house like a disease. She had run to the bathroom and seized her mother's lipstick. Heart racing, she had scrawled one word across the mirror, seeing the reflection of her own tear-stained face beyond it.

"Divorce," she had written, and the letters were blood red. Perhaps they had been blood in truth, for Posy's heart had certainly been bleeding. It was an ugly word—a horrid word. But something had compelled her to see it, to write it with her own hand, and face the truth of what she felt her life was catapulting toward.

And so now her heart was breaking for Kyran as well.

At last, she tried to speak with him, though she didn't know how to begin. "I am sorry, Kyran," was all she said, her voice little more than a whisper.

"Why are you sorry?" He turned immediately to scowl at her.

"I meant ... I only meant your father," she stammered.

"Oh, yes," his voice was careless. "Well that shouldn't surprise either of us, should it? No matter who may have talked him into the decision, it was his in the end. If he is taken from his throne because of it—even if he dies—it will be nothing more than he deserves. He is a weakling, and a weak man cannot rule the Kingdom."

"But he is still your father, Kyran," said Posy, feeling this was all wrong.

"Yes, and I cannot let that stand in the way of what I must do. He obviously did not let any such emotion stand in his way when making decisions about his own children. No, our goal now is to simply find my sister, then I will get to Alvar's side and lead the army against the king as soon as may be. Now he has officially declared war we will need to take action as swiftly as we can."

Posy understood; how could she not? But somewhere, in some part of her, she rebelled against it, against Kyran forming an army against his own father, against Kyran speaking of his own father's death as something deserved, anticipated. She did not know why, for everything Kyran said was true, even just. Still, the unease was there, the feeling that she would be sick with the sadness of it. But what could she possibly say to Kyran now that he would really hear? She knew there was nothing. And when she could not explain to herself the disquieted feeling she had, or wish it away, she simply locked her mind against it, turning from it so swiftly that it looked like guilt, even to herself.

* * *

Posy had never heard sounds of battle before, but she recognized them immediately. Amidst the dripping chill of the forest, she heard the distant clamor of armor, the clang of swords echoing off the canopy of leaves above them, and strange voices lifted in battle cries. Kyran drew up the reins and Belenus came to a stop, his ears pricked and head held high and watchful. The day was swiftly disappearing. The sun's already meager spackling of light was diminishing to a gray haze that hovered and shivered around the trees, infusing the forest with a ghostly glow. Posy felt her arms tighten around Kyran's waist as he nudged a nervous Belenus forward toward the sounds. It wasn't long, though, before the horse became impossible to ride. He began prancing in circles, his tail whipping sideways, lashing at Posy's legs.

Kyran dismounted and pulled Posy down after him in one fluid motion. He brought Belenus' head to him and stroked his ears, murmuring to him in a low soothing voice. The horse's eyes rolled around frantically, and Posy saw the muscles in his neck tense as he ripped his head away from Kyran's grasp and let out a blood-curdling scream, full of stark terror. Seeing Kyran's well-behaved, battle-trained horse behave this way made Posy's blood run cold, more than any sounds of battle. Kyran tied Belenus to a tree securely then turned to grab Posy's hand and tugged her toward the clearing. Posy's heart beat so forcefully she could feel the blood pulsing in every part of her body as she mutely followed Kyran through the increasing mist.

They crouched at the edge of the trees and saw before them a vast barren area with the forest growing up in a circle around it. Posy peered through the underbrush and felt her eyes grow wide and her breath stop in her chest. She knew this was a land of magic, a book like a fairytale with its kings and queens and creatures of myth. Still, she was not prepared for this.

Within the clearing was indeed a battle. The creatures that fought against each other were similar at first glance. In the chaos of the scene, through the swirling miasma that rose darkly from the earth, it looked like a battle of men and horses. It churned with arms and legs, thunderous faces, swords hacking against armor and flesh. When Posy stopped reeling from the shock of it, she saw that the horses were men—or the men were horses.

"Centaurs," she breathed.

Kyran nodded and leant toward her. "Not only centaurs, but centaurs and ipotanes. They are longtime enemies. At least, that is the story Evanthe and I always heard. It has been long since I have seen a centaur. Another time. Another story."

"But ... ipotanes? What are those?"

"They are the creatures that stand on two legs instead of four," he answered. "Do you not see the difference?"

Posy did see. The centaurs stood on four horse legs, with a large horse body and the torso, head and arms of a human man replacing the neck of the horse. But the ipotanes were different. At first Posy thought they were normal men, but with a closer look she saw their legs were also those of a horse, but they had only two. They reminded Posy of pictures she had seen of satyrs—but only in their general build. As she watched them slash and kill she knew this was a different creature altogether. Soft curved horse ears rose through the wild masses of the ipotanes' hair, a stark contrast to the steely bodies beneath. The ipotanes were broad and strong, and Posy could see the centaurs struggled to push them back. But the centaurs were strong, too—a play of shadows ran across their muscular chests and arms in the dimming sunlight as they fought—but the ipotanes seemed to be made of iron, and it took many blows to defeat one of them.

It seemed they watched for an eternity. Posy felt it was a dream, and though she saw the killing and the blood, it seemed far away. Was it truly real? She could hear it and see it, even smell the tang of blood and the dust and sweat of men and animals. But it seemed she watched a picture in a book, moving and dreamlike. She couldn't feel the horror of it, not yet.

"Why do they hate each other?" she asked Kyran.

He shrugged and shook his head. "I don't know," he admitted. "I only know the stories I've heard through the ages. It seems that I have distant memories of the centaurs themselves, and since we now know that they used to be the king's council, I suppose I actually do have. But the ipotanes ... I have only ever heard of them. What quarrel they have with the centaurs I don't know."

"Do you think ...?" Posy faltered, wondering if it was a foolish thing to suggest.

Kyran turned a questioning gaze to her, looking into her face for the first time. "Oh," he said before she could continue, as if he had read her question in her face. "I don't know if this has anything to do with the Kingdom's war." Posy knew he must have asked himself that question already in these past minutes. "The only thing I care about is the victor. The centaurs will be my father's enemies, so I'd be a fool to wish the ipotanes victory. And whatever the sympathies or cause of either army, the ipotanes are legendary for their cruelty and changeability. I wouldn't wish to be under their protection, especially should they learn I am the king's son."

So, something else to worry about. They had only just set eyes on this place, this battle, and already they found they had much to lose or gain by it. Posy sighed. She felt her eyes drawn again to the battlefield, and the numb wonder she had seen it with before seemed to fall slowly from her eyes. Her heart felt heavy as she saw one after another slain and dying, lying on the cold unforgiving ground. Amidst the untamed cries of the creatures fighting, a voice thundered above them all. At the edge of the field, an enormous coal-black ipotane stalked through the battle, ruthlessly cutting through those fighting near him with his massive sword. His armor gleamed ominously and his eyes were dark as he gazed across the field intently and made his way forward.

"What is he doing?" Posy asked, shivering.

"He must be the ipotane leader," Kyran whispered, intent on the scene. "And see, he makes his way toward the centaur leader." His hand rose as he pointed to the other side of the field, where a centaur fought in the thick of battle. He was large, sinuous and strong, and the horse part of his body was a soft dove gray color. His hair fell in long white-blond braids out from under his bright silver helmet and over his broad shoulders. It was impossible to know how old he was. His face was ageless, young and old. Even from a distance, in the midst of the teeming battle, Posy could see the determination in his face. It was an encompassing determination, focused on winning the battle and his cause, not the immediacy and thrill of blood-lust that lit the eyes of the ipotane leader as he struck each adversary down.

At last, the two opponents met, and the battle seemed to slow somehow. Every creature there sensed it had come to this. Silence and an eerie calm hovered in the glade. Swords lowered until there was only the scraping shift of armor upon moving bodies. The ipotane's voice came loud and deep, jarringly soulless. "Give up the glade and no more of your army will die today," he demanded.

The centaur leader grew dangerously still, his crystal eyes fixed upon his enemy. At last he spoke, and his voice was like a deep and swift river. "We will die to the last one if that is what is required to keep the glade from you and he who sent you."

"Him who sent me?" The ipotane's harsh laugh rang out. "You dare suggest someone commands *me*?" The muscles in his arms flexed as he gripped his weapon tighter.

"I don't suggest it. I say it as truth." The centaur angrily pawed the ground in front of him with one of his front hooves. "You are here at the command of one of that race, the humans, and you will only cross the threshold of the Glooming if you kill me and every last centaur in the forest."

"Then," the ipotane's voice lowered, slithered like a deadly snake, "that is what we will do."

He raised his massive sword above his head and lunged toward the centaur, a savage cry ripping from his throat. But the centaur was too quick for him, and with hardly an indication that he had moved at all, his arm shot out and his sword struck home deep within the ipotane's chest. It happened so swiftly that Posy felt her mouth drop open in disbelief.

A deadly hush fell over the glade then, and even the other centaurs gazed at their leader in astonishment. Then, like the rippling of waves, the ipotane army began crying out and running. At first Posy thought they were shouting in attack, but she realized they were shouting in fear, and running for their lives. It seemed their purpose had vanished with their leader's death.

"The cowards!" she cried, relief flooding her.

The centaur army let out a victorious cry and began to give

chase into the trees after the remaining ipotanes. The leader stayed where he was, wiping his sword clean in the grass and gazing over the field of slain bodies, a look of deep sadness in his eyes. He turned to speak to the centaur nearest him, a male with a flow of white hair and broad strong shoulders, who then turned and began swiftly making his way across the field.

Posy threw a look of panic at Kyran as she realized the centaur's path led straight to where they hid. Kyran made no move to run. Posy watched, but saw that his hand did not reach for his sword, a thing now familiar to her when danger threatened. His expression held nothing she could read but expectation, and when the resonant voice of the centaur called out to them to show themselves, he did not hesitate. He stood and greeted the beast in kind.

CHAPTER THIRTEEN
The Centaurs

Posy felt curiously unafraid as Kyran took her hand and helped her to her feet. They stepped from behind the undergrowth of the forest where they had been crouched and onto the edge of the glade, still with hands clasped.

"Greetings," called out Kyran in a voice like a king's. If he felt fear at all, Posy couldn't see it.

The centaur came to a smart stop. He pawed at the ground and turned a half circle, his dark gaze never leaving them. "Come, children." Then he turned with a swish of his tail and began making his way back across the field to his leader.

They didn't have a choice; not really. So, they crossed the glade together and came to the leader of the centaurs, who stood regarding them as still as stone. His ice blue eyes seemed to pierce straight through them. But Posy held his eyes with her own, and she saw the softness beyond the ice—hidden, but unmistakable. No, there was nothing to fear here.

"I am Kyran, prince of the Kingdom beyond the forest, and this is the companion of my quest, Posy."

"Greetings, children. I am Faxon, leader of the centaurs. We have been expecting you." His voice was gracious, kind, and it rolled over Posy like a song. "The Author told us you would come."

The two children stared in disbelief. Kyran finally spoke, his voice halting, "The ... Author told you this?"

"Yes." Faxon bowed his head in assent, sending his bright braids forward over his shoulders. "You do not know of him?"

Kyran's face grew troubled as he tried to find an answer. "Of course we know of him," he finally said. "But he does not speak to characters, not in the Kingdom, and surely not here beyond the Borders, where only outcasts find a home. The story does not extend into the Wild Land—why should the Author be here?"

"Ah, but we are not outcasts, Prince," Faxon answered with a sad smile. "Only in your Kingdom are we considered such, but not in this land. And your story, along with the Author's words, extends far beyond what its characters believe. But you know that, or you would never have come here."

"We came here," said Kyran, "to find my sister. Not to seek the Author or any other Plot than the one I know."

"Yes," the centaur answered quietly, "we know of the princess Evanthe."

"You've seen her?" burst out Posy.

"I saw her two days past," Faxon replied. "Here, within this very glade."

"And ... where is she now?" Kyran's face worked to keep a calm expression.

"She has entered the Glooming." Faxon's eyes flashed, a mysterious expression that came and was gone in an instant.

"The Glooming," Kyran's voice came miserably through Posy's swirling thoughts.

"I spoke with her," Faxon said, and Kyran's head snapped up in attention. "But she was intent upon her destination, and nothing I could say would prevent her."

"You could have stopped her," Kyran said. "You stopped the ipotanes from gaining the glade, and the entrance to the Glooming. Why not her? Why let her venture into such danger alone?"

"Evil must be stopped, by force if necessary, but enforcing something against someone's free will, when no evil is intended? It is not as the Author would wish, and it is not how we live. The plot here is unlike the Plot that has wound itself around your Kingdom, young prince. The plot here in this land beyond is one that may change and vary; it is one that is dependent on the choices of its characters themselves. It is not set; it is not the same every time the book is opened or the story told. That is its danger. And that is its beauty."

"But the free choice to walk into unknown danger—a girl alone? How can that be right or fair?" Posy heard the anger beginning in Kyran's voice, despite the centaur's calm words.

"Yes, Prince." Faxon's voice hardened as well, as if he were growing weary of explaining something so natural to someone who did not wish to understand. "Even if she must walk into danger. She was not ignorant of it; she knew what she entered into. Something was strong in her mind ... something she knew she must do, or try to do. We would not stop her from it."

Kyran shook his head, wordless, and walked a few paces away. Posy followed him without hesitation, grasping his arm. She didn't know how or why, but she had a sudden surety about what was happening. "Kyran," she said earnestly, "Faxon is right. It was meant to be, don't you see that? It's like the poem said, if we're to find the center and heart of truth, this is what we have to do. Evanthe had to go there, and so do we. I think this might be the answer to everything."

"The answer to everything? What are you talking about?" Kyran asked with a curl of his lip that reminded Posy unpleasantly of their first meeting. Posy wasn't sure what she meant. It was more of a feeling, a swirling sensation that she couldn't quite make out or explain but was sure of all the same.

"I don't know," she answered honestly, "But I feel that everything here is connected somehow. Haven't you had enough of lies and confusion? Don't you want to find something ... true?"

"Oh, but I already know what I am to do," Kyran said, shrugging his arm out of her grasp. "Nothing that happens will change my purpose, which is to take my father off the throne and free the Plot from his tyranny." Posy knew of Kyran's anger, and his grief over his father's cruelty, so his words did not surprise her. Still, she felt them bite into her with something that felt so close to betrayal that she caught her breath.

Faxon, who had missed nothing, walked to where they stood and said, "I believe the lady is right, Prince. The Glooming is a dangerous place, many times an evil place, but great truth and goodness can be found there by the right people—people with strength. Perhaps you will find something you never sought at all."

"I don't know what any of that means," retorted Kyran testily, "and what's more, I don't care. How can you feel the need to chastise me when I say I am to overthrow the king? You, who of all creatures have been most wronged by him."

"And those who have been most wronged have the greatest opportunity for forgiveness, young one. But it only comes from the truest, deepest part of you, and it is not something that is easily reached. Nothing true and good is."

Kyran had no answer for this. But as Posy looked at him, his face took on a subtle change, and his eyes lost a bit of their anger. Before either of them could speak, they heard noises from across the glade where the centaurs had been clearing the battlefield of bodies and armor. Two centaurs were on either side of a captive ipotane who was struggling violently between them. They dragged him across the field toward Faxon. Faxon stood, still as a statue, and his blue eyes glinted like steel as they approached and thrust the ipotane before him.

"Well," he said solemnly. The ipotane cursed at him and strained against his captors, the muscles of his upper human half-taut and bulging.

Faxon ignored this, and merely asked, "I have a few questions for you, and it would be best for you if you answered them truthfully."

"And if I don't?" the ipotane's voice came furiously.

"We shall have to see," Faxon answered calmly. "Now then, who sent you?"

"Ferreolus was our leader. He was the one we followed, as you well know. And now you have killed him! You—you—filth, you—"

"I know of Ferreolus," Faxon cut him off. "I also know that he did nothing without a reason. For centuries, the centaurs have been guardians of the glade. Why did he choose to attack us now, and gain entrance into the Glooming?"

"I don't ask questions!" shouted the ipotane angrily. "I trusted my leader, as did every ipotane who followed him. We needed nothing more than that to follow him wherever he had need to send us."

Faxon eyed him for a moment, as if trying to decide if he could trust what he heard. At last, he nodded and continued, "No matter how blind the trust, each creature has its own mind. What does your mind tell you, ipotane, of this battle fought today?"

Ashlee Willis

The ipotane gazed at Faxon skeptically. "You know we have never been at peace with you, nor you with us. What is different about this battle?"

"Ah, but it *is* different. You attacked the glade, and those of us guarding it. Ferreolus sought to gain entrance into the Glooming itself. This attack was not made against the centaurs; it was made for a purpose."

"And you think that if I knew the purpose I would tell you?" spat out the ipotane venomously. "You are a fool."

"Very well," Faxon nodded with finality, unruffled. He gestured to the centaurs holding him, and they took their prisoner away. "So then," he said, turning to Kyran and Posy and smiling, "you must be hungry. Will you come to our camp and rest and eat?"

"No," exclaimed Kyran immediately, "I thank you for the offer, but we must go into the Glooming as soon as we can—now—and find my sister."

"And you will go as soon as you can, but that time is not now, young one," said Faxon. "The entrance to the Glooming is not open continually. We will have to wait for its next opening."

Kyran's face was dumbstruck. "And when will that be?"

"Do not worry," Faxon said with a serene smile for them. "You have not long to wait. It happens at midnight this very night."

CHAPTER FOURTEEN
Painful Words

"I suspect," Faxon turned to look at Posy and Kyran as he led them through the trees, "that our captive was telling the truth."

"You mean that he knew nothing?" asked Posy, lifting her skirts a bit to keep up with Faxon's rapid pace. She wondered where they were headed. She and Kyran had finally made it to the entrance of the Glooming, and now they were walking away from the glade and back once again into the darkness of the forest. The forest seemed a different place, though, with the centaurs around them and Faxon leading them. He moved and spoke completely at ease. The forest may not be where he had come from, or the story he had been written into, but it was clearly his home now. He moved with confidence that only one deeply familiar with his surroundings would have.

"He may have had opinions of his own about the reasons for this battle," continued the centaur, "but he did not know anything for certain. It is like an ipotane to leave his soldiers in ignorance and expect them to follow blindly." He shook his head.

Kyran quickened his stride to match the centaur's, and came up to walk beside him. "May I ask if you have an opinion as to the attack?" he asked curiously.

"Oh, yes, although it is considerably more than an opinion," Faxon answered smoothly. "The owls—or the king, through the

owls—have been sending attacks against us since we left the Kingdom more than a century ago."

"What?" cried Posy breathlessly from behind them.

"Yes," Faxon smiled sadly at her over his shoulder, "When the
Council of Owls overthrew the Council of Centaurs, there was an
uproar in the land and we were banned from ever stepping foot
inside the Kingdom again. The king has made us fair game to any
character that might come across one of us." Posy noticed Kyran
wince when he heard this. "We have made our lives in the forest,
and we are no longer outcasts of the Kingdom, but true dwellers
of the Wild Land. Yet in recent years, that has not been enough
for the king and his councilors. They have sent violence into the
very forest to pursue us. The battle you saw is one of many we have
fought over these past months."

"But, the ipotanes live in the forest too, don't they?" asked Posy.
"They can't be part of the Kingdom, or under the rule of the king."

"No, they are not part of the Kingdom, that is true. It is likely
Falak has hired them as mercenaries to chase us from the land or,
preferably, kill our entire race."

"But why?" Posy asked, her eyes on the back of Kyran's head. She
felt pain for him at this further proof of his father's cruelty, even if
he would not admit to his own pain.

Before the centaur could answer her, Kyran said, "Isn't it obvious? They feel the centaurs are a threat to their rule. The Kingdom
has been restless these last years. Characters are somehow beginning to understand things they never understood before. If they
should begin to know too much—to remember too much—they
might demand the return of the centaurs to the Kingdom, and oust
the owls." His voice grew vehement. "It is not the king who does

this, but Falak and his followers. Only they would fear the return of the centaurs so much."

"I think they would not be the only ones who would fear it, young prince," Faxon said quietly, coming to a stop at last.

"What do you mean?" Kyran's voice was hard as a stone. His black hair fell over one of his eyes as he gazed at Faxon.

"These are things we will speak of," answered Faxon lightly, as if the conversation hadn't taken a dangerous turn. "But for now we must rest and eat."

"Rest and eat," Kyran repeated with a shake of his head. "Even with all that needs to be done."

"Yes," answered the centaur, stopping to look straight at Kyran. "Especially with all that needs to be done. Do not underestimate these things—they are not trivial, but the things that give us strength to continue. Never underestimate anything that gives strength, however small it may seem." He began walking again. "And we have many hours before midnight, though they will pass quickly with all that we must speak of and prepare for."

Posy finally forced her eyes from Kyran and Faxon and blinked as she looked around her. The small trees and underbrush of the surrounding area had been cleared and numerous tents stood tall around them. They were high and sweeping, regal almost, and made of heavy, richly colored material. Faxon led them past groups of battle-weary centaurs who had been making their way from the glade to the encampment. Some sat on the ground, their front legs folded beneath them, resting and talking in low voices; others were sharpening swords or taking off their armor.

Faxon led them to the tent at the rear of the encampment. It was at least twice the size of the others, and it was patterned with brilliant green, silver and gold.

"Our Summit Tent," he announced as two centaurs held open the thickly-draped flaps of the door and they entered. The room they walked into was enormous. The top of the tent rose far above them. The sides of the room were lined with silver and gold banners, rippling from the top of the tent to the floor. A wider banner of green, sewn with brightly colored threads, hung from the head of the room, on a raised platform. Though it was extremely different in many respects, the room reminded Posy of King Melanthius' Audience Chamber. That was almost certainly what this room was meant for, she thought. After all, hadn't the centaurs been the ones who advised from that chamber in times past?

"Come." Faxon led them through the large chamber and into a smaller, adjoining one that was obviously made for comfort instead of formality. He looked at them and smiled apologetically. "Centaurs have no need of chairs, of course, but this room has been made as comfortable as possible for you to rest in for a time. Please, make yourselves at home." He spread his hand invitingly and watched as they sat themselves down on the thick layers of blankets that covered the floor of the chamber. As he backed from the room, he said, "I will give you an hour to rest, then have food brought here for you before we meet in the Summit Room with my council."

The flap of the room swept closed, and Posy settled herself back onto the blankets. How long had it been since she had sat on something soft? Not so long, really ... but, oh, it felt like it! She was keenly aware of Kyran, so near her. She wanted to look at him, speak to him, but they had drifted apart somehow. She wondered if he could feel it, too, or if he even gave it any thought. She found she couldn't gauge his mood or read his expression. It was hard and blank.

At last, he threw himself back on the blankets and closed his eyes. "What do you think these centaurs are about? Living in the forest, outcasts, fighting continual battles. What can be their purpose, do you think?"

"Kyran," Posy said softly, sensing something she didn't like, "I thought you trusted them."

"I get the sense, though ... that they may think it is all my father's doing."

Posy took a breath. "He *is* the king," she said hesitantly. "Whatever the owls might talk your father into doing, as the king, it's his final decision."

Kyran sat up so quickly that Posy reactively lurched away from him. His dark eyes bore into her as he hissed, "So now *you* say my father is the one as well? After Falak sent soldiers and creatures of the forest to murder us, after he sent us blindly into the dangers of the Wild Land and away from the Kingdom's protection." He paused and gave her a withering look. "I never would have believed it of you, Posy."

Posy's first reaction was pain. It seemed this was a sort of betrayal from Kyran, this refusing to understand, especially when there had been so much understanding between them. Her next reaction was anger. It was her anger that spoke.

"Why can't you just be a man and admit it, Kyran? Admit your father has done all of this intentionally. He doesn't think of you or Evanthe or the characters of his Kingdom. He only thinks of himself. He only thinks about power. And if Falak has persuaded him to some things, it is only because Melanthius is weak, and selfish—things that must have been there inside of him all along." Posy paused to draw breath and had time to take in Kyran's furious expression before she plunged on, "But you know all of this already. I don't need to tell you, do I? The only difference between us is that I can admit it, see it for what it is. You are still trying to hide from it because you're a coward!"

Her voice had risen and her face felt unbearably hot as she leaned forward toward Kyran. She had the urge to grab him and shake him, pound her fists on him until she made him understand. She had faced it, hadn't she? She had written the horrible, ugly word across the mirror, not so long ago. She had stared at her reflection, her own tears, though she hated them. And it had meant pain to her—it meant the end of everything she knew. Still, she had looked straight at it.

Kyran stared at her for a long time ... such a long time. Posy felt her own anger abate, the urge to scream die down with the steadying beat of her heart. She watched Kyran's face, saw him struggling visibly with the feelings that played across it, trying to push them down. Moreover, she watched with pain and helplessness as those emotions retreated behind his eyes, somewhere far away, where she couldn't find them. She raised her hand as if she would seize his thoughts before they were gone, but then dropped it back on her lap heavily. She knew he had closed himself to her then, and she realized this was the last thing she had wanted to make him do. His face was shuttered, his eyes empty as he looked at her, and the words he spoke next were devoid of feeling.

"I'm going for a walk. You should get some rest." With that, he got up and left Posy alone in the room. She lowered her face into her hands and began to cry.

* * *

Posy awoke to the soft sounds of someone moving about in the chamber. When she opened her eyes, she saw a centaur placing platters of food on a low table in the corner of the room. Candles had been set on the table as well, and they threw gentle waves of light up the sides of the white tent walls. When the centaur was finished he merely turned to her and smiled slightly, bowing his head, then departed.

With a flood of dread, Posy remembered what had passed between herself and Kyran. She turned her face to the darkness of the blankets. *Is this how the story is supposed to go?* she asked herself. *It's a mess, and nothing makes sense.*

After Posy had eaten some of the food the centaur had left, she heard a soft voice from the doorway of the chamber and saw a woman's head poking through the flap. A horse's chestnut body followed her into the room. Her hair fell in lively auburn curls around her shoulders and her beautiful face smiled warmly at Posy. She said, "I am Caris, wife to Faxon." She gestured to the door she had just entered. "Will you follow me?"

The lady centaur led Posy to another tent, small and plain. It had a large washbasin full of warm clear water resting on a stand, with towels and clothing neatly folded on the floor.

"Thank you," breathed Posy as Caris smiled and disappeared behind the tent flap to await her outside.

The spring night sent a chill-fingered breeze through the small tent, so Posy washed quickly. The warm water felt blissful on her grimy skin. When she had finished cleaning her body, she poured

Ashlee Willis

the basin of water straight over her head, running her fingers through her tangled hair and scrubbing at her scalp. She looked around the small tent hopefully for a comb, but didn't see one. She ran her fingers through her tangle of curls until she felt it was presentable. After she was dry, she got dressed quickly. The clothing was odd, but it fit her well enough. A sort of robed dress that hung loosely down to her shins, with a cloth belt to wrap around her waist. Posy pulled it on quickly, stuck her feet back into her boots, and stepped outside of the tent.

Caris was there. "Someone will take your dress and clean it. I am sorry we can offer no better clothing than this," she gestured toward Posy's robe, "but as you can see, we have no need for such things." Indeed, none of them needed anything but shirts. The male centaurs had only had their armor on, and Caris wore a soft shirt made of animal skin, serviceable and plain.

Posy shook her head. It didn't matter. She looked around the camp, trying to spot Kyran amidst the dots of firelight shining through the now darkened forest. Caris stood before her, unmoving, and Posy realized she was being rude. She smiled at Caris.

"Thank you so much for the clothing, the food ... everything. You said ... I believe you said you are Faxon's wife?"

"Yes," Caris nodded.

"Do the other centaurs take their wives with them to battles?"

"Faxon has not brought me here," said Caris with a small smile. "All of us live here. The centaurs are now guardians of the glade. We protect the entrance to the Glooming from those who should not enter. It is the task the Author has given us now we are no longer part of the Kingdom's Plot."

"How do you know what the Author wishes you to do?" asked

Posy curiously. "Maybe it was never the purpose of the Author that you left the Kingdom to begin with—maybe you should rightfully still be there."

Caris' jaw tightened, and she shook her head vehemently. "Nothing is by chance, young one," she said, her voice trembling with emotion. "If we were to ever think we were not in the place the Author would have us be—if we were to ever lose faith that he is the one writing the story and not us—we would be lost. How could it be otherwise?"

They had come to the entrance of the Summit Tent. Caris turned her hazel eyes searchingly onto Posy's face, and Posy felt as if they saw all the way into her, to the depths of her soul. "There may be great decisions made today, now that you and the prince are here," she said quietly. Then she said, taking Posy by the arm, "We must join the council, for they are ready to begin."

CHAPTER FIFTEEN
Friends and Allies

Upon entering the Summit Tent, Posy found herself in a extremely intimidating situation. Before each unfurled banner along the edges of the long chamber stood a centaur, straight-backed and attentive. Faxon stood before the wide banner at the head of the room, his shoulders thrown back and his face set grimly, as if this were a task he would rather not undertake. When Posy and Caris entered the flap of the tent, Caris immediately went to her designated place in front of one of the banners amidst the other centaurs of the council. Posy was left standing alone.

Faxon nodded his head at her and motioned a hand to summon her forward. Posy swallowed and began walking the length of the room, centaur eyes upon her from every direction. She spotted Kyran at the head of the chamber already, standing at the foot of the platform on which Faxon stood. When she went to stand next to him and gave him a small smile of greeting, Kyran merely blinked and turned to focus his attention on Faxon without a word. *So, not forgiven*, Posy thought with a sinking feeling.

"Centaurs of the council and guardians of the glade," began Faxon, his voice resonating throughout the tent. "We have convened here today for various reasons, and to come to certain crucial decisions. Firstly, we have here among us two characters from the Kingdom which was once our home. They have broken with King

Melanthius and are seeking the princess Evanthe, who, as we know, has entered the Glooming."

Posy noticed most of the council nodded in understanding. Apparently, none of this was new information to them.

"We must decide whether or not to allow these two entrance into the Glooming as well," continued Faxon. "Do any wish to oppose this?"

A tall centaur with long white hair and a short-clipped beard cleared his throat. Posy recognized him as the one Faxon had sent to fetch them from their hiding place in the glade. "Yes, Stonus?" Faxon asked.

"We have no reason to trust these two," the older centaur stated baldly. Posy felt as if her heart dropped into her stomach. She had not bargained on opposition from the centaurs. She waited for Faxon to assure the other centaurs that he trusted them, but he only nodded at Stonus' words, saying nothing to refute them.

A soft lilting voice rose above the murmuring of the council, one Posy recognized at once. Caris said, "You will excuse me, Stonus, but I see no greater proof—that these children are with us rather than against us—than in the fact that they have defied King Melanthius himself and ventured into the Wild Land at great risk to themselves."

"That is no proof," Stonus said, shaking his head. "Many people may have many reasons for defying the king. It does not mean their reasons are the same as ours, or that they are with us."

"Perhaps," said Caris, "we should let the children speak for themselves."

Thirteen centaur heads turned to look at Kyran and Posy. Posy shifted uneasily and hoped Kyran had something prepared to say;

she certainly didn't.

"Friends," said Kyran, turning to face the length of the chamber. "King Melanthius is my father, but he is now also my mortal enemy." An almost indistinguishable intake of breath could be heard throughout the chamber at these strong words, but only Posy knew what they had cost Kyran to speak. He continued, "I have watched for years as the Plot has changed, worsened, and as the king and his councilors have sought more power for themselves, and have been less and less understanding toward the common characters. My sister, the princess Evanthe, saw it long before I did, I am ashamed to say. I have recently learned that the king himself changed the Plot to include the sacrifice of my innocent sister, in order that more readers would come, and thus secure his place as ruler. After learning of this evil, no one with any honesty or integrity would be able to ally themselves with the king. Indeed, I have not only broken from him, but am intending to lead a revolt against him."

Now the murmurs grew louder, and a few centaurs even spoke aloud, shaking their heads angrily, though Posy couldn't hear what they said. Faxon held up a hand for silence. He turned to Kyran and said, "In what way do you intend to revolt against your father, young Prince?"

Kyran's dark eyes ran the length of the chamber, meeting the troubled eyes of each creature there before he swallowed and answered, "I have a friend who is even now working in my name to recruit soldiers and characters and form an army that will march on the Kingdom as soon as it is possible."

Stonus' deep voice came across the room. "It is wrong," he said simply.

Kyran's face changed, and Posy thought his expression was much the same as it was when she had first met him. It held aloofness and pride. "And what right have you to say that to me? A prince of the Kingdom who has lived in it and seen the injustice there?"

"Every right," said Stonus calmly. "You forget it was not long ago that we centaurs counseled the king and lived within the Kingdom ourselves. The Author himself put us there in the beginning, for that is where we belonged, though since that time, we have been driven out by less pure forces."

"The Author?" Posy burst out suddenly, and she felt her heart leap. She hadn't intended to speak—but she couldn't stop herself.

"Yes," said Stonus.

She felt everyone in the room looking at her, and she could feel her face growing pink, but there was no going back now. "How do you know what the Author intended?" she asked boldly.

It was Caris who answered. "Because," she said gently, "he speaks to us."

Centaurs around the room nodded, their expressions softened, in response to her words.

Faxon said, "King Melanthius and the Council of Owls would have the characters believe that the Plot is unchanging, while they themselves change it to their own liking. This is how they keep power, by the ignorance of the characters. The Council of Centaurs, when we reigned in the Kingdom, knew the Plot changed. We knew that the characters had a right to make their own choices and form their own individual stories, as long as the Author would allow it. Only the Author has the true right to govern the larger Plot, and move the characters within it."

"Many of the characters of my Kingdom say that the Author has abandoned us," stated Kyran, as if daring someone to disagree with him.

But Faxon only nodded and said, "In a way he has, although in truth, it is much more the other way around. The Kingdom has abandoned the Author; therefore, the Author has abandoned the Kingdom."

"What a life to have," Caris said almost as if to herself, "to be a character, but not to have the strength or openness of mind to look up and beyond yourself, and see that you are not your own Author. What misery that must bring! To think that a weak king writes the words to your life."

"But that is what I am trying to do," said Kyran suddenly. "I lacked the strength for a long time, but now my eyes are open. I wish to bring about vast changes, to overthrow the evil in the Kingdom and replace it with what the Author intended."

"It is not as simple as that." Stonus shook his head sadly.

"It may not be," said Kyran stubbornly, "but it has got to be better than skulking in the forest of the Wild Land and doing nothing." This was obviously meant as a jibe at the centaurs, but they were too wise to rise to the bait. Faxon merely turned his piercing blue eyes on Kyran and looked at him intently for several moments before turning to the rest of the centaurs and saying, "It is not the way of the centaurs, violence and war. But as you know, we have had to change like everyone else over the decades. We have had to learn the art of battles and warfare, in defense of our own lives."

"And if it serves the greater good, we should fight alongside the prince," called out one of the other centaurs.

"Perhaps," was all Faxon said. "We shall see. You know our numbers are diminished since we came to the Wild Land. Our fellow centaurs who have fallen in battle do not come back to us as they did within the Plot, and if we join this war we will lose even more."

Posy felt as if ice was trickling down her spine. She looked at Kyran and saw his eyes widen with the import of Faxon's words.

"Do you mean," Kyran said slowly, "that outside of the Plot, characters may die, and not return?"

"Yes, Prince," nodded Faxon, his eyes solemn. "It is not as it is within the Kingdom. Sacrifices may be made there, deaths may be written, but none of it is final—none of it is real."

Kyran remained speechless, but Posy could see the thoughts flitting across his face, the doubt and fear, and finally, realization.

Faxon continued. "The council will have to meet at another time to decide about the war of the Kingdom, and our place in it." He turned to face the centaurs lining the chamber. "Now we must decide whether to let these two into the Glooming. Let me state, before we decide, that I believe that the prince and this young woman have the purest intentions for entering the Glooming, and that they possess the strength to navigate it safely. Now, let us decide."

Posy waited, holding her breath as each centaur down the long chamber gave his or her answer. All were in favor of letting them enter the Glooming. And so it was decided. She supposed it should have felt like a great relief, but instead she just felt dread.

* * *

"In what way does the Author speak to you?" Posy and Caris were walking together on the outskirts of the encampment after the meeting. They had only an hour until midnight, when she and Kyran would enter the Glooming. Torches and campfires glowed all around the camp, sending long shadows dancing across the ground at their feet.

"He has written me," answered Caris simply. "He not only knows me, he created who I am, and in everything I do and feel, I see him and hear him." She shook her head, making her auburn curls quiver. "This war between the Kingdom and the Wild Land—it is not just about the power between characters. It is so much more. But most do not see it."

"You mean it is about the Author," stated Posy.

"Yes," said Caris. "The king, Falak, even your young prince— none of them realize that even if one of them wins over the other, it matters little if the Author is not behind them. None of it will last if he is not the one invited to have power over them."

"In my world," said Posy, "authors write stories, and the characters do whatever the author tells them. It's not like this—the characters don't have minds and lives of their own."

"How do you know this?" was Caris' surprising reply. The corner of her mouth turned up in a playful smile. "You do not see the characters when the pages of the book are shut. Is there never a time when you read a book for the second time and you notice something that you didn't remember from the first time? Or hear a story told, and every time it is told it grows and changes in the telling? Change is the nature of everything." Caris' face suddenly grew solemn, and she stopped to turn and look into Posy's face. "You must know," she said quietly, as if she thought they would be overheard, "that the Glooming is a dangerous place."

Posy's heart leapt, but she nodded. "I know."

"It does not appear to be perilous," Caris went on. "And in that lies its greatest danger. It will appear to be a friendly, beautiful, even joyous place—but you must not be blinded by this. I only hope you find what you are seeking."

"You mean the princess?" asked Posy. "I hope so, too. Kyran is certain she's there."

Caris hesitated a moment before replying quietly, "Yes."

They both turned, hearing a great commotion from the encampment. A young centaur came galloping toward them and shouted out one word before he turned, his hooves throwing up a small cloud of dust, and rushed back in the other direction: "Attack!"

CHAPTER SIXTEEN
Into the Glooming

Kyran and Faxon had received the same warning only moments before Posy and Caris. They had immediately sprung into action, preparing for battle. Faxon had turned to the prince for a single moment after they had been warned of the attack, and had said, "They know you are here." Kyran had no time to ask who Faxon spoke of—no time to even wonder. He drew his sword and rushed to follow Faxon back into the center of the encampment, where the other centaurs were gathering already in vast numbers.

"Soldiers!" cried Faxon, his voice rising above the din of voices and clanging armor. "Form ranks and prepare to fight." He gestured with his sword toward where Posy and Kyran now stood together. "These two must be kept safe at all costs; they must not be kept from entering the Glooming when it opens. Who will protect them?"

"I will protect them," a voice rang out, and Stonus stepped forward from the crowd of centaurs. Faxon clasped his shoulder and looked into his eyes, nodding. "I will trust you, my friend," was all he said. He turned to Posy and Kyran. A sad smile flickered in his crystal blue eyes. "Stonus will guard your lives with his own. Trust the Author. Listen closely for the true story, the one that has been covered and hidden these many years. And when you hear it, follow it, for it is the story the Author intended from the beginning, and you will not go wrong with it."

Posy watched as Faxon turned his full attention to his soldiers. Stonus immediately took over. "Come with me," he commanded.

They followed him out of the encampment, away from the sounds of the approaching enemies, and into the woods, pitch black with night. Posy felt her heart pounding in her chest. As they thrashed through the forest behind the centaur, Posy tripped on a root jutting from the ground, and she cried out as she lurched forward. Kyran deftly swept in front of her and caught her before she fell. For a moment, their faces were so close that Posy could feel the warmth of Kyran's skin, and his breath on her forehead. She supposed it was this—and the fact that she was horribly afraid of both the danger behind and before them—that made her reach out and clasp his hand, forgetting any argument between them. He had forgotten too, it seemed, for he locked his strong, cool fingers through hers tightly.

At last, Stonus slowed his pace and finally stopped. He held a hand up to silence them and lifted his head, eyes sharp and alert. His armor gleamed dully in the weak moonlight that trickled through the treetops. "We have only minutes before the doorway will open," he said at last. "I must get you there, and through it, before the fighting reaches us."

"But where is the door?" asked Kyran suddenly. "Is it not in the glade?"

"Yes, it is in the glade," answered Stonus.

"But we are in the middle of the forest now. We will never have time to get back to the glade if we only have minutes." Kyran's voice came through the darkness, edged with panic.

"No, young one," answered Stonus calmly. "We have only made

a wide circle around the encampment. We are not far from the glade's edge. Come."

They followed him again, more slowly this time, painfully cautious, through the deep-shadowed forest until the trees stopped abruptly, and moonlight flooded their faces. Posy gasped as they emerged from the forest and stepped into the glade. It was a place wholly transformed. No longer a bloody battlefield—not even a common clearing within the trees—it was bathed with pearly white-blue moonlight, desperately still and silent. Posy watched as Stonus walked right to the center of the clearing, and she half expected to see the air around him ripple and move, for it was as if he walked into a picture and not a real place. He motioned for Kyran and Posy to follow.

"But where is it?" asked Kyran again. "Where is the doorway?"

"Faith," Stonus turned a look of gentle rebuke on Kyran. "It will appear when it is meant to, no sooner."

Posy stood shivering, waiting. She was faintly aware of the far-away sounds of the battle, and wondered if they were getting nearer.

"Remember, my children," said Stonus, his deep voice piercing the silence around them. "You go into a place of evil and treachery. What you think you can trust will deceive you; what pains you to do will perhaps be the thing that saves you." He lifted his eyes to the thick tree line surrounding them, and Posy knew she wasn't imagining it now; the sounds of fighting were very close. Why were the minutes passing so slowly?

Suddenly, a subtle rumbling came from the ground beneath their feet. Stonus stamped his hooves in anticipation, his eyes still raking the dark edges of the glade for danger. The rumbling became shaking, and the shaking gave way to the sound of earth ripping and crumbling apart. Posy and Kyran looked down to see two stone columns rising from the ground, pushing through the soil and rising high above their heads.

Kyran turned to Stonus abruptly and said, his voice urgent, "I must know ... why would enemies of yours, like the ipotanes, want to enter the Glooming? What has someone with evil intent to gain in that place?"

Stonus' eyes glimmered and darkened in the shadowy moonlight, and for a moment it looked as if he might not answer. His face a mask, his tone carefully controlled, he, at last, answered, "The Glooming has many outlets and entrances; this is only one of many." He gestured toward the raised columns. "Depending on where an army may want to attack, one of these entrances may be crucial in the winning of a war. And what's more, there are ... powers that lie sleeping in the Glooming that could prove useful to the ipotanes in battle, though they are dangerous and sometimes deadly to awaken."

"Why did Faxon not tell us?" Kyran asked incredulously, his dark eyes growing wide.

Stonus shook his head. "What has it to do with what you seek? What has it to do with the princess?"

"Everything!" Kyran's voice exploded. "It has everything to do with it! My father is at war with the Wild Land, in case you've forgotten. He wishes to kill all the centaurs, and probably now even me. What better way to ... to ..." his voice spluttered out angrily.

They all grew suddenly silent, though, when a new sound burst into the clearing. Posy barely had time to see the group of ipotanes and soldiers making toward them over Stonus' shoulder before Stonus turned, his broad form blocking her view, and said, his voice low and urgent, "Go—now."

"But—" Posy started, staring at the columns.

"It is a doorway. Simply walk through the columns." Stonus had one strong hand on Posy's shoulder, gently pushing her toward the door, and the other hand was at his sword. The ipotanes were nearly upon them. She turned quickly to Kyran, thinking they would walk through the doorway together, when she saw that he had drawn his sword and had his back to the door, facing their attackers.

"Kyran, no!" Posy cried, but he showed no indication of hearing her.

"Posy is right," Stonus' voice was so low Posy barely heard him. "You must go now, or you will miss it. The door only remains open for a few minutes' time."

"Then I will have to miss it. I will not run the other way and leave you alone to defend us, if that is what you are asking."

Posy felt certain that was exactly what Stonus was asking, and she waited for Stonus to make an argument. But he merely nodded his head once, his eyes on the approaching enemy, and unsheathed his sword. This was a race of creatures, she reminded herself, who did not push, force or bully, and she could see Stonus had accepted Kyran's right to make this decision.

"However," Kyran said, turning to Posy, "*you* will not miss the door because of me, and I will not have you standing here in danger. I will follow you as swiftly as I can, Posy—I swear to you."

Posy didn't even have time to process what was happening or what he meant. Kyran took her shoulders and gently but firmly spun her around and pushed her through the middle of the columns. Immediately Posy met with resistance. It wasn't a forceful feeling, but odd—as if she were pushing through an invisible web. She turned around to look back through the doorway, to see Kyran and Stonus, but all she could see were dim shapes moving as if she were looking through very old, mottled glass. She could hear the sounds of fighting, too, although they sounded distant and muffled. She thought she saw a blurred flutter of wings swoop above the fighting forms, but she could have been mistaken. Instead of moving forward, she decided to wait, suspended as she was and with the air around her pressing in on her uncomfortably.

"I'm waiting for you," she tried to call to Kyran, but it was as if her voice met with a solid wall, and no sound came. Whether the words were spoken or not, she stubbornly waited. She tried in vain to make out which shape was which through the other side of the door. Was that Kyran? Had he taken a slash to his arm? Was it Stonus who had fallen to the ground, or an ipotane? Just as she was beginning to feel the beginnings of true fear for the two of them fighting alone, something happened to cause her even more concern.

It began as a slight rumble, as it had begun before. Only this time, the columns began to move slowly downward. In alarm, Posy began trying again to call to Kyran, but it was no use. She stared through the thickened air around her at the distorted figures, a wild anticipation thrilling through her body. *Please, Kyran,* she said desperately to herself, *please don't leave me here alone.*

When Posy thought the columns were nearly too low to allow anyone to crawl in, she saw a figure running headlong toward them. When the form reached the entrance, it dropped down and slid forward, straight through the swiftly-shrinking doorway and toward her. The atmosphere slowed him the minute he was

Ashlee Willis

through the door; otherwise, he would have crashed right into Posy. As it was, his body pierced the web of air around her, his arm reached out to wrap around her and pulled her with him through the dense resistance until they were beyond the doorway and into the Glooming.

* * *

When Posy looked to her side, she thought she could still see distorted shadows of the glade as if they passed through it in a dense, dreamlike haze. But soon they began to descend, and it grew darker and more difficult for a while until, suddenly, the resistance ended and they came bursting into a narrow passage that smelled strongly of earth. It was impossibly dark, and they both had to feel cautiously around. They discovered that it smelled of earth because that was what the entire chamber was made of.

"We are underground," stated Kyran, wiping his soiled hands on his pants.

"Great. And how are we supposed to see anything?" asked Posy, making a face in the darkness.

"We don't."

"How do we know where to go? How do we know we won't fall off a ledge somewhere to our deaths?"

"We don't know, Posy," Kyran's voice sounded blunted as it thudded into the walls of packed dirt that rose around them. "No one said this was going to be easy."

"No," answered Posy, and she felt her shoulders droop, suddenly very weary. Though they could not see each other, it was as if Kyran knew her thoughts, and she felt his arm go around her in a brief, awkward embrace. "My sister has been here," he said, his voice full of forced hope. "She passed through this exact spot only days ago. We are close, Posy, I know we are. And we're together. I'm glad of that. I'm glad I'm not doing this alone."

His words flooded Posy with warmth, and she knew they were at peace again. Had it really been today that they had argued, met with the centaur council, watched the horrors of the battlefield? It all seemed so long ago.

"Yes," Posy said, straightening her shoulders and shaking her head as if she could shrug away her weariness and deny the fear that this place made her feel. "You're right, Kyran, we are close. We've got to be."

They walked for a long time down the narrow earthy passage. It was a slow process, for Kyran was walking ahead and using his hands to inspect every inch of the tunnel before they proceeded into it. He wanted to take no chances, now that they had gone this far. After they had been in utter darkness so long, it was hard to tell, but Posy began to imagine she could sense a faint light. When she could make out Kyran's silhouette in front of her, she let out an exclamation.

"It's getting lighter," she said excitedly.

"Hmm," Kyran said. "I thought so."

"Well, that's good, isn't it?" Posy said when she heard the skepticism in his voice.

"That depends on where the light is coming from and who or what is making it. We'll have to be extremely careful now. No more words, even a whisper, until we know it's safe. And stay behind me."

They continued down the passage toward the light, the sound

of their footsteps deadened by the damp earth all around them. The ground beneath them began to flatten and harden, and Posy looked down to see the floor of the tunnel was now stone. The light ahead of them grew brighter and brighter until there could be no doubt that it led to a room. Kyran stopped and squeezed Posy's arm when they both heard the voices that came from the room ahead of them.

"People—many of them, by the sound of it," said Kyran in disbelief. "What do they do here?"

As they crept closer to the narrow crevice of rock that led to the room beyond, Posy could hear the voices, and they reminded her of something. It sounded like the content and happy conversation of a relaxed gathering of friends. There was the tinkle of glass, laughter springing up here and there amidst the murmur of voices. It reminded Posy of the sounds at her house when all her family stayed for Christmas, happy in each others' company, laughing at each other's jokes. She felt herself warm to it, and straightened from her crouched position as if drawn to the room beyond.

Kyran grasped her arm and yanked her back down next to him. "What are you doing?" he hissed in her ear.

"Don't you hear?" Posy answered with a smile, unabashed. "Don't you hear how they sound?"

"Yes, I hear, all right," Kyran whispered, staring at her. "And I don't care for it. Why should a happy gathering of people be here, in this place, Posy?"

But all she could think about was the feeling she had while listening to those voices—as if she had come to a place like home. As if she was wrapped in comfort, and completely secure. As if nothing could shake the solid ground beneath her.

Kyran shook his head. "We're not going in there until we know what's going on." He latched his arm around her tightly—so tightly that any other time Posy would have cried out and tried to shake him off. But not now, for she was in reverie and she couldn't be disturbed by anything. Anything—except what they saw next.

Just as they came to the opening in the rock and peered through, and Posy was feeling as if she would have to break away from Kyran and rush into the friendly warmth of the room, the veil was torn away. Her senses seemed to clash together. What her ears heard and what her eyes saw were at terrible odds, and she stood rooted to the ground, her breath quickening and heart beating rapidly. Now Kyran's arm tight around her seemed the only security she had at all. She turned to him and saw the horror and disgust on his face, as it must have been on her own.

The room beyond was filled with the light of a thousand candles. It was filled with tables and chairs, the stone floor shimmering like waxed marble. A hearth was ablaze at one end of the room. All around the room were the people whose voices they had heard, reclining, laughing, and standing in groups all about the chamber, talking happily. People, yes, for people they must have once been. Posy felt a shudder run through her entire body as her eyes swept the length of the room.

When Posy and Kyran thought of it afterwards, it was hard to get a picture in their minds, although they vividly remembered the feeling of coldness and dread when they first saw the wraithlike creatures. They were not ghosts exactly—not skeletons either. They had skin, but not enough of it to cover all their bones, it seemed. It was stretched horribly across cheekbones and thighs, shoulders and ribs. The hollows of their eye sockets were large and shadowed.

Ashlee Willis

Their clothes looked like finery, only they were made of something that looked to Posy like cobwebs, and it trailed in a ghostly cloud behind the figures as they moved about the room.

"No," was all she could say, barely a whisper. "What are they?"

"I don't know," Kyran said with difficulty. "I only care how we are to get past them unseen. I've a feeling my sword would be no use against them."

"If we can't touch them, maybe they can't touch us," suggested Posy hopefully, but Kyran only grunted, his gaze sharp.

"There," he said with a slight gesture toward the far side of the room. "I see another opening similar to this one."

It was barely a shadow against the wall, a darkened gash running up the side of the stone that flickered with ghostly candlelight. "So ... do we make a run for it?" whispered Posy, her teeth beginning to chatter.

Kyran let out a dubious snort of breath, but said nothing; he had no other suggestion to make. He had never come up against something that his sword couldn't handle.

"Maybe," he said. "Let's wait and see if anything else happens, though."

"Anything else—like *what* else?" Posy asked incredulously. "We are *not* waiting for something even worse. I mean, look at it this way—at least they all seem happy right now. As far as this type of circumstance goes, that's got to be good, right?"

After a long silence, Kyran finally nodded once. "All right," he conceded quietly. "We run."

Posy's heart skipped a beat, but she quickly steeled herself against her fear. Kyran stood and turned his dark eyes on her face entreatingly. "I want you to run as if a nightmare were chasing you—as if hell were grasping at your heels. Don't look around you and don't try to go anywhere or touch anything until you get to the opening."

"And you?" asked Posy calmly, though her heart was beating so loudly now she thought he must hear it.

"Don't think about me—I'll be behind you. Just think about getting to that door and don't stop for anything, do you hear? Not *anything*."

"Fine," she bit her lip and felt her eyes slide to the light and warmth of the room beyond them, filled with such grisly horror.

"Ready?" Kyran said as they both edged toward the creviced rock. "Go." He pushed her lightly from behind. For a moment Posy felt as if she had frozen, then her legs sprung into action as if they had come to life on their own. She immediately wanted to turn for the reassurance of Kyran running behind her, but she knew she couldn't dare to do it.

It happened slowly at first, their noticing her. Even with her racing heart and her fear practically suffocating her, she could still sense the difference in the room. It became quiet for a drawn-out moment. The voices hushed, the music stopped, the clinking of glass was quieted. Only silence and a terrible coldness now filled the room. Still Posy kept running without looking anywhere but her destination. Until she heard Kyran.

When she heard him calling out, it was as if an icy finger had trailed down her spine. Her feet immediately slowed, and she turned to look, though she knew as she did it that she shouldn't. She couldn't help it. Kyran lay on the floor of the chamber, his sword lying some feet away from him as if he had drawn it to fight and had it knocked from his hands. He was curled oddly, almost like a child, and his black hair fell over his face as he leaned forward, wrapping his arms around himself and whimpering.

Not one of the wraiths in the room was near enough to be harming him. They all just silently watched as Kyran cried weakly as if in pain, or deathly afraid. Then Posy began to see shapes around her—faint at first and then stronger, brightly colored, terrifyingly dark. She knew the images at once for her worst fears, things she dreaded, nightmares she never wished to revisit. It was as if her very feelings had taken shape and put on faces. Helplessness and anger and an emptiness so deep it made her gasp – there they all stood, staring at her from empty eyes, as real as she. They began to circle in toward where she stood rooted to the ground. She heard her own voice as if from a distance as she cried out and tried to cower away from what she saw. Black thoughts and horrors swam around and through her, and she felt as if her body was fading, and nothing would be left of her but raw fear.

A flash of something flitted through the darkness in her mind, like the white wing of a bird in the dark of night. She grasped at it, tried to see what it was. It was a voice. Her mother's? Her father's? Kyran's? She couldn't tell. A person she loved. A bit of her heart thawed when she heard it, and she felt the rest of her body fight wildly in pursuit of it.

"Posy, darling, remember your coat."

Her mother, then. She must have said those words to Posy a thousand times, but why she thought of it now she didn't know. But her mother's voice, and the love she felt for her, were enough. With a groan, Posy opened her heavy eyes and gazed around the chamber, her eyelids drooping. They were gone. A swirl of mist, a sprinkling of dust upon the stone floor, was all that was left of the creatures who had surrounded them and infected them with darkness. Even the fire had turned into a pile of ashes in the cold hearth. Posy lifted herself up and looked over to where Kyran was moaning and rolling over on his side.

"Posy," he said faintly, reaching a feeble hand for hers. "What saved us?"

"My mother," Posy said, her voice shaking. "I thought of my mother, and how ... how I love her."

Kyran reached up to brush a tear from Posy's cheek, giving her a sad smile. "Your mother saved you, then. But it was you who saved me."

"What?" Posy looked up at him.

"You. It was you I thought of in the darkest moment. It was you who brought me back to myself."

Ashlee Willis

CHAPTER SEVENTEEN
Horrors, Inside and Out

They slept huddled together, under Kyran's cloak, leaning against a dirt wall in one of the many tunnels that wound through the Glooming. They did not take turns sleeping, but fell asleep together. Posy knew this probably wasn't a good idea, but they were both too utterly exhausted to be cautious now. Posy couldn't remember the last time they had slept—not since before they had reached the glade.

There was no daylight, and no way of knowing when morning came. Posy and Kyran woke several hours later. Posy felt the darkness of the Glooming seep into her before she opened her eyes, but there was something else in her now ... something new. It wasn't happiness—no, nothing so superficial—but it was something with goodness too strong to be frightened away by this darkness. For the moment, anyway, it was difficult for her to imagine anything worse than what they had come across already, and she somehow felt they must be near to finding the princess. She felt hope.

After some debate, they decided to venture back into the chamber they had come from the night before, to see if there were any embers at all on the fire, and make a torch. At first Posy had been completely opposed to this. She thought they would come across the creatures again. But Kyran told her they would be nowhere without some light, and he crept back to the chamber. He came back triumphantly a few minutes later, with one of the torches that had lined the stone walls of the chamber in his hand, lit from the embers of the fire that had burnt out in the hearth. There had been no sign that the ghostly creatures had ever been there at all.

So they set out again, through endless tunnels. Several times, they came upon chambers, and every time Posy felt her heart give a lurch, but they didn't come across anything more terrifying than a rat in any of them. At last, though, Kyran gave a snort of impatience and stopped short.

"We are going nowhere," he stated tensely.

"Nowhere?"

"One empty chamber after another, nothing changing, no perceptible decline or incline to the tunnels. We don't even know that we haven't been traveling in circles for the past two hours."

Posy had to admit that he was right. They had no way to gauge the direction they were going.

"I suppose we could do as Hansel and Gretel did, although I'm not sure what we'd use. It's not as if we've got bread with us."

Kyran's dark eyebrows shot up. "And who are Hansel and Gretel? Friends of yours?"

Posy laughed before she could stop herself. "No," she said. "Well, I mean ... they're from a story, in my world."

"A story, is it? Very interesting. People in books are generally quite intelligent, so I've been told." He gave her the hint of a smile.

Posy smiled in return. "They were a brother and sister, led into the forest and left to die, but they left crumbs behind them to mark where they had been, and found their way home."

"Hmph. Sounds like a fairytale," said Kyran dismissively.

Posy wanted to tell him they were in a fairytale right now, but after all the things that had happened to her, she wouldn't. It wasn't a fairytale any longer.

"Anyway, if we had something to leave behind us, we'd at least know we had already passed this way if we came across it again."

"Yes," Kyran considered it. "But we *can* leave something behind."

"Like what?" Posy asked.

"This." Kyran held the torch up to the cave's stone wall, making large scorch marks in the shape of a cross.

It wasn't long before their plan worked for them. They circled back on a tunnel they had come from, and turned the opposite way. Every time this happened, they would turn the way they hadn't been down before. At last, they came to a chamber that was different from the others. At first Posy couldn't quite picture what was different. The same dirty floor, the same stone walls jutting with roots. Then she saw the small depression in the wall, and something within it glowing dimly into the darkness of the room. Posy began to make her way across the room, but Kyran grabbed her arm.

"What are you doing?"

"I see something."

"Yes, as do I. What of it? You can't just go traipsing over there. I suppose you've already forgotten what happened only hours ago in another chamber of this cursed place?"

"Yes, you're right," Posy said meekly. "But look around. This room is like a dead end. There's no way out except the way we just came in."

"Hmph," was all Kyran said in response. He drew his sword and began to make his way cautiously across the room toward the gap in the wall. Posy followed closely behind him. When they reached it, they saw a small table with a golden cup on it, set with rubies, pearls and diamonds. It was filled with a deep red liquid, like wine, and the cup was so luminous it seemed to put out a light of its own.

"What is it?" Posy whispered, peering over Kyran's shoulder.

He shook his head. "I don't know, but I sense magic," he said with distaste. "We shouldn't disturb it." He began to back away from it, pushing Posy behind him.

"But what else are we to do?" Posy argued. "There is nowhere else to go. We can't just leave this room and follow the same tunnels we've been walking in all day. Not a single chamber has been different until this one—this chamber which doesn't have any other doors. It has to be significant ... doesn't it?"

Kyran rolled his eyes. "What do you suggest we do, then?"

"I think one of us has to drink it," she answered simply.

"Oh, no," Kyran immediately answered. "That we will *not* do."

"I'm not excited about it myself. But what else are we to do?" Posy was completely terrified when she thought about drinking that dark, blood-red liquid. What horrors would it bring? But she also knew that there was no other way. With this thought in her mind, and before she could let her fear get hold of her too tightly, she made her way across the chamber, straight to the golden cup.

"No!" Kyran cried, his voice breaking in fear. "Posy, don't!" He ran to her side and seized the cup from her hand before she could drink. "I'll do it, then, you infuriating, willful girl."

"Why you?"

"Because I won't let it be you, that's why. I must keep you safe, Posy."

At Kyran's tone, Posy looked up into his face. Without thinking, and with a rush of fevered thrill, she reached up and pressed her lips to his. She immediately felt fire shoot through her veins, and then felt so weak she thought she'd collapse. Kyran wrapped his arms around her so tightly that she gasped. When she at last pulled away from him, they stood looking at each other silently. Posy saw Kyran's dark eyes fill with something that scared her and thrilled her at the same time. Then without a word, he grasped the cup and put it to his mouth, tilting his head so that his black hair brushed his back, drinking to the last drop.

At first Posy thought nothing was going to happen. Then they both heard it. The room seemed to shudder around them, the very air shivered and ruffled like an invisible cloak, and they heard a deep rumbling sound. Posy looked at Kyran and had barely opened her mouth to speak when, to her horror, he began to change before her eyes. His body seemed to blur as the noise in the room increased. From somewhere—perhaps the walls—came a violent gust of air, and it seemed to blow Kyran apart. Posy saw the lines of his body and face dissolve and disappear into the wind that blew around the entire chamber. A full-fledged storm had broken within the walls of the room. Posy's mouth gaped in awe when she saw a fierce knife of lightning explode across the room, and she felt heavy drops of rain begin to splash her face.

"Kyran!" she screamed frantically, her eyes darting wildly around the chamber in search of him. But he was gone, vanished as if he had never been. She struggled around the chamber, searching every dark corner, determined to leave no gap unsearched. The wind howled mercilessly in her ears, seeming to swarm into her mind, and the rain soaked her so thoroughly she felt heavy-footed as she walked through the chamber, stumbling several times. She felt her mouth working, forming desperate words, sensed the tightness in her throat that felt like a rising scream.

Then she saw him. Kyran stood in the center of the chamber, smiling at her. Posy gasped his name in relief and began faltering toward him, but then her heart lurched. Next to Kyran stood someone else. She could scarcely believe her eyes, and she blinked violently several times as her lashes dripped water down her face. It was another Kyran. Two Kyrans standing next to one another.

One of Posy's best friends in her own world had been a twin sister, so she knew well enough the subtle differences to look for—ones that are obvious to fond and familiar eyes. But when she gazed at both of the Kyrans staring back at her, she saw no differences at all. They might as well have been the same. Then the horrible thought came to her, what if they *are* the same? What if the potion he drank had split him in two?

"Kyran," she called through the baying of the wind. "What is this? What has happened?"

The first Kyran looked calmly at her and smiled. "I suppose that cursed potion I took did this to me. It's pretty clear what you'll have to do now, Posy."

"And what's that?" she asked, incredulous at his composure.

"You'll have to choose, Posy. Choose which is the true Kyran. That's the only way for me to be whole again."

"But," cut in the second Kyran suddenly, "if you are wrong ..."

"If I'm wrong?" gulped Posy.

"If you are wrong," the second Kyran's dark eyes widened in an almost childlike fear, "I think I will be divided forever."

"Forever?" repeated Posy mechanically.

"I'm afraid he's right," nodded the first Kyran, giving the second a distasteful glance. "Although why he's so worried I don't know. I trust you, Posy. Implicitly." His black eyes sparkled as he gave her

Ashlee Willis

his most charming smile.

"Do you?" the second Kyran almost shouted, his voice panicked. "I don't."

"You don't trust me?" Posy asked, wondering if she trusted herself. She wanted to put her hands over her ears, with the storm raging around her head. She couldn't think, couldn't make sense of it.

The second Kyran looked at her askance, his dark hair hanging limply on his shoulders, dripping in the torrential rain. "No," he answered falteringly. "That is, I don't know. I don't trust anything in this room. Do you?"

Posy looked about her, squinting against the blowing storm. "No," she shook her head. She looked back at both of the Kyrans, and she was terrified. This was her choice, and if she was wrong, it would ruin Kyran forever. Would he truly be half a person, maimed in his soul and possibly his body, if she made the wrong choice? Her thoughts seemed to crescendo upward and out of control, as if the squall around her carried them with it. She shook her head, her wet hair slapping her cheek. She felt as if she could scream her frustration, but it wouldn't be heard above the din of noise that seemed to swallow her.

Closing her eyes against the flashes of lightning and the relentless sting of the rain, Posy tried to think. She tried to picture any place but this one. She tried to picture Kyran as she knew him, not as the two who stood before her now, who were somehow so like him, but both so completely wrong. But she couldn't see him. *If I don't know who Kyran is—who does?* She asked herself silently, almost frantically. And the answer seemed to float into her mind. The Author knew. For hadn't he written Kyran?

"But he's not here!" shouted Posy in helpless frustration.

Both Kyrans eyed Posy suspiciously at this outburst, but they seemed to blur from her vision. The wind and rain, the lightning and clouds, seemed to fade from her sight and grow quieter. A whisper, as light as the faintest feather touch, curled its way into Posy's conscious. Posy felt her being seem to release into the quiet bubble she was in amidst the storm, and she heard the words brush softly against her ears. *What you think you can trust will deceive you. What pains you to do will save you.*

A corner of her mind recognized the words, but she couldn't remember where she had heard them. It didn't matter. They were there, whispering to her, clearer and clearer, despite the rage of thunder and rain around her. Any other time she would have scoffed at their lack of clarity and called them a riddle. Somehow she knew what to do.

"Kyran!" she gasped, as if she had been holding her breath.

"Yes?" they said in unison, staring intently at her.

"You are both Kyran, but you are neither one Kyran at all."

A flash of something passed behind the first Kyran's eyes, but he visibly quashed it and said lightly, "My dear, that is a wonderful puzzle, but I believe you are trying to take the easy way out." His voice hardened. "Name one of us, quickly, before we *both* disappear."

His words gave Posy a start. Would they both disappear? If she did this wrong, would she ever see Kyran again? But she shook her head as if to rid it of the thought, and stated strongly, "I cannot trust either of you, but then, neither of you is Kyran. You are both part of him, but one without the other is not him at all. It is impossible to name one of you." Her voice became unsteady. "I *have* to name you both at once." Didn't she?

At Posy's words, the storm began to churn to an amazing pitch, swirling and screaming about their heads. "Oh, no," Posy thought, watching the blackened clouds swarm above her head with wide eyes. "I've killed him, *I've killed him.*"

As if to prove her right, the first Kyran let out a piercing cry that rose above the storm. The second began to whimper as if in pain, and Posy couldn't tell if it was the rain or tears running down his face. But he looked straight into Posy's face, and she saw his mouth form words—she couldn't quite make them out—just before they both disappeared in a violent flash of lightning.

The instant they disappeared, the room grew silent. The wind died as if someone had closed a lid on it, the black clouds dissipated, and even the walls and floor were completely dry. It was as if the storm had never been. But Posy looked down at herself and knew it had, for she was dripping with water from head to toe, leaving a widening puddle on the stone floor.

She put her hands up to cover her face, but she couldn't even cry. She felt turned inside out, with hardly the strength to stand.

"Posy," she felt a warm hand on her shoulder. She turned as if she were in a dream and saw Kyran standing close next to her, a half smile on his lips. She didn't say his name. She didn't say anything. She just leaned forward and put her head on his shoulder and gave a weary sigh, as if every emotion had been pushed out of her and she had none left. He put his arms around her.

Ashlee Willis

CHAPTER EIGHTEEN
Changing Words

A door had formed upon one of the stone walls of the chamber. The magic of the storm that had taken Kyran and then sent him back again had created the door, and they knew that the test of the chalice had been passed, and they were to proceed through it. The door towered high above their heads and the only indication that it was there was its faint gold outline, as if a line had been etched into the stone and filled with gold dust. The door would not open like any other door. Kyran pressed his hand flat in the middle of it, but nothing happened. Posy did the same. Only when they both put their hands on it did the door begin to moan and crack until its enormous weight shifted and it opened on invisible hinges.

As Posy took a step into the darkened threshold, she felt Kyran's hand whip out and grab her shoulder to pull her back. She looked down at her feet and realized a narrow, dark hole of a staircase descended steeply downward, right in front of her. Another step and she would have stumbled and fallen down the chipped stone stairs.

"Oh, no," Posy shook her head. She felt weary to her bones. The thought of descending into that blackness below them—she didn't think she could do it. Kyran nodded, understanding, but Posy saw the glance he cast over his shoulder. He had no wish to return to the room they had just come from. It was as if the two sides of himself that Posy had so obviously seen before had come as a surprise to him. Perhaps he was not eager to be haunted with the memories of his own extremes again. Posy tried to imagine what it would be like to see herself in such a way ... split down the middle, with her fear in one body and her stubbornness in the other. But surely it hadn't been only bad—surely the goodness that she knew was in Kyran had been in those two who had stood before her—hadn't it? To lose oneself, and be left only with a distorted, corrupted shell of whom you had been .... Posy shuddered, a feeling like sickness wrapping around her mind.

"We won't go back into that chamber," Posy said, keeping her voice light. "What if the door were to close on us again and we were locked in? No, we can sleep here, on this landing." They both looked down at the stone floor. Perhaps three feet of it stretched between the doorway they had come from and the first descending stair. It would have to do.

Without another word, Kyran removed his cloak and spread it on the floor. They both sat, leaning against the wall. Kyran pulled some food from his bag and they shared it, huddled together like fugitives in the shadowed space. Posy drew her water flask out of her own bag and drank deeply. She knew she should try to conserve what they had, but she couldn't seem to stop herself. She felt the water go down her throat, and it seemed the only pure and clear thing in this dark place.

The enormity of their experience seemed to seep into Posy's conscience in a kind of haze. She could not be sorry for it; she was no longer even much surprised at it. But she knew it all had significance somehow. She suddenly wondered if the Author knew she was here, in this book. And if he did know, what must he think of her, and of Kyran, trying to change his story, rearrange the words?

　　　　　Ashlee Willis

"Do you think he approves?" she murmured, half to herself.

"Mm?" Kyran's groggy voice came to her in the semi-dark, and she realized he had almost been asleep.

"Oh," she shrugged, "I was just thinking of the Author, and what he must think of us changing his tale."

Posy felt Kyran's body shift next to her as he sat upright. "I have pondered that myself," he admitted quietly. "But I have no answer. The Author is like a faraway fairytale, not truly real." The irony of this statement only faintly touched Posy. "We have never seen him or heard him. There are only stories."

"But the centaurs," Posy began. "They know he is real. They speak of him as if they *know* him."

"Yes," Kyran nodded slowly. "But they are different than we are. They no longer live in the Kingdom. They no longer have to answer to my father."

"Whether the characters answer to the king or not makes no difference in the Author's existence," Posy said carefully, wishing she could see Kyran's features better in the darkness.

Kyran gave no answer for several moments. "If the Author is real, and if he has created this story and our world," he finally answered slowly, "then he cannot approve of my father as king. Perhaps it is the Author's plan that we change this story—for it is truly in need of changing, Posy. We have to trust that what we do is for the best, some part of a mysterious and complicated purpose of which we can't see the whole." His voice was calm and reassuring, and Posy sighed, relaxing her head against his shoulder. It was the first time she had heard Kyran speak of his father without anger and bitterness in his voice.

Not truly real, Kyran had said. A faraway fairytale, he had said.

But Posy wondered, suspected, even began to believe, that sometimes reality was too solid and too hard, and that perhaps sometimes the clearest and straightest way to truth was through a fairytale.

* * *

A million stars studded the night sky, miles above and away beyond where Posy and Kyran slept. A cliff towered above the water, and the sea crashed below, thundering waves colliding against sheer rock. Across the water, winged creatures flew silently by, like noiseless shadows against a moon wreathed in gray clouds. Owls, a dozen of them, swept down to an almost invisible crack in the side of the cliff, their wings giving a hushed sigh before slowing and disappearing into the face of the rock.

The entrance gave way to an enormous cave, a ceiling disappearing into unfathomable black, and an irregular stone floor, deep with water-filled gashes. The walls dripped with frigid water, the air tingled with chilling secrecy.

"Fellow councilors," Falak said, his steady voice echoing through the chamber. All the other owls settled down from their various perches on jutting shelves of rock, and the rustle of their feathers grew silent. Eleven pairs of large and gleaming eyes stared at Falak, his gray feathers reflecting the moonlight that filtered through the cracks in the wall.

"We have come here to speak of the Kingdom tonight, and to decide what our course of action will be now that war is inevitable. We've no time for formalities, for we must return to the castle before sunrise, or we will be missed by the king." Falak's wide eyes searched the faces of his fellow creatures. "Who has a report to give me?"

Egbert cleared his throat. He inched forward from where he perched, his dark feathers melding with his surroundings. "The glade was attacked successfully, Chief Councilor."

"Ah, yes." Falak's voice held pleasure. "Details, please."

"The ipotanes failed, as you know, but the centaurs were attacked again that same night, by a quickly gathered army of the ipotane deserters, together with soldiers of the Kingdom. It was a success." Egbert's eyes gleamed maliciously.

"So all the centaurs were killed or taken captive?" Falak's voice was sharp.

"Well," Egbert faltered. "Many were killed, yes, and we took their leader captive, as well as his mate. He calls her his wife, but they are animals. What do they know of such things?" Egbert laughed derisively.

"I suppose animals should never rise above themselves, and forget the mindless creatures they are," Falak said smoothly.

"Yes—er—that is ..." Egbert's eyes widened as he realized his mistake. "Not all animals, Chief," he ended weakly.

"Hmm," Falak eyed him briefly, then turned his attention to the rest of the gathering. His eyes turned to a small, sharp-eyed owl, with night-black feathers and yellow glinting eyes. "Quintus." Falak's voice struck the walls of the cave. "You have been following the prince and the imposter princess. Where are they?"

"Oh, that is no problem," sniveled the owl with a small smile. "They make it very easy on me, indeed they do. They were last seen in the centaur encampment, just before it was attacked."

"What did you say?" Falak's voice had become deathly quiet.

Quintus jerked his head sideways nervously and blinked once. "Yes, they were there. I even spotted them during the attack. Running through the forest with one of those filthy centaurs."

"Running away from the battle, then? Where did they go?" Falak questioned him sharply.

"They ran into the glade, Chief, near the opening of the Glooming. I can only think they entered it, although I do not know how."

"You didn't see them enter the Glooming?"

"I—the battle was—there were many fighting around them. I cannot be sure, although I will say I am almost positive ..."

Falak gave a slow sigh and made a tsking noise. "Quintus, Quintus, what are we to do with you? Our best scout, or so I thought, and you cannot even tell me the whereabouts of two children? Battle or no, they could not have disappeared into thin air."

"But that is exactly what they seemed to do, Chief!" burst out Quintus with a tinge of indignation. "I *am* the best scout you have, and you know it. I would not question something unless it was truly a mystery. And this is a mystery. No one knows for certain where the Glooming is, or in what manner you get there. No one but the centaurs. How can we know what truly happened? No," he shook his head, "the most we can do is assume they are in the Glooming now. And even I could not follow them there."

"No," Falak agreed. "You could not. But you can wait for their return. For return they must. If they find the princess Evanthe within the Glooming, and they bring her safely back into the Kingdom, our plans are overthrown. You, Quintus, will be the first to taste my anger if such a thing happens." Quintus' dark eyes stared emptily into Falak's face. "Station guards at every known opening to the Glooming. Do whatever it takes to stop them from reaching the Kingdom alive—all of them." Falak spoke now almost as if to himself. "They must die outside the Borders of the Kingdom."

A quiet voice spoke up then, barely audible above the hooting and murmuring of the owls as they spoke to each other. "But must we kill them, Chief Councilor?"

Falak turned to look at Nocturne, a white owl with gray-tipped wings, his eyes black as the night.

Nocturne continued. "If they were merely driven into the Wild Land, or even beyond, into the Unknown Land, would that not be enough? Can it be wise to begin your reign with murder?"

The owls in the chamber had grown silent with anticipation and awe. Their leader and his decisions were not to be questioned.

"Perhaps," answered Falak after a long silence. His eyes glinted for a moment before he smiled amiably at Nocturne. "You are young yet. You have much to learn. Perhaps you would like to keep watch outside of the cave until our meeting has ended?" He asked, but it was a command. Nocturne bowed his head briefly, spread his wings and flew from the chamber. With a glance from Falak, two large owls followed swiftly behind him.

Falak turned, smiling, to the others. "Anyone else with questions for me?"

But he was met with silence.

"We know that things that pass for treason and murder in the Author's world are merely actions that must be taken to ensure safety for all characters of the Plot, do we not?" Falak's statement was met with murmuring hoots of agreement. "We know that in order to overthrow the king and control the government of the Plot, we must do things that, to weaker creatures, might seem unpalatable. But we know," he stood taller on his perch of shadowed rock, chest thrust forward, "that what we do is strong, and right—indeed, it is good! The age of the owls has begun! So I say, down with the humans, and up with the owls! Death to the king!"

His words were met with thunderous shouts and hoots, beating and flapping of wings, and cries of "Up with the owls, up with the owls!"

"Death to the king, who has no one's interest at heart but his own!" continued Falak in a booming voice. "And death to the Author, who only lives in the feeble minds of those weak enough to believe in him at all!"

At these last words, there was a faltering of the cheers that rang through the chamber as if something unspeakable, unthought of, had been spoken. But one look at their Chief and leader, and the flinty intensity of his fiery eyes, and the owls took up their cheer once again, louder than before.

"Up with the owls! Down with the humans! Death to the king and the Author!"

* * *

Outside the cave, on the shore by the crashing sea far below, Nocturne groaned, lying helplessly on his side. A broken wing and a smash to the head had been his reward for questioning his leader. His body ached with the beating, and his heart ached with the treachery of which he now wanted no part. *Get away, get away,* he told himself over and over, *before they return and finish the job.* For he knew Falak would kill him in a heartbeat.

He began painfully dragging himself with his one good wing along the sand and toward the overhang of a cliff beyond. His sharp ears could hear the cheering above, and it made his insides roil with anger. Halfhearted as his participation had been to begin with, he now knew there was no turning back. Not now. Not after this. Therefore, he gritted his teeth and tried not to cry out in pain as he gave one last push that sent him under the slab of rock protruding above the sand. He did not stop there; he kept going, deeper and deeper into the rock until he could barely discern sunlight, barely hear the crash of waves on the shore. *Just until they are gone,* he told himself wearily. *Then I must go—I must find a way, somehow, to warn the prince, warn the king, find the Author ....* The thought wavered in his mind, then faded as darkness more profound than that of the cave came over him, and he was lost to all conscious thought.

CHAPTER NINETEEN
Love and Hate

Posy started awake, remnants of a dream clinging to her mind like a cobweb. It seemed she could still hear echoed hoots of derision and angry flapping of wings as she shook her head to clear it.

"Bad dream?" Kyran was awake already, seated across the small space they shared and gazing at her in the weak light.

"Yes—no ... I can hardly remember," she answered uncertainly. It was unsettling to wake in darkness, after what seemed like a night's sleep, and not be sure of the time of day. She felt she yearned for the sun already, and they had been in this underground labyrinth barely two days; at least, she thought they had. Perhaps it had been shorter ... or longer.

"This place is full of bad dreams, I'd say. They climb the walls here," Kyran said, his dark eyes roving around the chamber, lingering at the top of the staircase they soon must descend.

"It wasn't a dream so much as a feeling. A terrible feeling." Posy realized her voice was shaking. Kyran quickly moved to her side and placed a tentative arm around her shoulder. She wasn't sure if it was the darkness of the place they were in, or the lingering dream. Perhaps it was that she finally saw their situation as reality, here in this black place, with a yawning unknown before them, and she found she had lost the feeling that everything would inevitably be all right. They were in a book, she told herself repeatedly, but it was no good. The other world—the one she had come from—now seemed the unbelievable story. Kyran, saving the princess and the Kingdom—these were the things that mattered now. Tears slid silently down her cheeks, and she turned her face to Kyran's shoulder.

"There, there, my darling," Kyran whispered softly against her hair. "I swear nothing will happen to you. I am here for you as you have been here for me." He took Posy gently by the shoulders and turned her so that she stood looking straight up into his face. "As sharp as you are, I'd have thought you would have noticed by now, but I suppose I will have to tell you straight out." Now Kyran's voice shook. "But I love you." He leaned down and kissed her. It wasn't the hard, impassioned kiss they had shared the first time. This was soft and unhurried. It gave Posy plenty of time to think about the sweetness of Kyran's mouth on hers, and the tenderness with which he held the back of her head—and best of all, the words he had just spoken to her, words she had only dreamed to hear from him. Warmth started from her head and spread throughout her body. She was drinking magic ... swimming in it. She was feeling it seep into her bones.

"Kyran," she breathed, but seemed unable to say more. Her thoughts seemed to swirl, then come sharply into focus. Long before she had fallen into this story, she had longed for such a security to wrap herself within, the surety of knowing beyond a doubt that she was loved. Here, it stared at her out of Kyran's dark eyes, and what she felt was ... fear. Oh, joy as well, bliss, exhilaration. But fear was there, lurking. A deep instinct within her told Posy that the most wonderful things in life would never come without this dread of losing them. But in this moment, it didn't seem to matter.

She pushed the thought away, a mere flicker across her mind. She reached up to cup her hand around his ear, then ran her fingers down his jaw, rough with the beginnings of a youthful beard. She couldn't think what to say to him. What would possibly be sufficient to tell him what she felt?

In the end, she whispered, "I love you," in return, just before reaching up to kiss him again. And it was enough.

* * *

King Melanthius burst through the doors to his bedchamber with a furious growl. Queen Valanor lifted her eyes calmly from the needlework she held in her long white fingers, and raised an elegant eyebrow. She had no need to spend her breath asking him what was wrong; she need only wait until he told her. The look on his face told her it was inevitable.

"I have had enough of stalling and politics!" he shouted. "That blasted bird had better show me some results soon, or he will be banned along with the centaurs!"

"I've no need to ask who 'that blasted bird' is, for you only call the creature a 'bird' when he is in the greatest disfavor. What has he done, Majesty?" Valanor's pale gray eyes lowered once again to the work in her hands. Melanthius moved from where he had stopped indignantly in the middle of the room. He stood near her in front of the large fireplace. His eyes were shining dangerously, and Valanor wondered fleetingly if he was truly as angry as that, or if perhaps he had taken a bit too much wine at supper. She sighed and put her work down, focusing her attention on him. He placed his hands on his hips, his face like thunder, resembling an overgrown spoiled child more than a king.

"He does not respect his king as he should, that's what," he said. "I told him days ago to bring my children back to the Kingdom, whatever the cost, and it has not been done."

"But, Majesty, you told me that Falak explained the reasons—"

"Not good enough! The reasons, I see now, were most likely stalling tactics because he knew he would be incapable of bringing them back here. Now I shall have to send someone else after them, and that blasted usurper, Pruny—"

"Posy," inserted the queen.

"Yes—that's what I said. And we've lost two more precious days in the meantime!"

"Falak did win the battle against the centaurs and won you the glade of the Glooming," Valanor reminded her husband.

"Yes, well, he might have, but from reports I received, my own son could very well have been killed in that battle. It was only sheer good fortune that he escaped as he did."

"Good fortune?" Valanor stood from her chair now, knitting her delicate brows together. "Good fortune that Kyran escaped? I thought you wanted him captured? How can he now be considered an ally with the Kingdom? Melanthius, if you succeed in capturing him, you will have no other choice than to imprison him, at least for a time. He cannot be allowed to cause more uprisings and trouble."

The king grumbled something under his breath, his eyes fixed to the floor.

"Majesty," Valanor said, her voice becoming stern. "You understand this, do you not? You understand there is no other choice? Just as there was no other choice for Evanthe's role in the Plot?"

"Yes," the king conceded. The anger had drained from his face, and in its place was an odd uncertainty. Valanor was quick to see this; her first urge was to cringe from such weakness. Instead, she smiled sweetly at her husband and placed her long cool fingers on his arm. "If we don't have the Plot, we have nothing," she said softly. "If we don't have readers, what good is the Plot? The characters must be taught to obey. They must do things as you decree—no one else. You are the king—*you*. Not Falak. Not your son. They too must obey you, and if they do not, they must be punished accordingly."

Melanthius nodded, his expression muted, the red flush on his face draining slowly. "I do wish ..." he started falteringly, then stopped, shaking his head. He strode across the chamber once again as if to leave. As he put his hand to the door, he turned to look at his wife across the length of the room. "I wish at times it was not necessary to take many of these measures. The Plot is important—it is the most important thing—but I have been king for so long, Valanor. It is a long time to uphold something alone ... to see my own children turn against me because of it."

Valanor shook her head and raised one hand to stop him. "No. They do not turn against you. You are the king and their father. They are misguided, as are many of the characters in the Plot. It is your lot to lead them—it is what you must do. We must not have the characters turning to the ancient myths of the Author. They will lose their faith and obedience to you if this is allowed." She fixed the king with her gaze and said slowly, "You must be ruthless if you love them—merciless if you wish to save them." Then she turned from him.

The king left the chamber silently. Valanor took her seat by the fire. As she plucked her needle from the arm of the chair where she had placed it, she threw a derisive look across the room at the empty space in which her husband had just stood. "Fool," she hissed scornfully, shaking her beautiful head and settling to her work once again.

* * *

And so, the staircase; it stretched below Kyran and Posy like a fathomless cavern, an open mouth ready to swallow them into its darkness. Each of them had a torch from the chamber behind them, held before them like a talisman against whatever evil they might encounter upon the stone stairs, or at the bottom of them. Their free hands were clasped together. Kyran's hand in her own left hand gave Posy more courage than the torch in her right. Somehow she knew—and Kyran did, too—that this was the final length of their journey in the Glooming. They were close—she could feel it—close to what they were looking for. But what they were looking for had changed shape since the start of their journey. Princess Evanthe was their destination, but Posy now knew there were things beneath the surface, unseen and intangible, that they must find as well. Things that flitted through the grasp and just beyond sight, like a wood fairy, or a wisp of cloud.

So, hand in hand, they descended. It wasn't long before they became tired with the descent. It seemed to Posy to go on forever, and her legs began to ache and cramp.

"What if this is a magical staircase?" she spoke her fear at last. "What if it never ends, and we are stuck here on it for the rest of our lives? No top, no bottom?"

"But we know there is a top. We just came from it," Kyran reasoned wearily, stopping to rest on a crumbling stone stair.

"But what if we were to turn and try to go up the stairs again, and found that we just kept walking, kept climbing, going nowhere?"

"Posy," Kyran said, "that kind of thinking doesn't help. Perhaps this staircase is enchanted, like you say. But perhaps its enchantment is to make the person upon it only *believe* there is no end, and thus despair. We must press on. But first"—he patted the hard stone beside him—"rest here with me for a while, sweet."

Sweet. Posy smiled despite herself and settled next to Kyran, his arm slipping naturally around her waist and her head dropping to his shoulder. Her eyelids fluttered and drooped. Much too soon, Kyran was urging her up again, and so they pressed on. The staircase began to show a subtle change eventually. The crumbling stairs gave way to smoothly-cut ones. Then the smooth ones turned to glossed marble. When Posy saw this, she felt a shudder of foreboding.

"Kyran," she whispered, "I think we must be watchful from now on." She didn't know where the feeling of dread came from. But she remembered the feeling of comfort she had before they entered the room of ghostly creatures, and she knew this was a place where nothing was as it seemed.

In his usual way, Kyran seemed to read her thoughts, and nodded, understanding her meaning without words. "I do not forget Stonus' words to us of this place, Posy," he said quietly.

They kept descending, and the staircase widened. Before, it had barely fit the two of them shoulder to shoulder; now it would have fit a dozen people or more walking parallel. Posy glanced over her shoulder at this point—she didn't know why—and stopped dead in her tracks. Kyran felt her body stiffen next to his and turned swiftly, his hand flying to the hilt of his sword. But it was not something he could fight against that they both turned to see. A wall now stood behind them, solid and seemingly invulnerable, blocking the stairs they had just descended. It was odd, Posy thought, but there were no words to say about this. There was only the look of fear in her own face, and the determination in Kyran's dark eyes as he sheathed his sword and continued. No thoughts of turning back now.

"Well"—Posy pushed past her fear in an attempt to make Kyran smile—"at least we know now that the stairs aren't enchanted—at least in the way we thought."

Kyran did smile at this, but it was fleeting. His eyes were directed sharply ahead of them now, and his stance was that of the warrior-Kyran that Posy felt she was beginning to know too well.

The staircase had ended at last. Posy was on the alert the instant her eyes took in the room. Luxurious furniture was arranged in an enormous chamber that stretched before them in a great expanse of marble floors covered with vast sumptuous rugs. Ornate and detailed tapestries covered the high walls. A small fountain bubbled in the center of the room soothingly, the only sound to be heard other than the thumping of their own hearts.

"It's not as it seems," warned Posy quickly, desperately almost, in a low whisper. Kyran was silent beside her. "What are we to do?" she finished.

Before Kyran could answer her, a ringing voice said, "What are you to do? Why, you are to be our honored guests, and come sit with us a while."

Posy's eyes shot swiftly around the room and she saw a woman, an astonishingly beautiful woman, sitting upon one of the couches. Posy would have sworn that only moments ago she was not there. The moment the woman's lovely voice called to them, she felt a difference in Kyran, who stood close beside her. He relaxed his grip on her hand, and his shoulders lost their rigidity. "Come, Posy," he whispered, "We must at least speak with her if we are to get through this chamber."

Posy felt her mouth drop in bewilderment, and started to protest, but she had no other alternative to this plan. After all, they couldn't stand at the foot of the great staircase forever. "Kyran—" she started, wanting to repeat her warning, but he was tugging her swiftly across the chamber to where the woman sat waiting for them, a smile on her beautiful lips.

"Welcome, children," she said as they approached. Her dark silky hair hung in rippling waves over her shoulder and spilled onto the couch beside her. "Forgive me, I didn't know when exactly to expect you. The princess was rather uncertain of when you would arrive."

"The princess?" Kyran breathed, his voice wavering. "Is my sister here? Is Evanthe here?"

"Oh, yes, our lovely Evanthe is here. What a brave girl she is, to traverse the Glooming alone! We are very proud of her." The woman's dark liquid eyes danced, light glistening on two shadowy pools.

"Oh, Posy!" Kyran turned to Posy and squeezed her hands in a painful grip. "She is here! We have found her at last! I knew it—I knew we were close."

The woman beamed upon them as if they were amusing children. But Posy didn't take her eyes off the woman's face. "Who are

Ashlee Willis

you?" she asked, ignoring Kyran. "And what do you mean, 'we'?"

"Oh, how remiss of me! I am Seraphine," the woman answered, touching a slender white hand delicately to her chest. "And these are my sisters, Limnoreia and Adamaris. We have been keeping watch over the young princess these many weeks, have we not, sisters?"

Posy and Kyran turned and saw two more women, as lovely as their sister, sitting composedly on the couch behind them. Posy knew this time, with foreboding in her heart, that they had most certainly not been sitting there moments ago.

"Wha—" Kyran started, and Seraphine interrupted him with a laugh like a ringing bell.

"My sisters have just come from your own sister, Prince. Do you not wish to hear of Evanthe?"

This got Kyran's attention. "Yes, of course," he answered. "But—pardon me—I wish to *see* her even more than to hear about her. Is she near?"

"Very near," said Limnoreia. Posy silently stared at the women, all so exquisitely beautiful. She knew something was wrong here. She could feel it. She just couldn't see it. She turned to look at Kyran. His face was open and trusting, and he gazed from one sister to the next in open admiration. Posy felt annoyance rise in her. *I suppose every danger is forgotten if the woman is pretty enough,* she thought to herself angrily. She pushed away her feelings, though, and tried to concentrate every thought on reality. *This is not as it seems,* she repeated to herself. *Not as it seems ... why can't I see it for what it is?*

And suddenly she saw it. She didn't know what it meant, exactly, but she knew it was a clue—the first loose thread, ready to be pulled to unravel this veil that covered their eyes.

As Posy looked at Seraphine, her eyes traveled down to the couch, and she saw that Seraphine's lovely hair looked ... wet. At first it seemed the very tips of her hair were dripping slowly onto the couch beside her, forming a tiny puddle; then, as Posy's eyes traveled up, she blinked in disbelief. Seraphine's entire body was drenched with water. Her dress clung heavily around her shoulders, her breasts, her thighs. Drops of water hung, like glistening diamonds, from her black eyelashes. Posy felt her breath quicken as her heart began to beat harder. She turned to look at the other two sisters and saw that it was the same with them—wet from head to toe. She saw a piece of something that looked like seaweed in Adamaris' hair.

"You can speak to the princess yourself, Prince Kyran. You must only follow us," Seraphine was saying calmly. *Follow her where? And why does she not rise from the couch?* Posy's thoughts were in a frenzy as she tried to work out this puzzle. She glanced at Kyran and saw that he discerned nothing of what she now could see. The veil still covered his eyes, it seemed. Ah, well, so it was up to her, then.

"Then stand and take us to her," said Posy suddenly, cutting into the conversation. She was met with silence. Kyran turned to her to give her a look of reproach. "But they don't!" she said to him, not missing the sudden flame that seemed to spark in Seraphine's eyes. "Don't you see? They don't take us to her. They only speak of her."

"Oh, but we will," said Seraphine, her voice dangerously serene. A smile still played at the edge of her lovely mouth, but it was tight.

"You have to do it now, then. We have waited long enough. We have traveled a long way. Stand and take us to the princess Evanthe. Please," she added as an afterthought, and because Kyran was now gaping at her in astonishment. "Oh," she said to him in a burst of frustration. "Don't look at me that way! You never showed me even an ounce of courtesy when we first met, but here you are *drooling* over –"

Kyran grabbed Posy's arm roughly and pulled her away from the women, near the fountain. "What are you doing?" he demanded in a harsh whisper. "Are you going to offend the only ones who can take us to my sister—out of ... out of *jealousy*? What are you trying to do, Posy?"

"Please, Kyran," Posy said, and she knew it was important now to chose the right words. "Listen to me for a moment. We know we are in a place of deception. That is what the Glooming is. We have been deceived before this, and more than once. Why do you trust these women so much? Is it because they are beautiful? Is that it?"

Kyran let go of her arm abruptly and took a step back from her, the old disdain and pride taking hold in his expression and voice. "It is because they know where my sister is. What other choice do I have? Beautiful or not, Posy"—and he gave her a scathing look—"I am here to rescue my sister. Nothing else. Or have you forgotten that?"

"No," Posy said, keeping the anger and pain she felt from her voice. "I only thought *you* had, that's all. Nothing is as it seems. Didn't we agree on that?" But Kyran was no longer listening to her. He turned from her and strode back to where the sisters sat waiting calmly.

"Kyran, please," Posy pleaded. "Remember what Stonus told us. You said you'd remember his words!" But she spoke to his back, and he would not turn to her again.

Posy turned to stare into the waters of the fountain for a moment to collect her thoughts. Why must she do this alone? Why was Kyran so blind? The waters swirled with more motion than Posy would have thought possible for a small fountain, and she bent over to look more closely. She saw that the water was deep—fathoms deep, blue disappearing into darkness miles below. A creature with many tentacles swam slowly by and seemed to gaze up at her. Posy felt her breathing still, her face felt frozen as she stared down. Then she turned from the fountain and ran.

She did not spare a word for Kyran; there was no point in that. She ran straight to Seraphine and lunged for the foot of her couch before she could move, a mad instinct guiding her.

"Posy!" shouted Kyran, pouncing toward her to stop her. But he stopped dead in his tracks when he reached her. Posy had lifted the bottom of Seraphine's dress to reveal the thread that unraveled it all. A tail, and fins.

Kyran's eyes widened in horror, but he immediately sprang into action. He swung Posy up from the floor and thrust her ahead of him. "Run for the stairs," he cried behind her, and as she obeyed him, she heard Seraphine's furious scream.

As she ran, Posy felt the floor beneath her giving way, dissolving into nothing as if the beautiful room had been made of clouds or dreams. She reached the foot of the stairs, panting, and turned quickly to see Kyran give a great leap and land sprawled beside her. Water lapped the edge of the staircase, and green-black depths of it spanned the entire chamber, licking gently, almost silently, at the walls of the cavern. The enchantment was gone—there were no more carpets and tapestries, just cold stone walls, dimly shadowed waters, and darkness.

CHAPTER TWENTY
Cruel Memories

"Oh, Prince," called a watery voice, a voice like an eel slipping through the deep. "What a mistake you have made, you and your worthless companion. You won't get away now, you know."

Seraphine's shining wet head emerged at the water's edge next to where Kyran and Posy stood at the foot of the stone stairs. The tips of her shimmering tail fins curled and uncurled slowly beside her as she eyed them with an amused detachment. Kyran's left arm was tightly wrapped around Posy, and his right brandished his sword, though neither of them could see much more in the dark chamber than Seraphine's face. *A mermaid, then,* Posy said to herself. *A cruel mermaid. What does she want with us?*

"I only seek my sister," Kyran's voice came strong and clear across the cavern. "I promise no harm will come to you or your sisters if you will release the princess to me now."

Limnoreia and Adamaris materialized beside their sister, gentle smiles on their blood-red lips. "Sweet of you," said Adamaris almost regretfully. She shrugged her slender white shoulders, "But you could do us no harm anyway. Your father has done enough al—"

"Hold your tongue!" Seraphine's voice grew, her face contorting furiously. But the damage had been done.

"My father?" Kyran leapt on Adamaris' words. "What has my

father done to you? If he has hurt you, or treated you unfairly, I can help you. Indeed, I have vowed after I rescue my sister to lead an army against him."

Too much, Kyran, you are telling them too much, and too soon. Posy's thoughts flew through her head, and she reached down to squeeze his hand, willing him to hear her thoughts.

The mermaids exchanged subtle glances with one another, and Seraphine's expression immediately mellowed. "Yes," she whispered. "I suppose you might help us. For my sister is right; your father has done us great harm. But first, tell me—why do you oppose him? You, who are his own son?"

Kyran smiled coldly. "He is a tyrant and a manipulator, selfish, untrue and unkind to those he should be caring for."

Seraphine nodded acknowledgement, her face serene. "We, too, feel this way, young prince. I will show you how it was." The three beautiful faces disappeared suddenly beneath the water, leaving three rippling circles where they had been. Moments later Posy and Kyran could see brightness, a glowing deep within the water. It shone brighter and brighter, closer to the surface, until it burst upward from the water, a twinkling mist that filled the cavern and hovered over the water's surface. Two figures gleamed before them, created by the mist, and Posy recognized them at once: King Melanthius and Queen Valanor. She heard Kyran's slow intake of breath beside her.

The king and queen seemed not to notice them, but stood facing each other angrily. Posy felt somehow that this must be a memory, bottled up and released, or recreated, within the haze that hung heavily in the chamber. She watched as the scene before them unfolded.

Ashlee Willis

The king and queen appeared to be much younger than they were now, though Posy knew that couldn't be true—for they remained the same age always in this story. Yet the king didn't wear the hardness in his face that Posy remembered. The queen had an openness in her countenance that held passion, very unlike the subtle flickers of repression and grief Posy had seen in her eyes before. Yes, they were both infinitely different from what Posy had seen with her own eyes not long ago. From the corner of her eye, she saw Kyran shake his head as if to dispel a lingering dream.

"You," the queen shrieked at her husband, her pale skin flushed and fevered. "If you cared for me at all, or the Plot, you would banish them."

"Banish!" Melanthius crowed. "Oh, Valanor, you speak in the heat of passion. We can forget what they have done and continue with the Plot. Let it lie in the past, my dear. For"—and he hesitated, a look of something like shame crossing his face—"you know that you are the only one I have ever loved."

"You forget, husband," Valanor's voice hovered between anger and wild tears, "there is no past here, and never has been. Anything you have done ... anything those creatures may have done ... will not fade in my memory. Not now—not ever."

A cloud passed across the king's face then, and he moved his hand across his forehead absently. "Yes," he said at last, "there is no past within the Plot. Only the Plot, over and over again."

Valanor nodded as if encouraging a child who recited his lines. "Over and over again, yes," she repeated. "An endless beautiful circle. We know who we are and what we do. There are no questions for anyone, no need for confusion or deviance. Only the Plot, husband. And any who disturb it ..."

"Any who disturb it?" Melanthius' eyes sharpened as he turned his gaze to his wife's face.

"Well," she shrugged her shoulders and crossed her long slender arms across her breast, unconcerned. But the glint in her eye was hard as a hammer driving the nail home. "You are the king. What happens to those who disturb it?"

King Melanthius turned to her and stretched out his arms. His great bulk of body pulled her willowy one close. His muscled arms encompassed her. "I have been wrong," he smiled over her shoulder, but his eyes glistened with tears and fleeting sadness shone from them. "And you, my dear wife, have been right. We cannot forget the Plot."

"My king." She reached up to trace his jaw with one long finger. "You are the ruler of it all. From days of old you have ruled here, and now you are so mighty the Author himself could not gainsay you. An ancient legend cannot overthrow you. It's only you, King. So make your decision," she whispered close to his ear. "And make it a strong one."

The mist before Posy's and Kyran's eyes swirled madly now, smearing and erasing the forms of the king and queen. Posy had a fleeting awareness that Kyran was crushing her hand in his own until it pained her, but she pushed all other thoughts aside as a new scene churned thickly and took a new form before them.

Now a bright landscape seemed to stretch beyond where they stood for miles. A glistening lake shone in the warm sun, surrounded by towering, age-old trees, and flanked by an enormous white mountain. She thought she had seen that mountain before, far in the distance, from the stone window of the princess' room in the castle. She had not seen its wonder then, within the fog of the

Plot that had become a fog in her mind as well. But her clear eyes saw it now, and she gasped at the beauty of it.

Across the distant field were black dots at the edge of the horizon—a party of men came, riding horses. As they drew closer, Posy saw they wore the colors of the Kingdom, and she knew they must be the king's men. All held weapons except one with a large scroll tied to his belt. They approached the lake and dismounted. Everything Posy saw seemed to take place at a distance, through a cloud. She could hear no voices, nor the splash of water on the banks. She could only see.

One of the men walked to the water's edge and called out. The group waited, moments, minutes. At last, one by one, heads and shoulders began to appear across the lake; a hundred—two hundred—and more; men, women, children. The merpeople swam toward the bank to where the soldiers stood waiting. The man with the scroll took it from his belt, unfurled it, and began to read. As he read, Posy saw the faces of the merpeople change. Curiosity gave way to surprise. Surprise turned to anger, and tears. The mermen raised their fists and shouted angrily. The women held their children close.

Posy was startled to see a familiar face amidst the many. Seraphine. She looked the same, and as beautiful—but there was something different in her face, and Posy recognized it immediately. Kindness, and happiness. Both were alight in her eyes, even as the soldier proclaimed whatever terrible sentence was to befall her people.

She saw a merchild huddling in the protective curve of Seraphine's slender arm. Seraphine bent her graceful neck to touch her lips to the top of the child's head tenderly. Posy saw that, though

Seraphine was smiling, tears flowed from her lovely eyes, and her mouth trembled with the sobs she was fiercely holding down.

The scene seemed to become muddled in the haze. Posy saw flashes of things. Mermen raising bright flashing swords in defiance. The king's soldiers securing merpeople with thick, cruel ropes. And, lastly, Seraphine being torn from her weeping child, her face set like marble, misery swimming in her dark and fathomless eyes. The mist itself now seemed to weep for them, and it ran rivulets down across the vision until it was washed from the air of the chamber.

* * *

After the vision, they knew they had to trust the mermaids, this beautiful trio of sisters. They shared a bond of pain with them, and pain inflicted by the same person—King Melanthius. Posy knew now, though, that the queen was equally to blame, and it made her wonder how much Valanor had to do with every decision the king had made. *More than Falak gives her credit for, I'd bet,* thought Posy. She wondered what the king had meant when he had told the queen he loved only her. Could he have fallen in love with Seraphine or one of her sisters? Was that why Valanor had urged him to banish the merpeople? Or had they done something more serious to threaten the Plot? Posy looked at their beautiful faces and knew it wouldn't take much for any man to fall in love with one of them. Kyran himself had not been immune to it.

"So," Seraphine urged, a strange crooked smile on her lips, "you will help us?"

"I will do all that is within my power, lady," said Kyran with a bow of his head. "The king's behavior is unpardonable, and he must be taken from the throne."

"But what of the Plot?" asked Limnoreia with a flip of her corn silk hair, and a sideways look at Kyran, "If you make yourself king, will you uphold it?"

Kyran paused. Posy knew he fought against everything he had ever known. What a leap it must be to abandon the only thing you were certain of—what courage it must take! For he had lived within the Plot for lifetimes, longer than his eighteen years. His childhood had been spent, generations ago, within the only story he knew. She knew she could not blame him if he chose to follow it still.

Decision swept across his face, and he nodded, "I will only uphold it where necessary. I cannot—I *will* not—make the cruel decisions my father has made. There are characters in the Plot, but they *must* have voices of their own."

"And what of the Author?" Limnoreia asked quietly. "What power will you give him?"

"Power?" scoffed Seraphine before Kyran could answer, bitterness edging her voice. "He has no power. If he did, he would have stopped my child being taken from me. He would have stopped the king's cruelty long ago, before it had destroyed so many lives and made a misery of the Kingdom and the Wild Land both. The Author has no power within the Plot at all—not anymore. And if he has power, he misuses it by allowing such evil to persist. Only the characters have true power, and we must do something to take it in our hands now. It must lie in the hands of many—not one."

Kyran listened intently to her. Posy heard the raw pain in Seraphine's voice, even now, even after so much time had passed. She knew that she spoke through that pain, too, and it was all she could see. She looked at Kyran, trying to trust her love for him, and have faith in the answer he would give. He didn't disappoint her. "I cannot give you an answer for that, lady, until I have found the wisdom for it. The only thing I can promise you now is that, if I reign at all, I will reign with kindness for all characters, within the Plot and without. You will not see such a thing as befell you ever happen again, if I am king."

Seraphine studied him a long while before deciding. She nodded once. "Then I will take you to the princess," she said shortly, and dove beneath the water, her tail throwing a string of waterdrops through the air, like glittering diamonds.

Ashlee Willis

CHAPTER TWENTY-ONE

Scout

Quintus sighed with boredom. Chief Councilor Falak had sent him on a futile mission. Following Nocturne was the easiest thing he had ever done, and was a waste of his superior scouting abilities. What could Nocturne possibly do that would be of interest to anyone, especially Falak? He may be a traitor, but he was a weak traitor, and could do little harm.

Quintus stretched his sleek black feathers and blinked his piercing yellow eyes. *It was almost painful to watch Nocturne's progress,* he thought with a cringe. How determined he was, walking, walking, holding his pathetic wounded wing against him. Nocturne's fevered voice came up to him now from far below on the forest floor, repeating, as it had done the past two days, "Must find him, must find him! Have to ask him what to do—yes, that's it." Quintus thought Nocturne must be mad, or close to it.

Yet his burning determination had begun to shine a pinpoint of doubt into Quintus' mind, though the owl was slow to admit it to himself. Where *was* he going, after all? Mad or not, he had a firm mission—that much was clear. Would he lead Quintus to the king's children, as Falak suspected?

Thinking of the king's children and their disappearance in the glade made Quintus push his head down into his shoulders and wince. He was a good scout. He knew that—the best there was to be found in the Kingdom. Even King Melanthius had used him for his own purpose ages ago when stirrings in the Plot had to be crushed. Why, then, had the children vanished before his eyes? No one knew for sure what that dark place truly was, he reasoned to himself. No self-respecting character of the Plot had ever ventured long into the Wild Land, let alone the Glooming itself. It was an empty place in his mind, the Glooming; somewhere that even his imagination couldn't conjure pictures of. All he now knew of it was that it could eat people up, make them dissolve into air as if by magic.

Magic. Quintus straightened up on his high branch, trying to block out the sounds of Nocturne's desperate mumbling below. He had never seen magic up close. He knew that Falak experimented incessantly with it in his secret room in the castle. Some things he did on the king's orders; others, without the king's knowledge at all. Whatever the case, everyone knew that magic flowed, untamed, in the Wild Land and beyond. Magic was the answer, he suddenly knew.

He turned to look up to the sky flecked with a million stars. The moon shone bright; the next night it would be full. What better time for magic than that, Quintus asked himself with a shudder of self-satisfaction. Alert now, and hungry for the unknown, his sharp eyes focused with renewed interest down to the silvery spot on the forest floor that was Nocturne. Falak, he thought suddenly, had already worked this out. Quintus noted a newfound respect for his leader, followed closely by a prickling unease that felt very close to fear.

Ashlee Willis

CHAPTER TWENTY-TWO

Into the Deep

"She is ready," said Limnoreia suddenly, as if hearing a silent call from her sister beneath the water. Posy froze in anticipation. This was what they had come for. This would be the end of their quest for the princess Evanthe. Her eyes roved the surface of the water, still and shining as black glass. Nothing happened.

"Here," Adamaris beckoned a slender hand to them. "We must ready you to enter our home."

"Pardon me?" asked Kyran, confusion written across his face. Posy almost laughed at the courtesy in his voice at such a moment, though she felt a quick sting of foreboding.

"We may not bring the princess to you," explained Limnoreia, her pale blue eyes wide. "As you can see, there is no way out for you here. The only way out is the other side of the Glooming. And you may not find *that* any other way than through the water."

Posy did laugh now. "And as *you* can see, we don't have fins and tails as you do," she stated, an edge of mistrust resurfacing into her conscience.

Limnoreia smiled sweetly at her. "Of course not, my darling. That is why we must ready you. You must don these."

Posy and Kyran both gazed to where Limnoreia gestured by their feet, but saw only slick wet stone. The mermaid's tapering fingers reached to pluck something from the rock, and as she raised her arm, a filmy, glistening thing hung from it, visible only because of the glint of light reflecting off it.

"I'm most definitely not *donning* that," Posy exclaimed, and crossed her arms as Kyran turned to smirk at her.

"It will allow you to move swiftly and smoothly through the water," stated Adamaris calmly. "And most importantly, it will allow you to breathe. It is not as it seems."

"Huh," Posy rolled her eyes. "So I am beginning to understand."

"These garments contain magic in them," Adamaris' voice took on a slight note of defense. "Our offering of them is not to be scoffed at, young maid."

"I'm not scoffing at your offer," Posy said apologetically. "I—"

"Posy—that is, we both—are overtired and more than a little overwhelmed by our journey," Kyran cut in, directing his most charming smile at the mermaids. "We accept your offer and thank you. What must we do?"

"You need only drape the garment over you, and it will do the rest, Prince." Limnoreia lifted her arms, and Kyran bent to take the silky mantles from her. Kyran placed a hand on Posy's arm and nudged her back. She knew that he meant to put his cloak on first, to save her from any danger that might be hidden within it. She snatched the second cloak from his hands before he could stop her, and she watched it unfold, rippling like liquid from her hands to the stone floor. In a single moment, without another thought, she had swung it around and draped it over her shoulders.

She could see Kyran still, and the frown on his face as he watched her, struggling to unfold his own garment. But he was not the same. He swam before her eyes as if she saw him through a watery mist. A pleasant warmth spread from her shoulders, upward to her face, and all the way to her feet. Suddenly, she felt her lungs seem to grow heavy, as if the atmosphere pressed on her. She was nearly gasping just to pull a breath into her body. Posy's panicked eyes found the outline of the sister mermaids in the water, and she could make out the laughing smile on both of their faces. Did they mean to kill her this way—was that the trick in it? She tried to speak, but could not. She could only pull the air around her with all her strength, trying to force it into her lungs.

"You will not learn so quickly, my dear," said Adamaris brightly. "Though you try ever so bravely. It would take years for you to become accustomed to breathing out of water, in this horrible shallow air. Hurry now, jump into the water and all will be well."

Kyran had his own garment on now, though the moment he had placed it on his shoulders it had seemed to disappear as if it had become a part of his skin. He grabbed Posy's hand and in one violent movement pulled her off the stone ledge. Both of them plunged into the icy black water below.

The water should have pierced them with its cold, should have shocked and frozen them from any movement. Though Posy could feel its chill caress on her skin, it did not penetrate any deeper. Her body remained pleasingly warm, and she could feel a tight, smooth resistance on every inch of her new slick skin. She looked down at her hands and body in curiosity, but could discern no difference. She took an experimental breath and found that water flowed into her mouth like air, soft and effortless.

"Very good, very good!" exclaimed Limnoreia, clapping her small hands together like a pleased child. Posy could clearly see her now—so clearly and intensely that it almost hurt her eyes. Limnoreia's beautiful blue eyes shone like sapphires, and her hair floated around her like a cloud of spun gold. If the mermaids had been beautiful before, they were radiant now, here in their true home.

Kyran's voice broke through Posy's wandering thoughts. "Lead us to my sister now." His voice was courteous, but there was no mistaking the command.

Adamaris bowed her gleaming auburn head and flitted away.

Posy and Kyran found how natural they were now, beneath the lake. Its darkness became weightless and clear, its icy depths only a cool touch to their skin, its dense waters easily pierced as they plunged after the mermaids, deeper and deeper.

How deep are we? crossed Posy's mind in wonder as she trailed the mermaids. She and Kyran had already descended so deeply in the earth before even entering the lake. What a weight of water, land and stone must sit above their heads now! The thought made her shudder and suddenly have an odd premonition, as if they were being led into a trap. Had it been only two days ago that she had been in the camp of the centaurs, sleeping and eating, breathing the fresh forest air, walking through the forest talking with Caris and speaking of the Author? Posy wondered, with a darkening of her heart, if the Author had written this place they were in now, this lake with its black, shadowy beauty, and if he watched as she and Kyran tore through his story and changed every word.

"Here is our home," Adamaris' voice rang like a bell over her shoulder as she pointed one long finger.

Posy saw before them a great rise of stones on the floor of the lake, like a chain of small mountains. She exchanged a glance with Kyran. This was no mere rise of stones, his look said, and she had felt it already. It was a palace, a kingdom within itself, that lay beneath those deceptively natural rocks. Perhaps it was the magic in their glossy cloaks, now closer than their own skin, that allowed Posy and Kyran to see it for what it truly was.

Soon they were swimming through a pair of mammoth doors, into the side of the rocks, entering the palace of the mermaids. Posy clung to all the trust she could muster. It was too late now, wasn't it, for second thoughts? They were entirely in the keep of these sisters. They must hope the purpose that united them was strong. Strong enough.

Posy's last thought before the heavy doors grated shut behind them was a question—a simple one, but one that sent an ominous chill through her. She took a breath and put it into words. "Why do the three of you need such a large place to live? Were you not banned from the Plot alone?"

Seraphine seemed to materialize from the stone walls of the palace. Her white arms moved gracefully beside her and her shapely hips and tail glistened like a water serpent. Her eyes held sadness, but a glint of her small white teeth shone behind her smile, like a wordless warning. "You are correct, of course," she agreed slowly, with a nod of her dark head. "But that was long ago. You will find we are far from alone now, my dear."

CHAPTER TWENTY-THREE

The Mermaid Palace

Posy reached for Kyran's hand, its familiar grip strange and slick in its watery skin. Kyran said, his face unchanging, "You will take us to my sister now. We have waited long enough."

"Long enough?" Seraphine stared at him, her eyes bottomless dark pools. "You do not know what it is to be separated from someone long. How long have you been separated from your sister, Prince? A few days or weeks? Even many years would not come close to comparing to what I have lost, and the time I have waited to hold my little one again. This enchanted lake keeps my sisters and me prisoners in unending pain. We have been here many lifetimes ... too many."

"And I have promised to help you," Kyran answered calmly. "I will overthrow the king, and I will do all in my power to restore your child to you, lady."

"No," Seraphine's voice came quiet and bitter. "You will not do that. Not unless you can bring her back from the dead."

Limnoreia gave a tiny gasping sob. Adamaris swam swiftly to Seraphine's side to stroke her hair in comfort, before turning a face ferocious with pain to Kyran and Posy. "It is true," she said huskily. "My sister's daughter was sent beyond the realm of the Kingdom, out of the Plot, and died there. Those who die outside of the Plot never return to it. My sister's pain is beyond anything you would know. She has lived centuries, lifetimes, knowing no turn of the Plot will bring back her child, knowing no king or king's son can ever make right the wrong that has been done to us and our people. And we know—we learned long ago—that if you cannot get back what you lost, you may at least let your revenge fall on the heads of those who took it from you."

"No," Posy said, her voice sticking in her throat. Yet she had known, somehow, it would come to this, hadn't she? In her heart she had seen it, though she had denied it. *Some hurts don't heal,* Posy thought, and the thought struck something within her like a gong, hard and deep. She felt her eyes burning with the threat of tears, and knew her whole body was shaking.

Kyran reached down to gently extricate his hand from Posy's tight grip, then he calmly unsheathed his sword. "I have no desire to hurt any of you," he said, his voice tinged with profound sadness, "but I will find my sister, as you have promised me I would. I must insist you fulfill that promise now. I am sorry in my heart for your loss, but it was none of my doing, and your revenge is not for me." His face changed as he spoke and he seemed to be lost in his own thoughts, almost speaking to himself now. "I suppose a cruel thing may be done, and its doer never knows the many wrongs and pains that happen because of it, falling one on the other, toppling like an avalanche on a mountainside. Can it only end in the ruin of everything in its path?"

Seraphine looked up suddenly, her eyes fastened on Kyran's face. "Yes," her voice was low. "I see you know more of pain than I thought, Prince." She shook her head. "And that makes what I do even harder for me, but I cannot go back. I will not. Don't you see?"

"Go back?" Posy finally spoke, her voice unnaturally loud in the hushed palace hall. "What do you mean? What are you going to do to us?"

"Do?" Seraphine gave a weak smile. "I will do nothing to you at all. You are here now, in my palace, and the princess is here as well, just as I told you. You may find her if that is your wish, and take her back to the surface and out of the Glooming. But you must do it alone. I am done with this now. I see what I must do."

"Seraphine, no!" Limnoreia swam to her sister and seized her arm.

Adamaris had an equally panicked look on her lovely face, but she only cast an anxious glance at her sister and swam to where Kyran and Posy stood. Her voice low and quick, she said to them, "My sister has her own path to follow now, and I do believe she means to do it."

"Do what?" Posy asked in alarm.

"It does not concern you, little one," Adamaris said. "What does concern you is finding the princess before it is too late."

"Before ... it's too ...!" Posy sputtered, fear gripping her.

"My sister would not do you harm, for all her talk of revenge. She has decided to summon a deep magic and end her imprisonment here once and for all, though at what cost only the Author may say. She will do it soon, I think." Adamaris threw a glance over her shoulder once again at the solemn face of her sister. "So you must find Evanthe quickly and leave this place. For I believe our little kingdom here will be destroyed." Her voice held sadness, but Posy noted with surprise that it held a trace of something like relief as well.

"And the garments?" Kyran asked, his voice so calm that Posy stared at him.

"Yes, they are only temporary, as all magical things are," the mermaid nodded. "If they dissolve, you will no longer be able to breathe and remain under the lake. You *must* reach the surface before this happens."

"Where is the surface? How do we leave the Glooming?" Kyran pressed.

Adamaris' look was distracted; Seraphine and Limnoreia were gliding out of the chamber now. "When you leave the palace, here," she gestured toward the doors they had just entered, "you must follow the way you are *meant* to go. No man leaves the Glooming alive if he does not know his own self, his own soul. There is no other way to leave such a dark place than by a light such as this. Words could never show you." The mermaid leaned forward and kissed Posy's cheek suddenly, her expression more open now than ever. She grasped Kyran's strong hand in her own small one. "Do not blame my sister, when you see what she has—" She hesitated, biting her lip, and started over. "Remember, Prince, there is good and bad in everyone. Dark and shadows depend so wholly on light that it is impossible sometimes to see where one begins and one ends. Not a soul in this world or any other is ever completely lost to darkness—not unless they choose to be."

The palace walls seemed to groan, then, and Adamaris threw an anxious look around her. One last word she gave them, her emerald eyes large with urgency.

"Go," she said, pushing them toward the depths of the palace. Before Posy could take it all in, Adamaris had darted away after her sisters through the water, leaving only a rush of sparkling froth behind her.

CHAPTER TWENTY- FOUR
Through the Water

Kyran did not hesitate a single moment, and Posy could see the fierce light of determination behind his dark eyes. He swam to the stone pillars between which the mermaids had disappeared, Posy close behind him. The sisters were nowhere to be seen. Posy knew they would not see them again. She looked about her and seemed to feel the chill of water a bit more, pushing on her body like a coldness that would seep into her bones. The palace was a place of darkness, and a place of despair. How could it be anything else? It had been created by Seraphine, who had lived lifetimes in regret and sorrow for her child, in anger, amidst thoughts of vengeance for those who had wronged her. What an anguished place to live in, Posy thought. She turned and saw Kyran watching her and, as had become their habit, knew her eyes spoke to him at that moment more than her mouth could have. He nodded, a look of sorrow still on his face.

"Yes, Posy, I feel it. I see it. Yet this is not the time to dwell on these thoughts. Be strong against them. We must find Evanthe." He crossed to her and reached up a hand to cup her chin. He leaned forward and kissed her, hard and quick, and when he pulled back, his face was set. "We must separate."

"What?" Posy cried. "Separate?"

"It's the only way we can find her with so little time." His brows furrowed. "The only question is, how will one of us let the other know if we have found her?"

"Separate?" Posy repeated. "Not in this place, Kyran, please!" The coldness of the water lapped around her, mocking.

"You will be safe in the palace, though it holds such horrible things. The things that lurk here cannot harm your body, I think," he said wryly. "We have no time to discuss it. I will go this way, you go that. Stay to that side of the palace, search every floor and room and corner. If you don't find her, leave the palace and wait for me near where we entered. Don't linger here."

"I ... Kyran, I ..." Posy heard her own voice choke. "I can't ..."

"Yes, you can. Because you must. Be brave, little one." He kissed her forehead briskly, gave her one last piercing look, and was gone.

* * *

Posy didn't know when she had last been so frightened. *Never,* she admitted to herself with a shudder. Darkness and emptiness, it seemed, terrified her more than a danger standing solidly before her. She knew she had to move before the seeping coldness she felt made her incapable of any movement at all. So she pushed her arms through the water and began.

She searched, high and low, room after room of the palace. Some rooms were ornately decorated, fit for any castle in the world. Some were empty and seaweed-covered, small, wide-eyed creatures peeking at her from darkened corners, flitting away when she came near. Nothing harmful, nothing even alarming ... yet she couldn't shake the feeling of something growing within her until she had to scream. *Not yet,* she told herself desperately, willing her mind to hold her fear down. *Not yet.*

The palace kept groaning as it had just before Adamaris left them. It sounded like a great creature in the throes of a terrible pain. Posy knew, in the depths of those endless empty rooms, that it had held its sorrows closely for too long, and it was ready to drive them out forever. She suddenly understood the fleeting look of relief on Adamaris' face before she had gone. The strong stone walls shuddered, and the furniture trembled, and Posy's searching became frenzied. She swam from rooms to hallways to towering balconies overlooking the darkened floor of the lake, and saw nothing, and no one. She began to feel a creeping suspicion that Kyran was not here at all; she felt certain he must have gone from the palace, and left her alone. No one could feel so alone as this, so alone you begin to question the thoughts in your own mind. She was the only person in the world—or so it felt—and though she was the only person, she didn't know who she was.

She didn't know when she had started crying, but Posy's sobs seemed to be a part of her and she barely regarded them as she searched and searched through the emptiness. At last, she reached the top of the palace, a spiraling tower wending its way upward, folded into the mountainside. Before she opened the door to the small room at the top of the tower, she knew that it was empty, too. With a feeling like falling into nothing she stepped across the threshold. She knew she must truly be alone in this horrible place—aloneness so deep that even she did not seem to be there. Then the emptiness pushed on her, invaded her being and pierced her skin, with a coldness like icy death.

Kyran had felt pain when leaving Posy and seeing the look of childlike fear she cast at him. He had felt that something was tearing off him, when he had to leave her. *This is the first time we have been apart on this journey,* crossed his mind with a jolt as he swam swiftly away from her. But his determination to find his sister overcame everything else, and with a warrior's single-minded purpose began searching his half of the palace.

As far as he could tell, as he performed his swift and methodical exploration, it appeared to be a normal palace. It was, in fact, startlingly like his father's castle in the Kingdom. He wondered, with a feeling of unease, if the similarities were deliberate. He didn't know what it could mean, but something within him became wary at the thought.

The first room in which he saw people was like all the others, richly decorated and comfortable. And that was the troubling thing; for they were people—not merpeople at all. As he swam slowly into the room, he gazed about him guardedly. No one seemed to notice him; they all were preoccupied with what they did. Two people were sitting at a small marble table playing a game of chess, laughing and pointing at the stone pieces as they moved them. Two ladies were sitting on a couch; one reclining slightly and seeming to drowse, the other intently reading a book. A man was sitting in a chair across from the ladies them and was raptly conversing with the one who held the book. Kyran stared at them a moment. Why would the lady not look up from her book, and pay the man some attention? And why, yet, would the man not seem to notice that she ignored him so completely?

Kyran shook his head as if to clear it, and walked carefully past them, his eyes alert. Nothing changed, and no one seemed to see him, or even notice anyone else in the room. Kyran opened the door at the far side of the room to enter the next chamber, and was met with a scene disturbingly similar to the one before. A roomful of people, all absorbed in what they did, but no one seeming to notice anything else. Kyran attempted to speak with a few of them, but it was no good. He even touched a few of them, and once or twice someone would glance at him. He got an unfocused gaze from one man, a nod from another, a slight smile from a woman; but nothing more. He began to feel a coldness creep under his skin as he entered room after room down the long corridor and was met by only different renditions of the same thing.

One room, though, was different. He felt it as he opened the door, and instead of nothingness, like all the others, there was a vibration in the air, a feeling, and a cry. He rushed frantically into the room, disregarding the two or three people who looked up long enough to give him a look of annoyance as the door swung open and hit the wall with a loud crack. He searched everyone's face, looking for his sister, but he didn't see her. He had felt it; he knew he had. His shoulders drooped, and he sat on a settee next to a woman who rocked a baby in her arms. "Well, really!" she breathed crossly, and turned her back on him, continuing to coo quietly to the sleeping child.

Kyran leaned forward to put his face in his hands, covering his eyes from the emptiness around him. "Where are you?" he spoke aloud. "Evanthe, you are here, but you must help me! Where are you?"

Here, Kyran! Here!

Kyran shot from his seat as his gaze swept frantically across the room.

"Evanthe?" his voice faltered.

Here, the faint voice came again, and this time he saw where it had come from. He ran to the darkened corner of the room where his sister sat, huddled on the floor, hugging her knees like a lost child, her tangle of golden hair falling over her knees and onto the floor around her.

"Evanthe, Evanthe," Kyran sobbed, crushing her in a wild embrace. But she didn't embrace him in return. She didn't even look at him. Her body was limp in his arms.

"I thought I heard him," she said aloud, shaking her head as he released her. "I thought ... but I was wrong. Wrong, wrong, wrong, wrong .... Kyran, why don't you come for me?" Tears streamed down her pale face.

Kyran drew back from her, a dawning horror flooding his mind. "Evanthe?" he said slowly. "I *am* here. Don't you hear me? Don't you see me?"

The princess hugged her knees closer to her and shivered, her violet eyes staring across the room, the endless tears dropping from her face to the floor. *She has cried those tears for so long,* Kyran thought suddenly, *that she does not even bother to wipe them away.*

His mind stopped, then, as if hitting a solid wall. He did not know what else to do. He did not know how to help her. "Posy," he said, "I need Posy." He turned as if to run and find her, then turned back to Evanthe. He could not leave her here, like this. He felt the palace walls heave and it seemed the very foundation rumbled beneath him; there was no time. He did the only thing he knew to do. He leaned down and scooped up his sister, light as a flower, and held her against him.

"I can't get to your mind, Evanthe," Kyran breathed in her ear. "I suspect it is no one's choice but your own to come back to me. But I *will* save your body and take you from this horrible place." He held her fiercely to him and buried his face in her shoulder, stilling the anguish that fought to burst out of him.

He lifted his wearied eyes and gazed about the glittering room, the people smiling at what was before them. He shook his head slowly, grief like a stone sitting in his chest. He saw only a waking sleep here; a living death. Holding to his sister like a lifeline, he hastened from there without a backward glance.

* * *

Posy was alone. Her search had halted, because she didn't have the heart or strength to swim anymore. She floated, frozen as a statue, before one of the great windows atop the tower room, staring sightlessly across the barren sea floor. The surrounding yellow-green water seemed to reverberate and ripple with anticipation, and Posy saw tiny waves beginning to spread outward from the palace. The waves seemed to speak of a doom, in Posy's mind. After a fleeting glance around the chamber, seeing it was empty, she had become mysteriously calm. The weight of emptiness and sadness was still on her, but she no longer fought it. She felt how easy it would be to give in to it, to let it overtake and drown her. How blissful just to let it pull her down, to stop her frenzied struggle. She knew this must be the end of the journey for her, and she almost laughed. So close to the goal, but not to reach it. Was it tragic ... or pathetic?

A shaft of light shone suddenly on a hidden part of her mind, and she remembered her parents and her sister, as if they were fairytale creatures from another world. She knew she would miss them—if only she could feel anything at all.

Her eyes finally recognized something moving on the sea floor, far below her. A person had come out of the palace doors and was swiftly moving away from it. Kyran? So he had left her, after all. The thought of that was like a hammer hitting a numb spot. The pain was there—she just waited to feel it. Then she saw that he carried something—a person! Posy's mind worked sluggishly ... it was—it had to be—the princess! He had found her.

Slowly, so slowly Posy almost thought something else must have been guiding her hands—she reached for the latch of the window before her. It sprang open almost before she touched it. She pushed her fingertips on the screening of seaweed and it swung open for her, inviting. But she needed no invitation. She climbed over the sill and prepared to jump, her heart giving a horrible flutter. There was no time to leave the castle the way she had entered it. This was surely the only way. Perhaps she would die in the fall, but her only other choice was to remain in this place, and she would not do that.

Only as she pushed herself off the ledge, the decision made, did she remember, feeling foolish, that she was swimming, and could come to no harm doing this. She had thought the escape from such emptiness would be a difficult one—she had been prepared for it to be so, for the pain and more that may have come of it. And it was as simple was pulling a latch ... opening a window and stepping out.

She escaped the mermaids' palace, and its horrible coldness, even as she heard its groaning reverberate deeper behind her. She swam down, down, closer and closer to where Kyran was swimming away. She tried to shout at him, but the garment she wore seemed to be losing its magic, and her voice wouldn't obey her. She looked behind her at the castle. The climax would come soon, the end of the palace, whatever end that might be. She was too near it. The groaning and rumbling stopped suddenly, and in the horrible, hanging silence, Posy heard Kyran's voice shouting her name. He was swimming quickly toward her, but still so far away—too far.

A deafening roar struck Posy then, like a blow to her body and ears and mind, and the palace walls fractured and fell apart before her eyes. A brilliant light exploded from the destruction, right from the tower she had leapt from, and shone upward for a single moment, a fleeting beacon. The roar continued, and everything was in it—fury and grief, relief and joy, ecstasy and peace. Posy had a thought to put her hands to her ears, to shield herself in some way from the terrible force of it, but the thought barely crossed her mind before she lost consciousness altogether.

* * *

But the ending was not to be so easy. Posy heard a voice within her, calling her by name, pushing through the hollow places within her, shining a glaring light on the loneliness she felt and chasing it away. It was a father's voice, deep and calm. It said her name, over and over, calmly, but so firmly she knew it meant for her to awaken. She felt so peaceful now, with the voice spreading through her whole body, that she had no wish to wake. She knew also that she must. She had what seemed to be long-ago memories of a handsome black-haired, dark-eyed boy whom she loved, and a lost princess.

Ashlee Willis

She awoke to pain, gasping helplessly. Kyran's face, pale from fear and exhaustion, peered at her in torment, and joy flooded it when he saw her open her eyes.

"Posy, Posy," he kissed her forehead, her temple, her eyelids. "I couldn't have stood it. I couldn't have."

Posy looked around and realized they had not gone anywhere at all. She still lay on the sea floor where she had fallen. Kyran was here with her. The remains of the palace lay before them, so horrible she had to turn her face from them. She saw a girl, looking terribly young and pale, with ropes of golden hair falling over her slender body, lying near her. Posy rolled over to reach a hand out and touch Evanthe's cheek lightly.

"Yes," Kyran nodded, his face grim. "She lives," he said quickly, answering the question in Posy's face. "But what kind of living this is, and how to wake her, I do not know. Right now, all I know is that we must go. Our shrouds will lose their enchantment soon, and we will die if we do not reach the surface quickly." His dark eyes analyzed their surroundings.

Posy shook her head, feeling she had just come out of a deep sleep, but her mind flew sharply to a thought, and she spoke it without hesitation, "We must find the way we were meant to go."

Kyran turned to look at her and said, "That is what Adamaris told us. But what does it mean?"

Posy sat silently, staring ahead blindly. She wasn't thinking, exactly, but things inside of her churned and worked as they had never done before. She knew she had not undergone such horror for nothing, and she was right.

"Up, from where the tower was—the one I came out of," she said finally. "That is the way out of the Glooming."

"How do you know that?" Kyran asked, trying to keep the skepticism from his voice. "And how will going up from there be any different from going up from here?"

Posy remembered the emptiness she had felt in the mermaid palace. It had been like a black hole, deep enough to swallow her soul, dark enough to make her forget who she was. But then she had seen the devastated palace, and the pillar of light rising from its ruins. The light had risen from the very place she had thought would be the end of her. No, there was no doubt in her mind. They were things that flashed within her for a moment and were gone, but it would take much too long to tell it all to Kyran. They had to leave.

"You will have to trust me," she said, holding his gaze. She knew beyond a doubt she loved him the moment she saw the decision in his face, the immediate trust. He nodded, bending at once to lift his sister into his arms, ready to follow her.

Posy swam ahead, glancing frequently behind her to be sure Kyran kept up. Straight up, where the brief beam of light had pointed the way, they swam for what seemed to be hours, but it was only minutes. The rocky mountain beneath the lake formed a wall on one side of them, and soon Posy saw that the wall surrounded them, narrowing. This was the only way, she told herself. This funnel they swam through could have been reached in no other way than the one they now swam.

But Posy knew her arms and legs could not endure much more of this swimming. She seemed to feel the coldness in the water more; she thought the water pressed around her body with more force. Her limbs felt heavy and awkward, and her breathing became labored and choked. The magic garment she wore was losing

Ashlee Willis

its power. In panic, she looked behind her. Kyran was struggling also—more so, for he carried the weight of his sister.

"Hurry!" she tried to call to him, but water came rushing into her mouth and her eyes began to blur and sting.

Posy knew there was nothing she could do for Kyran. He would have to save himself. Trying to save each other now would only drown them both. She struggled to swim, ever upward, until her head spun wildly and her lungs were like fire in her chest. Every pretense of the shroud was gone now, and the icy water nearly paralyzed her body. The voice came to her again, then, amidst the chaos of her body and mind: "Fight, Posy."

She fought. She fought until she knew she couldn't do it any longer. And then she fought some more. Her mind screamed angrily at the voice within her, since her voice could not. *What use is fighting now, when it's impossible?*

"Fight," the voice commanded, returning her anger with a mighty anger of its own.

And she broke through the surface of the water at last, gasping and nearly weeping with pain and fatigue and relief. Sun splashed onto her face, blinding, and she closed her eyes against it. Posy pulled herself onto the bank, collapsing before her feet were out of the water. Kyran was close behind her, lifting his sister onto the bank first before pushing himself out of the water to fall beside Posy. Posy felt him kiss the top of her dripping head before she lay it down on the sodden grassy bank and sleep overwhelmed her.

CHAPTER TWENTY-FIVE

The Author's Words

The cold woke Posy. The sun had dried her dress and hair, but the night air seemed to creep inside of her, and the cool ground was like a soulless stone beneath her. She raised herself up to a sitting position with a groan, every inch of her aching, and peered cautiously around. They were in a tiny clearing, surrounded on three sides by thick forest, and on the fourth side by the deep pool of water they had emerged from only hours before. The full moon hung like a brilliant silver ornament in the sky, larger and brighter than any moon Posy had seen in her own world. It flooded the glade with a white light and flung deep shadows into the trees.

Kyran was a small distance away, attempting to start a fire. He had carried Evanthe away from the water's edge and had covered her with his own cloak. If Posy had not known it was the princess, she would have thought the small lump next to Kyran was a bundle of blankets, it was so tiny, so unnaturally still. Kyran's dark head turned as he heard Posy stirring and he rushed to her side.

"I have not been awake for long," he said, "but I believe this place is enchanted."

"What?" said Posy, feeling her legs tremble weakly beneath her as she tried to rise. "Why do you think that?"

"I cannot start a fire here, no matter how I try." His voice was hushed. "And the wind has not blown even to flutter a leaf, nor has the surface of that pool moved since we came out of it. There is magic here."

Posy shivered and nodded. "Then what should we do?"

"I think," said Kyran, his black eyes gazing upward, "that something will happen here soon. The moon is full tonight, and that is when magic happens, so all the old stories go. We could wait ... wait until the moon is risen high."

"And then?" Posy asked, watching the shadows move on Kyran's face.

"Then we shall see," was all he would say.

"Your sister?" Posy's eyes moved to the small form on the ground next to them.

"The same," Kyran answered, jaw clenched. He told Posy how he had found the princess, and what he had done. He told her the words she had said before she had gone into the deep slumber she was now lost in. "She breathes, and shudders now and then, though she does nothing else. She will not speak now at all or even open her eyes. But as long as she lives, there is hope. We have not rescued her for nothing." His voice held stubborn determination.

Posy hoped this was true, though looking at the princess, it was hard to have any faith in it. She looked like she was gone from the world already. Her lovely face was ashen and stony as death. Not a muscle of her face or body moved, and Posy wasn't sure how Kyran knew she breathed—she couldn't see Evanthe's chest rising and falling. She remembered with a sudden peculiar thrill that the princess had indeed died many times before, in this strange story—a sacrifice for the Plot. Then she recalled what the Centaurs had told them—that any who died beyond the Borders of the Plot could not come back from death. Posy turned her face from Kyran to hide the hopelessness that she knew was written on it.

The slow scrape of Kyran's sword made her turn swiftly back around. His eyes were fixed on the edge of the surrounding trees where a small shape moved along the ground there. Posy's heart beat faster, and then she saw that the shape was that of an owl, pearly white in the moonlight, bright eyes dimmed by something like misery. Or pain.

"Nocturne?" Kyran said suddenly, stepping toward the creature and lowering his sword slightly. Posy recognized him too. He had been the one who came to her room on the night of her rescue.

"Yes, yes, it's me, Prince," came the small, weary voice. "Please don't kill me, I've come so far!" and the owl collapsed into a feathery heap.

Kyran and Posy only had time enough to run to the owl's aide, take in the extent of his pitiful injuries, before they saw a large shadow on the ground before them, so large it seemed to block out the light of the moon for a moment. Posy gasped and turned around, but it was upon them. A large bird swooped straight over them as they both fell to the ground. Posy only saw the flash of a sharp black beak, heard expansive wings thrusting air aside with a hiss. Kyran rolled where he had fallen and sprung to his feet again, sword held out before him.

The creature swept past them and landed in the still pool of water, sending gently skidding waves before it, its vast white wings held wide and high to slow its flight. It slid silently across the water, its head tilted downward toward its white slope of neck, its eyes, glittering like black diamonds, fixed upon them.

"A swan." Posy's words were more like breathing than speaking.

Ashlee Willis

"I am a swan this night, yes," said a voice Posy knew. She walked toward the dark pool, her heart pounding. She didn't know what she felt, exactly, but she knew she feared this creature, and yet didn't fear it. She felt in some part of her that she should run from it, but every fiber of her body seemed to long for it all the same.

Kyran grabbed Posy's wrist before she could walk far, trying to pull her back to his side. "No," was all he said.

Posy heard fear in his voice, too. She shook him off gently and whispered, barely knowing what she said. "Put your sword away, Kyran. I know who this is."

The swan ruffled its wings at this, and its beautiful head lifted. "Yes, you know who I am, child. You would think the young prince would recognize the one who wrote him as well."

"Who wrote ...?" Kyran's voice was incredulous. "You can't be! You cannot be the Author."

"I suppose I should ask, 'And why not?'" The swan's voice seemed to laugh as it spoke these words. "But, you know, you would have no answer for me. Why shouldn't an Author be able to enter into his own story when and how it pleases him? Many have done so before me."

"But I ..." Kyran's voice shook. Posy instinctively turned to take his hand, limp and cold within her own. "I didn't know you were real. No one does. They all think you're a myth, or a legend from long ago—a story no one believes anymore."

The Author ... a story within his own story, thought Posy.

"Hmm." The swan's black eyes seemed to darken even further as it glided beneath the shadow of a tree. "And is this what you believe, Prince? That I am a myth?"

Kyran's eyes never left the swan's face, but his answer was long in coming. The silence of the night seemed to drag on until Posy thought he meant not to answer at all. Finally, his voice barely more than a whisper, he said, "No."

The trees seemed to sigh and the moon, high above them, shone brighter.

"But," Kyran continued unexpectedly, "though I believe you are what you say, I cannot pretend to understand why you have left this story for so long? *Your* story. Why have you allowed it to fester and rot until it is so far from what it was meant to be, so long ago when it was written?"

"You remember when it was first written, then?" The swan's voice was not eager, but hopeful.

"Yes, I do now." Kyran bowed his dark head. "I didn't while I was within the Kingdom ... I didn't remember much of long ago. But it has been coming back to me, slowly, these many days I have been in the Wild Land. And the more I remember of the beginning of the story, the more I know how it has been twisted."

"And the more it breaks your young heart, yes," murmured the creature, emerging from the shadows, magnificent in the moonlight. "Who better to know that than I?"

Posy heard a rustling noise, followed by a squeak of dismay. She turned to see that Nocturne had regained consciousness and was staring, wide-eyed, at the swan. "I knew it!" The owl hobbled unsteadily toward them. "I knew magic would happen in this place! I knew I would find you here!"

"Yes, little owl," the swan's voice smiled. "And how brave you have been! Come."

Nocturne didn't hesitate at all, but went stumbling toward the bank where the swan was now rising out of the water. It lifted one great wing and gathered the owl to him beneath it. It bent its head in a fluid, soothing movement, as if it would whisper secrets to the little creature tucked beneath its wing. Posy and Kyran both stood, still as statues, watching. At last, the swan lifted its wing and Nocturne walked away from it, his injuries gone as if they had never been.

Posy gasped, and knew that if she had a question in her mind before, she didn't now. Only the Author of this story could have such absolute power over it. Kyran watched Nocturne thoughtfully a moment, then nodded, turning his eyes to the swan.

"You didn't answer me," Kyran said. "I need to know where you have been for so long, and why you left the Plot and its characters helpless?"

The swan lifted its neck high and let out a trumpeting call that hit the trees and bounced off the water's surface. "I *need* not answer any question you have, boy." The voice held the same tinge of anger that had urged and commanded her to fight for her life only hours before. "I wrote you, you are mine," it continued, its voice as hard as its diamond eyes. "But I do not write everything you do and think. I do not write every decision you make. Not because I cannot—but because I *will not*. Perhaps someday, when you are a father, Prince, you will understand how empty is your heart if your child is a hollow toy that you can move where you will him to be. No—there is no joy to be found if you cannot watch as he struggles to become himself, finds the borders and decides to cross them for himself, sees the enemy and finds the strength to fight against it."

Kyran's face was stony. He made no response.

"I would not love my characters," whispered the Author, "if I did not let them live. They must live, though it means making many mistakes."

"Cruel and fatal mistakes, Author." Kyran's voice shook, like a child who struggles to keep up a face of anger when all he really feels is sorrow.

"Yes, cruel. And, yes, many have died. This is the price of freedom, and of choice, and of wisdom. And when you have gained wisdom of your own, young Prince, you will know that no one can make a choice other than this for one that he truly loves. There can be no other way. That is the law of this and every other story ... if it is a true one."

"But they are your characters! *We* are your characters!" Kyran exclaimed. "I—I don't want to be a puppet, but—but ... couldn't you have at least helped us when we needed it? My sister, look at her!" he shouted. "She is nearly dead from what she has been through, and none of it was her fault. And my father—the one who caused this suffering—sits on his throne now and he feels no regret or sadness that he has lost us. No remorse for the many cruel things he has done to us."

Posy could feel the words in the air, though the Author didn't speak them. *How can you know what your father thinks and feels?* Perhaps the question came from her, though, and not the Author at all.

Tears streamed down Kyran's face now, and Posy felt her heart breaking for him. He knew what true emptiness felt like, as did Posy—indeed, as did many people in many worlds. It seemed to overwhelm her, this thought of so many people, all of them alone with their sadness. She stood and cried her own tears, for her own grieving heart as well as Kyran's. It was like a cup full of poison was being poured out, emptied, ready now for something new—something good. She looked up and saw, with a sting that felt like both pain and joy, that the swan's eyes dripped tears black as blood in the moonlight, and the deepest sorrow was etched across its noble face.

"My children," said the Author, its black beak like a slash of midnight across the background of soft water. "Someday you will understand, someday you will know ... you have to learn for yourselves, just as you have to fall and triumph for yourselves. If I do it for you, if I write the words for you to follow blindly, and the decision is not made in your own heart, then you are mere characters indeed. If you can choose to forget me, as many have done, that means you can choose to remember me as well."

"Oh, yes, yes!" Nocturne piped. Posy started; she had forgotten about the little creature standing at their feet. "And the characters *are* remembering, Author. They are coming out of the fog! The Plot no longer holds them!"

Posy and Kyran both looked down at him curiously.

"I met with creatures in the wood, as I came here to find the prince, and they told me ... they hear things from the Borders. There are uprisings everywhere in your name, Author!" He turned to Kyran, "And in yours, Prince. There are people who are standing against the king and calling for changes in the Plot."

"Yes," said the swan. "Great changes are coming about in the Plot, and in the Wild Land as well."

"But"—Nocturne's face fell—"many have been put to death for speaking against the king."

Kyran's hand clenched tightly onto the sword he still held. "That is something my father is good at," he said through his teeth. "Killing."

"But it is also on the queen's command that they die," said Nocturne quickly. "Your father the king is out with his army, battling along the Borders. So say the woodland folk I met along the way. Queen Valanor is left to rule the castle and its prisoners on her own."

"What else do the folk of the Wild Land say, little owl?" questioned the Author gently, though Posy suspected that he knew very well already.

The creature ruffled its feathers a bit in excitement. "They say ... they say now that the characters are rebelling, and ... and"—His voice fell to a hush—"the words of the story are changing. *Changing.* No one ... no one ever believed such a thing could happen before!" His eyes were huge with wonder. "But now it is whispered of everywhere. And they are calling you, young lady, and you, Prince Kyran ... they are calling you the Word Changers."

"The Word Changers?" Posy repeated, feeling an unexpected thrill going up her spine.

"Yes." The owl nodded his head vigorously. "For they say the Plot is changing because of your quest."

"Our quest?" Kyran asked wonderingly. "But how do they know of our quest?"

"Oh, they don't, not really," said Nocturne quickly, "But they know you left the Kingdom, and they discovered that the poor girl they put in the princess' role was a fake ... and, well, stories will crop up, won't they?"

"That was Olena, my maid! Well—" Posy blushed, remembering she had also been a fake princess not so long ago. "*Evanthe's* maid," she amended. "So she escaped?"

"Oh, yes! Olena's father abandoned his duties as a character

Ashlee Willis

when he found out they meant to put her in the princess' place, and ... and sacrifice her. He broke into the castle with several others and took Olena and his entire family into hiding, beyond the Borders and into the Wild Land. Yes, everything began to change quite quickly after the two of you left. After Olena was rescued, that is when the king took his army out to the Borders. There have been one or two small battles already."

"I wonder ...," said Kyran thoughtfully, his voice trailing. "Nocturne." He turned quickly to the owl. "I think you came to us as a friend, since you tell us all these things."

"Oh, yes! Yes, I did. I left the Council of Owls and came to warn you—oh, yes, I *must* warn you that Falak is planning –" But Nocturne turned his dark eyes upward suddenly, as if he had heard or seen something. Posy heard it, too—a faint rush, like wings. She looked up into the trees where the owl's gaze was fixed and saw a shape, black against the moon, fly above them and swiftly out of sight.

"Quintus," whispered Nocturne shakily, his sharp owl eyes following the disappearing form. "Oh, what have I done? I have led them straight to you!" His voice was panicked. "He will go back and tell Falak where we are!"

Kyran and Posy exchanged a look. "It's all right, my friend," said Kyran soothingly to the owl. "You did what was right. You came to this place and found us. You have warned us of what the king is doing. That is all that matters."

"I didn't know where you would be," admitted Nocturne, "but I thought ... that is, Falak has sent owls to guard each opening of the Glooming. I remembered this one, from ages past, and had the smallest hope. You see, we owls do not forget the past as easily as the humans do. The magic of the Kingdom doesn't cloud our eyes as it has yours these many years. We have known of this place, and its magic, since the time the Plot was written."

"You have done well," the swan said, the warm smile in its voice again.

Kyran nodded. "And so Falak sent you to guard this outlet?"

Nocturne's round face darkened. "No," he said. "I was cast out of the Council of Owls. I questioned Falak, and his desire to kill you."

Kill them. They had both known it for some time, really. *So*, Posy thought, *Nocturne's injuries must have been Falak's parting gift*.

"Was Falak's wish that we were killed *outside* of the Border?" Kyran asked slowly, his voice telling them he already knew the answer.

"Yes," said Nocturne miserably. "He wanted you completely eliminated from the Plot. You see, that is what I came to warn you of. Falak wishes not only to kill the three of you; he wishes to kill your father the king as well. He wants to ..." The owl swallowed with difficulty. "He wants to become the ruler of the Plot himself."

Posy looked quickly at Kyran, and what she saw in his face surprised her. It was a look of fear. A fear she hadn't seen when his own death was mentioned, but that he now seemed to feel at the thought of his father being killed.

"So what are we to do now?" he asked solemnly, turning to the swan, which was waiting silently.

"You have a friend who waits for you, now you have found your sister," said the swan calmly.

"A friend?" Kyran asked.

"You forget what Alvar has done for you so quickly, then?"

"Alvar! No, I do not forget him," Kyran's voice sounded tired.

Ashlee Willis

"We were to meet his army as soon as we could," said Posy. She turned to the Author. "You can tell us where they are, can't you? Or …" she hesitated. "Perhaps you could take us there?"

"I could take you there," the swan agreed, "but I will not. There is no need, and I have places to be, now that the Wild Land has awoken, and the characters begin to remember. A battle must be prepared for, and the Wild Folk need a strong leader. They have lived on the outskirts of the Plot for so long they are accustomed to living in the dark of the forest, and need someone who will awaken their bravery. But never fear; you will reach Alvar's army in safety. And all I speak to, I will send to you, to fight with you."

"But—" Kyran began.

"No," the Author said, stopping him. "The time for questions and words is over. I wrote you and made you what you are, but it's because I have such a great hope for you, and such a love, that I will step back to see what you are made of. I long to see my own characters come to life and make decisions and words of their own. Tell me, what Author doesn't wish that? But you must promise me," he continued soberly, "that though you set the course of words in a different path, you will yet remain faithful to the original Plot—the one I know you now remember deep within you. The Kingdom must be restored to it before it can live at peace again."

Kyran gave a silent nod. *How simple,* thought Posy as she watched the exchange. *How deceptively simple is such an enormous responsibility sworn to.*

The Author now walked on his webbed feet to where Evanthe lay on the dewy grass, and he laid a great wing across her small body, just as he had done for Nocturne. He said words, low and sweet, inaudible to the others, into her ear. Posy saw in her imagination how it must be: a book open, a page of words. The words begin to swirl and change, making way for a new part of the story, a change in the plot that sends ripples flowing outward, like a stone thrown into water. An author's words, which can change everything.

They saw the princess stir and murmur, and Kyran surged forward to her side, grasping her hand, quick tears escaping from his eyes. "She will sleep now," said the Author, "but when she wakes she will have come back to you."

The swan stretched its neck again and trumpeted to the sky. Soon, the outlines of three more swans appeared against the moon. They landed next to the Author, who nodded wordlessly at them.

"These fine creatures will take you where you need to go," the Author said. "Farewell, Word Changers."

The swan took flight above them before they had a chance to say or even think anything more. The Author seemed to melt into the moonlit clouds as he flew higher and higher, and then was gone.

Ashlee Willis

CHAPTER TWENTY-SIX
Spies and Plans

Quintus flew like a swift black shadow throughout the night, tireless, a ferocious triumph burning like fuel in his veins. His sharp owl eyes spotted a mouse far below him once or twice, but he ignored the twinge of hunger he felt, and the urge to swoop and kill. He could not waste a moment with the news he had to give—no, not a single moment.

As he sped above the thick trees of the Wild Land and neared the Borders, he came upon small lights dotted here and there, a rustling as if an enormous beast slept under the trees. Campfires, soldiers sleeping. An army, but not the king's. It was a large one, he thought, peering down, and this would be important to Falak. He knew then his news of the prince must wait a little longer, for he had scouting to do. He would have to wait until dawn at least, when the soldiers would be stirring from their tents. Only then could he get an idea of how many were camped here, ready to cross the Borders and attack the Kingdom.

Quintus landed silently in a tree at the center of the camp, gazing thoughtfully down at the glowing embers of the scattered fires. Perhaps, he thought, it was the army of this Alvar whom the prince and the swan had spoken of.

That swan. Ah, now. There was another thing. Here he was, rushing back to make a report to Falak, but exactly what report was he to make when he arrived? Was he truly to believe the swan and the Author were one and the same? He couldn't countenance it himself. And he had no wish to appear a fool to his leader, or even to King Melanthius, whom he held little enough respect for anyway. He made a swift decision that he would tell only the cold facts, the words he had heard and the things he had seen. Nothing more. He would have faith in his leader, who would accept the truth of things with his usual cool reason; Falak would not blame Quintus, who was merely the messenger of the news.

Dawn came tiptoeing quietly over the horizon, the colors of it spreading thinly through the trees. The light cut weakly through the drizzling mist that hung about the trees like ghostly garments. Quintus cast his eyes upward and saw the moon, full and large, losing its luster as the brighter sun slowly outshined it. Men had been gradually emerging, waking, speaking in low voices. A few began to prod fires back to life. Quintus spotted a large man walking purposefully across the camp, his bulging muscles and flame of hair setting him apart from the other men. The owl knew whom it must be even before he heard another man call to him as he passed: "Alvar! How long are we to wait here for the prince?"

Not a challenge; at least, not quite. Quintus allowed himself a smug "hmph!" of pleasure to see that Alvar's soldiers questioned him. What could be better to see than dissention in an enemy camp? That was sure to make Falak happy.

Alvar stopped and turned slowly to face the man who had spoken to him. He didn't speak. The man decided the silence was an invitation to question his leader again. "The prince could be dead for all we know, and his sister with him. If they are deep into the Wild Land and have not been seen these three weeks, surely we cannot believe they will ever return. The creatures of the Wild

Ashlee Willis

Land may have"—and here his voice dropped and he sent a watchful glance over his shoulder—"they may have killed them—eaten them! Perhaps worse."

"Worse?" Alvar spoke now, his voice steady. "I pity the thoughts in your head, man, to think of things worse than being killed and eaten." He gave a cheerless smile and made as if to turn away.

"Plenty of things are worse if you listen to the stories that are told, Alvar," the soldier puffed up indignantly. "The Wild Folk can do things to you ... to your body, and your mind that would make death seem like a gift." A crowd of soldiers had begun to form silently around the two men, listening.

"The Wild Folk do these things?" Alvar turned again, a hint of warning in his voice. "You refer to the Wild Folk—the ones who are willing to fight with us? Who have come out from hiding for all these ages to help us overthrow a king who has little to do with them?"

Doubt crossed the man's face now—perhaps a trace of shame. Quintus knew shame in the face of a leader, and he recognized it now with a bitter pang. Yet the man opened his mouth to continue.

"We don't know for sure –" he began.

"I will stop you there, my friend," Alvar's words were not angry ones, but the mere sound of his voice seemed to hold an unspoken threat. And if that hadn't worked, Alvar's face surely would have. He took a step nearer, his eyes boring into the soldier's. "We will have no words said against the Wild Folk who aid us, not from you, nor any one of you." He threw a dark look into the crowd of soldiers surrounding them. "And you," he pushed a large finger into the man's chest, "will await my command of this army. Now fix some breakfast there." He finished with a wave of his wide hand toward the fire, his anger gone as suddenly as it had come.

Quintus could now see the size of what Alvar called his army. It was really no army at all, he thought with relief. Between two and three hundred men; nothing to concern Falak greatly. He had no idea how many of the Wild Folk would come to help, and he had to admit to himself that part troubled him. The Wild Folk had stayed in their forest and their tree-thickened land of exile for ages—were scarcely heard of or seen. Quintus could not even remember what sort of creatures they were. Yet the traitor Nocturne had told the prince that the folk of the Wild Land spoke of the Author now, after all these long years. They *stirred*.

Yes, it troubled him.

He had seen enough. With a swish of black wings, he took to the sky.

* * *

Posy had never had such peace, or such rest, as she had that night. The glade seemed a place through which life flowed. When she lay on the dark mossy ground, after the Author had left them, she felt she could not tell the earth's heartbeat from her own. All seemed right, and no pain she had felt before now mattered. She and Kyran were together, and alive. They had found the princess, and she would soon be well. The Author had come to them, spoken to them. Her sorrows seemed so far away. Nothing could touch her in this place; not tonight.

Tomorrow, she thought fleetingly, her eyes drooping toward blissful sleep—*I suppose I will worry about tomorrow when it gets here.*

Trumpets sounded as Queen Valanor stepped onto the great balcony overlooking the Judgment Square. A small enough space; not meant for the numbers that had assembled and crowded here now, surely. But then, the Plot had not been written with this part in it, she thought bitterly. Her eyes narrowed as she gazed down at the two creatures held in chains below her. *Centaurs.* She didn't even like to think the word, and she refused to say it. "Monsters" was more apt. Misshapen beasts that had trespassed into the sanctity of the Plot. They had been banned, yet still they crossed the Borders.

These two were some of the few who had survived the battle in the Wild Land several weeks earlier. They had formed yet another band of fighters and attacked a Border army. The queen tasted the sourness of scorn at the thought of such blatant disobedience and disrespect. Thankfully, they had failed miserably. The queen nearly laughed to recall how simple it had been to capture them. One of the centaurs turned his head to cast a look up at her, crystal blue eyes like razors searing through her with their contempt, white-blond hair flashing bright as a challenge.

Her laugh caught in her throat and dissolved.

"Send them to the prison with the others for execution."

CHAPTER TWENTY-SEVEN
Escaped and Escaping

The Kingdom never had seasons, of course, Kyran had told Posy. How could they, stuck in time as they were? They had only one season, a sort of truce between winter's end and the beginning of spring, which merely replayed over and over within the Plot each time a reader read their story.

But here in the Wild Land there was no such truce, no in-between. Spring thrust from the earth and sprung from the branches in a frenzy of life, as if eager to prove itself. Posy awoke to bursting shades of green everywhere she looked. When she turned to see where Kyran went, she saw that he was sitting cross-legged on the ground near where he had slept, his arm draped over the shoulder of his sister, who was now herself sitting up and awake, looking very tiny and frail next to her brother.

Posy's heart leapt at the sight. She admitted to herself that she didn't know what to expect from this princess for whom they had come so far and done so much. "But she is Kyran's sister," she whispered aloud to herself, "and I will love her for that if nothing else." She straightened her rumpled dress as she stood and combed her fingers through her tangled curls, suppressing a groan at the thought of what she must look like.

"Posy!" came Kyran's animated voice when he saw she was

awake. "Come!"

Posy walked to them, her eyes on the princess' face. It was a lovely face. She had violet eyes, as light and gentle as Kyran's were black and fierce. Her small pale face with its sharp chin seemed childlike, and her eyes large within it. She was slender as a reed, and golden ropes of hair hung around her shoulders and down her back in soft snaking curls.

Posy curtseyed as gracefully as she could, and as she knelt forward, she felt her dull brown hair brush her cheeks. Her ears burned as she thought of the contrast she must make to this princess, and suddenly she was conscious of Kyran gazing steadily at her. She rose from her curtsey, keeping her attention upon the princess, avoiding Kyran's eyes.

"Princess Evanthe," Posy found her voice, although the words came in a sort of whispering croak.

"Please," Evanthe said quickly, stepping lightly toward her, "please don't do that! I can't stand it, my dear!"

Posy looked at Kyran in a moment of confusion.

"She does not wish you to bow to her, Posy," he explained with a smile. "Not after what you have endured to save her. I have told her everything this morning while you slept."

"Everything?" Posy asked, able to think of nothing else to say.

"Well ..." Kyran winked at her. "Everything she needs to know."

Posy looked down quickly and felt her face flush again.

"Brother!" Evanthe exclaimed, her voice bubbled with a hidden laugh. She walked to Posy's side and took her hand, her expression becoming solemn. "Kyran has told me how faithfully you searched for me. Indeed, he told me you were the one to begin the journey in the first place! How can I thank you, my dear? I know I never can."

"Oh," Posy shook her head, "I—" Why could she think of nothing to say?

Evanthe's small warm hand on hers gave her unexpected comfort, and Posy raised her eyes to the princess' face. "I would go to any length to save someone so close to Kyran's heart," Posy said, not knowing where the words had come from.

Evanthe nodded in understanding, her crystal eyes bright. "Well, he loves you. That much is clear," she said calmly, to Posy's utter surprise and discomfort. "I suspected it, when he spoke to me of you, but I had only to see him looking at you just now to be sure of it."

This is the princess, Posy reminded herself, *who says and does things that no one else dares.* She shouldn't have been so shocked at Evanthe's stark words.

"But we will say no more of that now," the princess continued with a smile. "Kyran tells me you both spoke with the Author, and we have somewhere to be?"

"Yes," Posy hesitated. "But, should you not rest for a while yet? You've been through so much!"

Evanthe's gaze fell, and a shadow crossed her face. "I have seen much sadness," she agreed, then lifted her head. "But nothing worth jeopardizing the future of the Kingdom and the Wild Land. We must go."

The swans the Author had sent in the night stepped forward as if summoned from the edge of the trees. As they came close, Posy saw how large they were—many times the size of swans in her own world—and how powerful their wings looked.

"One for each of us," Kyran said, reaching out a hand to stroke the neck of the one closest to him. He helped Posy and Evanthe mount two of the swans, and in another moment was astride his own. "And now to Alvar and his army," said Kyran resolutely.

The swans took wing, rising swiftly above the tiny glade, and in no time the place where so much magic had happened was only a speck below them, and then, at last, no longer visible at all.

* * *

King Melanthius strode from his tent and toward his troops, who lined the field for inspection. He had slept little the night before—well, he had not slept at all, really. He, his Chief Advisor and two more close council advisors had been closeted within the heavy drapes of his tent, scouring maps of the Kingdom, talking of the best ways to defend against an unfamiliar enemy army and, as Falak felt were most important, methods of attack. They had discussed, questioned, argued, discussed again, until he had grown so weary of it, he barely knew what he was saying and had sent his advisors from his tent with words that were, he admitted, sharper than he intended. He had been half-asleep, yes, but something about the look in Falak's eyes as the king sent him away had caused a faint disquiet in his mind. Melanthius had snatched what seemed to be moments of sleep, his large body sprawled across his bed within the tent, and upon awaking thought nothing more of it.

Now he suppressed a yawn and tried to push away his bad humor as he walked through the camp among his soldiers, Falak flying alongside his shoulder.

"Majesty," Falak said quietly to him, "we must come to a decision from what we talked of last night." Melanthius' eyes closed for a moment as he tried to control his annoyance. He kept walking and did not answer the owl. He was sick to death of talking, especially to this confounded bird.

"I believe we must make a move before the enemy has the chance to make one," Falak continued.

"I am well aware of your opinions, Falak," the king said stiffly, wishing he could swat this provoking creature away from him as he might a fly. The corner of his mouth twitched at the thought of that.

"So? We have been encamped here for four days now, and all we do is inspect the soldiers every morning, watch them go through their drills, and keep a tight watch on the Borders. Two small skirmishes are all we have to show as yet of our dominance."

"And?" Melanthius growled, spinning now to face his advisor. Falak stopped short and was forced to land on the ground far below the king. Melanthius felt some pleasure at this; he knew how the owl hated to look up to anyone, even his own king.

Falak shot him a look of stark frustration, and said slowly, as if talking to a small child, "*And* ... these are good things in themselves, of course, Sire. But where does that leave us? Waiting. Waiting for something to happen to us. I say *we* are the thing that happens! *We* charge across the Border, find the enemy, and destroy it."

"Oh, as simple as all that?" Melanthius began walking back toward his tent now, the inspection finished. "And just how are we supposed to find this enemy army? I won't have half of my men wandering lost in the Wild Land for days on end searching for an enemy we aren't even certain exists."

"It exists," said Falak simply, orange eyes snapping. "And we need only wait for my scout to make it back and inform us of its

Ashlee Willis

location. But attack within the Wild Land is necessary. Victory will do us no good if all the men we have defeated appear again the minute a reader opens the pages."

"I see. Well, I will make that decision when I speak with your scout upon his return. Until then, we continue as we are. No!" he thundered, seeing Falak open his mouth to speak again, "that is the final word from your king. Go see to ... your duties." He waved his hand and turned from the owl.

My duties, sneered Falak to himself as he flew away. *My duties indeed. My duties are watching him, making sure he doesn't ruin everything, destroy his own pitiful Kingdom. Well, what does it matter if he does? And what's another day or so of waiting, I suppose? If the battle will only reach into the Wild Land, where death can take him and never let him come back, I will be content. And that failing to happen ... well, I will have to take matters into my own hands, then.*

Shouts erupted from across the camp, and Falak turned sharply to see what was the matter. He saw a group of soldiers wrestling with three centaurs bound in heavy chains. *Ah,* he thought with satisfaction, *here is diversion for the morning.*

"Yes, yes," he said, flying above the commotion. "Get them under control, men, or you will answer to me."

"Answer to you, eh?" King Melanthius' voice boomed up to him with sarcasm. "I suppose that thought puts more fear into their hearts than answering to their own king."

Falak felt a moment of surprise at being caught thus; he had thought the king was heading back to his tent. But his surprise quickly changed to anger at the king's words.

"Stop flying around in circles and get down here and tell me what this is all about!" shouted the king. "I never ordered these prisoners out to the battlefield. Your explanation had better be a good one."

"Majesty." Falak schooled his voice to respect, though he seethed inside. "I ordered it. These beasts have been sentenced to die, and I thought perhaps it would be wise to question them and get more information about the enemy's plans before they are killed. Perhaps"—he lowered his voice so only the king could hear—"they have news of your son or daughter."

The king froze at these words, the protests on his lips silenced. "Very well," was all he said. Falak turned from him, hiding his look of smug triumph, and faced the centaurs.

They were magnificent creatures, Falak admitted begrudgingly to himself. Large and strong, even the woman, with an overpowering beauty in their stormy countenances. To restrain them, Falak had ordered contraptions similar to halters, attached with strong lead ropes as would be used on an ordinary horse. The thought had crossed his mind to set up a temporary arena here at the camp and have the soldiers attempt to ride the beasts for entertainment—he knew centaurs hated to be ridden—but he had cast the idea aside, not wishing to distract the soldiers from the battle close at hand. With a quick glance, he noted the bruised and gashed faces and backs of the centaurs; he had given the order to avoid killing them, and to feed them very little. A hungry beast was a weak beast.

"Well, now," his voice came sharply. "Which of you will tell me what you know of the prince and princess? We must waste no time. Their father the king wishes to find them so they may not be caught in the middle of the ensuing battle."

The largest centaur, a male with a white body, light-colored braids and fierce blue eyes, pawed a hoof into the ground and snorted angrily. "You," he said slowly, "are a fool if you think we would believe a word from your lying tongue, Owl. And more of a fool if you think we would ever tell you anything you want to know."

Falak, used to hiding his anger, suppressed it now and merely nodded once, no emotion reaching his wide round eyes. He turned to the king. "May I have your permission to kill the female beast, Sire, if these creatures do not oblige us with information?"

King Melanthius laughed as if entertained. "By all means!" His massive shoulders had relaxed; he was enjoying this change of scene, and had no objection to Falak's cruelty if it was directed at someone else.

The female centaur turned as far as her bindings would allow and said, "Faxon, do not let this stop you. You know you must not say a word."

Faxon's eyes had clouded, and he stared at her as if in a trance, as she spoke. He shook his head vacantly at her and said only her name, quietly, "Caris."

"Faxon!" she repeated, more urgently. "Do you hear what I say? Let them kill me if they must ... remember what we agreed? My life is not worth the destruction of the Wild Land. We all agreed. Topaz as well." She motioned to the centaur at her other side.

"Well, what a touching regard you have for the Wild Land and your leader, lady horse," Falak said coldly. "Let's see what your friend does now ... will he save your life, do you think, even after such a lovely speech as that?"

Three soldiers surrounded her to hold her still while a fourth stepped forward to place his sword at her throat. It seemed Faxon could not speak, for he only stared at her.

"Now, will you tell us what the plans are in the Wild Land? The whereabouts of the children? The forming of an army? What about you?" he spoke now to the third centaur, standing silently by.

"I can say nothing." Topaz shook his dark head steadily. "And it is no good to threaten my life or anyone else's. Faxon knows this as well." He directed his golden eyes upon Faxon's face intently, as if willing a message to him. At last, Faxon came to life.

"Yes," Faxon said, "I will never speak to you. Do what you may." He turned his face to Caris, and she nodded to him bravely.

The soldier whose sword was at her throat looked to Falak, and Falak nodded almost imperceptibly, permission given. He tightened his grip on her and pressed his sword to her neck fiercely, preparing to draw it across. He had no more time than the half-second it took him to prepare, and he was dead. Topaz swung around and kicked outward with his back legs, straight into the soldier's chest. It sent him flying backward like a lifeless toy, and he fell to the ground with a solid thump, a heap of crushed limbs. His sword had gone flying from his hand as he fell, and Faxon reached a muscled arm to catch it smartly by the hilt.

The soldiers, Falak and the king all stared, dumbfounded, at the broken body on the ground. The silence lasted only a moment, and then chaos rained down on them all.

"Kill them!" screamed Falak at the same time the king was roaring Falak's name in fury. With the sword before him, Faxon came hurtling toward the group of soldiers. He killed three more before any of them knew what was happening, and then swung to slash through the chains holding Caris and Topaz. "Run," he told them, and they obeyed without a word, making for the Border at a flying pace.

Ashlee Willis

Faxon turned, however, and approached the king slowly. Neither of the two remaining soldiers moved to protect their king. Melanthius made a noise in his throat like gagging, his eyes practically popping from his face as he stumbled backward away from the centaur. "If—if you kill me now," choked out the king, "my entire army will be upon you. You cannot escape."

"I have no fear of you, nor your entire army." Faxon's face shone with anger. "I will tell you this: you have several of my fellow centaurs in the dungeon of your castle. Release them at once."

"At once?" stammered the king. "I have no way of doing that now ... I am here....and they—they are there."

"Send a messenger now, as I watch." Faxon took another step toward the king, sword pointed at his throat.

The king nodded to Falak, who had been watching, both incensed and horrified. Falak motioned to one of the two soldiers, standing and staring at the scene, and he began to mount a horse to deliver the message.

"Give him your ring," said the centaur calmly.

"My ... my ring?" The king's hand went straight to his other, and he placed his fingers upon his ring as if he would protect it.

"He must have proof the message came from you. You know that, King."

"Well, yes, I—yes, of course." Melanthius' face darkened, but he handed over the ring, and the messenger was gone.

"As for killing you," said Faxon, eyes never having left the king, "I will not do so today. But only our love of your son has saved you, and the knowledge that your death would bring him sadness. The next time I see you, you *shall die*." He backed away from the king and then turned to gallop across the field away from the camp, to the edge of the forest where Caris and Topaz had disappeared.

Several soldiers who had seen the commotion from the camp had come running to the outskirts of the tents, and they now arrived. "You fools!" screeched Falak at them as they gazed around in confusion at the bodies of their fellow soldiers. "You wretched good-for-nothing fools! What good are you now? *You are too late!*"

"Silence, Falak." The king, breathing heavily, hefted himself toward his tent.

"But, Sire!" Falak continued. "Will you not send soldiers after them?"

"No," the king answered, his voice a low growl. "You must be a fool yourself if you think I would do that after what just happened. One centaur, bound in chains, killed three of my armed men in a matter of seconds. No, I will not have them hunted. Young man!" he addressed a soldier near at hand. "Quickly get a horse and ride after the messenger I just sent in the direction of the castle. Tell him to come back to the camp at once. No message is to be sent after all."

Falak nodded in agreement. "Yes, yes, that is good thinking, Majesty." He nodded his owlish head quickly. "But I still don't see why –"

"Enough." King Melanthius turned slowly to regard his chief advisor. "I need no approval from you, Advisor. Indeed, I believe I have had enough altogether from you for now. You may return to the castle until I have need of you." And he turned his wide back to the owl and entered his tent, letting the drape sweep down in Falak's face.

"Wh—" began Falak incredulously, eyes round with disbelief. But he quickly snapped his beak shut and nodded to himself.

Ashlee Willis

Without another word, he took flight and soared upward, over the camp and toward the Kingdom. When he had gone over a hill and was out of sight, he veered west, instead of south toward the castle. He was through with the king. There could be no more bowing, scraping, pretending to be loyal. It was finally at an end, and he could openly pursue his own course.

"I will not return to that castle until it is mine," he said aloud to himself. "He will pay, oh ... he will pay," he said over and over until it began to sound like a spell, or a curse.

* * *

King Melanthius watched through the crack of his tent flap as Falak flew out of sight. He sighed as if a weight had been lifted off his chest. He didn't know how it happened, but whenever that owl was around he felt less of a king, and more of a child. It wasn't un-like the way his own wife made him feel. He shook himself like a huge bulky animal and ran his large hands over his face. "I'm the king here," he whispered to himself. "I need no advisor, I need no queen, I need no Author, to tell me what to do with my own Plot and my own people."

He saw in his mind the hatred in Falak's eyes, the disrespect of the centaurs, the derision in his queen's voice, the betrayal of his own children. His chest constricted painfully as fear gripped him. He had lost control somewhere along the way. *Where?* He asked himself desperately. But no answer came. So, he ignored his fear, and the small bit of wisdom he may have won if he had listened to it more closely. Instead, he did what came most naturally to him.

"Attack," his voice came loud, dying abruptly as it hit the walls of his tent. "If they will not listen and obey me, they must learn their lesson, even if it kills them. After all," he questioned the silver goblet on the table before him, "I must protect my Kingdom from the Wild Land, mustn't I? We must go to battle, we must attack. It cannot be too soon." He slammed a heavy fist down on the table before him, and then bellowed for a soldier.

"Have the army ready to march at dawn," he shouted into the man's surprised face. "We will find this pathetic Wild Land army and obliterate it, do you hear?"

CHAPTER TWENTY-EIGHT

Alone

Faxon, Caris and Topaz arrived at Alvar's camp that very after-noon, and found that Kyran, Evanthe and Posy had arrived only an hour or two before.

"And sent by the Author himself, so they say!" whispered one of the soldiers confidentially to Faxon as he led him to the tent where the children were resting. The centaur merely nodded.

The reunion was a happy one, and a sad one. Posy felt such an overwhelming sorrow knowing that so many of the centaurs she had seen only days before were now dead. She hadn't even known most of them. But their hearts had wanted the same thing she did, the same thing Kyran and Evanthe did, and it seemed unbearably cruel that they should be gone now because of it. Stonus, too, had died in the glade. Posy remembered his hesitance accepting Kyran and her, yet he had helped them still, led them, given them wise advice. The thought that he had died in their defense seemed too much to bear. But it seemed also to drive home the importance of this war, and their vital need to win it.

"Sadness is natural, child," Caris said resting her arm over Posy's shoulder, "so long as it flows out again with the tide. We must not keep it with us. Our friends knew the risk, as did we, and they were happy to lay down their lives for the Wild Land and the True Story."

"The True Story?" Posy asked shakily through her tears, looking up into Caris' beautiful, bruised face.

"Something far different from the Kingdom's Plot, I'm afraid," Topaz said, shaking his black braids. "It is the name the Wild Folk have given to our cause. It is the story the Author intended us to be a part of; not the one fabricated by the council and the king."

"Yes," Posy nodded, and again her mind heard the words the Author had spoken to them—the promise he had extracted from Kyran. "Yes," she said again more strongly. She would do much to see the triumph of the True Story. But die? It wasn't a question she wanted to ask herself right now. She still felt the tug of her own world in the back of her mind, and a sort of numb wonder that she had been so quick to forget it. She wondered if she died within this story, would she ever be able to return to her family.

Caris ran a soft, strong hand over Posy's cheek and smiled sadly at her. "We hope it will not come to that, child."

Only after she had walked away did Posy realize Caris had heard and answered her fear, even though she had not spoken it.

* * *

The prince and princess were closeted with Alvar, Faxon and Topaz for a long time within one of the tents. Planning, Posy knew. She tried not to feel left out, now the princess was here. What good could she do in planning a battle? Not so very long ago she *would* have been part of that meeting. Now that the princess was back, she felt herself seem to slide toward the edges of this story once more. Perhaps it was just her own feeling, she told herself. *The princess was bound to return eventually; that was our quest, after all!* Posy told herself. *It's not as if I haven't had time to prepare for this.*

She let her eyes wander through the camp. More men and Wild Folk showed up every hour, adding to their army's numbers. She watched as the Wild Folk hovered around the borders of the camp. They were uneasy around men, around fires and tents and clanging swords and armor. Their willowy figures, ferny hair, skin like moss-covered bark, seemed unreal in the shadows. No, they were not at home here. But they were here all the same; they were willing to fight for a cause that had become their own. Posy knew the Author must be somewhere in the Wild Land, stirring its creatures to action. He had told them bravery must be awakened. Well, it looked as if the waking had begun.

When Kyran and the others finally emerged from the tent some hours later as darkness was falling in the forest, Posy did not rush to meet them and question what had been decided. She made herself stay seated by one of the campfires and hoped her face didn't betray her sharp curiosity. With a pang, she saw Kyran glance her way and smile at her, but then turn and walk away somewhere within the camp. She had not missed the weariness and strain on his face, though, and she wished she were brave enough to chase him and find a way to wipe it all away.

Evanthe came to sit next to her at the fire. After a few moments, her soft voice said, "It has been decided. We will march tomorrow."

"So soon?" Posy couldn't conceal her surprise.

"It seems a couple of soldiers spotted one of the owls spying on the camp. He will already have told the king our size and location. We really have no choice, for they will surely attack us within a day or two anyway."

"I see," said Posy, her heart sinking. It had to come to this. It had to, she repeated to herself silently. *But I want more time. I need more time to be with Kyran. I can't leave him yet. It will rip my heart in two.* She knew, somehow, that the end of this war, whatever the outcome, would be the end of her time here. She let out an abrupt, involuntary sob. The princess lifted her slender arm to place it around Posy's shoulders. She squeezed her tightly and said, "I understand, darling. You may not think I can, but I do."

Posy wanted only to shake Evanthe's arm off her, to shout at her. But she knew she couldn't do that in the face of such kindness. She stood up, and the princess' arm fell away from her. "Thanks," Posy said through clenched teeth, holding in her tears. "I just ... I can't ..." She shook her head. Why finish? She couldn't even explain it to herself. She turned to walk away into the darkening trees, away from the camp. She had always hated for others to see her tears. And she had many of them to shed now.

* * *

Posy awoke, stiff and chilled to the core, staring into blackness. She had wandered outside of the camp, crying until she knew her eyes must be red and puffy and her face blotchy. Into her mind had crept a memory, a time a few years ago. It was a night like so many others, and Posy could hear her parents' angrily raised voices down the hall. She had wept desperately, face pushed into her pillow. Posy knew now, looking back, that she had been trying to hide the sound of her crying from herself more than from anyone else in the house.

That night had been a strange one, and maybe something evil had descended on their house. But for some reason, when Posy's tears had run out, she got out of her bed and crossed the room. She turned on her small yellow lamp. Her mother had put the lamp in her nursery when she was a baby. Now it was on her dresser and out of place with its frilly gingham border in her 13-year-old bedroom. She had walked to the mirror. She had leant in, hands flat on her low dresser-top, her face inches from the mirror, and stared into the face of her reflection. Dark shadows, magnified by the lamp beside her, pooled under her eyes, and her young cheeks had looked hollow, like those of an old woman. An idea, more than words themselves, came into her mind then. *Grief,* it said to her, *must change a person into something awful.*

Aloud, she had said coolly to her reflection, "I hate you."

Unbelievably, her tears stopped after that, as if a well had dried up. She lay at night hearing her parents argue, listening with a sort of cold observation that turned out to be short-lived. She wasn't old enough, nor had she seen enough, to become so hard—not yet. And her tears came back a few months later. But she hated to cry unless alone. She hated to think of anyone else witnessing the secret distortion of her face in such horrible sadness. And she never again would go near a mirror while crying, or after, until she could feel her face fall safely back into the face she knew.

She sat beneath a tree, leaning against its smooth trunk, so deep in remembrance that the forest was far away. She had finally sunk into sleep, like a refuge to drown in, and she awoke now to true night. She couldn't even make out the dancing orange dots that would have been campfires through the trees. All was silent, and a sudden bitter and painful thought shot through her: *No one has even remembered me, or noticed that I've gone.* She stood up, more angry than sad now, and strained her eyes fiercely into the shadows, trying to see something, anything. The thought crossed her mind that she should be afraid, but she barely had time to work up any fear of her situation before she heard, quite close to her:

"Now, if you stay still and keep quiet, this will be quite painless."

Ice shot through Posy's veins. She opened her mouth to scream, hoping desperately that someone in the camp was awake to hear her, but a rough, foul-smelling hand roughly clamped down on her mouth before she could utter a sound. She began to struggle violently in the steely arms that came around her. The man made a *tsk*ing noise. "Well, that's too bad, that is," he said in mock regret. "I thought you was a smart girl, especially escaping like you did from the castle. But I see I was mistaken. Tie her up, Lem."

Two of them, at least. Perhaps more. She had no chance of escape unless she could get her mouth free long enough to scream. It was her only hope. She fought fiercely, twisting and thrashing, trying to slip out of the man's grasp. But his hands were like iron clamps on her arms—she could feel the bruises already tender there.

"I did warn you to keep still, lass, and I don't warn twice. You're lucky I said it once, you are."

It was the last thing Posy heard before what must have been a large fist smashed into the side of her jaw, sending pain through her like an explosion, and blackness darker than the night bursting in her head.

Ashlee Willis

CHAPTER TWENTY-NINE
Preparations

Dust swirled in the opening of Kyran's tent as Evanthe threw back the flaps and swept in. She knelt next to the cot where he slept and shook him gently. No need for haste now, she thought sadly, and took a deep breath as he rolled over and looked at her. He sat up, and his sharp black eyes immediately saw what she was carrying draped over her arm.

"Posy," he said, snatching the cloak from his sister. "Evanthe?" He stood quickly and began to head for the door of the tent without waiting for an answer.

"Please, Kyran, wait," Evanthe called after him. "She is gone, my dear."

Kyran stopped before the opening of the tent, his back to his sister. She heard the harsh whisper of his voice, but she could not make out the words—only the bitter sound of them.

"She's gone back," he said at last, turning.

"Back, Kyran?"

"Back to her own story. Her own family." His face drained of color, and emotion. "I always knew she would."

"I don't think so." Evanthe stood and put a delicate hand on his arm. "Alvar has his men searching the vicinity of the camp already, but the place where they found her cloak showed signs of a struggle. See, her cloak is torn."

"Curse him," Kyran hissed, and Evanthe didn't know whom he spoke of. He shook off her hand and burst out of the tent.

Alvar was standing outside waiting for him. "Prince." His deep voice was gentle. Kyran rushed past, ignoring him. "There is nothing you can do," Alvar called after him.

Something in Alvar's voice made Kyran stop. The distressed look on his face melted away, and hardness replaced it. "It was my father."

Alvar's silence and sudden downcast eyes told Kyran the truth. "We followed Posy's trail into the forest. The horseshoe tracks surrounding the area had the king's mark on them. There was a struggle," Alvar hesitated, but continued, with a direct gaze at Kyran, "and we found blood on the ground."

Kyran made a silent, violent movement, his face like thunder. Evanthe thought for a moment that he reminded her of their father. Kyran looked around the camp, at the men emerging from their tents. The tree folk creaked as they lifted their acorn and mulberry eyes to their leader's face, their leafy hair whispering as it moved. The few centaurs in the camp, never far from the prince, turned their heads to him expectantly.

"Be ready, men," he called out strongly, his expression tight with pain and anger, "For we march within the hour."

*　*　*

Melanthius' dark eyes rested on the Borders. He watched the forest trees sway lightly in the breeze like a crowd of nervous creatures. They glowed ominously with the arrival of the morning sun.

Ashlee Willis

His son—no, he corrected himself—his enemies, would come from there soon. He knew from the many chapters and ages of his life, the many replays of the Plot, that these thoughts were of no good before a battle. He should be sitting hardening himself to the thought of impending death and possible defeat, but never admitting to his soldiers or even himself that anything but victory could happen for them here today.

What a fool he had been to put his trust in the owl, Falak, who had abandoned him. He realized he was putting most of the blame for this war on his Chief Advisor and the Council of Owls. And he meant to see that every other character in the Kingdom felt that way as well after all was said and done. But something whispered to him that if he had been a stronger king, a better man, a kinder father, perhaps none of this would have happened. But it was just a whisper; so easy to ignore that he had forgotten it before it had finished itself in his mind.

The king knew now that Falak would not be coming back. There would be no news from the scout he had sent out to the Wild Land. He knew also that he didn't have room in his mind to worry about those things now. A battle was at hand, and that very morning he had given orders for his men to be ready. If any of the tales of the Wild Land was true even in part, there was no telling what manner of creatures would emerge with his son's army.

His battle-hardened mind steadily banished any tug of feeling for his son and daughter. They had chosen to turn against him, and they would have to pay the consequences, however terrible. *And*, Melanthius thought, his mouth twisting into a shape some would have taken for a smile, *they would be terrible*.

* * *

The dungeons smelled of fear, death, and urine. Queen Valanor grimaced as the stench hit her like a solid wall, but she was no fainting maid. She hadn't brought a scented cloth to hold to her nose as most women would have, and she didn't regret its absence now. She was concerned about more important things.

The guard lifted a torch from its hold in the stone wall and led her down the uneven stairs. The light threw wild shadows on the pocked walls, hiding and revealing in turn the crevices, gaps and scratches etched in the ancient stone. A terrible, unbidden question materialized in the queen's conscience: were the shadows that hid things, or the light that revealed them, more horrifying? She shook herself angrily for thinking such superstitious nonsense, and stumbled on the hem of her dress. The guard turned quickly to steady her, but she irritably shrugged him away.

"Here we are, Your Majesty," he said at last. She hadn't counted how many narrow passages they had come down, how many crooked stone staircases they had descended, but Valanor knew they were deep beneath the castle's foundation. The hall they were in was the darkest and most foul smelling of all. It was lined with cells on either side. The guard passed a half-dozen empty cells before stopping and holding out the torch toward one of them.

"Ah," breathed the queen, staring at the shadowy heap in the far corner. "Here she is at last. The usurper *princess*. How much trouble the Kingdom has had since her ill-fated arrival! More trouble than we have had in a thousand years, I think. Pity we couldn't have captured my daughter or son along with her."

"The king's orders, my lady," said the guard.

272   Ashlee Willis

"Yes, yes, I know he wanted her for some reason. I wonder if his advisor put him up to it? Ah, well. I'm sure there is some explanation." *Though he felt no need to inform his wife of his reasons,* she finished to herself bitterly.

"You want me to wake her?" the guard asked eagerly.

"Is she sleeping?"

"Unconscious probably. I believe she had rather rough handling." He grinned.

"She had better not be dead, or the ones who killed her will also die."

That wiped the grin off his face. Now it was the queen's turn to smile. "No," she continued, "do not wake her. Bring food and water for her, though, and if her condition is bad, bring the physician down to see her as well. Now take me away from here."

When the queen was safely above ground, and the guard back at his post, he said to one of his fellows, "Who'd a thought the queen would have such a compassionate heart, eh? She was threatening to kill anyone who harmed the prisoner girl. Wonder why she wants her in prison in the first place, then, if she feels so sorry for her? She even thought to bring the physician down to tend to her!"

"You dolt," the other guard sneered at him. "Of course she doesn't want the girl alive out of sentiment! You haven't got a brain in that head, do you? She wants the girl alive for the ceremony. They're going to sacrifice her!"

* * *

Posy woke to searing pain and the faraway snapping sound of a whip. Her whole body ached and her head and jaw throbbed with a pain she hadn't known was possible. She released a groan that was more like a cry, but making the sound only sent more waves of pain through her head. The place she was in was dark as a moonless night, but from the feel, it was a close place, and from the smell, a vile place.

Again, she heard the whipping sound. It echoed as if coming from down a long corridor. This time she heard taunting shouts and laughter with it. She hoped it wasn't the captive centaurs that were being beaten, but she feared her hope was futile.

A dungeon, she thought. *That's where I am.* She tried to think of the world she had come from. Was it really a different world than this one? She grasped her head and tried to think through the steadily throbbing pain. *I had a mother once. And a father. A sister as well.* She tried desperately to remember them, and for a moment their faces floated in a sort of unfocused blur before her eyes, but her mind didn't have the energy to keep them there, and they floated away again out of her reach. The old fog had reached its fingers into her mind again, and she knew she must be within the Kingdom.

She wanted to cry, but knew that would make her head hurt even worse. And she remembered that crying was what landed her here in the first place. Running into the forest alone ... what had she been thinking? And why hadn't Kyran come after her?

"Author!" she said aloud, though it sent bursts of pain erupting in her head. "If you wrote this story, you can hear me. I'm sure of it. I'm one of your characters now, whether you wanted me or not. So help me! Can't you write something that makes this story turn out for the best? I thought," she faltered, her voice breaking. "I thought you wanted to help us."

It felt like talking to herself, and again, she had to choke down the urge to cry.

Then she noticed that she could see. Only a little, but enough to make out hazy shapes. She searched around and saw that her cell had a tiny barred window, and the light was coming from it. The moon shone through it and cast a misshapen square of light onto the dusty floor in the corner of the cell. The moon must have been there all along, she thought; it had just been behind the clouds. She stared at it, enormous in the night sky, and two eyes seemed to gaze at her from its surface. One of them winked at her.

Posy's eyes widened. So was this it? Was this the chance the Author was giving her—this small square of light? She knew she had no room to complain. She had to spend her energy on using this chance for the best. She looked at the place the light fell. There was nothing there. Dirt, straw, something that looked disturbingly like bloodstains, dried and blackened upon the uneven stones. She walked to the corner, every muscle in her body crying out. She stubbornly ignored the pain and got to her knees upon the hard cold floor. She ran her hands through the filth there, rubbing her palms against the floor for a sign—any sign. She reached up to the bars of her cell, shook them, twisted them, beat at them with her fists.

The moon disappeared behind a cloud once again, leaving her in darkness. Posy felt tears on her cheeks. That was it? That was the chance she had been given? Her body sagged in disappointment, and she sat with her back against the stone wall. That's when she felt it. Only a slight movement, a tiny noise—barely discernible. She turned quickly and ran her palms across the wall she had just been leaning on. Yes, the stones were crumbling there. A larger portion of the rock teetered back and forth like a loose tooth in a giant's mouth. She jammed her fingers into the crevices around it and pulled. Nothing happened.

"Fight," a voice said, just as it had when she fought her way up through the water of the Glooming. But this time the voice was hers. The Author didn't need to urge her to take this chance, not this time. She kept tugging at the stone, kept scraping her nails at the tiny crumbling rocks around it until she could feel a warm trickling and she knew her hands had begun to bleed. Even then she didn't stop. At last, the larger stone gave way with a loud scraping noise and fell onto the floor of the cell.

The moon peeked out from behind the gray night clouds, and Posy cast her eyes up to its eyeless face once again. "Thank you," the words came on a breath. She found there was just enough room to squeeze through where the stone had been lodged. A moment later, she stood panting outside of the prison.

But where to go now? she asked herself with mounting apprehension. She had been carried to this place unconscious. She had no idea where she was.

Why, that's easy, dear, said a strangely familiar voice. Posy felt a gentle cloud of mist settle around her.

"You!" Posy exclaimed, relief flooding her.

Yes, I, the mist admitted cheerfully. *Now, I will take you wherever you want to go, but I must tell you, I suggest you make your way to the tower, to where the owl performed his magic to bring you here. That's the only way you'll ever be able to get back, you know. I'm sure of it. Why, I was there the day he pulled you from your own world.*

"Oh, well ... I don't know." Every part of her wanted to rush to Kyran's side as soon as she was able.

This may be the only chance you have to visit the owl's tower alone, the mist encouraged.

"Yes, very well," Posy said at last. "You may lead me to the tower. But," she added with conviction, "I have no intention of going home yet."

* * *

The black cave echoed with the steady drip of icy water. A musty, damp odor hung in the air. Once again, Falak shivered and regretted that he had gotten so used to life at the castle, with his own large dark rooms and a roof over his head. It had made him soft.

"Now." He turned his large eyes onto the small group of owls with him. "If I give the signal, you each will lead your group into the battle for attack. But only if I give the signal. We do not wish to be part of this war if someone else can do our fighting for us."

"Yes, indeed," snickered one of the other owls.

"We need the king dead for certain, and if possible the queen, the prince and the princess as well. But the king must be our first priority. We will wait and see how the battle goes between him and his offspring, and if he is killed in the battle—well, it's one less thing for us to worry about."

A chorus of agreeing hoots answered him.

"But if the battle seems to be going in the king's favor, we will need to finish things ourselves. You know what to do when I give the signal."

Owlish heads bobbed up and down in eager comprehension.

"Well, then," Falak finished. "Let us be on our way. There will be no sleep *this* day."

The Word Changers

They made their way, one by one, to the narrow opening of the cave and dropped off the ledge into the gray of early morning. As they glided downward, more owls spilled from crevices in the mountainside and followed them, blackening the blushing horizon with shapes like winged arrows, flying toward the battle.

Ashlee Willis

CHAPTER THIRTY
The Battle Begins

Sneaking through the castle had been easier than Posy supposed it would be. She guessed that the Plot's upheaval and impending war were reasons enough for things to be awry. The halls were blessedly devoid of servants as the mist led her upward toward Falak's tower. Lack of food, exhaustion, and the aches in her body and head made her feel a sort of nervous confusion. She wasn't sure what she would do when she reached the tower. The mist had said she needed to find the way she had arrived so that she would have a way to return to her own world. But she wasn't at all sure she even wanted to return. She could barely remember her own world, and the ones there that loved her. She did see Kyran's face, clear and sweet as a song in her head, and it was more real to her now than any other family she had known.

Hurry, hurry, dear, the mist urged. *There is no one about, that is true, but it is only a matter of time before your absence in the dungeon is noticed.*

"Oh." Posy hadn't thought of that. She rushed up one last twisting staircase, recognizing the tower in which she had once visited Falak. It seemed so long ago now. She pushed the heavy door open and peered cautiously into the great high-ceilinged room.

Here, here, called the mist as it floated soundlessly across the room toward the towering row of shelves on the far wall. *There must be something here somewhere.*

Posy felt her jaw drop as she walked across the room. The shelves were crammed full of glass bottles of every shape and size, filled with liquids and gasses of every color she had ever seen—and some she hadn't.

Do you see anything that looks familiar?

"Familiar? How do I know?" Posy felt herself becoming desperate, and a little irritated. How was she to find what she needed? Nothing was labeled. Even if it had been, it probably wouldn't have helped.

You won't know until you look, the mist said sternly.

"All right, all right," and Posy leant in toward the shelf, wishing she had remembered to take a torch from one of the walls. Only moonlight guided her now, coming from a high round window far above. But, she thought suddenly, moonlight had just led her to escape from the dungeons. She supposed it would be better to trust it than to complain.

That's when something on one of the tall shelves caught her eye. It was much too high to reach, and almost too high to see. But it captured her attention for some reason. It was a small round bottle with a sort of blue vapor swirling slowly within it. She knew immediately she had to see it better. After casting a critical eye over the ledge of the shelf, she put her foot on it and lifted herself to reach the bottle.

Ooh, have you found it, dear?

Posy stared into the bottle as if in a trance. She saw everything there, amidst the curls of blue fog. Not this world, but her own. She saw her town, her house, her own bedroom, and her parents and sister. Memories swam by in the bottle, jumped out at her like things alive, ready to pull her into them. They threatened to overcome her, and washed across her body like waves, making her shudder.

"Yes," she answered past the lump in her throat, tearing her eyes away from the visions. "I've found it."

Let's leave this place, then, quickly.

"Yes, all right," Posy agreed. She reached for a cloth lying on a table she passed and wrapped it around the bottle, then stuck it into the pocket buried in the folds of her skirt.

"What are you, exactly?" Posy asked suddenly, directing her question to where she had last heard the mist.

Whatever do you mean, dear?

"I mean, are you a sort of magic? Falak gave me a potion to take to make you appear."

Oh, no. That potion was not to make me appear. It was for you, so that you could hear me. For I've always been here. I suppose you could say I'm the spirit of the Kingdom. I don't go beyond the Borders anymore than the characters do. And nowadays I don't even go much beyond the castle walls.

"Why is that?"

I don't really know, darling. I only go where I'm wanted, I suppose. Where I'm needed. And the characters have forgotten me these many years. I'm afraid they have despaired—and it's ever so hard to hear me above the sound of despair, you know. So here I've stuck, in the castle. I used to guide people to greater things, but Falak has made me into ... well, now all I do is guide people through the corridors of the castle.

"Does the king hear you?" Posy asked.

Oh, not anymore. I don't speak to those who don't wish to hear. Even if I did, they wouldn't be able to hear me. The longer they block out my voice, the less likely they will hear me at all.

"I see," Posy answered, feeling a sadness she didn't understand. "I am sorry."

Oh, think nothing of it, dear, the mist returned with cheer coming back to its voice. *I have a feeling changes are afoot.*

* * *

It didn't feel much like an escape, for Posy saw no one as she left the castle. It was like a ghost palace, guards nowhere to be seen, the villagers locked up tight in their houses. She had to leave the mist behind, but she thought she would be able to recognize things enough to know her way, even in the chill semi-dark of early morning. She crept through the courtyard, out into the castle grounds near the stables where she had first met Kyran. The thought gave her a pang, as she remembered him as he had been then. Her hand sought the lump in her dress that was the bottle.

Posy kept a sharp lookout all around her as she continued, and she was soon beyond the castle grounds. The bottom of her skirt brushed the dewy field as she crossed it, and her eyes searched through the fog for the line of trees that was the edge of the Wild Land.

The sun had begun to rise at last, its weak rays burning away the fog hovering like a blanket over the fields. As the haze disappeared, Posy saw what she was looking for, and more.

She caught sight of the Border, and she saw the king's army. How many were there? A thousand, at least. No wonder the castle was empty of soldiers. She shivered. They were all standing battle-ready, facing the dark of the forest, waiting for something. They were silent and still, as an army of statues, and her spine tingled as she watched them. What did they watch for? And then she saw.

"Kyran!" Posy's voice screeched in her ears, but she barely noticed. She was running now, her breath coming in short gasps of panic. She saw Kyran and Alvar on horseback, emerging from the edge of the trees like spirits. She knew it must be them. She recognized Kyran's slender body and black hair, the way he held himself and turned his head. And no one but Alvar had such broad shoulders. Yes, it was them. The battle was beginning, and she was too late.

"Stop, stop!" she screamed from the hilltop, and realized she was weeping. If this was how it was all going to end …?

A familiar sound—like a cry— came from above, and sharp claws wrapped around her shoulders. Then she felt her body being lifted. She looked up through her tears and saw one of the giant swans that the Author had called to the glade. It was carrying her as if she weighed no more than a leaf. Downward toward the battle they swept, past the king's troops, over Kyran's slowly emerging army. The swan dropped her gently onto a wide thick branch of a tree, then it was gone. She wrapped an arm around the trunk for balance and looked through the thinly-budding branches to the battlefield. She had a clear view from here. She looked down the trunk of the tree and felt her arm tighten around it. She was much too high to get down unaided. Her eyes swept the field around them and, some distance away, she saw a small lake on the outskirts of the trees into which a river from the forest emptied. It had begun to sparkle like diamonds with the rising sun, and Posy had to turn away from its brilliance.

She watched as if in a dream as Kyran and Alvar rode out ahead of the army, and the king rode out ahead of his. The three men met midway and began speaking. Posy wished she could see Kyran's face now. She could see Melanthius', and it was carved in stone.

It wasn't long before Kyran and Alvar turned from the king and began riding back toward their men. The look the king threw at their backs was one of rage. *He looks like a child ready to throw a tantrum,* Posy thought, and shivered to think that this man held so much power.

Then the king did an unspeakable thing—something even Posy would not have thought him capable. Before Kyran and Alvar could make it back to their own army, with their backs still turned to him, Melanthius drew his sword and bellowed, "Attack! Attack!" He spurred his great horse forward as his army surged up around him.

Kyran turned swiftly, and Posy saw the surprise on his face, but he was ready in a moment, his own sword drawn. "For the True Story!" Alvar roared, and the men and creatures of the army cried back. There were a great many more in their number than Posy had remembered, and she was glad of it. A great clattering and creaking signaled their movement forward as they went to meet their enemies.

Posy watched from her tree. She had never felt this helpless. It was as if she was watching a play. If only she weren't stuck here. But what could she do? She saw the king's men in their strong shining armor, their helmets pulled low—a faceless army—and she knew she would never have been able to fight them. She watched now as Kyran did just that, swinging and hacking. Nothing Posy had ever imagined about battles did justice to what she saw now. It made her stomach churn, but her eyes wouldn't turn away from it. Swords slashing bodies, blood running thick, anguished cries of pain.

She had seen the centaurs fight the ipotanes, but it had been different from this. Now it was human flesh, and somehow her skin seemed to feel it too. Every nerve in her body was attuned and watching. Would these people come back to life when the Plot began again? They were fighting on the very edges of the Border ... hovering at the perimeter between the Wild Land and the Kingdom. Now on one side, now on the other. Who knew what would become of them?

It stretched on and on, or at least seemed to. What an eternal clashing of metal! Would the blood ever be washed from her eyes? Two or three times Posy had to lean out from her branch to be sick. She could feel the tears running down her face, but she didn't bother wiping them. Only more would come.

At last, she began to see a change in the battle, but not the one for which she felt every inch of her body straining, hoping. The creatures of the Wild Land were fighting with their souls, she could see that—but it wasn't enough against the numbers in the king's army. And they began to fall behind. She sought out Kyran in the throng of gore and saw exhaustion wiped across his face with the grime and blood of the battle. Her heart soared when she saw he appeared to be unharmed ... and then plummeted when she realized one stroke of another man's weapon could be the end of him. She wouldn't be able to bear losing him.

A horn sounded. Posy lifted her eyes to see where it had come from. Out of the lake behind her, a man's head and upper body had risen. He held a silver horn, and slung over his naked back was a bow and a quiver full of arrows. A merman.

Then many more heads began to rise from below the water ...

dozens, scores, hundreds! Both mermen and mermaids, armed with bows and arrows. They lost no time taking aim. For one panicked moment, Posy wondered for whom they fought. Then she saw they aimed for the flanks of the king's army, well away from any action where an arrow might hit one of Kyran's men.

Thank you, thank you, breathed Posy, and she thought she must have been speaking to the Author. Even amidst this death and impending defeat, there was hope, and a change only the writer of this story could have made.

A multitude of arrows arched through the air and rained down on the enemy like deadly falling stars. Before the king's army had a chance to regroup and defend themselves from a different angle, many of them were dead. King Melanthius turned bright red, and then pale, as he watched his men fall, and something like panic flickered across his face. Posy could see it even from a distance. It was perhaps more due to the king's panic than the loss of his men that the battle now turned against them.

A cry struck up amidst the fighting, and before long, so many men were shouting it that even Posy could hear it: "The Border is broken! The Border is broken!"

What? Posy couldn't wrap her mind around what it might mean. She watched as men fell on this and the other side of the trees, and it dawned on her. Death had been permanent only in the Wild Land before. Now it had spread to the Plot as well. Any who died in this battle would not be seen again. She knew with a terrible certainty that it must be true, and slow dread crept through her heart at the thought of it.

Posy felt her throat tighten as she once again sought out Kyran, but she couldn't see him. In dread, she began to look around for a

Ashlee Willis

hold so that she could climb out of the tree. There was none. The trunk was sheer up to where she sat. She cried out in frustration, then made a decision. She would have to jump. She looked down and tried to gauge how far it must be. Twelve feet? Fifteen? *Just do it,* she told herself, and before she could think and change her mind, she jumped.

Her next sensation was like being sucked into a vacuum, and her stomach felt like it had risen into her rib cage. Then a shock as her body slammed into the hard earth. Posy heard a sharp *crack,* felt horrible pain shoot from her ankle up her leg, and knew without a doubt she had broken something. She heard a scream of pain, which must have been her own, but even above her pain she could only think of the hindrance this would be to finding Kyran.

She immediately started forward in an awkward combination of a hobble and a sort of drag, making her way toward the slowing battle. She was agonizingly slow, and sharp shafts of pain shooting up her leg made her cry out with every step she took. But she had one thought overshadowing all the others—only to get to Kyran. What was a broken ankle or leg? There were people dying here, dying right before her eyes. It wasn't a book anymore, wasn't a story that could be opened and closed. These characters wouldn't come back to fill their roles when the next reader came, and if Kyran was one of them ... if he was ... No, she wouldn't think of it now.

Posy stopped when she got near the battle, and grasped a tree trunk for support. Peering out from behind it, she scanned the thinning battlefield. Many were dead or dying. She saw many of the king's soldiers lying where arrows or swords had struck them down. She saw the men and Wild Land creatures of Kyran's army lying still in the bloodied grass. A man with tree-bark skin and mossy hair groaned near her at the edge of the trees. When Posy looked down at him, he seemed almost to be melting into the earth. The creature turned its acorn eyes up to Posy's face and said, "He only weakens himself by killing us. With each one of us he causes to die, he strengthens the seal upon his own fate." Posy realized her face had contorted in fear, in horror, in pity, and in helplessness. She watched as the man disappeared, with only a mossy spot in the grass remaining to mark that he had ever existed at all.

A cry went up then, and Posy's blood ran cold at the sound of it.

"Fall back!" Alvar's deep voice bellowed above the chaos. "The prince has been taken!"

CHAPTER THIRTY-ONE
Change of Heart

And so he was. Posy saw midway across the battlefield three of the king's soldiers restraining the prince. She saw Kyran struggling in frustration. She saw his mouth move as he tried to shout toward where the king stood nearby. Melanthius gave no indication he heard his son; he made a slight gesture to one of the soldiers and the man turned to throw his fist forcefully into Kyran's stomach. Kyran doubled forward. They had taken his sword and shield and tied his hands with a thick rope behind his back. Melanthius nodded, and the three soldiers drew their swords and pointed them at Kyran.

"Good people!" the king's voice rolled across the field to where Alvar and his army had separated from them, and now stood apart. "Lay down your weapons and surrender, and the prince will not die. Promise to obey me, your king, and return to the Plot, and I will spare his life."

Alvar's great shoulders dropped a fraction, but his face did not reveal his defeat.

"If we drop our weapons, you must abide by your promise, Melanthius. If you do not, you will die."

"Oh!" the king laughed. "Such an insolent threat from a conquered man. And a rather difficult thing to accomplish when you are surrounded by an army twice your size, weaponless."

"It takes but a moment to lift up a weapon, and another to loosen a deadly arrow—and that is all the time I would need. If I am unable to do it today, another would do it tomorrow, I assure you." Alvar's voice held a deadly intensity as his hooded eyes bore into the king.

Alarm flickered through Melanthius' eyes just before his features hardened and he bellowed, "Drop your weapons! I am the king, and what I say, I will do."

Silence, then, until Alvar nodded his head, eyes still fixed on the king. Then the men and Wild Folk and other creatures of the army laid their weapons down in the grass before them. Posy began to cry, watching their faces, for they lay down much more than weapons.

The king's army swiftly surrounded them, pushing them forward toward the king, and away from their weapons, which lay scattered on the grass.

"Well, now," Melanthius visibly relaxed. Then he squinted at the hill that sloped upward toward the castle some distance away. A small group of people made their way down it on horseback. As they got closer, Posy could see it was several castle guards. Queen Valanor sat astride her horse among them, tall and rigid. The sun caught a strand of her white-blond hair and seemed to make her whole face and head glow.

She would look as beautiful as an angel if I didn't know differently, Posy thought bitterly.

As they cantered through the crowd, the soldiers made way for them, and the queen graced them with her cold smile. The king held out his hand to help her dismount. "I see you finally managed to do something right," she said under her breath as she smoothed out her dress. The king turned a blank face away from her.

Posy watched from the edge of the trees. They were not far from where she hid, but she knew she had to risk danger and get nearer. She made her way falteringly on her damaged ankle past the bodies scattered on the field. She tried to shut it out, somehow, but it was impossible. Her eyes were drawn to the faces of these men who would never see their own land again, and she fought down the sobs that rose in her throat.

She came to the edge of the great crowd of the two converged armies and pushed her way through the king's soldiers who surrounded the perimeter of the group. They barely noticed her, so rapt were they on the king and his family. She made it some distance before a man's voice clicked "Eh, eh" in her ear as a hard hand grasped her arm, jerking her to a stop. "No further than that, if you please." The man eyed her sharply, eyebrows drawn together.

He recognizes me! thought Posy with rising panic. But the man only shook his head and said, his voice disapproving, "I'd never have thought the prince was so desperate as to employ women in his army. A shame is what it is."

Posy let loose a silent sigh of relief as he turned away from her. She looked around her and realized she had gained what she wanted—a view of Kyran.

After the queen and king consulted quietly together for a few minutes, the queen held up her hand for silence, and announced, "We will be having a trial here, to determine the guilt of the prince Kyran."

"A *trial?*" Alvar roared.

"Why, yes." The queen didn't blink an eye at the outburst. "Oh—perhaps you think his guilt is so obvious we should forego the trial? Hmm," she pretended to consider. "Perhaps you are wise."

"The king has just sworn the prince's safety to us," Alvar continued, his anger rising. "A trial judged by the likes of *you* can lead to only one thing."

"Indeed?" the queen's eyebrows lifted. "And what is that?"

"His death," spat out Alvar with contempt. "And isn't that just what you've wanted from the start?"

"Silence him," the queen said calmly. "He has caused enough trouble already and will pay for it in due course."

Posy strained, but she could not see Alvar through the throng of people. She could hear a violent struggle ... then silence. Had they killed him? Her heart beat like the wings of a trapped bird within her rib cage.

It was then she felt something tickle her leg, feather soft. She looked down. Sitting at her feet was a tiny gray field mouse. It gazed up at her with intelligence and feeling she had seen before, in another creature's eyes, and before she knew what she did, she bent down and picked it up.

"Thank you," it squeaked, and leapt nimbly from her palm to her shoulder. "We do not have much time," it continued. "You must be ready for what will happen next. You will have but a moment to act."

"Ready for what?" she whispered, trying not to move her mouth.

"Ah, now," the mouse's voice seemed to smile. "That cannot be told. Does a character know at the beginning of the story where he will be at the end?"

"But then ... how am I to be ready?" Posy questioned.

"You must be ready for anything," the mouse breathed in her ear. "For *everything*."

Then the Author scurried down her dress like a flash and disap-

Ashlee Willis

peared into the tall grass. *Yes, the Author,* she thought. There was no mistaking him, whatever form he took. Posy allowed herself a small smile, for now she knew there was hope. Kyran looked up then and caught her eye, and he instantly mirrored her smile. It caught at her heart, for she knew he did it to assure her.

Be ready for everything? How was that possible? The Author never revealed the full plan to any of his characters. But then, she thought, wouldn't it be ridiculous if he did? The characters would lose hope ... or perhaps gain it too soon. She had to act on what she knew, on where and *whom* she was—not on a far-off ending that may change in the course of things anyway. The Author knew the end, and the characters would get there, but not until they began to do things *now* to make the pages turn. She must take the chance given her, however small—just as she had done in her prison cell.

"... death," the queen finished as Posy came out of her reverie. Posy's heart skipped a beat at that word, and her gaze searched the crowd, looking for a clue as to what had just happened. "You must, my lord," Valanor said to the king. "It was our daughter before, for no crime at all. How much more must it be the prince now, for all the wrongdoing he has committed against you."

So she was sentencing him to death, then, and Alvar had been right. She was trying to push the king into passing the judgment here and now, before he could change his mind. But the king had promised ... well, Posy knew it didn't matter. He wasn't a strong enough man to keep his promises. All the same, Posy glued her eyes to Melanthius' face as he paced before them. His boots thudded on the ground and his armor and sword clanked against each other. His face was thoughtful. Posy squinted at him. He was truly thinking about this, and she could see that it troubled him greatly.

It was the first hint of anything good she had seen in him, and her heart leapt up in hope before she could stop it.

Queen Valanor saw his indecision as well. "You must—" she began, but stopped short when the king turned a slow, hard gaze on her.

"I *must*?" he whispered, and the queen's eyes widened in surprise. A heartbeat later, her surprise slid swiftly into a gentle smile, and she walked over to him and put her arm through his. Posy reeled at the speed and ease of the change. Surely, the king could see it for the deception it was?

"You must do nothing you do not wish, of course," her voice came softly. Only those closest to them could hear. "But you know as well as I that the Plot requires a sacrifice or it cannot survive. And it cannot be just anyone. That is what is written, Your Majesty."

"Written? By the Author, do you mean?"

"No. For you are the author, husband. The ancient laws that hold the Plot together—that is where it is written."

And who wrote those laws? Posy wondered.

Then an unbelievable thing happened. Melanthius' eyes, as he gazed at his queen, changed. It was subtle—nothing even to detect by those who saw only surface things. But Posy saw it. It swam below the surface, in a dark and secret place, but she saw it all the same, recognized it for what it was. And she knew instinctively that it was a great change—a change that would save Kyran's life.

"Yes, I am the king, as you say," he said slowly. "We follow the Plot that was written because that is what we have always done. I cannot blame my son for wanting something different ... something more. Can I? After all, Queen, we have changed the Plot in many ways over these ages ... perhaps we have forgotten."

Ashlee Willis

"*Chosen* to forget!" shouted one of the Wild Folk from the crowd.

The queen tried to hide her panic and horror, but Posy could see she struggled. She opened her mouth once more, her pale face even paler than before, but the king stopped her.

"No, there can be no trial today. No sacrifice or death," he said, his voice strong with decision at last. "For I am no more innocent than my son. Nor, I think," he finished quietly, "are you, my queen."

The battlefield was silent, so silent that Posy began to feel tingling in her spine. She thought everyone must have stopped cold at such a sudden change in the story, by the person they least expected it from. They were frozen with disbelief. She saw that Kyran's face beamed through his matted hair and the dried blood on his face. Posy knew his joy was more for his father's heart than for his own saved life.

Someone cried out then. Posy didn't know if it was one of the king's men, or one of the prince's. She thought it was the first cry of joy at the king's words—the start of a celebration at this new peace. She was wrong. It was a cry of alarm, and it was not long before there were many more. Someone shouted—someone pointed to the sky. Posy cast her eyes upward and saw a black cloud darkening the sky, blotting out the sun, moving and pulsing like a living thing.

No, she saw clearly now. Not a cloud. Owls. Hundreds of them. And with their deadly talons spread, they descended.

CHAPTER THIRTY-TWO

Victory and Defeat

They went first for the king. A tightly-knit group of them made a straight line to him, bearing down on him until he lay on the ground, screaming.

Posy knew she had only a moment—that's what the Author had said. Only a moment to do what must be done. So she ran toward Kyran as swiftly as she could, forgetting the pain in her leg and ankle. She immediately crashed into the solid body of a soldier and went sprawling across the grass. She was up in an instant, a single purpose in her mind. When she reached Kyran, he was ready.

"Hurry, Posy," his voice was tight with desperation as he watched his father struggling, the owls so thick on him he was barely visible. "A knife, a knife!"

Posy cast her eyes around frantically. She didn't want to do it, but there was no other choice. She made for one of the soldiers lying dead on the grass not far from them, and pulled his sword from his lifeless hand. Kyran thrust his hands out and away from his back as she returned and she set the blade against the rope that bound them. If she weren't careful, she could cut him badly. Kyran had no patience for it, though.

"Just hold it steady," he commanded. Then he swept his arms upward against the sword. The rope dropped at Posy's feet. Kyran turned with terrible speed and seized the sword Posy held, saying, "Run. Into the trees. *Run, Posy.*"

He was gone in a flash. He lifted his sword as he went, then descended on the throng of owls assailing his father, hacking and swinging with strength that came from somewhere beyond his own body. Posy stood frozen for a long moment, watching him. Then his words hit her, and she ran.

Posy was only halfway across the battlefield when she was knocked heavily to the ground. She felt claws like knives in her back. She screamed. Rolling swiftly to the side, she bypassed the next swooping attack. She got to her feet as swiftly as she could manage, her ankle still throbbing dully, and struck out with her fist, the only weapon she had. It met with the side of her attacker's head. The owl lurched sideways, and before it could get its bearings and attack another time, Posy was running again.

At last, she arrived under the cover of the trees, and sunk into a bed of ferns to hide. As her breathing steadied and slowed, the pain in her ankle and leg grew. The places where the owl's talons had torn into her felt like paths of fire trailing down her back. Her body had a distant longing to lie down, to simply go limp, and fall into a dreamless sleep. But the pain that went through her in waves kept her body rigid and shaking.

"Posy!" she heard her name, and the sound of someone running through the forest undergrowth. She poked her head slowly out of the ferns.

"Evanthe!" she cried out as the princess fell to the ground next to her, and they wrapped their arms around each other.

"Oh," Evanthe exclaimed when she saw Posy wince. "Posy, you're bleeding!" Her violet eyes were wide with concern. "How did this happen?" Her gentle hands turned Posy around, and she gasped in shock.

"It's nothing," Posy said, turning back around quickly. "An owl attacked me before I could get here and hide. Anyway, there's nothing we can do about it now." She tried not to think of the inevitable scars that would remain.

"My poor dear," Evanthe said. Somehow, Posy always felt like a child with Evanthe, though she knew they were near the same age. It had given her a tinge of annoyance in these past days, but it was strangely welcome now, with pain and death and fear around her. She slipped her hand into the princess' and allowed herself a fragment of comfort.

The battle—the second of the day—went on. The cries and shouts of battle seemed almost too much to Posy. How much would they all have to endure before this would end? Yet this was different ... and it did not take the two girls long to see it.

Something happened that Falak had not considered. When the king had his change of heart, so did each of his men, many of whom had been hesitant about the prince's capture and death to begin with. Now instead of one army for the owls to fight against, there were two. A horrible—a fatal—miscalculation on Falak's part. But then, how could he have seen? How could he have possibly known? Posy admitted to herself that none of them would have expected it to come to this.

It was short work, really. The girls watched, hands clasped, as the owls were finally driven away. Posy wondered fleetingly if Falak had been killed, or if he would fly away to hatch plans once again in some dark faraway place. He had been evil from the start, and she had been too blind to see it. Yet he had been the one to bring her

Ashlee Willis

into this story, and she could never, ever regret that.

There seemed a horrible sense to it all; it looked like confusion, with the good and bad floating together, merging and parting. But all the pieces were there before her eyes. Posy had an odd, creeping suspicion that this thought applied to more than just these circumstances. Perhaps they applied to everything she had ever known or done. And if she could once see those scattered and broken pieces for what they were, guess at the sense and order of them, the whole world would shift and nothing would ever be the same again.

* * *

Kyran found them some time later. The sun was high in the sky; it could not be far past noon. Posy thought this must be the longest morning she had ever spent. He came into the trees, and when he called out to them, the two girls went running.

Evanthe embraced her brother. They looked at each other, and the thoughts ran palpable between them, though they did not speak. They had won, and won more than they ever dreamed. "Our father?" Evanthe asked at last, her calm voice belying the unease beneath.

Kyran's face became grave. "He has been seriously injured. He is being carried to the castle as we speak. You and Posy must go back to the castle as well. You will be safe there, don't worry. And our mother is not to be allowed from her own rooms."

"The king's soldiers agree to this?" Evanthe questioned, raising her eyebrows.

"Oh, yes," Kyran smiled grimly. "They are completely ours now, sister. I'm not so sure they wouldn't have joined us even if the king had not made the decision he did. The Wild Land has not been the only place of unrest and discontent."

"Good," the princess nodded. She glanced at Posy and gave her a quick smile. Then she walked a distance away from them, beyond the edge of the trees, discreetly waiting. Posy couldn't seem to lift her eyes. She looked down at the mossy forest floor. The smell of damp earth and green life was all around her. The smell of fear and blood was still on her, though.

"Don't cry, Posy," Kyran's arms came around her and he kissed her hair. "It's all over now, little one."

His words only made her cry harder. She wrapped her arms around him and tugged him as close as she could. Her fingers clawed into his back, her face pressed into his chest. She couldn't seem to pull him near enough to her. She felt the sudden urge to share a skin with him—nothing else would seem to quiet this strange mixture of sadness and joy she always felt when she was near him.

"Posy," he whispered, "when I found out my father had sent men to take you ... when I saw that you were gone ... I ... I think I might have murdered him right then if he'd been near me."

"No, Kyran," Posy shook her head against his chest. "You would never do that, not for anything. I've watched you, I know you ... and you love him. Don't you?"

He nodded silently, tears slipping past his dark lashes.

"Oh, Kyran," was all she could say.

When she pulled away from him, it was as if someone were pulling off part of her own body. It hurt far worse than a hundred talons in her skin, a thousand broken bones. How could one person need another so desperately? She had never known it was possible.

Ashlee Willis

"You must go back to the castle now," Kyran said with a weary sigh. "You must have your wounds seen to, and rest. I will be there soon."

"Can't you come now?" she choked out, feeling a sudden fear at leaving him once again.

"I have to stay with my men and clear the battlefield." He gently took her arm and began to walk with her out of the forest. "So much has happened here at this Border, Posy," he said distantly. "And now there is no Border at all. It is broken, and we are all the same. Nothing will ever be as it once was."

"No," Posy answered simply.

Kyran stopped and took hold of Posy's shoulders. He leaned down to kiss her softly. She melted at the softness of his lips. The difference between this incredible tenderness and the hardened warrior she had seen on the battlefield amazed her. It seemed like a beautiful thing, somehow, such a difference, and she loved him for it.

"I will be with you soon, love," he said again, his dark eyes looking into hers one last time. He turned to walk away.

* * *

Posy awoke to one great ache. She couldn't specify where the pain came from—it seemed to come from every inch of her. Her head throbbed, her muscles were tight, the skin on her wounded back felt horribly stretched and stiff as leather. She groaned and tried to roll over. She opened her eyes into the glare of the sun shining boldly into her bedroom. *Her bedroom?*

No, it was the princess Evanthe's bedroom. How it seemed like ages ago she had been here, yet it was only a matter of weeks. She gazed around the large high-ceilinged room at the tall windows, the white stone walls, the great rug before the fireplace that roared now with a fire. Posy forced her legs off the side of the bed and tried to stand. She found that her damaged ankle had been wrapped tightly and expertly, and though it pained her still, it felt much better. She walked slowly to the fireplace to stare into the blaze. How long had she been sleeping?

Eleven hours, that's how long! The mist descended upon her, swirled lightly around her shoulders.

"And where is Kyran?" Posy asked quickly.

Oh, he has come to see you many times, but he only peeks in so as not to wake you. He has snatched an hour of sleep here and there, but most of the time he is pacing around the castle, working and talking, talking and working. He has much to do now, dear. He is King Kyran now, you know—or will be soon.

"King?" Posy exclaimed. Happiness and dread seemed to hit her at once. "Oh! Has his father died, then?" Her heart beat faster, knowing the pain this would cause to both Kyran and Evanthe.

Oh, no, not dead. Injured, yes. Saddened, yes. But not dead. No, he listens to me now, does the old king—and not just to lead him down a hallway, mind. He listens to me telling him about the magic of the Plot. He grows well again hearing me whisper of the breathtaking possibilities that may now unfold. No one hears his thoughts, though—only me. He does not appear conscious to anyone—only I know what things are working and spinning in his mind while he lies in his sleep. And he knows, alas, that he can no longer be king. He does not wish to—and even if he did, they would not let him. The mist drooped gloomily.

"They? Who do you mean?" Posy asked.

Oh, the people of the Kingdom, of course, dear. The characters themselves! The mist leapt up cheerfully again and danced above Posy's head. *They insist upon crowning Kyran. They will have no other! And it will all be as it should be.*

"Oh, my!" Posy said. "How much can happen in eleven hours! But you," she said to the mist, recalling something, "you say Melanthius listens to you now? Does that mean you can leave the castle? Does everyone hear you now?"

In time, darling, in time they will, I have no doubt. Already I feel stronger every minute, and feel myself growing. Yet I will never be loud, you know—I cannot stand the thought of shouting at people! Oh, no. I must be heard because I am wanted only.

"We all want that, really, I suppose," said Posy with a sigh.

* * *

Kyran and Valanor faced each other in silence. Kyran's dark eyes saw a woman defeated, but too proud to face it; they saw a face of stone that bespoke of isolation and grief. And his heart felt sympathy, and even love, though she had caused him so much pain. He wondered what must have happened to her to cause such bitterness and unhappiness. He was sorry for it, whatever it had been, and wished he could do something to take the pain of it away from her.

Valanor's pale eyes gazed disdainfully at her offspring, and they saw a mere boy, though admittedly much changed since she had seen him last. Oh, he was the same as he had been on the outside with his black hair falling to his shoulders and his dark snapping eyes. But there was a certain strength in his eyes now, a determination in the way he held himself. Valanor thought bitterly that it was a pity his father had shown none of these signs. Her eyes traveled up and down the prince, assessing coldly. Any seed of hope she had in her past, any whisper of love she had ever felt, had been trodden on or scorned, and her only and strongest defense had proven to be this cold face, and this heart that felt ... nothing.

"I will forgive if you ask it, Mother," Kyran's voice came both soft and strong. "And I will love, even if you do not ask it."

"Love?" she scoffed before she could stop herself. "Such weakness. Love can lead nowhere, son, except to destruction and humiliation."

"Is that where it led you?" he asked quietly.

She could hardly stomach the look of sadness and sympathy in those black eyes. She turned away from him. "You may choose to do what you will with your love or forgiveness. I will never ask for either of them."

"Very well," said Kyran. "And so I will."

Instead of turning to go as she had expected, he paced over to her and grasped her long beautiful hand. He pressed it to his cheek and kissed it before she could protest.

When the door closed behind him, Valanor took long strides to the window and gazed blindly out across the green spring fields and budding trees. Her face contorted and she made a choking sound, clutching and pressing at her chest as if to keep something down that would escape.

Ashlee Willis

CHAPTER THIRTY-THREE
Forgiveness

Great doorways shining with embossed gold images, cobblestone floors that threw footsteps and voices off the lofty ceilings, stone walls with slits for windows that glimpsed the sprawling kingdom beyond. Everything was as Posy remembered from that first night she had been in the castle, when she had crept through the darkened passages to spy on the king and his councilors. Never mind that it was a few short weeks ago. Posy knew it had been an age past—another time completely—and that this was a new story.

It had been two days since the battle, and Posy felt much better, in part because she had been pampered and waited upon without ceasing since she arrived. Hot baths, beautiful clothing, and curls in her hair made for a wondrous difference. Her ankle had been bound tightly, and the physician had given her remedies to ease the pain.

But no matter how well her body mended, her spirit still felt tattered. *Why have I been brought here?* she thought bitterly. *Why have I been dragged through all this pain and love, which feel so much the same? What is the lesson in it all?* Her soul felt tired beyond imagining.

Now she made her way with the prince down the corridor that led to the king's chambers. Melanthius had been in bed since the battle; he had only just regained consciousness. His wounds had been many, and deep. The guard that stood before the towering door stepped aside silently as they approached, and they entered the room.

It was dark. The blinds were all drawn tightly against the sun, and only candles lit the chamber, throwing long shadows across the walls and the king's vast bed. The sharp sweet smell of burning herbs met Posy's nose, but underneath the odor she could smell sickness and pain. She imagined she saw the mist hovering quietly above the bed, just high enough to be hidden by shadows.

The physician walked forward from his place at the king's bedside. "He is awake, but seems to tire easily. Don't be long."

"No," the king's rasping voice addressed the doctor. "They must stay to hear all I have to say, no matter how long it takes."

"Yes, Majesty," the man bowed and quietly took his leave.

Posy grasped Kyran's hand as they made their way to the king's bedside. He was bandaged heavily—arms and chest, probably his legs, though they were hidden from view under the blankets. His face had long deep lesions, the scars of which would undoubtedly be with him for the rest of his life. Impossible to determine the extent of his injuries, really. Posy wondered how much of his weakness was due to guilt and regret more than any physical hurt. His shadowed eyes had changed from the man she remembered, and his large frame looked small and sunken, there in the bed heaped with blankets.

"First, my dear Posy, is you."

Posy started at the king's words. She hadn't realized he had even known her name.

"Yes, yes." He gave the suggestion of a smile. "Come here, child, and take my hand."

Posy walked closer and hesitantly took his bandaged hand in her own. The only skin she could see or feel were his fingertips, which were warm and alive. "There would be much to say to you if I could say it, child. But I am not a man for those types of words— at least not yet. I think if I ask you to forgive me, you would understand all the rest."

Posy felt a sudden indignant anger flare up within her. He could ask her this, after all that had happened? But she tried to ignore it, and forced herself to say, as kindly as she could, "Yes, I forgive you." For wasn't forgiveness more an action—a decision—than a feeling?

"I thank you," the king spoke sincerely. "For I do not deserve it, my child. And now ..." Melanthius' dark weary eyes turned to his son, standing solemnly behind Posy. "We must speak."

Posy knew the many things that might pass between them, and she knew she must leave them alone to speak them. She made her way quietly to the door. Just before she closed it, she turned and saw Kyran smoothing his father's hair away from his injured face. She could only feel the injustice of such mercy, and she turned quickly to shut the door behind her.

She waited in the wide corridor. A window alcove with hanging drapes was across the way, and she went to sit there and gaze out across the fields toward where she knew the Border was, and the Wild Land beyond. Yet there was a Border no more. Kyran had told her they were all the same now, Wild Folk and characters of the Plot. Were they, really, though? He would have his work cut out for him as king, reconciling his people, getting them to live at peace together.

Her eyes drooped with sudden weariness, and she leaned her

head back against the stone wall behind her. A moment later, she was swooping like a winged creature across fields and villages.

Things passed by her at an impossible speed, a sort of smearing cloud of memories. She tried to make sense of them, but she was flying too fast and couldn't slow herself. She saw flashes of beasts attacking in a darkened wood; ghostly skinless faces that stared with hollow eyes; the clash and gleam of swords on a battlefield; a loneliness that clutched her by the throat until she felt she couldn't draw another breath; the ripping sound of claws across flesh; the king holding a knife to the heart of his son with a smile on his lips that made Posy shudder even in her sleep. Then everything stopped abruptly. But before her mind could halt along with it, she was flying again. Now she saw a door slammed, heard the shout of an angry voice, felt the isolation of withdrawn love, and a brokenness that left her empty and raw. She had to escape. If dreams could kill, she was sure this one would kill her. The sky suddenly became glass, and she flew into it, wings flapping wildly, once, twice, then broke through with a horrible crash.

She was awake, but found she had not escaped at all. For she knew before she opened her eyes that everything she had dreamed was real, part of her past, or part of her future. So much pain—rivers of it, oceans of it. Would it pursue her the rest of her life?

Well, my dear, I suppose there are words I could say to you ... many of them. The mist floated through the drapes of the window. *But I believe you know the answer to your own question. And after all, I only ever tell people what they know already.*

"Well, not me," Posy answered angrily. "I *don't* know." She leaned forward to press her forehead against the windowpane.

Only weak people put the blame on another, my dear, and only faint hearts say they have no choice. You must learn to rise above the hurt that others have caused you. You must not remain a slave to it forever.

"I've tried," said Posy, tears coming to her eyes. "I've tried. I don't know what else I can do."

Oh, but there is more to do, you know. Because once you have risen above it, you still don't have freedom ... not until you love.

"I have to love the pain that I go through?" Posy asked skeptically. "I can never do that."

No, darling, not the pain, came the mist's patient voice. *But you must love the giver of the pain.* It dissolved through the glass of the window and merged with the spring wind that wafted and twirled around the castle like a carefree child.

Well, wasn't that what Kyran was doing now? For Posy had seen the way he looked at his father, heard the way he spoke to her of his mother—and they were both the givers of his pain. She felt she had no right to withhold forgiveness from her parents, when she saw how completely Kyran had forgiven his own. She knew also—something faint and secret whispered to her, something she had ignored for a long time—that her parents had never meant to give her pain—not like Kyran's.

Melanthius and Valanor had made mistakes, taken evil counsel, deceived, mistreated and killed. Any love they might have had for their children was drowned in their own schemes and trickery. But it didn't matter to Kyran, for he had a different love now, one that didn't need anything in return. Posy knew it, because she knew him, loved him, could read his face like the dearest story she had ever read.

Yet how could she know him so well, and not understand where this strange mercy had come from? What had he found that she couldn't?

The door to the king's chamber opened, and Posy peeked around the drapes to see Kyran's dark head ducking quietly out of it. When he reached her, she didn't give him a chance to speak.

"Why, Kyran?" she burst out. "Why do you still love him? It's not … it's not fair."

"Fair?" and he gave a sad, sighing smile. "Oh, Posy. But that's what mercy is. If everything was fair, mercy would have no place in this or any other world. For it has nothing to do with justice."

"But it's not just mercy. Mercy I could understand … but … but there's more. You *love* them, your mother and father, and they have hurt you so badly. I have hated them for your sake. *Why don't you hate them, too*?" her voice broke in anger.

Kyran paused, gazing at her for an unbearably long time before he said, "Because there is no room in me for something so poisonous. Such a thing does me more harm than it could ever do good. Can't you see that? If mercy is undeserved, how much more should love be?"

Posy shook her head, feeling tears burn behind her eyes. She looked down at her feet, and Kyran grasped both her hands in his own.

"Anyone can love something that is good and right," he said quietly. "It's easy. And even empty, sometimes. And that's not the life for me, Posy," he continued, leaning toward her. "Neither is it the one for you, I think." He reached a hand up to brush her hair away from her face, then pulled her close. "No," he said, looking beyond her through the window. "We choose to live for greater and deeper things now."

Ashlee Willis

Posy closed her eyes. Kyran had loved his father through unthinkable betrayal and cruelty. And it hadn't harmed him or taken away from him; it hadn't shamed him. It had made him bold, and it had set him free. Posy now understood that, and she could see that Kyran felt it as well. For it had given him power over any threat or enemy he may ever have. It made him strong beyond believing. Posy felt she held a stranger in her arms. Yet his words had hit her somewhere she hadn't known existed, a place so deep she thought it must have been shrouded in sleep since the day she had been born. They crept through her, making their way to her center, and awoke the place that slept. Her heart took in Kyran's words like a balm, like a secret she must protect with the last breath of her life.

Kyran released her and looked down into her face again, his dark eyes seeking hers. "You must leave soon, Posy." His words gave her only a moment's surprise, then she nodded.

"Yes," she said, and waited for the tearing feeling that had become so familiar to her: the feeling of heartbreak. But it didn't come. She sighed, and knew it was this knowledge, this new secret she held within her, that would give her the strength to leave this place she now loved so much. Not much strength—but enough.

CHAPTER THIRTY-FOUR

Farewell

The characters all came out to feast their new king, and the Wild Folk with them. It caused some stir among the villagers to see a tree-man walk across the meadow, limbs creaking and patched with moss, ferny hair sprouting from his head; or to see a centaur canter across the cobblestone courtyard, noble head held high and proud. The villagers thought of these creatures as fairytales for centuries. But Posy knew what they felt—she knew what it was to have a fairytale come true before your eyes.

Great long tables lined with silver and green cloth were set up in the castle's largest courtyard. A hundred extra servants were hired from nearby villages to help with the cooking and readying of the castle. Everything was bustle and work, and Posy tried to help as best she could without thinking of when she must leave. She knew she was putting it off, but she told herself she would know when it was time. Everywhere she went, she carried the glass bottle that would take her home. She would sometimes slip a hand into her pocket to touch her fingertips to the smooth crystal. She didn't like to touch it, this thing that would take her away from Kyran, but she had to know it was there all the same. The mist had been right to urge her to find it, for Kyran's soldiers had destroyed everything in Falak's chamber that hinted of magic as soon as they gained the castle.

A sunny afternoon two days after they had spoken with the king, Posy sat with Kyran in one of the small gardens surrounding the castle. He had paper, quill and ink before him, working on a short speech he would deliver to his people before the feast.

"How can I ever find the words that need to be said?" he asked wearily, looking up from the paper in front of him and rubbing his eyes.

Posy smiled.

"What?" he said with a ready smile in return.

"It's just that ..." she began. "Oh, I don't know ... you can't find the words, you say. You *changed* the words, Kyran."

"Did I?" he asked, his face now solemn. "I'm not sure of that at all."

"Not sure?" Posy looked at him. "Kyran, they called us the Word Changers. The story has changed—only look around you. Of *course*, the words are different now. How can you question it?"

"But they didn't change because of me," he said quietly. "No." He stopped Posy before she could speak. "I was one among many who started those changes. You, my sister, even the owls and my father ... we all did it, and that is how it was meant to be. And do not forget the ones who died defending the True Story. Their noble deaths changed the words to our lives more than anyone."

"Yes," Posy said slowly. "You're right. We all did it. We were all the Word Changers."

Kyran's dark eyes turned to look at her, then past her, to the land beyond the garden and past the castle. He sighed. "But how much more has changed than words."

* * *

The feast day passed in a whirl. Posy's body was there, but her mind strained ahead of her like an animal on a leash, and it took all her strength to keep it with her. The day dawned green and brilliant; it opened like a flower with the sun's touch. Posy knew it was perfect, and she watched as if in a dream as Kyran and Evanthe performed their duties, greeted their people, and took joy in their new Kingdom.

Kyran's speech came before the meal, and before the people were drowsy with good food and wine. He stood from his seat on the low balcony overlooking the courtyard and raised a hand. Silence descended like a blanket. Every man, woman, child and creature of the Wild Land had eyes only for their king now.

Kyran's strong voice rang out into the corners of the square. "Not long ago," he said, "we lived in darkness. Nothing can enslave a person more than his own thoughts ... his own ignorance of the choices before him ... his cowardice to face down what he knows is wrong. No ruler on earth can have more power over you than this. The Plot told us who we were, what we were to do, how we could live, and even die. But no more.

"The True Story can now begin. It also knows who we are and how we will live and die, just as the Author wrote it. But there is a difference. The magic of the Kingdom does not hold us now. It cannot confuse and blind us as it once did. The mist has driven it away and can live among us once again, reminding us of who we once were, and whom we can become.

"There are things a king cannot decide for us ... and things an Author *will* not. The Author knows what will become of us, but he

Ashlee Willis

will not reveal all. We were happy to leave those things hidden for so long. But when we decided to reach out a hand and lift the veil, we found what we were meant to find all along—what had been there, next to us, all the ages of our lives. And we had not seen it, or we had forgotten it.

"This war, these deaths, have had a true and noble purpose—for now we have found it, now we have remembered what we had so long forgotten. This is a new world, my people." Kyran cast his eyes over the crowd as if he would look into each man and woman's eyes. "And I will tell you in truth … defeat will be more sorrowful now. But victory will be more beautiful, and love will be deeper. What a thrill it will be for us to not know what turn the story may now take, or what wonders it will lead us to!

"We can live now as we were meant to, and only once. The Border has been broken, and with it, the continual replaying of our story. A reader may come a thousand times to turn these pages of ours, but he will only find the flat memories of us, for we will be moving now, ever onward. And who is to say? Perhaps the True Story may have an ending … and perhaps not. Perhaps one day we will discover what is beyond the Wild Land—perhaps we will visit the Unknown Land, and it may be a new story will begin there.

"But in this story we are no longer slaves of a merciless Plot. We are free characters who were brave enough to push away the darkness that we came to recognize, brave enough to welcome that strange, mysterious light that comes from each of us—that the Author placed there when he wrote us—that will change the words and make our story into what it was always meant to be."

Posy found she had been holding her breath—she didn't know how long. She released it in a long sigh and turned to look around her at these characters whose fate had been wound tightly with her own. She looked into their faces, and saw what must have been written on her own. They were eager to agree, desperate to believe, and Kyran barely finished his last words when they all sprang up and roared, clapping and shouting together, so thunderous that Posy thought the courtyard walls must be rattling in their foundations. She couldn't help but smile, and cry, and raise her hands alongside these people who meant so much to her.

* * *

Posy had always hated goodbyes. It was no different here. In fact, it seemed a thousand times worse. For she knew when she said goodbye here, it would be forever. She had a kiss for Nocturne as she ran her fingers over his silky smooth feathers affectionately. She had tears and embraces for Faxon and Caris, two of the king's new councilors alongside a variety of creatures and people including owls, Wild Folk and characters.

Evanthe had taken her aside to hold Posy's hands within her own while tears streamed down her pale childlike face. But as childlike as she was, and despite her tears, Posy saw her strength and knew Kyran would not lack for help with any of the difficulties ahead that he may face. Posy gazed at the princess. *She is the reason I was brought here, not long ago. And now I am bidding her farewell for the last time. I've barely had time to get to know her at all.* Posy found she was crying, too, but the tears were somehow full of something good, not the desperate sadness she had expected. When she reached to put her arms tightly around the other girl, she felt nothing but reassurance and happiness.

"My brother won't be the same without you, dear one." Evanthe ran a hand over Posy's curls. "And neither will I. You saved me ... a person you had never met. You risked your life for mine, and a debt like that cannot go unpaid."

"There is no need," Posy faltered, shaking her head. "You are thankful ... you are alive. That's all the payment I need, Princess."

"All the same, Posy, I think we will meet again. The Author knows a loose end like this cannot be left in a story."

"Come now," Kyran's voice came to her from where he stood holding the reins of his horse. "It's time we went. The sun will rise soon."

He swung up into the saddle and deftly pulled her up to settle behind him. She wrapped an arm around him as Belenus' hooves clattered on the stone courtyard. She had decided ahead of time she would allow herself to turn once, as she left, to watch the people and creatures she had come to love. More than that would be tempting an unnecessary pain. Therefore, she turned now to take them all in, standing scattered across the backdrop of the castle. The last of the moon's fading beams made puddles of light trailing from where they stood to where she and Kyran now departed. She didn't need to raise a hand in farewell. She didn't need to call out any words to them one last time. The suffering they had all been through, along with the triumph, passed between them, written in their gazes, more than any words could have communicated. For they all knew—they understood each another. And they all felt the same.

* * *

Posy held onto Kyran tightly as they broke into a gallop across the outer fields of the Kingdom. She had felt when it came time for her to leave, it could only be in one place—so they now directed their path there: the Wild Land. She looked up to see the moon glinting off Kyran's black hair. She watched across the meadow as tiny lights flew up, circling, then plunged back into the tall grass. There was much about this world she would never know. But undoubtedly—and she almost laughed—there was much she would never know about her *own* world.

Her own world. She closed her eyes and leaned her cheek against Kyran's back. Memories flooded her mind. Not the ones that made her cower and cry, but ones that made her long to return home. She thought of her mother and father, their faces and voices. The familiar scent of her father's aftershave seemed to rise to her nostrils from nowhere, and she took in her breath sharply. She felt the soft brush of her mother's hand on her face, as she had felt it so many times before. Lily's face also swam before her, with its sweet smile, and suddenly Posy ached to see her sister—to touch her and be sure she was real. To talk to her—return to the person who had always been her other half. Posy began to think—she began to suspect—that her blame and her anger had been magnified, and perhaps not so deservedly as she had thought. She began to believe that, however much she feared the things that waited for her in her own world, she would never see them in the same light again.

Kyran's horse began to slow, and Posy's eyes snapped open to take in their surroundings. They had reached the forest's edge.

"Kyran," she said quietly. "What's beyond the Wild Land? Surely, the forest cannot go on forever? Is it another place entirely? Or does it just ... end?"

"No one in the Kingdom knows for sure, Posy. We have always called it the Unknown Land. But I will tell you." His voice grew soft, as if he was about to reveal a secret. "I intend to find out one day. When my kingdom is fully at peace once more, when the crinkles of our pages have been smoothed into the story it is meant to be, I intend to take some men and go there, into the far reaches of the Wild Land. For the forest must end somewhere. We will discover if it ends in nothingness ... or in a new world altogether."

Posy shivered against him. What *was* beyond the Wild Land? Perhaps—and her heart leapt ... but no, that would be impossible.

Kyran urged his horse into the sheltering darkness of the trees, right into the thick mist that hovered like a ghostly shroud on the forest floor. When they had gone some distance, Kyran dismounted and reached his hands up to grasp her waist as she slid from the saddle. She watched his face, so open with its sad, crooked smile—sweetness that was like a knife in her heart. So different from the haughty and sneering smiles he had given her little more than a month ago, Posy thought. Loving each other had made each of them into a new person. And she wondered with something like shock if that had been the purpose of her journey all along.

"Well," Kyran looked at her, his black eyes and hair darker in the shadows of the trees. "The sun will be up any moment." He paused; then, in a rush, "You could ... you could come back with me, Posy. You could be my queen. Everyone would love you—they do already! And I ... I love you. I don't know what I'll do without you." He sounded like a child suddenly, not the warrior she had seen, terrible and strong on the battlefield. Posy lifted her hands to hold his face. She looked at him and felt that looking at him forever wouldn't be long enough.

"Your sister," she said slowly, "felt sure we would meet again. But you know I have to go now. I love you, Kyran. But there are others I love, too."

"Yes," he said, nodding, understanding. "Yes, I know."

And who could know better than he? thought Posy sadly.

He leaned down to kiss her, and they both knew it was the last time. Posy had felt she had been strong to hold back tears until now, but this undid her, and she tasted her own tears mingling between their lips. She embraced him, feeling the familiar hardness of his muscles, the warmth seeming to emanate from him.

"Go," he said at last. If there could be both courage and heartbreak in a single word …. He kissed her hand so softly it was like a butterfly landing for a brief moment, and of everything, that was what almost changed her mind. But she pulled her mind back from the memory of the first time he had kissed her hand, bowing before her for forgiveness there in the forest, and she returned to the task at hand.

Squaring her shoulders and taking a deep shuddering breath, Posy reached into her pocket to grasp the crystal bottle. She backed away from Kyran, just a few steps, for she didn't know what would happen when she removed the lid. Really, she thought gazing down at it, she wasn't sure what she was supposed to do at all … was she to drink it? Why hadn't she thought of it before?

She didn't have to worry about that, though. The first narrow rim of bright sun was emerging atop the hill beyond the forest, and as its rays spread like fingers through the trees, Posy knew the moment had come. She looked up at Kyran, and found she suddenly felt fear. Her hand hovered uncertainly over the bottle. He nodded and smiled, and before she could think anymore about it, she pulled the cork from it.

The rays of sun seemed to flee. Then Posy realized they had only converged together, into a great orb, pulsing and glowing ... and growing larger every second. It was bright, brighter than any eyes should be able to withstand, but she and Kyran both stared in amazement as it took shape into a great beast.

It was a creature that crackled with fire and surged with water. It deepened with the blackest shadows even as it shone with blinding brilliance. Through the pulsing light, Posy could make out the shape of a great beast, tall and proud. And wings, wide and powerful. A face with eyes that were ... less than human? Or more?

"So it is time for you to leave this story and return to your own," said a voice Posy knew well.

Posy only nodded, still awestruck at the sheer gigantic size and overpowering presence in which the Author had chosen to cloak himself this time.

"Well, then, child," the voice sparked and fizzed with flames. "Come, and I will embrace you."

Embrace? Posy stood frozen for a moment, her eyes watching the leaping flames and moving shadows that flowed like waves over the creature. Then she thought fleetingly of all she had been through, the terror and joy both, and knew this one last thing should not frighten her. She walked closer to the Author, feeling his fiery breath as she neared him. He spread one enormous wing, blue and white as a wave, and she stepped into the shadows beneath it.

It was like both drowning and breathing more clearly than she ever had. It seemed the Author found pleasure in writing things that were at odds with each other—things that seemed to oppose, but could not exist without each other. Posy turned within his wing to rest her eyes on Kyran one last time. She saw him in the distance, his clothing and hair blowing as if a strong wind was suddenly whisking through the forest. She reached out a hand to him, hoping he would see it and know everything that was unspoken between them. He did not wave back, but put his left hand up to cover his heart, and Posy knew he was showing her the place she would remain with him.

That was the last thing she saw before a flood of water and flames completely crashed over her head.

CHAPTER THIRTY-FIVE
Changed

She woke from a sleep like death. The story's power still pulled her down, even as the Author pushed her up, up into her own world again, commanding, insistent against any weakness she may give into, just as he had been once before.

Her eyelids wouldn't seem to open, her arms and legs felt like lead. Posy could hear something, though. Something unspeakably familiar and comforting. She realized, not knowing if she wanted to laugh with relief or cry with sorrow, that it was the soft buzzing hum of the electric lights in the library. Her eyes obeyed her at last, and she opened them slowly to soft yellow light and tall unending shelves of books.

So here I am, as if nothing happened at all, she thought, and she suddenly felt tired to her bones. Thoughts flashed through her mind, memories tore through it mercilessly, and she closed her eyes against them. She put her face in her hands and began to shake with silent sobs.

"I'm sorry," a soft voice came to her through her grief. "I'm sorry, but ... is there anything I can do to help?"

Posy hadn't known anyone was near to witness her tears. She quickly choked them back and rubbed her palms across her face to wipe it dry before looking up into a pair of dark eyes. Her heart did a strange turn inside of her, but then she began to see all of him. He was a boy from her school. She had only passed him in the halls— never spoken to him. But she didn't speak to *many* people. He was tall—a bit lanky, perhaps—and wore round-rimmed glasses. In his long arms, he carried a stack of books so tall Posy feared his slender body might topple over under the weight of it at any moment. He must be a year or two older—she had seen him studying and talking with the other juniors and seniors.

But why did it matter? She had just wanted to cry in peace, to mourn for the place and people she had lost. But something in his look stopped her from giving a sharp retort. It was kindness. He wasn't just being polite; he was worried about her. And if she looked beyond the glare of light on his glasses, deep enough into his eyes, she thought she could see a trace of ...

She smiled suddenly. He backed a step away from her and cast his eyes down. They had lost their look of concern, and now he only looked embarrassed.

"Sorry to bother you," he mumbled, and began to turn away.

"No!" Posy quickly set the book on the table next to her and leapt from her chair. "Please don't go. I wasn't smiling because ... I wasn't laughing at *you*! Is that what you thought?"

"Well," he said, looking cautiously up at her again, and she knew she had guessed right.

She sighed. "I was only smiling because ... well, because I like looking at you." Her eyes widened as she heard the words come out, and she clapped a hand over her mouth.

Now it was the boy's turn to laugh. She watched his face transform, his dimples and his flash of white teeth giving him something like charm.

"As long as I know you're all right." His face took on its serious look once more. "I had been watching you read … oh, well, I suppose I shouldn't have told you that … well, I saw you reading, and it looked as if you weren't ever going to come out of that book! I can tell you, I've felt the same way before. But after a while … something seemed to be not quite right. You …" and he paused, unsure of continuing. "Well," he said at last. "You were *too* far away."

"Too far?" Posy asked faintly.

He shook his head. "Never mind." He smiled again. "Can I help you carry any of your books?"

"No," said Posy quickly. The sudden image of Kyran's face flashed through her mind, and she felt her heart sink, and something like shame. Should she be speaking to this boy at all—even smiling at him—when she had just left Kyran, whom she loved so much? It felt like a betrayal.

"But thanks anyway," she mumbled.

He seemed to gain some confidence from her uncertainty, and said, "I'd offer to walk you home … but I can see you'd rather be alone right now."

They had begun walking together down the aisle between the bookshelves, treading the zigzagging path toward the stairs. Posy remained silent, still in the grip of her longing. *It's not his fault,* she reasoned with herself. *He has no idea what I've been through and where I've just come from. And,* she cast a sidelong glance at him, *he's nice. Nice enough to be a true friend.* She knew instinctively that he wouldn't judge her or laugh at her. She even had a fleeting thought of sharing her experience with him … at least, maybe one day.

Normally she could barely talk to a boy, especially one she had never met. But this wasn't normal, and she wasn't normal. She had changed unspeakably because of the things she had seen and done, and she felt older, wiser, braver.

"Maybe," she ventured, "tomorrow? I'll probably be here—I am most days, anyway. Maybe I'll see you then."

"Yes," he said, his eyes shining. "Yes, all right." He ran long fingers nervously through his unkempt brown hair.

They had reached the lobby and Posy turned to him. Thoughts of anything else were quickly receding as she thought of her family, her home. "I'll see you tomorrow, then," she said and made to turn from him toward the large double doors.

"Ethan."

"What?"

"Ethan," the boy repeated. "That's my name."

"Oh." Posy felt herself flush as several people turned to look at them. "My name is Posy."

"Posy," he said with a nod, and she liked the way it sounded when he said it. "I'll see you soon, then, Posy."

* * *

The trees were greener than they had been, the sky had been washed a brilliant blue. It probably was noon or not long after, but Posy could see the moon in the sky, and it was large, larger than it used to be, she was sure, shining stubbornly against the sun's greater light, a dull marble white. She had stepped back into the world that was hers, and she found it wasn't the one she had left— not really. Would nothing ever be the same again?

Posy walked down the street, her feet unexpectedly slow. Word

Ashlee Willis

changers, that's what they had called Kyran and her. The wonder of it was that the words to the story hadn't changed at all ... it had been the characters themselves. For the words had already been changing all around them, every age, every day. They had awoken from a dream and found they had a choice—one that had been there all along. Posy wondered if she would ever stop thinking about the story and what would happen there now that she was gone. She wondered if she would ever stop looking for Kyran's face around every corner.

But she had a secret now, the one that had led her home, and she was impatient and terrified to tell it and to live it. *You can't die from the lack of something when you have so much of it to give yourself,* she thought. Why did the words seem so familiar, when she knew she had never heard them spoken before? She would never have to fear again, never wonder if she would shrivel up or simply disappear from love not given, or not felt. Kyran, the Kingdom, the Wild Land, the Glooming, even Falak and the king and queen—they had all forced her to open her eyes to what was already in her.

No one can open your eyes but you, child. The voice was on the breeze—or had it come from the click of her shoes on the pavement—or the beat of her heart? She knew the voice, of course, would always know that voice, and warmth like a blanket settled around her. *Others can shine a light, but you have to choose to see it.*

She rounded the corner at last to see her achingly familiar house. *Here I am,* she told herself, gathering her courage like armor, *here I am. I've come from so far away. So far. They don't know my secret,* she thought, and it gave her a thrill of happiness. *They can't guess it, but I'll show it to them every way I can. Mom, Dad, Lily.* Her love for them pulsed through her heart and into her veins. It was a part of her as it never had been.

So Posy walked up the stairs she had descended hours ago—lifetimes ago. She grasped the doorknob with a shaking hand, drew her breath, and walked into a new world.

~ end ~

Ashlee Willis

CPSIA information can be obtained
at www.ICGtesting.com
Printed in the USA
LVOW03s1711070817

544126LV00004B/966/P